Operation Green Arrow

KELLY PRIAULX

This novel is a work of fiction based on real life events. All references to names and characters, unless already in the public domain, are entirely fictional. All incidents portrayed in it – unless recorded historical events – are the work of the author's imagination. Any resemblance to actual persons, living or dead, events or locations are entirely coincidental.

ISBN: 978-1-0684226-1-4
First Edition
Cover artwork independently sourced by khindir

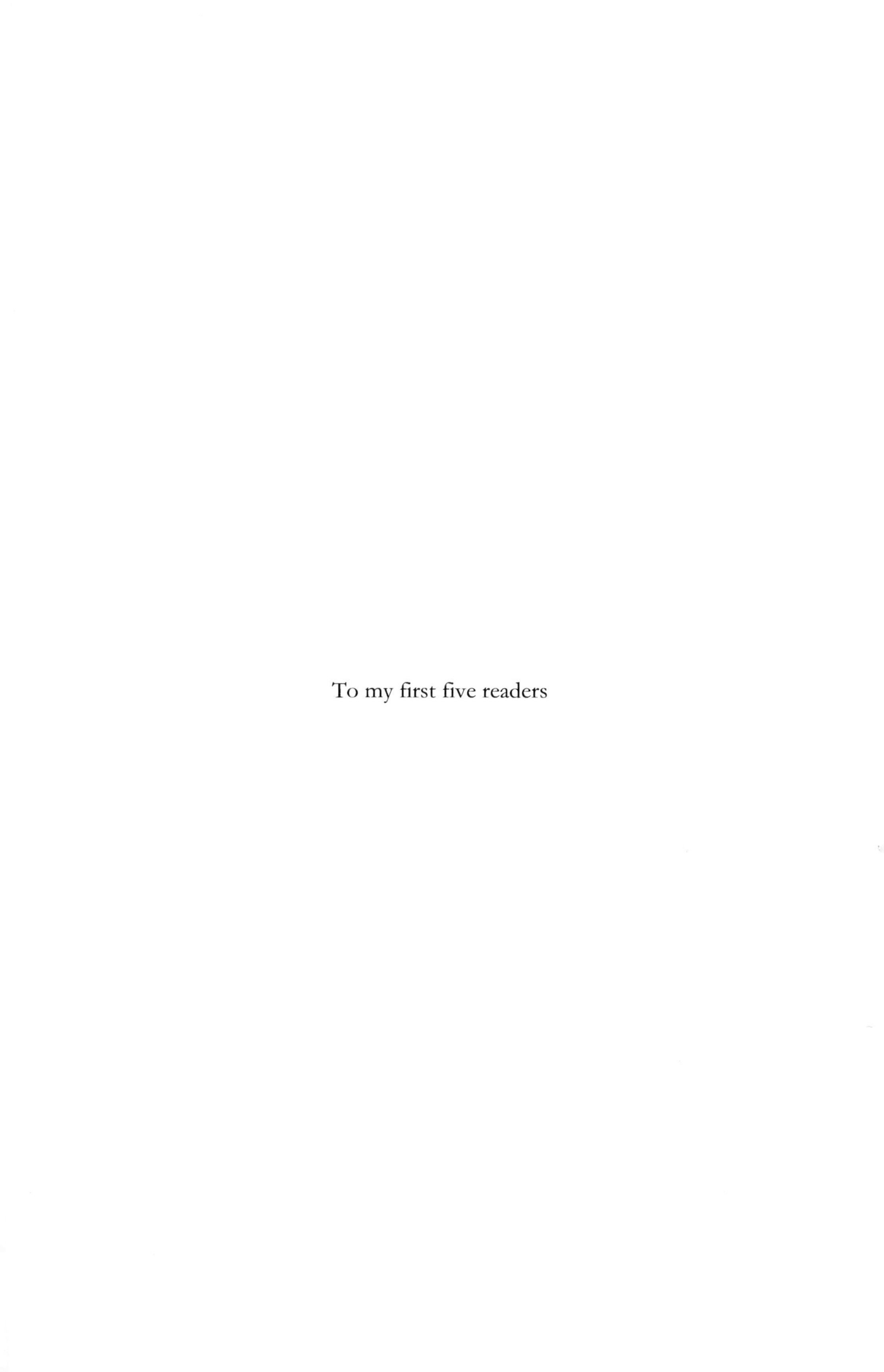

To my first five readers

Operation Green Arrow

Heaven was here,
had we but known it.

V.V Cortvriend
Isolated Island

Operation Green Arrow

Preface

There are different ways to save a life.

One can physically protect another from an act that would otherwise have broken them. Then there are the other more subtle - but equally valuable - ways. There are ways present only in the mind, or only the body. There are ways of which you cannot give clarity to or justify. A life can be saved by an arrival, a departure, or a return. You can save your own, if you are brave enough, or give it to another like a gift.

A life can be saved because of love.

A life can be saved out of duty.

A life can be saved without meaning to be.

Operation Green Arrow

In 1940, the German forces prepared to carry out the seizure and occupation of the demilitarized Channel Islands. They gave this invasion the code name *Operation Grünpfeil.* Operation Green Arrow.

Operation Green Arrow

PART ONE

FREEDOM

Operation Green Arrow

1

They were aggravating from the start, those bothersome tame and orderly boys who took bi-annual summer visits to our island. They were the boys who could not skim stones, ride bikes or jump haybales. They came from somewhere far afield – I was never inclined to ask – and smelled too clean to be on Guernsey, our small unassuming island nestled in the Northern Coast of France. We ended those hot and hazy days slick with exertion and sandy toes, yet they always smelled pristine. The way they spoke bothered me, too; one in clipped short and sharp English, the other sounding out his words with a lazy drawl.

I'm not sure they particularly liked us at first either, now I think about it. To them we were the small island ferals, civilised enough to sit around a table to eat dinner but wild enough to climb trees barefoot.

The boys had been visiting with Elka and Doug Reid for as long as I could remember. When I think back on the summers of my childhood, they were mostly what I remembered of them. I had hazy memories of my parents building up to their bi-annual summer visits for months before, stocking extra food to feed them and carving room for them in our old farmhouse. They were flashes, mainly, unremarkable moments which came back to me when they first arrived on the island, say, or when we waved goodbye to them at the harbour jetty.

I knew their names – Otto and Tomas – but for a long time had little idea or care for which name belonged with which boy. I rarely, if ever, spoke with them directly in those early days. I hovered on the outskirts of our play; in the cornfields but never in the centre, on the haybales but always the last to jump, and paddling in the shallows but never swimming deep into the blue with them. I was happy that way.

My little brother Pierre – just one year my junior – and my cousin Mariette, were not. My family were intrigued by the boys exoticism and, as we all grew older together, the infuriating dynamic where one of the boys made the rules and the other followed, obediently.

I had no idea, then, that one of those boys would love me, and the other would kill me.

↔

Summer 1928

Today is a typical blue-sky day in the summer of 1928, the type where the heat settles on the roads in a hazy mirage and there is a band of blue on the horizon so deep it plays on the cusp of indigo. The heat wraps itself around your skin and clings damply to your hair.

The Reid's – Elka, Doug, Tomas and Otto – are on the second day of their visit. Whilst the grown-up's set themselves on a blanket nestled against the sea wall seeking shelter, the children wade down to the shore desperately seeking some salt-water respite.

I join the others for a paddle in the shallows, enjoying the way my feet sink into the thick sand like mud. My toes wiggle up and down and I let the white spray of the breaking wave tumble through my fingers. They wade out deeper, with Mariette latching a squirming Pierre onto her hip so she can continue on with the boys and not fall back into the shallows.

"He is too old for your hip," I grumble, at the same time the Reid boys call back, somewhat resigned already to my answer, "aren't you coming?"

I shake my head, chewing at the little piece of skin around my left thumbnail that stands prouder than the rest. Her voice gets lost under the undulation of the incoming wave, but I am certain I hear Mariette telling them "she is a baby, she is scared of it."

You're only a year older, I think.

After a while I leave them and make my way back to where my parents and the Reid's sit. I relish in the *pat-pat* as my wet feet hit first the damp, tide-drenched sand and then the soft powder. When I have dried off a little in the heat and can brush off the grit clinging to my skin, I take hold of a nearby stick of seaweed – the hard kind, the ones that, when the tide goes down, stand up from the sand like pillars. I pull hard and, pushing the layer of dry light powder away, start scrawling in the sand.

Margot La Joie, I write, sketching lines and patterns on the beach, *6 years of age*. I let the six be a little bit bigger, because it is a big number, after all.

I glance across to Elka, sat like a swan, lips painted in rouge lipstick so bright and bold against her exotically translucent skin. I wonder airily when Ma will let me wear lipstick like that. Elka intrigues me, with the clipped abrupt English that is so obviously not her mother tongue. She is quite a fascination to be around. She speaks in a way I have never heard anyone speak before.

Papa ruffles my brunette curls as he strolls past, on his way to join Pierre, Mariette, Otto and Tomas in the sea. "Are you joining us, Margot?"

I squint down to the shore and the salt air picks at my eyes. The sea looks quietly turbulent today, like her gently undulating waves are just a mask for what lies beneath. I shiver and shake my head. *No, Papa.* Before he goes, he kisses the top of my head and the black hairs on his big bear arms tickle my cheeks. I wave him away, giggling.

Later the boys chase Pierre and Mariette across the sand holding crabs (which I think are alive, but I can't be sure) and seaweed that looks like mermaid hair as it floats behind them.

Ma widens her arms for me as I fall onto the blanket in a sticky mess, and she delicately wipes a damp strand of hair from my face, watching as I follow the children's path along the shore. "You don't want to join them, *ma p'tite souée*?"

"Not today," I sulk, propping up my elbows and leaning my head on my hands, gazing adoringly at Elka as much as I can without it looking obvious. She is curious and utterly captivating, this enchanting princess from a far-off magical kingdom.

↔

The dust blows up in our wake as we march along the earthy cliff tracks like soldiers, the adults trailing behind us. I glance back at Elka every once in a while, to check that she is still among us. She and my mother are head-to-head, giggling, sharing a story as they walk that I won't be privy to.

Pierre leads our march along with one of the Reid boys. Mariette behind them, beside the other. I hang back a little, in a void between the children and the adults. My comfortable place.

We make our way around the southern coast of headland, the gaps in the ancient trees giving way to views of the crystal blue ocean. It is so close I could throw a pebble and watch it hit the water. I shudder, pressing my toes harder onto the earth, checking the solid ground is still underfoot. An old fisherman's hut sits nestled in the valley, breaking up the sloping heather and craggy cliff edges.

"Renoir painted this very area you know."

"Oh my. I can see why. Such beauty! Look at *that*, Elka darling," I hear Doug call to his wife, pausing at the particularly beautiful viewpoint. The sun is hitting at just the right time, sending golden shards of light between the tree trunks and swaddling everything around us in a warm glow.

"I love ze sea," Elka croons. "We do not see zis at 'ome. Not easily."

Where is home, I wonder? I've never asked. Elka belongs in a castle, somewhere nestled among ancient trees and lush green landscapes.

After showing the Reid's what feels like most of the island's cliff path, we shuffle down to the pine forest, where the grown-up's take a rest on one of the green benches that break up the monotonous terrain. I perch in one of the ancient pine trees and watch the children, chasing each other across the clearing and through the thicket. I inhale that sharp and musty pine needle scent and feel the coarse bark on my back, sighing in satisfaction.

One of the Reid boys is chasing the other. I scrutinise them, try to work out which is which. I do not try too hard; it seems a lot of energy to expend on something that will not affect me, one way or the other.

In the end I grow tired of watching my brother and Mariette fall about themselves over the boys, so I amble down the clearing. This spot in the woods is on a steep incline, so I angle my feet horizontally as I descend, giving myself an internal high five when I make it down unscathed. Pierre, Mariette, Otto and Tomas look like ants on top of a hill from down here.

We are just on the cusp of the season for pinecone collecting, but I manage to gather a few early babies that have dropped off from the thick branches overhead. I lift one of them to my nose and breathe in deeply. Ma will be pleased; I can dry these out and will only have to wait a few weeks before they will be needed to keep the fire burning at home. I have almost reached full capacity in my pockets when I hear a low yelp from above. I look and see a rush of colour moving towards me at a rapid speed. It is one of the Reid boys, rolling over and over amongst the pine needles, tumbling down the hill.

I start to look away, willing to leave them to their games, when I realise that he probably isn't playing. It is easy to lose your footing on the pine needles; fine as they were they held little grip, and once you stumbled it was almost impossible to right yourself. At that point your best bet is to hand yourself over to gravity. I see the impact before I hear his cry; the boy has rolled into the trunk of a thick tree, with incisions on the rough bark so deep you can insert a finger almost whole. I know. I've tried. He lies in a crumpled heap against the tree only a few feet from where I stand, a pinecone still frozen halfway to my pocket.

"I hope you haven't hurt the tree," I mutter.

Pierre, Mariette and the other boy don't seem to have noticed his fall.

He is groaning - *very much alive then*, I think - but he is not moving. The idea of leaving him there, pretending not to have seen, briefly enters my mind. But Ma and her damn *manners* rise up, so I cautiously make my way over the net of pine needles towards him. He is wheezing a little by the time I get there.

"Are you quite alright?" I crouch down, careful not to get too close. I nudge him with my foot when he does not move.

He tries to talk but cannot catch his breath.

"You've winded yourself, that's all." A few gentle breaths and he will be fine. Lord knows I've winded myself plenty of times whilst out exploring these woods.

His eyes fill with panic, though, and he continues to gasp at the air as if it is running out. "Calm down," I bite, frowning. "Haven't you ever been winded before?" He shakes his head. He must be from a city. I ignore the disappointment in my chest. I can't imagine Elka's castle looking right in a city.

"It will pass." He tugs at his stomach and when his shirt lifts at the edge I see a crisscross of angry red marks on his skin, the perfect imprint of the bark. I grimace. "That will need to be cleaned, though."

He stands gingerly and rests on one of the fallen boughs of a tree. When he finally catches his breath (after a long time, these boys are quite dramatic) his eyes crinkle at the corners, and he smiles. "Thank you."

I shrug – *it was nothing*. But there is a warmth in my stomach that I quite like.

2

Summer 1930

There are three lower branches to the ancient oak tree we treated as our own. The higher branches are impossible to climb, though many have tried before us and incurred scraped knees and broken bones in the course. Mariette always sits atop the uppermost of the three accessible branches, as she does now, with her back against the tree's wide trunk and both legs outstretched. She rests a book on her lap, but I suspect she isn't really reading. Mariette does not read.

Pierre sits on the lowest, the one closest to the ground, as he is the youngest. He does not like that and argues that as the male of our trio he should have the upper most seat. We naturally do not relent.

I nestle comfortably in the middle, one leg dangling down, almost skimming the top of Pierre's sandy blonde head.

It is so quiet in the tree, so peaceful. We talk a little, sigh a lot. In here, it is just us and the birds. They occasionally rustle the leaves overhead and we get a fluttering of them land in our laps.

It is hot out, has been relentlessly so for three days, and the island has fallen into a still, sleepy and almost drunken reverie.

"Shall we dunk our heads in the trough?" Mariette asks sleepily from above.

"Too tired to move," Pierre grunts from below.

"The *douit* then?" The stream.

"We could roll," I suggest.

The idea of rolling down the shallow bank into the stream that runs through the purple meadow tickles us. Our shoes are off before we hit the ground.

The relief of the cool running water on our bodies is too much to bear and one by one we strip off whatever layers we can, eager to get more. I feel the water turn to steam as it hits my clammy skin, pouring handfuls of it over my face. The stream bed underfoot is brimming with pebbles and silt and my toes play with the textures.

Still dripping - but fully satiated - we climb back up the stream banks to the openness of the meadow. The purple flowers are still in bloom, delicate little pops of colour dotted among the grass, sending the clearing into an indigo haze.

"The Reid's are here!" Pierre calls suddenly, running ahead.

My stomach drops at the same time as Mariette claps her hands together. "A day early! Summer can begin!"

A fire starts somewhere in the pit of my stomach as I approach the oak tree. The two boys have taken to the upper two branches and settled themselves comfortably in the shade, and by the time I arrive at the foot of it Mariette and Pierre are on the lowest. The Reid boys smirk down, challenging me.

There is nowhere for me to sit, so I thrust my hands into my pockets and walk away towards the farmhouse.

"Ignore her, she is hot and bothered."

My cheeks flare and I am grateful they cannot see them.

↔

After dinner that night with the Reid's, the adults remain at the table and play a game of cards, drinking wine from bottles with no names and getting all the merrier for it. We leave them in peace and head out to the garden, where the air is still clammy and smothering, the suffocation of heat only just beginning to lift.

The blonde-haired boy holds his hands up and the others instantly fall silent. He smirks, and I smolder. "I am the prisoner, and I have escaped. Catch me if you can!" With that he runs off into a cut out in the bush which leads to an adjoining field where, in the morning, a farmer will almost certainly find trodden stalks of corn in the wake of their game. Pierre runs after him, snaring his shirt sleeve on a rogue twig, and Mariette lifts her skirts and does the same.

I hang back, clutching a book loaned from the library in my hand, waiting for them to be out of earshot and fully involved in their game before I sit down and open it. I turn back to the wooden table beside the rose bush to find it already occupied.

"Oh!"

"Sorry," he jumps. "You want to sit?" The way he talks is more like his mother than his father's lazy drawl – his '*s*' becomes a '*z*' – and I feel dim witted as he watches me translate what he said.

I bring my thumb up to my mouth and begin to chew at the skin around the nail as I think it over. I just want to be alone; to read my book, to be able to hear the distant echoes of the others' play but not have to endure it myself. There is a certain safety in that. Besides, I'm still angry with him for taking my place on the tree. It was *my* place, didn't he know.

"I leave, if you want?"

He must be older than me, this one. I hadn't noticed that in the woods last year.

"I-I was just going to read." I hold up my book to give evidence to my claim.

"I gathered."

I slide into the bench opposite him, turning to my page and trying to pick up the story, but my mind keeps drifting away and before I know it, I have read the same page three times. I shut the book and go to leave, but something is simpering in the back of my mind, uncomfortable and probing. I realise it is the manners Ma is forever instilling in us.

It would be bad manners, *Margot, to leave him here without a word.*

Where are your manners, *darling, he is a guest in our home.*

I clear my throat. *Fine.* "You don't want to play?"

"Not tonight." He eyes me cautiously.

"Are – are there trees where you are from?"

"Trees?"

"Yes." I blush furiously into the evening air, shying at the way he regards me like some idiotic island girl.

"Yes, Margot," he says, slowly, "there are trees in Canada."

So, Canada. The Reid's are from Canada.

"I never knew that you were Canadian."

"You never asked," he points out - quite validly, I think. "But I not Canadian. I move from Germany when I am younger. Germany has trees too," he adds with a smirk, then waves at the farmhouse where the noise of merriment from the kitchen is getting louder. "*Meine* aunt and uncle, they take me in when I am small - *kleine.* They are only family I have left."

I sit back, stunned. "Elka and Doug are not your parents?"

"*Neine.*"

"I thought -"

"My parents dead."

"Oh. Well...."

"And Otto is my cousin. You thought he was my brother, *ja*? He and I are too different."

"So, you are…" I surmise, feeling an unexpected relief at no longer having to guess at who was who.

"Tomas."

"And Otto is…" I point in the direction of the corn field, where the shrieks of gameplay are just distant sounds.

"Elka and Doug's son," he confirms, obviously seeing the effect this new family revelation has on me. "Four years we have been visiting Guernsey, Margot, yet this is first time you speak with me." He laughs. "We thought you dim, at first. Then realise you just painfully shy."

"I wouldn't quite say *painfully…*"

"You did not know which was Otto and which was Tomas, did you?"

That wasn't shyness, I want to say, *that was intentional ignorance.* Instead, I bring my thumb back to my mouth and gnaw at the skin again.

"Is alright. Is easy to tell us apart. Otto younger and 'andsome, blue eyes, blonde hair. I older and rather not."

"So you are not a Reid then?"

He laughs, and the sound is surprisingly low and throaty. "No, I suppose I am not."

I drop my thumb, but am not quite sure what, if anything, I can say that won't incriminate me further.

↔

Two days later, we leave the grown-ups at a disused coastal fort and follow a small path to its left. The compacted ground soon turns into a cobbled stone slope, leading through a pebbled beach and straight into the sea. The way it disappears under the gentle lapping waves always reminds me of Moses parting the red sea.

"Let's skim stones," Pierre suggests, immediately dropping to his knees and starting a hunt for the best skimmers.

"Sure," the boy I now know is Otto agrees, picking up a stone and throwing it into the water.

It is clear he has never skimmed a stone in his life. The way he is holding it is all wrong; he is clutching it like an apple and throwing them in with such force that it is little wonder they are tanking through the surface like a bullet. I scowl. Why is no-one correcting him?

I see Tomas eyeing Otto subtly, then he, too, picks up a pebble – the wrong kind – and lobs it into the sea.

What is wrong with these boys? Surely it is a rite of passage to learn how to skim stones. I am about to say something when Mariette's shrill laugh rings out across our otherwise silent and secluded bay.

"What god-awful throw was *that*?" She directs at Tomas.

I know that laugh anywhere. There is an undertone of scoff and belittlement. It makes my blood boil. She had seen Otto's dismal throw. I know she had. But she had not taken it upon herself to comment on *that* one.

"Christ, T, remember you're trying to float the ship, not sink the damn thing." His elongated *damn* rings annoyingly in my ears.

I narrow my eyes to Otto's back, hoping the power of might and sheer willpower will be enough to make him turn and see my annoyance. He doesn't, though, so I find a pebble I know is worthy of skimming and stride past him, deliberately knocking his shoulder as I do.

"Here, Tomas, I will show you how."

I hand him the pebble and can see for a minute that he scans the faces of the others. Will he be ridiculed accepting help from a girl? Something must tell him yes, as he doesn't take the pebble.

I curse under my breath – thankful that Ma and Papa are still sauntering around the fort remains with Elka and Doug – and pull my arm back ever so gently. I finger the smooth flat pebble between my thumb and forefinger, bending slightly at my knees to drop position. I taste the wind, making sure the direction is right, and then launch it with a flick of my wrist. With a satisfying smile I watch as it skims once, twice, three, four times at even leaps over the surface of the sea, before sinking gracefully into the dark. It is all I can do not to rub my hands together in glee.

"Not like it's difficult," Otto mumbles, picking up another pebble – again, the wrong kind, and continuing to do a terrible job of it.

I turn to stomp back up the beach, but a hand grips my arm and stops me. To his defence, Tomas does have the decency to look sheepish. "Would you – uh – could you show me which one is good?" He gestures to the variety of pebbles at our feet.

I spend the next hour teaching him the basics in pebble skimming. He is a quick learner, and we high five when he manages a triple skimmer, even if it does descend with an ungraceful plop.

"So, you are quite good at this, *ja*?" He asks later as we sit on the rocks.

"You don't skim stones in Canada?"

"We are not close enough to the ocean. My aunt and uncle they – *we* – live in the city. Calgary."

"Ah."

"You spend a lot of time at the sea?"

"Yes. Or the woods, or fields, but mostly the sea. No-one complains if you trample their crop or scare their cow."

He snorts, and I realise I quite like the feel of making someone laugh.

"But," and his eyes drop to the ground, which makes me a little nervous. "But you are afraid of the sea, no?"

My chin juts a little higher, surprised that he had noticed. "I am. But a great deal of people are. It is not that unusual."

"It is strange, is all. You are good with the sea, but you are afraid of it."

I chew the inside of my cheek, about to admit that the sea terrifies me because the vast majority of it is unknown. Beyond my head height, beyond my eyeline, is unknown. But Mariette interrupts.

"Sorry to break the two of you apart, Margot, but the grown-ups are here."

Otto sniggers as they walk off, so Pierre does to, of course, but at least he is close enough for me to clip around the ear.

"*Baisse mon chou*," I hiss in his ear.

Kiss my –

3

Summer 1932

We have been stood on the jetty at the White Rock harbour for an hour, the frigid wind biting at my bare ankles, my cheeks red raw. I could have stayed at the farm – my parents trusted me enough - that was the truth of it. They had given me a choice but staying meant milking and picking and feeding and mucking. At ten years old, the thought of freezing on a jetty waiting for a boat to arrive seemed more appealing.

"That is the thing about sea travel," Papa muses, as if I have asked the question, "all it takes is a little inclement weather out there on the ocean and everything runs a little delayed."

"This weather is an awful shame," my mother says. "Dear Elka and Doug, arriving in this." She shakes her head. "It's hardly Summer weather, is it."

I rub my hands together in agreement with this, crossing my arms and letting them warm in the folds of my overcoat.

Thirty minutes later, with the first sighting of the ferry boat on the horizon, the gloom slowly lifts. Despite the incoming grey cloud and the even cooler shift in air temperature giving sign that rain was imminent, we were all, for different reasons, excited for the arrival.

Ma and Papa would see their best friends for the first time in two years.

Pierre would see Otto, who was fast becoming a hero in his eyes with his brazen confidence.

I would see Tomas.

I had received my first letter from him six months after the Reid's had departed Guernsey in 1930 and headed back home, to Canada. Lord knows how he got my postal address, as I certainly did not give it to him but, nevertheless, there the letter was one Monday morning. It had not said much, mostly reiterating that he had enjoyed talking with me about books on his last visit to Guernsey and learning to skim stones. From that first letter however, there had been others, back and forth between us, for the next eighteen months. We spoke of the latest novels we had read and shared thoughts on the stories. He would speak a little of Canada, about how he missed Germany, and I would regale tales of Guernsey life.

The boat approaches, and blurred colours slowly materialise into the familiar faces of the Reid family. Beneath my overcoat I have stowed a new book – *Mary Poppins*, by P L Travers – that I hadn't yet had opportunity to write to Tomas about.

Hours later, around a crackling fire that Ma had lit to combat the bitter wind blowing in through the single-glazed farmhouse windows, I give it to him. "It's just a little something that I thought you might like," I blush, handing it over, the gesture suddenly seeming like something more telling than a friendly gift.

He looks at the cover of the book and the corner of his mouth twitches. He shakes his head and laughs. I really do not see anything funny. And he still has not taken the book. I recoil a little, embarrassed.

"Well, if you don't like it…" I trail off. "It was only a thought."

I begin to withdraw it, but he puts a hand on the cover, stopping me.

"Is not that…" he laughs again. "Is a nice gesture. I…well…" He puts a hand behind his back and presents his own copy of the very same book. "I have same idea. This for you."

We exchange the books, laughing wildly.

↔

The following day the weather is back to its Guernsey finest; a cloudless blue sky and dazzling sunshine, as if the passing storm had never even made landfall.

Papa is a second-generation farmer, mainly supplying the mainland with Guernsey's famous juicy red tomatoes, and when he has some deliveries to make at the harbour, he asks us if we want to tag along.

I almost burst with pride sitting beside Tomas in the back of Papa's old rickety delivery truck. The open boot is bursting with the fruits, and he lets us each have one to eat on the ride. I laugh wildly as Tomas spits it out almost instantly and gags. Otto seems a bit more receiving of it, but it is hard to tell truthfully what he thinks when he is holding court with Pierre and Mariette, as he does now. Pierre is in the front passenger seat beside Papa, turning awkwardly in his chair to listen to whatever it is Otto is saying.

"Mariette is practically drooling at Otto," I pull a face at Tomas, who laughs so hard tomato juice comes out of his nose, which then sets us both off even more.

Papa can see how important we feel being able to help deliver the tomatoes for export, so he lets us stay in the truck, all the way to the harbour. Only once or twice has he let Pierre and I stay – we must usually wait for him on a bench at the Weighbridge, a historical clock tower that sits almost central to our main town of Saint Peter Port. I am almost certain it is because of the colourful language the dock workers use. I try telling him that we have heard it all before (particularly from the farm workers who help pick the fruit at peak times in the season), but he has none of it.

The dock workers make a big deal of the five children in the truck, showing off and trying to make us laugh as the tomatoes get taken aboard the waiting ships, which will sail later that evening for England. On the way home, once we are in the safe nestle of the rabbit-warren country lanes, he idles the truck and lets us out. It is a game we have played since Pierre and I could run; we race through the adjoining fields, and he drives through the lanes, racing us home. He always wins, of course, as we get distracted by hay bales or chasing butterflies with our bare hands.

This time is no different. The wafting scent of freshly packed hay bales greets us as soon as we are in the field. Pierre dares us to take our shoes off and run across the coarse and spiky stumps, where the hay had stood tall only a few days before. Otto and Tomas remove their shoes with enthusiasm, and it makes me wonder if they have this freedom at home in Canada. Can Elka and Doug safely let them run wild through country fields, trusting them to get home safely? Mariette grumbles a little, but soon we are all screeching across the field like feral animals, pausing only to jump across the mountainous hay bales like spring-loaded toy pistols.

↔

Later that evening, as we settle down to a picnic on the beach and I flick grains of sand from my sandwich, Tomas presents me with something.

"But you have already given me a book," I exclaim, holding the lightly wrapped parcel in my hands.

"This is different." He chuckles at my raised eyebrow. "Just open it."

A linen covered book drops into my sandy lap, and I delicately wipe the coarse grains from the title.

"*10,000 Leagues Under the Sea*," I read. "William Robinson. Tomas, what is this?"

But Tomas does not say anything - he simply stands, leaving me sitting half buried in the sand, and jogs down to the shore to join the others.

I casually flick through the wafer-thin pages, catching sight of several grainy photographs of boats and the ocean. When I turn back to the inside cover, a familiar scrawl has written *Margot, because you should be afraid of nothing.*

↔

"What time are we meeting the grown up's Margot?" Pierre yells into the air a day later as I cycle behind him, hoping I will hear it. I catch the odd word.

"Half past four!"

I chance a look at my watch, letting my feet hover on the pedals for a moment. The watch is ghastly, according to Mariette, but I am proud of it. Ma had picked it up from one of the small stores just off the market - a place that sold all sorts of ladies' purses, timepieces and men's wallets.

It is fifteen minutes past four. We have fifteen minutes to get ourselves back down to the beach to meet Ma, Papa, Elka and Doug, where the tide is at just the right height for an evening picnic and swim. Or paddle, in my case.

"Wait, wait," Otto calls from up front, braking on his cycle and holding his arms outstretched. We all stop, staggered awkwardly behind him, on the cusp of the long hill down to the beach. I frown at his back, the ache burning the back of my legs. "Who wants to race to the bottom?" He has a glint in his eye. He knows that no one will say no. No one ever seems to question Otto Reid.

"It is really quite – it is not the best hill for - there are a lot of blind corners," I reason clumsily, having been victim of a few narrow misses myself.

"Are you – chicken?" Pierre asks, tucking his poor hands under his armpits and clucking. I give him my hardest silent stare.

I win, naturally. I am smaller than Mariette, so I am faster, and bigger than Pierre but leaner. It is obvious that the only time Otto and Tomas ride a bike is when they visit Guernsey and borrow our old ones, and they are not particularly good at it when they do.

I glide through the air like I am weightless, that glorious downward motion pulling me faster. Many years later, I remember this moment.

I win.

4

Summer 1934

The arrival of the summer months brings with it a number of Guernsey celebrations, my favourite of which is The Western Agriculture and Horticultural Show, so called because it draws together the western parishes of the island in an homage to traditional farming and growing. It has all manner of animal judging, exhibitions of fruits, vegetables and baked goods, local games, heritage pageant shows and a variety of stalls selling foods and crafts. It is a day we wait for, dressing in our finest skirts and tying our hair back in the prettiest ribbons.

A part of me is excited to show Tomas – and even Otto – the show this year. It is the first time Ma and Papa have left us go unchaperoned, and it is all I can do not to skip through the gate as we arrive. The minute my feet sink into the spongy yet crisp sundried grass of the aerodrome field, I sigh happily.

I turn to begin my guided tour for the boys, certain I am glowing with pride – we will start at the tombola – but Otto pushes through my outstretched arm and takes the lead.

"Follow me. I say we start this way." He points to the right of the entrance gate, where the show is laid out in a circular arena, and sets off, expecting us to follow.

It is fine, I think, *Mariette will surely tell him that we start at the left of the gate, always going in a clockwise motion.*

"Great idea," she says, speeding up and linking her arm through his.

My feet do not move, and I do not have time (nor inclination, if I am honest with myself) to wipe the frown from my face before Otto turns back. "Aren't you coming?" He has that awful, crooked smile - half a smirk, half a challenge.

But – it is my show! I want to cry indignantly, tempted to stamp my foot.

Tomas looks from me to Otto and back again, the air tingling with tension.

"We start this way."

Otto makes a show of looking around him. "I do not see a sign."

"There isn't one." My chin juts a little higher.

"Then we can start whichever way we please."

"It makes more sense to start to the left."

"If it made more sense, there would be a sign telling you to do so."

My jaw falls open and Tomas tenderly puts a finger beneath my chin, closing it. Mariette takes in the painful spectacle wearing a grimace.

"Oh, for heaven's sake, we will start to the left if we must." She gently pulls Otto to follow who, for a brief moment, seems like he is going to refuse to move.

"Who cares if it makes sense," I hear him mutter.

"Margot does." But for once, Mariette has my back. It is rare, but on the occasions it does happen, I realise that blood can run thicker than water. She is spiky, but loyal.

"Let's go," Tomas prods. "Really piss him off and walk in front of him." We eye each other mischievously and do a quick step around Mariette and Otto to be in front. Then I see what lies up ahead and I think of an even better way to get back at the overly assured and bold Otto Reid.

The Fur and Feather exhibit tent holds all manner of animals and their babies; chickens, goats, giant pigs and cows to name a few. And the minute we approach the tent Otto wrinkles up his nose and goes to take a step back. Tomas slinks in behind him, and whether he means to or not, pushes Otto onwards towards the thick and musky aroma of farm animal.

Even Pierre and Mariette - who hold the boys on some pedestal I have yet to understand - have to cover their smirking faces when Otto and Tomas dry retch. Tomas looks in my direction with teary eyes and flushed cheeks but smiling. He understands the infliction; it is for the cause. It is satisfying to see Otto's confident and unruffled composure crumple.

"You have had your fun, now I am getting them out of here," Mariette storms, taking both boys by the arm and steering them out of the animal tent. Pierre dutifully follows.

I stick around for a while, whispering to the placid pigs. "You're misunderstood," I tell one particularly large and bulbous swine. "Everyone thinks you're rather smelly but actually you're one of the cleanest animals around." I sigh, give her rear end a pat and take a deliberately slow stroll to meet back with the others.

By the time I get to them, Otto and Tomas are nowhere to be seen.

"They went back to the farmhouse with Pierre, thank you very much" Mariette fumes. "Clever move."

"Oh, it was hardly an ordeal, it was the animal tent!"

"That they could not cope with! You knew that. They are from the *city*, Margot, not this damned island where every living thing smells like it has spent its entire life rolling in muck. Poor Otto, he said his stomach had taken a turn. He was awfully pale. And now what." She flings her arms up as if we had never been at the show alone together before. "I'm just going to go back to the farmhouse. Why on earth can you not just be nice to them?"

"Mariette don't do that," I race after her. "I'm nice to Tomas, aren't I. It's just Otto, he makes me *furious*..."

The fury radiates from her with each sashay of her hips and swishing of her hair. But I almost bump into her back when she stops suddenly beside a small, curtained tent.

"Have you seen this one before?"

I scrutinise the dark tent, the inside entirely hidden by dense heavy curtains. "No."

She goes to pull the curtain back, but I put my hand on her arm. "Wait. This isn't one of those fortune tellers, is it?"

She makes a weird noise with her mouth, a bit like a huff but more of a snort. "Oh Margot. Must you be afraid of everything, including your own shadow? Let us just take a look. This is clearly meant to intrigue, and it has worked, I am intrigued."

Before I can stop her, she pulls back the curtains and dives in. I follow, if anything, to save her from herself. The air is thick inside the tent but pleasant and cool, in spite of the humid air outside of it. There is a scent in the air, something floral. My eyes are just adjusting to the change in brightness – the tent is on the cusp of total darkness – when I sense a movement to my left and startle, knocking into Mariette.

"For goodness -" she starts at the same time as a slow voice says "*Baon-jou*, girls." *Good day, girls.* "Have you come to see what lies ahead for you?"

"I told you," I whisper from the corner of my mouth. "A fortune teller."

"Oh no, not me, dear." The old lady stands up, leaning on a gnarled wooden stick for support. She looks vaguely familiar; one of those familial matriarchs who keep the traditional families together with our island-specialty Guernsey Gache and a stern flick of her wrist. "The La Joie girl, am I right?" She points a bony finger in my direction. "And the Shaw girl, correct?"

Mariette nods. "Mrs…"

"Tostevin, dear. Of Torteval."

The tent is sparse; a handful of tattered books on a makeshift bookcase unsteady on its feet and a desk with a chair either side.

"If you aren't a fortune teller," Mariette begins, to which Mrs Tostevin tuts and sits back down, "then what is this?"

The old lady doesn't speak right away, and we can hear her rattled breathing breaking up the silence. Something tingles in the air, and I brush away goosebumps from my flesh.

"A fortune cannot be told by anyone but the one asking for it. No, I am not a fortune teller. But *you* may be."

Mariette and I catch each other's eye, and I can tell she too is struggling to suppress a giggle.

"Well, I ask it," she pushes in front of me suddenly. "I want to know my future. So, tell me how. Please," she adds as an afterthought when Mrs Tostevin raises an eyebrow to her impoliteness.

"Did you know that folklore has foundations in every community, but in small ones, historical ones like ours, folklore is more than just lore. It has truth.

Viability." She pauses for a moment, looking to us both before continuing. "You say you want to know what the future has in store for you, but I see only one question you want answered. And it involves a boy."

I screw my nose up, but Mariette brings her hands in a clasp to her chest.

"Wait -" I interject before Mariette can continue asking what I suspect she is going to ask. "What does folklore have to do with someone wanting to know who they will m- something about a boy."

"All manner of love potions and charms have roots in folklore. For example, did you know that in the 18th Century a Guernsey woman was said to bake bread containing her own blood to find out who her husband would be?"

"That sounds rather dramatic."

"Or that by killing two pigeons and skewering their hearts over a fire in complete silence you could determine whether you were destined to marry at all. Should marriage be in your fortune, your future husband would come to your door. Should it not, men carrying a coffin would visit instead."

This one turns my stomach.

"Perhaps too dark," she notes, somberly, but I catch the corners of her mouth turning up. "Something gentler, maybe. Well, there is one thing you may consider," she says to Mariette. "But for it to work, the person asking the question must want to know the answer." She dramatically turns to the small bookcase behind her, surprising me with her seamless agility for a woman of such age.

"Why else would they ask the question?" Mariette whispers so only I can hear.

"Here, this is it." She withdraws a deep brown book from the shelf, and I take notice of the familiar stirrings in my stomach, watching her flick the aged pages with a delicate wrist. The heady scent of old paper overtakes the florals, and I breathe it in, satisfied. "Yes, this one, here we are. To find out who your marriage partner is to be – this *is* the question you seek an answer to, am I right?" Mariette nods keenly, eyes as big as saucers. "Very well. Take a Golden Pippin apple – it *must* be a Golden Pippin, no other kind – and pass two pins crosswise through the centre. Remove the stocking from your left leg -"

At this I have to cover my laugh with a cough.

"– using it to wrap the fruit. Lay the wrapped apple down on your pillow at night. Now this, this part is absolutely necessary for the charm to work. Get into bed backwards -"

The thought of Mariette with only one stockinged leg retreating into bed backwards is too much and I burst into a fit of giggles. Mrs Tostevin of Torteval throws me a stern look and continues.

"– you must repeat the following incantation to St Thomas three times." She proceeds to relay the charm in our ancient romantic dialect – *patois*. The words play across her tongue seamlessly, stirring in me both pride and guilt. I hadn't bothered to learn much of our island language beyond the curse words and a handful of basic greetings, but it was now falling out of use. It isn't until she is finished that she takes note of our confounded faces.

"You young 'uns really ought to keep this dialect alive." She shakes her head, ashamed. "Very well. In *English*, then." She makes Mariette repeat it back several times before we leave the curtained tent, and by the time we do I have it as much stuck in my head as in hers.

"Saint Thomas, you say?" I ask. "St. Thomas' Eve…December?"

"Oh yes indeed, dear, do not attempt the charm before then. St. Thomas' eve is when the barrier is down for love charms to take effect."

One look at Mariette and it is clear she will be saying the charm this evening, St. Thomas' or not.

"And remember. Not a single other word is to be said before you fall into a slumber. Not a single one. Your future husband will come to you in your dreams that very night."

↔

Squeezed into my bed later that evening, she waits until my eyes are heavy lidded, and I am at my weakest before jumping up, startling me.

"We don't have any Golden Pippin's," I say sleepily, stifling a yawn with the back of my hand and shivering in the draft Mariette leaves in her wake.

I am not surprised when she pulls two from her night gown sleeves.

"Two?"

"One for you, one for me. You must be intrigued, Margot."

I shake my head. "Not in the slightest."

"It is this or the pigeon hearts."

I wrinkle my nose. "Fine. It won't work anyway. It isn't St. Thomas' Eve."

She waves a hand in the air. "Poppycock. Charms like this work at any point in the year. What does she know, anyway." I raise an eyebrow. "Alright, likely quite a lot, but what is the worst that can happen? We don't dream of him. Simple. Here -" she throws my stockings from earlier in the day at me - "and take these -" She reaches behind her ear and pulls out a hair clip, removing two pins from the clasp and handing them to me.

Concentrating so hard on not stabbing myself with the pins in the navy twilight of the bedroom I can feel my tongue lolling out of the corner of my mouth, something Mariette would usually deride me for.

"There," she holds hers up and compares it with mine, then we proceed to wrap our left-footed stocking around the fruit, feeling faintly ridiculous.

"Remember," she says, letting the apple hover above her pillow and encouraging me to do the same. "You have to want to know the answer."

"But I don't…"

"*Pretend* then, Margot. I won't have any dream of my future husband dashed because of you. And not a single word after the incantation. Promise?"

We link our pinkies. "I swear it."

With as much tender care as you would to a baby, Mariette places the apple on her pillow, turns her back to the bed and proceeds to get in backwards, repeating the charm three times –

Saint Thomas, Saint Thomas,
Shortest day and the lowest,
Let me see in my slumber,
He who will be my sweetheart,
Be he handsome, or be he ugly,
Such as he is, I will love him,
Saint Thomas, grant me this grace,
He to see and to embrace,
Amen.

She lands in bed with a flump, waving her hand at me to do the same.

I land with an equally ungracious flop on the other side, pulling the covers up to my chin, trying not to laugh. I turn my head to face her, and she does the same, placing a finger against her lips. *Hush.* Her eyes, though, swim with amusement. She snorts against her hushing finger, sending us both into a fit of silent giggles that hurts my stomach and burns my throat.

I am certain I fall asleep with a smile still on my lips.

↔

"Well, that was disappointing," she moans before my eyes are even open. "Did you dream of him?"

"I dreamt there was a chicken in my bed." I stretch my arms, welcoming that pleasing warmth of my muscles waking up from their slumber. "What do you think that could mean?"

We are just dressed and ready to go down to breakfast when there is a sharp *rap-rap-rap* on my door. Expecting Pierre on the other side both Mariette and I take hold of the handle, tugging at the door ready to surprise him.

Greeting us, instead, is Otto, his sandy unkempt hair falling delicately over his sharp and glistening blue eyes – always challenging. To his side stands Tomas, a broad grin stretching from dimple to dimple.

Mariette stiffens beside me and grabs my arm so tightly I wince. "It worked."

I scrutinise Otto and the way Mariette gapes at him, open mouthed. Her fingers dig deeper as his eyebrows pull together. "What did?"

5

Summer 1936

This time, when they arrive, the sun is high in the sky and the air at the White Rock harbour is humid and dry. A flock of seagulls speak to each other, circling the crowd of welcomers on the jetty.

Mariette has joined us on the jetty this time. Her mother - Ma's sister – had passed from Tuberculosis the year before, and Mariette had become commonplace around our table at mealtimes. In that time, she had become a woman. Not only has her body changed, but her mind has, too.

I do not understand at first why she has been so keen to join us. As Otto emerges from the boat and she runs to him, presenting his cheek with a single kiss, it becomes steadily clearer.

Rather more sheepishly, Tomas emerges behind him, and it becomes clear that in the two years in which Mariette and Otto have grown, Tomas has not. There is a noticeable height difference between the two boys where once there had not been. He carries himself more awkwardly than I remember, as if he is no longer sure what to do with his hands.

I make straight for him and, seeing how Mariette has greeted Otto, feel somewhat timid in embracing him with nothing more than a hug.

"What book do you have for me this time?" He asks with a knowing grin.

"Worzel Gummidge," I thrill, certain he won't have read it yet. "It's about this scarecrow who -"

"- is half human, and a wizard." He laughs out loud and pulls out the very same book from his satchel.

His English is much better, I notice. He still talks with a lilt, his words slightly clipped, but his sentences flow more like mine.

"We really must become more original."

He laughs. "But where would be the fun in that?"

↔

Several days later, with the sun still burning bright on our days, we spend another day on the beach. This time we head for L'eree bay, a rocky outcrop to the south-west of the island, renowned for not only its infiltration of beached seaweed at a high tide, but also of its excellent rock-climbing opportunities.

In the last two years, whilst Mariette's body has been developing into something rather voluptuous, mine has lengthened, and I've discovered a love of movement. The chance to do rock climbing and feel a heat in my legs and arms is too opportune to miss, so even though Otto is the one to suggest it and I would rather not give him the satisfaction of agreeing to his idea, I am the first to leap up.

Mariette frowns in what is becoming a particular resting face for her. Pierre jumps up second after me – of course he does, it was Otto's suggestion. Otto could suggest jumping off of the seawall at high tide completely naked and Pierre would be first in line, though I imagine he would have to fight Mariette for it.

Tomas squints at the rocks, then at me. "Margot, perhaps we could -"

"Come on Tomas, let's go." Otto, Pierre and I have already started walking in the direction of the rocks at the end of the bay.

"We are just going to climb the rocks." I call to Ma, who is enjoying a cider with the other adults. Imported fresh from France, I can vouch that it is rather delicious.

"Your parents are quite lenient, aren't they," Otto remarks when Ma waves us off. "You have so much freedom here, to do as you please."

Tomas decides not to join us, for reasons I do not entirely understand. Mariette, however, hitches up her pristine skirts, kicks off her shoes and joins us with a barely disguised scowl.

The boys lead the way up until we reach a narrow inlet of almost vertical rocks. As they are assessing a route up Mariette finally catches up. Red in the face, she blows a wayward curl from her forehead.

"This is *not* my idea of fun, Margot," she hisses so only I can hear.

"Then why did you come?"

Before she can answer, Otto turns to us and her face evens out. It is almost pleasant.

Oh. She is really rather sweet on Otto.

"Your future husband?" I mouth.

She smiles sweetly at him. "I suppose we head back now, do we? Maybe ask the grown-ups for some of that cider." She lowers her voice so only I can hear, "I sure could do with some of *that*."

"Go back? Heavens, no!" exclaims Otto. "We didn't come all of this way for nothing. Look around, we're at the end of the world!"

From where we stood, if we looked straight ahead at the waves crashing over rocks in the distance where only blue stretched out to the horizon, it truly did feel like we were at the end of the world. Ignoring the island behind us I let the gentle sea breeze swim over my skin. I was an explorer, then, an adventurer on a deserted island. I look up at the vertical wall of rocks we have paused at.

"Let's climb to the top," I suggest.

Mariette inhales sharply. "What are you *doing*?"

I ignore her and look to the boys for confirmation. "Well? Shall we?"

"Brilliant idea, actually," said Otto, startlingly impressed. Something in me stirs – a miniscule feeling, but noticeable. "Pierre and I were just discussing our options to get to the top. Can you imagine the view from up there? We will have to sort of shimmy on up, using our feet and arms. Are you sure you girls are up to it? It won't be a delicate job." And there it is. He raises an eyebrow and narrows his eyes, a smirk playing at the corner of his mouth.

"If I can't make it to the top, I doubt either of *you* will." I push past him and kick off my shoes, silently cursing his inane level of arrogance as I grasp hold of the rocks either side of the narrow shaft.

"Uh, Margot, don't you think we should go first?"

"*Why* Pierre, because you are a *boy*, and I am a *girl*?"

"Well. Yes. Precisely that."

I growl and kick off with my feet, using my upper body to pull myself up and my foot placement for stability, continuing until I reach the top. I am an island girl. *This is what we do.* I do not show it to them, but it takes me a few seconds to properly regain my breath at the top. It takes all I can manage not to clutch at my side.

I stand and take in the view around me. It is almost emotional, how beautiful the island is. One way is just miles of uninterrupted, navy-blue sea and a few flocks of seagulls going about their business. The other, as I turn, is predominantly green woods and meadows, with an occasional cottage dotted along the coastline.

Spotting Ma, Papa, Elka, Doug and Tomas on the beach, like little ants I am so high up, I wave enthusiastically. I am almost shaking with pride. I see Tomas look up from his book. He doesn't seem sure at first, then drops his book and stands. I watch as he runs to the grown-ups and points in my direction.

Do they think I am in trouble? I wave my hands above my head. *I am fine!*

The group on the beach start to make their way over to the rocks. In the rush to get down and clear up the situation, my footing slips, and I find myself sliding down the almost vertical wall of rocks so fast my cheeks don't even have time to blush. My behind bumps over small notches in the rocks and my feet scramble blindly to find some foothold. It is hopeless – the rocks are frustratingly smooth, aiding my fall rather than slowing it down. I can see the bottom of the shaft coming closer and the sharp, jagged edges of the rocks waiting to slice or impale me.

Before I can understand what is happening Otto steps into my path and throws his arms up beside him, palms on either side of the shaft. Rather than falling on to the piercing points of the rocks I fall into his arms. He stumbles back a little, grunting on impact.

He does not let me go.

I swallow hard, slowly opening my eyes. I hadn't realised I'd closed them.

His face is inches from mine, noses almost tip to tip. His eyes are an unusually exotic blue, this close. I search them rapidly, in time with my breath, waiting for him to say something, as I certainly cannot. Several strands of honey blonde hair dance around his eyes and he blinks them away, oblivious. What is the word I am looking for, I think, as I breathe in his salty, exerted aroma. His shirt sleeves are rolled up and it is the first time I notice just how strong his forearms are.

Intoxicating. That is the word.

"How old are you?" I breathe out, remarkably aware of how his arms still wrap warmly around me. His heart pumps just as much as mine, a vein in his neck throbbing to its beat. I watch his mouth, waiting for him to smirk or grin as I had become so used to seeing. He does neither. He looks, I notice, caught unawares – a mask down, truth revealed. I imagine it is how he wakes in the morning before he presents the world with himself, a raw canvas. The thought makes me blush. His lips pout and the breath coming through them is warm, tickling my cheek.

"Sixteen, Margot. I am sixteen."

Mariette, having seen enough, masquerades breaking us apart as coming to check on me. If she had not come, if she had not put her arm around Otto's waist and pulled him away, how long would we have stayed like that, I wonder.

We clamber back over the rocks in relative silence, something unfamiliar formed between us, neither of us sure how to move with it, but fully aware that it is there. We are met halfway across the sand by the adults and Tomas, all of them in a blind panic.

Ma runs straight at me, enveloping me in such a tight embrace I can barely take a breath. "Oh Margot, what on earth happened?"

"I am *fine*, truly Ma," I say. "I wasn't in trouble."

Tomas looks somewhat sheepish. "Your arms. They are grazed. Did you fall? Are you alright?" He walks back with me to our blanket and picnic.

I nod, feigning shock.

Am I alright?

No. I don't quite think I am.

I think I have just fallen – quite literally – into love.

6

Summer 1938

His eyes are on me as I walk across the pebbles and sharp nuggets of slate – I can feel them. I chance a glance over my shoulder. Yes, Otto is looking, from beneath a curtain of wayward, sun-tinged hair.

More aware now I know I have an audience, I walk across the Bathing Pools shoe horse walkway and dangle my feet into the water, cautiously. Tidal pools built in the 1800's, the railed pools are designed to fill with seawater at high tide and retain it at low. They were Tomas' brilliant idea to help me overcome my fear of the sea, six years earlier. He had taught me to move with the water rather than struggle against it, and had gripped my feet as I held on to the edge, only letting go when he was happy I had the power to sustain myself.

I look for him now, as I always do at times like this around water, but he sits on the stony bay, infatuated with baby Alice. Now almost two years old, the babbling, toddling little girl is equally as enamored with him. They have found themselves an amusing game; Alice wandering unevenly across the pebbles and collecting some treasured gifts to return to Tomas, who claps his hands and tickles her with glee.

He has fast become my best friend. Letter after letter we send to each other in the two years we are apart. When he stepped off the ferry this time a week ago, I noticed how much he had grown. His cheekbones more chiseled, dimples more pronounced, his hair somewhat longer. I had almost knocked him off his feet as we embraced. The years had been kind to him.

Ma has tried to imply something else, naturally. She cannot understand how we could have so much love for each other but not be *in* love. It doesn't help that Pierre, at fifteen, is already courting a girl from our lane. This is an over-exaggeration, of course, designed to make me panic. Though, when I think back on what has happened in our family over the last two years, I can understand why she thinks me older. I have had to be. Baby Alice arriving unexpectedly has meant that I have had to step up and help Ma more in the house, play the big sister rather than spending all of my time on the farm. But really, I am just trying to change the subject when she broaches it, because I know something she does not.

Neither Ma nor Papa – nor Mariette, for that matter - are aware of the exchanges between Otto and I. Every four weeks, for the last twenty four months, we have sent letters, back and forth, from Guernsey to Canada and back again.

The tone of these letters are entirely different to those I share with Tomas. In them we speak of the future. We speak of buying a ranch in Canada, using my skills learnt on the farm to raise cattle and sheep. We speak of each other; what we love and what we have not yet learnt. In every letter we ask a question, something simple and mundane. What is your favourite colour? What animal would you be? What music makes you cry? We ask them in an effort to learn everything there possibly is to know about one another. It never seems enough. There is one thing, in particular, I wish I could talk to him about. Of all the things I want to say, there is one that cannot be said in a letter.

I see a side of Otto that is soft, honest and vulnerable. In person he is full of wise cracks and quips, a smirk that says 'I don't care,' and a walk like he owns everyone and everything. He is undaunted, unafraid and unapologetic. In our letters he allows me a glimpse beneath that mask.

Yes, I can see why Ma would press so much for Tomas to be the object of my affections. Tomas is much more sensible, studious and practical. He makes sense, to my mother. Otto does not.

I wave Tomas in to join us as I slide off the walkway and tread water with trepidation. "Not this time," he calls. I see him glance at his wristwatch, making sure we do not miss the bus home, probably.

The Reid's are in awe of the freedom we have as teenagers on the island. There are little to no safety concerns and we are free to roam as we please. The boys see it as a revelation when they visit.

I watch him. When he is not playfully entertaining Alice, he falls into a somewhat melancholy reverie, watching the land, the sea, *us*. After a while, I run out of the water and throw myself next to him whilst he lies on his front, reading. Alice is napping under an open umbrella nearby. I close my eyes and enjoy the sizzle of the suns heat on my goose bumped flesh.

"Welcome back to the land of the living," he quips.

My smile falters a little. "Whatever do you mean?"

He gestures at the pool, as if that explains it. I shake my head. "You could have joined us, you know. Alice loves the water."

He is silent for a moment, before closing his book and sitting up rigid, almost in defiance for my lying down. He softens, eventually, as I suspected he would. Friendship always endeavors.

"You have changed a lot in the last two years, Mar, that's all."

I prop myself up on my elbow. His eyes drop down for just a flicker – a quarter second of a beat – then they find mine. His cheeks colour a little, which is unusual for Tomas. I want to say 'of course I have changed, Tomas, so *much* has changed.' Instead, I ask, "How so?"

"You are…confident. I like to see it, I do. I worry, though. I worry about where it has come from." His eyes unmistakably drift to the area of the pool where Otto and Pierre are diving in.

"Otto?"

"I know about the letters. He showed me."

"Well," I pick up a few loose pebbles and drop them, trying to be casual. "The letters are not a secret, Tom."

"But…Otto?" He looks ahead with a fixed, firm jaw. Then, he breaks and laughs. It is hearty and pure - it makes me smile. "Of all the people, Mar, *Otto*? He is my cousin and I love him, but you can do so much bloody better." He puts an arm around me. "I still love you. Just…be careful."

"Careful?"

"If Otto wants something, Otto gets it. And when he is bored, he isn't afraid to throw it away."

↔

Tomas may not think his intentions are pure, but as Otto meets me in the garden after dinner when the others have retired to the living room, his knowing smirk replaced with something altogether more solemn and serious, I disagree.

"There she is," he smiles, pulling me into a tight embrace. He steps back, replacing a wayward curl behind my ear. "Well, that was torturous."

"What was?"

"Fending off Mariette's advances."

I do not remember Mariette being in the farmhouse when I'd finished washing and drying the dishes. "Where is she?"

"Gone home, I imagine. She's not our biggest friend right now."

"You told her!"

"It's been two years, Margot, it was about time," he says dryly, barely concealing a grin.

I nudge his shoulder. My cousin would hurt, for a while, but it will pass. This is Mariette – affected by nothing. The memory of the love charm threatens to surface but I push it away.

Taking my hand, he leads me to the wall bordering the bottom of the garden. He sits with his back against the stone, drawing me into him so I face away. He pulls my hair from my neck and runs his nose along my nape.

"I spoke with your father earlier today."

"Oh?" I frown. I had known about his intentions to tell Mariette, but not Papa.

"I had to."

"You did?"

"There is an unspoken rule, is there not, that once a man has finished courting a girl, he asks her father if he can make her his wife."

Oh, this glorious feeling, bordering on painful, as my heart swells and fills my chest with a blinding warmth. I smile so broadly it hurts my cheeks. "And what did he say? Did he give his blessing?"

"Of course he did, it was me doing the asking." As I turn, I see his eyes sparkle with mischief.

"Really? He did?"

I feel his chest slowly inflate against my back. In that moment, as he exhales, his façade breaks, and his hard edges soften. "He did. I could have cried, Margot," he whispers. Then, loudly clears his throat. "I *will* cry. Later. When I am alone. Incredibly masculine." I nestle into him, keen to get closer.

"We've not gone about things conventionally, you and I, have we." He says wistfully. I hold my breath, wondering if now is the time to tell him, to tell him everything. But then he continues, and the fleeting moment is gone. "What with you hating me for years."

I wince. "Hate is a strong word. *Dislike* is perhaps more fitting."

He throws his head back and lets out a low laugh. It makes his whole body shake. "Oh, you hated me. It is quite alright. But that moment, when I gallantly saved your life," he puffs his chest animatedly, "it all changed then. There was a spark, wasn't there, that couldn't be ignored, even if we had wanted it to be."

I remember the feeling that day, the way it washed over me wholly uninvited. It had to be listened to. It was Otto. Always Otto.

"Tomas has told me to be careful."

"Tomas needs to keep his nose out."

"He cares about me -"

"- *I* care about you."

"- he does not want me to get hurt."

"*Every heart sings a song, incomplete, until another heart whispers back. Those who wish to sing, always find a song*. Plato," he explains with a sigh. "My cousin thinks this way because I had not met you when he formed this opinion of me. Your song whispers to me, Margot, and I will always answer it."

He folds his arms across me, and we sit like that for a while, his chin resting on my head.

"Will you, Margot?"

"Hmm?" I murmur, dreamily.

"Will you be my wife one day?"

↔

Mariette has not gone home.

When I turn in for the evening she is in my bed, as we had spent most summers since we were four years old. I climb in carefully, keen not to disturb her.

She does not turn to me, nor does she move an inch to make me believe she is awake before the air around us tingles. "He is not the one meant for you."

↔

Shortly before dinner the following night, Papa makes a grand entrance carrying a rather battered and beaten brown box. When he sets it down on the table in the living room where we sit playing a card game of Snap, Ma jumps.

"Frank!" She exclaims, holding a hand over her heart. "What on earth -"

"A wireless," he declares proudly.

"Yes, I can see that."

Elka and Doug are sat in front of me, just a little to my left, otherwise I would have missed the look between them. It speaks a thousand words, none of which I understand.

"I've always wanted one, you see."

"Have you?" She sounds incredulous.

"And Mr Mahy from the grocers was selling one. So, I thought, why not."

"Was he now?" Ma doesn't appear to believe him.

I watch a myriad of silent exchanges between them, then Elka mumbles something to Doug, who stands and looks apologetically at my mother. "Lucille, I am afraid I must take responsibility for Frank's purchase here." He glances at Otto, Tomas, Pierre and I. "I suggested it may be prudent, for the future, if he had one to hand."

Something is being said between the four of them, without it being said. Something we are evidently not privy to.

Pierre starts to fiddle with the wireless. It is large and cumbersome. How Papa had brought it from Mr Mahy to the farmhouse on his own I will never quite know. There is a central dial, and two knobs either side of some buttons. I wouldn't have the slightest know-how to use it.

By the end of 1943, I will be an expert.

7

Winter 1938

Only six months have passed when the Reid's return. This time, as we wait at the White Rock harbour, the atmosphere on the jetty is far from jovial. My parents are tucked in as tight to their woolen overcoats as they can be, Alice swaddled tightly against Ma. My hands are clad in the finest Canadian wool gloves that Otto had sent me only four weeks ago. He had never experienced a Guernsey winter, but I had written to him about the frigid cold and the intense coastal wind that reaped regular havoc on trees and winter crops.

"An exposed position such as yours deserves the finest wool one can buy," he had written. A week later, Tomas had written much the same thing, enclosing a similar pair. I tuck my gloved hands into the pockets of my overcoat, watching as their ferry makes shape on the horizon.

Not only does the island lay at the mercy of the wind and almost permanent rain showers October to February, we are also prone to thick fog which drifts up from the beaches or down from the highest tip of the island. In truth, winter on Guernsey is quite an isolated place to be.

"Papa," I ask for the tenth time, "tell me again why the Reid's have chosen February to visit?"

The fact that historically the Reid's have visited every two years, always in the summer, is not lost on me. Ma and Papa are hiding the real reason, whatever it may be. It only makes me more determined to find out why.

"They just can't stay away from us, can they Lucille," he tries a wry smile, one that only a man like Frank can get away with. In the frigid and bitter cold, however, it comes off as more of a grimace. It seems appropriate, with the lie. My mother shakes her head silently, tucking her chin in deeper to her coat and avoiding my scrutiny.

"I know it is more than that." I don't meet either of their eyes as I say it. "I just wish I could find out from you and not them."

Pierre hops from one foot to the other in a vain attempt at keeping warm. In the last six months he has had an adolescent growth spurt, almost towering over me.

Twenty minutes later, as the ferry docks and the passengers begin to disembark head first into the coastal elements, Pierre tugs my hand, pulling me back as Ma and Papa head towards the crowd.

"I may know why the Reid's are visiting now."

I wait for him to continue, but he doesn't. "Well?"

"It will cost you."

I roll my eyes. *Are all little brothers so infuriating?* "You know I can just ask Otto. He will tell me." I point out.

"Will he, though?" He runs his forefinger along his chin, pretending to think. "What if the truth would terrify you? Would he tell you then, or would he protect you from it?"

I analyse my not-so-little brother. He isn't one for dramatics, in truth. Pierre will usually tell you as he sees it, which makes this little show all the more confusing. Or worrying.

I sigh. "I will give you my upcoming weeks wage, how about that?"

I had been approached by a member of staff at Boots Chemists only two months earlier, asking if I would be interested in working for them on their beauty counter. I felt flattered; Boots notoriously employed only the prettiest girls to lure in customers. Mariette had already been employed there for a year.

He nods. "Fair trade." We stop walking altogether, letting the hustle and bustle continue around us. I keep one eye trained on the ferry, waiting for those familiar faces I have come to think of as second family. "Before I go to meet Ma and Papa on the farm in the mornings, I pretend I am not finished in the bathroom." I screw my nose up. "In truth, I sneak into Papa's study and turn on his wireless set. I listen to the BBC broadcasts for ten minutes, maybe more, depending on how long I believe I can get away with it."

"What does Papa's wireless set have to do with the Reid's?"

As I say the words, I remember an exchange, six months earlier. One that I knew then was an omen to something, something hidden.

"The BBC says that there is an impending invasion on Europe. They say a man, Hitler, is going to war."

I scoff. War, of course, is never off the table, I know that. Our Channel Islands had sacrificed many men to the Great War only years earlier. But an impending war, in Europe…I can't believe it. Has the world not already learnt its lesson that fighting achieves very little, except avoidable death?

"What would a war in Europe have to do with the Reid's visiting us from Canada?"

I look over Pierres shoulder to the ferry. Through the salt-stained windows I see rows of passengers still waiting to disembark. The Reid's haven't yet made landfall.

"Hitler is the leader of the Nazi party. A dictator, in Germany."

Elka - the majestic, powerful matriarch of the Reid family - is the first to take steps on to the jetty. Unlike Doug and Otto, Elka had been born and raised in

Germany. Tomas had been made an orphan when his mother and father – Elka's brother – had died, a result of infections picked up in post-wartime Germany.

"I'm not sure I follow. Pierre, do you believe the Reid's are coming here…for safety?"

For once, my brother looks sombre and serious. "No, Go-Go, I do not." My brothers affectionate childhood term for me seems oddly out of place, on this freezing, wind-bitten morning on the jetty. "My theory is – and I should request payment of another half weeks wage for this but, I like you, so I shan't – the Reid's are heading back to Germany."

↔

The truth, I shortly find out, is that Elka's father is ill. Germany is troubled, as is most of eastern Europe, and the future unsettlingly uncertain. Elka's father is elderly and lived alone.

"We have been back and forth," Elka whispers to Ma after dinner, though she makes a poor show of it. We can hear every word from where we sit, across the room. "But what can I do Lucille? I cannot leave him there."

"Will you bring him back to Canada with you?" Papa asks, running a hand along his stubbled chin. In the evening Winter light, one side of his face illuminated by a hearty fire in the grate, it strikes me how handsome he is. He is a big man, a bear. I cannot imagine him living somewhere far away, sick and alone, and having to make the decision to bring him somewhere away from the home he has always known, somewhere safe.

"If he will come," she sighs. "He is like you, Frank. Stubborn as hell." The adults around the fire laugh at this, but it is tinged with a horrible sadness. It doesn't sound right, and it frightens me.

"Elka, what if he is there?" Ma's voice drops. It is hollow and cautiously tinged, I realise, with fear. The four of us – myself, Otto, Tomas and Pierre - sit motionless around the table, uncomfortably aware that we can all hear every word.

"I certainly hope he is!"

"Not your father, Elka," she says, gently. "You know who I mean. What if he should find out you are back in Germany? What if he -"

"Doug will be with me, Lucille."

"Damn right I will. And if he dares to even come within an inch -"

"*Doug*," Elka warns, casting a look towards Otto.

"The house is not big, mother, I can hear you all loud and clear." Otto startles us all.

"Lucille," Elka continues, waving away Otto's comment but no longer speaking in a hushed voice, "if he finds me, I shall do what I should have done, seventeen years ago."

From here the adults fall back into a hushed chatter. I know better than to push Elka – or Otto – on what they mean.

The Reid's, I find out, are using Guernsey as a stepping stone on their route through Europe and down to Germany.

"Mar, are you in?" I turn back to the table, where Tomas waves a deck of cards at me. "Are we dealing you in?"

Tomas, of them all, looks the least troubled and preoccupied by what is to come. *He is going home*, I remind myself. Tomas had only been young when made an orphan, but old enough to remember a home he hadn't seen for many years. On paper, I suppose, it is a simple trip to pick up an ailing relative and bring him safely back. In truth, the more I listen to them talk of what they should expect, it seems a perilous journey to take. I fear for them all.

"Yes…alright."

Pierre and Otto are already dealt in for a Canadian card game I've been trying to learn the rules for. Mariette, this time, had not come to welcome the Reid's, nor had she joined us for dinner. It is unlikely she will see them now before they depart; they leave on the ferry to France early tomorrow morning.

We had played one round, and Tomas is setting up the second, when Otto's chair suddenly scrapes along the wooden floor and, without warning, he storms outside. Silence hangs in the air between all of us. The adults, too, have paused their whispered conversation and now look to where Otto has just departed. My eyes meet Elka's. She seems to deliberate something, then nods at me. I take this to mean I should follow.

I find him sat at the table outside the rear door, looking over the empty and barren cornfield. "Everything must look quite different to you, at this time of year." I take a blanket from the willow basket by the door, flicking off a comfortable spider, and close the door on the others.

He waves a cigarette at me. "Do you mind if I do?"

I shake my head. I am frightened, of course, by what is waiting for them in Germany, but nothing terrifies me more than seeing this somber change in Otto. I watch as his shaking hand puts the cigarette to his mouth.

"Are you cold?" He gestures to the blanket.

"I thought you might like it. We could sit here, together, if you wish to talk."

He shakes his head – not in refusal – laughing sadly and pulling the blanket across the two of us.

"Do you know what I am most afraid of?" He doesn't wait for an answer. "Not getting back home. I have heard the stories of wartime Europe, I just hope we don't…I hope we make it back to Canada, is all. If we do not make it back, to Canada, to…*anywhere*," he whispers, "I want you to know that this – this is not just a summer romance for me. You are not someone I just pick up when I visit. I – I'm always thinking of you. Contrary to what Tomas believes -"

"I never thought that, Otto. It is not for me, either. Will you write to me, when you are over there?"

"Of course."

"I shall pretend you are just back in Canada, that is what I will do," I proclaim, deciding on a plan of action to stop myself worrying. "It will be no different to when we go twenty four months without seeing one another."

"I wish I could do the same. How can we, Margot? Germany is not Canada."

We sit in silence, the inhale and exhale of his cigarette the only sound falling into the cold, silent night air.

"Everything *does* look quite different at this time of year." He offers, finally. "It is quite foreboding really, is it not. Is this weather an omen for what we are about to face, do you think?"

The air temperature seems to plummet in that moment, and what feels like a thousand needles stab at my exposed cheeks. "Snow," he says, in awe, amazed at how this winter weather can befall us on this little island.

"They had forecast it for tomorrow; it has come early. It is rare, here. There is too much salt in the air for it to settle. I find it quite magical," I say, looking up as the tiny flecks of white fall silently on us. I stand, forgetting the bitter cold, and hold my arms out to either side, almost as if I am in the middle of a folk dance. "I'm sure in Canada you see it all the time but here -"

So quick and swift that I haven't even noticed him move, and quite without warning or invitation, he kisses me. Otto needs no invitation. The force of it almost knocks me off my feet. I put my hands on his shoulders, pushing back ever so slightly. The snowflakes slide down into the small gap between our parted mouths and the warm air melts them instantly.

"I cannot leave without…" he breathes, his hands cupping my cheeks. I close my eyes, feeling the tips of his fingers bury beneath my hair, brushing my neck.

"Do it again," I whisper. "Do it again, and this time, do not stop."

8

March 1940

The intoxicating scent of approaching Summer fills the air as I cycle to the White Rock harbour. I race down the *Val Des Terres* as quick as I can pedal. The hilly descent into Guernsey's main town is notoriously difficult to get back up, but at this point, nothing can deter me from my intentions.

In the basket of my cycle is a letter and, as it always does, it feels like it carries my heart as well as words. It had taken three months for Otto's first letter from Europe to arrive. In it he spoke of his families uncomfortable but uneventful journey to his ailing grandfather. Unfortunately, his health was worse than expected, and they were to be in Germany with him for a while longer. Nine months later, it was to Germany that the letter in my basket is addressed. I hope, for all their sakes, that the next one will be to Canada, to their safety.

The news of Germany's invasions across Europe and the subsequent declaration of War has not gone unnoticed on our small, isolated island. We rely a great deal on import and export of goods to sustain our livelihood - Papa, in particular, is feeling the effects of the disruption in the chain. Other than in this area our island is, thankfully, little affected.

There is a certain element of safety in being set away from the continent. We hear the rumours over Papa's wireless (a purchase I suspected long ago was down to Doug and Elka's doing, with their knowledge of what was to come) often enough, but with all that ocean between us and the alleged atrocities we can, to some degree, feign ignorance.

If only Otto and his family can get back to Canada I can continue to play the concerned observer, rather than feeling some personal investment in what is happening over there. They have my betrothed, and I would quite like him back.

I pedal faster as I cycle along the flat stretch of harbour road, passing offices and tiered homes in a blur. On one side, the town of St Peter Port is built into a steep, hilly landscape, where narrow, cobbled streets meander at times almost vertically through townhouses, small shops and specialist grocers. On the other I cycle almost level with the crystal blue sea, where the busy port and harbour of the White Rock are home to an army of mariners and dock workers. It is here, at the harbour, that I watch the mailboat depart only minutes after I ditch my cycle and run to the sailor on board with my letter.

"This should have been posted, Miss," he had said sternly. A shrug of my shoulders and a battering of eyelashes and the kind sailor had popped my letter into the mailsack marked for Europe.

A tiny little thing, the mailboat appears, chugging away on the sea. Yet it carried so much of people with it; letters to loved ones, to far away friends bearing news of joy or sharing moments of sorrow. I watch as it carves its way through gentle waves soundlessly, with a smile on my face. Another piece of me is on its way to him. It will cross several oceans, touch land in several places before reaching him. Quite an adventure.

I pull my eyes away from the mailboat when it shrinks to a speck on the horizon and jauntily hop on to my abandoned bicycle. But my eyes catch something unusual on the ocean, and I pause.

"What on earth -" I breathe.

An old fishing boat is working its way into the harbour. People on deck are waving to me – to *anyone,* it seems – stood on the pier. Small figures – children, perhaps - are jumping, running from side to side to get a better look. There is an air of frantic joy on deck. Frankly, it looks chaotic.

"I don't recognise that one," grunts a dock worker as he passes, his arms laden with light machinery for the boats. He walks several paces from me then pauses altogether, eyes fixed firm on the boat. "What's got 'em all in a tizz, d'ya wonder?"

"I'm not quite sure," I muse. "Perhaps I'll take a walk down to the jetty, just to see. Point them in the right direction when they make land."

I climb down the jetty steps to the lower platform, taking care not to slip on the wet gangway. The boat is closer now, and I squint to the deck as it approaches. I raise my hand to wave back, offer a warm welcome if nothing else, but my arm stops halfway.

It cannot be…

Bodies – *so many bodies* – are horizontally stacked atop of one another on the open deck. Limbs from one mingle in with another, gruesome swollen parts distorted beyond recognition. I cover my mouth with the back of my hand, swallowing a knot of something awful rising in my throat.

I draw my eyes from the lifeless to those who are still alive. If one can call it that.

Ma would call them "skin and bones." There is little to them – walking skeletons, if that. These people have not seen food for a long time. Their jumping in joy and frantic waves, I now see, is the result of what little energy they had left to alert us to whatever horror they had endured. The sheer act has exhausted them and they all but collapse on to the salt-rimmed rails of the tiny fishing boat.

By now more people have joined me on the jetty, sharing in the horror as the boat gets ready to tie in. Dock workers scramble to assist the captain. Already the stench from the bodies is in the air, fueling it, thickening it.

I try desperately to lock eyes with one of them, but their bulging eyes are cast down, down to the sea. Finally, one, licking her lips against the salt air, meets my gaze. She opens her mouth to speak but at first no sound comes, just a rattled croak of someone minutes from death. She tries again.

I hold my hand to my ear. "I can't hear you," I call. French…is she speaking French?

She groans, and with a great strength I would not have thought possible, grips the railing, straightens her arms and draws her body upright. "*Le mondes est…*" she levels my gaze with hollow eyes and draws a single finger across her throat. No language barrier in the world could misinterpret that action.

The world is…

9

Early June 1940

That fishing boat carrying a hold full of French refugees was to be the first of many that would seek shelter on our island. On an island so small there were wild rumours, naturally, of ten boats, twenty even, over the course of the next three months. In truth, there were fewer than ten. No matter the number, as with the arrival of the refugees came the horrors of what they were fleeing.

Starvation – something so unimaginable in itself – is the least disturbing of the stories they bring. The German soldiers, it is said, will resort to all manner of means to get what they want, including brutal torture, murder and rape.

We have watched on as Germany invaded Norway, the Netherlands and Belgium and is now steamrolling its way with horrifying speed across France. According to newspapers, they have already blitzed their way into Paris.

Guernsey sits nestled geographically close to the coast of Northern France, and our vulnerable proximity to the impending German army is not lost on any of us. Our haven, our island of peace, has never felt more isolated and exposed.

Talks of a possible invasion on the island differ wildly from district to district. In the country parishes – where our family farmhouse, growing fields and cattle are – it seems so obsolete, so wild of a suggestion, that it is almost laughable. To the east of the island where there lies the main town, the shops, the harbour and, on a clear day, a direct view across to France, it seems more than possible.

The daily markets that Papa and I travel to become a breeding ground for gossip and hearsay.

"Why would they invade and occupy our island, Edith? What could little ol' Guernsey possibly bring Hitler and his army of madmen?"

"*British soil*, Raymond. Hitler would sell his own limb to occupy a piece of British territory, no matter how small."

"I shan't believe it."

"You can believe those damn airplanes though, can't you?"

The presence of aircraft flying overhead across the island is undeniable, though whether the planes are German or British can, on most occasions, not be determined.

For the most part, since war had officially been declared in the September of 1939, we had felt like sitting ducks. We fully expected to be subject to stray bombs or aircraft casualties, sitting as centrally as we did between England and France. Thankfully they had, thus far, failed to materialise into anything other than the things of panicked nightmares.

The irrevocable fear that grows daily in the pit of my stomach is not solely for my home. It is – more predominantly so – also for Otto.

I have not heard from him since February – almost four months ago. My letter to him in March has gone unacknowledged. It is the longest I have gone without contact. With every newspaper headline and BBC broadcast on the war comes another thud to my chest. I wish for nothing more than to be able to cover my ears and cower in a corner until it is all over. At which point Otto can sweep in, lift me back up and assure me he had been safely seeking refuge in Canada all along. The thought of him and his family being amongst the terrors on the continent makes my stomach roil.

This is not how our story is supposed to end. We have so much more to act out. We are going to live long lives, entwined in daily rituals together. We will do simple things; go to the market or the beach, or drive with no destination in mind, one of his hands on the wheel, the other linked with mine. My comfort, my reassurance, will be feeling the softness of his skin and the gentle scratch of his stubbled chin on my cheek. Our story is not supposed to end without knowing where he is. I have to find him again; it is not fair if he is lost to me before we really begin.

I had spent an entire childhood being told that I was old before my time. As a young adult, my no nonsense, no fuss attitude was lamented and extolled. My mind has always felt fuss-free, as if the answer to everything is always clear as day, and the inability for others to come to the same conclusion is at best baffling, at worst tiresome. Yet now I have no clear answer. My heart is cloudy. It hurts. It aches. It is true that our story should not end this way, that it is unfair, illogical, torturous even, for it to just cease. The reality however – of which I try my upmost to ignore – is one where he is caught in warfare and could be anywhere. It makes my head spin. My only blessing is that I will not move. I will be the constant. This island, my paradise, is where I will stay. That way, he will find me. He will find me when he can.

↔

No war can deny that summer is upon the island. To do such normal activities such as picnicking on the beach feels ignorant on our part. Life, however, seems to go on.

On one particularly hot summer Sunday, the sun burning brightly overhead (the sky clear, for once, of any lingering aircraft), Mariette joins Pierre, Alice and myself at the beach.

By now Alice is four years old. The same age, it occurs to me, that I had been when I had first met Otto, even if those memories are now merely flashes of moments that once were, or could have been.

Mariette is laying out on a beach towel under the blazing sun. I am knee deep in a hole Alice has requested Pierre and I dig. She claps with glee as every spade full of sand flies through the air.

"One of these days Margot you will grow up," Mariette grumbles.

I roll my eyes and hold out my hands to tickle Alice beneath the arms. She giggles infectiously, and even cool Mariette cracks a smile. Pierre stands and pretends to lecture us on abandoning our hole-digging posts. His tanned skin gleams with exertion, and I swallow pride at how handsome he has become. He is fifteen, still a child, but years of hard labour on the farm has brought undeniable strength to his arms and legs.

"Come on," I say, "let's sit down for some lunch."

My feet though, do not move. My hands grip Alice's arms to keep her steady, as if somehow by her staying still everything else will make sense. The high noon sun has been eclipsed and everything on the beach falls under a ghostly shadow.

"Is that -" Pierre starts.

"What on earth -" Mariette sits upright, blinking into the disappearing sunshine.

All around us people put hand to brow and watch the strange sight across the ocean and into the sky unfold. A pall of smoke rises from the horizon like a column, overpowering the sun's rays and sending us all into shade. The cloud grows increasingly dense and dark with each passing second.

My stomach involuntarily lurches and grips; I have to use all of my strength to stop from doubling over. Still, I keep a hold of Alice. Pierre has edged closer and together we form a triangle, watching.

"That's France, isn't it, Go-Go?" I sense he wants to hold my hand too, but he refrains.

"I believe so."

Yes. It is.

An awful silence has descended across the beach, with not one person uttering a sound. Babies, toddlers, young children, all of whom moments ago had been delirious in the throes of beach day fun - none of them have to be told to hush. Even the gulls overhead do not caw. They just know.

The eerie silence is disturbed by a mild tremor underfoot and the unmistakable sound of rapid fire, drifting to us from the continent like a ghostly whisper. It is resigned looks that flit between the adults, and I know what they say without need for words.

"France is burning."

↔

For weeks we continue to see evidence of the war reaching the Normandy coast. Smoke often drifts across Guernsey's skyline, and with it more signs that even the most stoic and defiant Islander can no longer question where we stand in the warpath.

Growers and farmers, like Papa, feel the effects of this odd in-between in particular.

Towards the middle of June, we are stopped by one of Papa's friends enroute to the harbour, our truck laden with overflowing crates of the juiciest local tomatoes ready for export to the mainland. Papa leans out of the window to speak with him, keeping their voices low. I can tell that my father is not pleased.

"*A la perchôine*, Etienne," Papa grunts, keeping his truck window open but pressing the accelerator with gusto. *Good day*, Etienne.

The romance of our ancient Guernsey dialect feels at odds with his harried behaviour. He runs a grubby, weather-toughened hand through his surprisingly thick hair as he drives, shaking his head to something.

I expect Papa to turn home – I suspected we were no longer taking the tomatoes to the harbour – but he continues on into the town. He drives us to a place locally dubbed the Blue Mountains viewing point. Of course it is not a mountain, neither is it blue, but it does have one of the most impressive views in the island. In particular, on a clear forecast such as today, you can see the harbour and the surrounding area in unrivalled clarity.

"I knew it," he grunts, stepping out of the truck and leaving his door ajar. I weigh up my options – Papa is a friendly bear, but has a temper easily lost – and decide to follow him. "They're taking everything away." He leans against the mid-height wall above the steep, vertical descent into the town. "Every*thing* and every*one* who could protect this island is upping sticks and leaving."

"Papa," I whisper, shocked. "Truly? How – how can you be sure? The British Government haven't said anything about -"

"Every man with half a brain and a pair of eyes can see it, Margot. They're leaving nothing – nothing at all – with which we can protect ourselves from an attack."

His words, though not meant to hurt, make my stomach roll and my eyes sting. I look again. He is right. He is always right. Armoured vehicles, trucks – large and small, and military men are gathering at the White Rock harbour like ants to an apple core. They load truckloads of armoury and equipment on to waiting vessels. Then, themselves. From here, it is silence. From down there, I can only imagine the noise.

"Papa, let's go," I tug at his navy blue knit – the traditional Guernsey jumper. As is the case with all traditional Guernsey men, however, he stubbornly refuses. He keeps watching them, shaking his head – a masochist awaiting a different outcome.

"The cowards."

"Perhaps they have a reason for it. Think about it, Papa, without a military on the island the Germans won't see us as a threat," I try, willing my words to be true. "Madam Martel says that Germany would have no use for us, anyway, we are so small, so *unimportant*. She says they will just bypass us on their way to -"

"Madam Martel – and all the others who say the same – need their heads clunking together. The British Government may have demilitarised us but it's not to save our bacon. They're just leading the lambs to slaughter."

And so it is that all arms, uniform and military equipment leave our island.

We are defenceless against an attack.

For by now, I know enough to be sure that an attack will surely come.

10

Mid June 1940

"That's unusual," Pierre notes, pointing a finger at a small congregation of men and women, walking together, heads down, towards one of the towns school buildings.

"Hmm." I agree with his sentiments, of course: it is unusual. But the clandestine act of the adults on our island, particularly ones in esteemed positions, meeting together was becoming a common occurrence.

We had come into the town on our bicycles, with baskets laden with tomatoes to sell at the local market. Exporting beyond the island is still not permitted, so we had taken to selling some of our wares to local neighbours and friends. Now, we sit on one of the low-level walls in a narrow, cobbled and hilly lane, snacking on a large red juicy tomato each, giggling as the juice drips down our chins.

"You animal," I laugh, as Pierre makes a show of grinding the juice into his chin.

"Good for the complexion, you know."

A silence falls between us, Pierre munching on his tomato in a boyish fashion, and I watching the group of headteachers – for which I knew for sure four of the six of them were – entering the school. The loud but charming gaggle of schoolchildren on lunch reverberates off the buildings.

"What do you think they are discussing?"

Pierre looks from me to the headteachers and back. "I wouldn't worry about it."

"I'm not," I lie. "I just think of Alice, that is all. She is in her first year of school. It would be a shame, wouldn't it, for anything to happen to her education because of what is happening on the continent."

"I don't see how education will change. Even if something does happen to us here -"

"*When* it happens."

He sighs and shakes his head. "Ever the pessimist, aren't you Go-Go? Look, *should* anything happen to the schools, Alice will get just as much of an education from the farm as she would stuck in any old building. Come on, let's go." He throws the pithy core of his tomato to the ground and mounts his bicycle. "Race you to the top."

↔

We dawdle on our way home, racing each other through the country lanes, and by the time we get back to the farmhouse it is well into evening. If we are lucky, we may have just made it in time for dinner.

Ma is standing at Papa's side in the kitchen, reading the evening newspaper over his shoulder. Neither of them notice as we enter. It is only the look on their faces – the scrunched together brow and set line of their mouths – that tells me anything is wrong at all.

"Who died?" Pierre jokes, but it falls flat, and no one smiles.

I can hear Alice banging around in her bedroom above the kitchen; the thin floorboards hiding nothing.

"She sounds…spirited," I point out, when only her thuds break up the awkward silence that has fallen between the four of us.

It doesn't strike me as unusual – not immediately, anyway - that Alice isn't at my mother's skirts. You could usually find her in two places; with me or attached to Ma.

"Is she displeased because she couldn't come with us to deliver the tomatoes?"

Ma sighs and her eyes meet mine, filled with an inexplicable concern.

Something bad has happened.

"What, then?" All of a sudden I can hear the blood behind my ears, thumping and pumping. "Is it Otto? Ma? Has something happened to Otto? Oh my, please don't -" My eyes are already swimming with tears when my father puts the newspaper down on the table. I blink them away, trying to make sense of the words roaring at me in print.

Pierre leans his head past me, towards the paper. After two seconds his composure breaks and he roughly pulls it closer to him. "Evacuation?" He looks up to Ma, Papa, lingering on me. "Is this – is this for -"

"They are evacuating our children to the mainland. *All* children. School age and under." Alice, as if hearing us, thumps a bit louder in her bedroom. "She doesn't know," Ma says, reading my thoughts. "She's not happy because your father and I told her to go to her room for a moment. She thinks -" she puts the back of her hand across her mouth, looking down, shaking her head. "She thinks we are mad with her, and she does not understand why."

Pierre and I huddle closer together – so close I can smell the tomato juice still tainting his skin - taking in the smaller print of the front page. My eyes skim fast, too fast, and I have to read it several times before any of it makes some semblance of sense.

"It says we need to report to the school tonight, by 7 o'clock."

"Yes," Papa – who has remained silent throughout all of this – says, pulling his pocket watch from his pocket. "In one hour."

I can barely catch a breath. There isn't enough time, surely, to make a decision such as this. My eyes glaze over the ration lists of food, the articles of clothing to pack for the journey ahead. An image, then, appears in my mind of Alice, with a case of limited clothing, a basketful of food to last her, alone in the hustle of England. Her dark hair, braided, trailing down her back as she boards the boat to take her away. Her eyes – betrayed, terrified…

I close my eyes and let the tears fall down my cheeks. I push the newspaper away. "It says if parents desire it."

"Yes," Ma says, and I see her grip my father's shoulder harder, until the tips of her fingers embed deep into his soiled work shirt. This is the moment she has been dreading.

"Do you desire it?" I force the words out, pushing them past the tears, past a disturbing gripping sensation in my chest. In spite of all the power behind them, they come out as nothing more than a meek croak.

"Margot," she says, releasing her grip on my Papa and coming to place a hand either side of me, caressing my arms gently. "You and I both know that it is not I who has to, truthfully, make that decision." The three pairs of eyes in the room – all filled with the same indescribable torment of indecision – are all of a sudden upon me. "So, what it is going to be *ma p'tite souée*. Will your daughter stay, or will she go?"

11

Mid June 1940

I had never told them who the father of my unborn child was, though I was sure they had their suspicions. I had told them little, in truth, of the circumstances that led to Alice arriving one wet and windy April day, and they had asked few questions.

The five of us, including Mariette, had made a pact. When Ma and Papa were over the shock of finding out their fourteen-year-old daughter was with child, there was only one thing to do. It was out of the question that I could be seen to be the mother; I would be shunned by our community unless I feigned that something undesirable had happened to me. Which, I do not believe had been done, and to say otherwise would go against my word, months earlier. The same would be said for the baby; she would be tainted with the bastard title from birth.

Not once did my parents tarnish me with shame. Not once did they show any sign that they were disappointed, though I know they must have felt it. Whatever her circumstances getting here, she was an extension of their family and to my parents - like all families from close-knit communities - family is life. My parents are nothing if not pragmatic, practical and rational. They saw sense where there was none to be made.

It was Papa who first suggested it. We were to say that Ma had had a surprise birth – not a wholly uncommon occurrence - with the baby arriving entirely unexpected. It was lucky that the latter months of my pregnancy were in the dark, dank depths of winter. Both my mother and I layered ourselves in woolens; she for deception, I for concealment.

Alice was born in my childhood bedroom and expertly delivered by my mother and Mariette (who was still shocked that I had – willingly – lost my virginity before her).

I could see her father in her straight away, naturally, though if my family did, they refrained from commenting on it. To the world outside of our farmhouse – and to Alice herself – I had gained a sister. But she had always been so much more to me – a bond forged the moment I realised I carried her within me.

↔

Alice, whose future now lay upon my decision.

To send her away would be to an unknown and distant – but arguably safer – life. To keep her would be to leave her at the mercy of an inevitable invasion and all the horrors that the occupying forces would bring.

Ma goes along and registers her at the school, irrespective of a final decision, and at a very overdue teatime we broach the subject with Alice herself.

"Alice, sweetheart," Ma looks to me as Alice shovels a fork full of mashed potato into her mouth like she hasn't eaten for days. "I think – well…I'm not sure how to -"

"How do you feel about an adventure, Al?" I force my voice to sound more excited, more enticing, than I really feel.

Her eyes widen – such innocence – and she pauses with her fork to her mouth, potato dripping off either side. "What sort of adventure?"

"One far across the sea. On a *boat*, Alice. Not just a dinghy on the shore either, a real big boat. You would get to share the adventure with lots of other children too, lots of your new school friends."

The fork is now down, her mouth open a little. "When could we leave?"

I hesitate. *We*. The newspapers and the school have stressed that mothers are only to accompany children under school age – babies, toddlers, an age which Alice had only months before grown out of.

Or we evacuated as a family. Papa had already, in all his stubbornness, refused to leave his cattle, his pigs, his chickens, and the fields full of crops awaiting harvest. Ma would never leave him. I imagine being placed in the unthinkable position of choosing to leave Otto behind to the mercy of the Germans, and shudder. Pierre has the option, as all children do, to leave with Alice. I can see the havoc the choice has on him. He is at the awkward junction of childhood and manhood; the boy in him longs to run off with the next boat and explore England, but the man in him feels the pull to stay and help Papa. Who knows what farm aides would be left to do it after the evacuations? We may end up losing everything we had worked for. He has registered, as have I, so that the option is not taken from us, but we all know that he will stay.

As for myself, I cannot leave Guernsey, not even with the threat of a rabid Nazi army descending. Where will Otto find me, when all of this is over, if I leave? I know that Alice will be safer in England; our food supplies will eventually suffer, and young children will be the ones to hurt the most.

"This is so unfair," Pierre breathes, but Alice is so thrilled at the thought of an adventure now she does not hear him.

"That is the *best* thing about this quest, Alice. *No parents*. Just you and your friends."

"Grown-up's?"

"A few," I shrug it off. "Teachers. They will all be just as excited for the journey."

"When does it start?"

"Tomorrow. Tomorrow morning, in fact, so not a lot of time to prepare. The surprise adventures are the very best kind, don't you think?"

She chews the inner left corner of her mouth for a while, thinking. We wait with bated breath, no longer hungry for the food on our own plates.

"So, you won't come with me?" She looks at Ma when she says it, whose own eyes fill with tears before my own. She swallows them away.

"Not right away, darling, no. As soon as we are able, we will come and join you."

"But, where will I live? How long will I be gone for?"

The alluring premise of an adventure is beginning to wear off, we can all see it.

"There are some truly wonderful families in England who will look after you until we can get there."

Alice drops her eyes back to her dinner and finishes it in silence. She puts her elbows on the table – something Ma would usually have called her out on, but ignores this evening – and says, mimicking an adult, "I suppose this adventure could be fun. Am I most definitely going? Can I take my toothbrush?"

Glances are shared between Ma, Papa, and Pierre and I. No one answers. No one quite knows what the correct answer is.

Over the next few hours, way past the time when Alice is tucked up in bed for what could be her last night in Guernsey, friends and neighbours drop in unannounced with only one thing on their minds; *what are you going to do?* It is all anyone wishes to discuss, and yet no one can give a clear answer.

I know I have a long, sleepless night ahead. Ma and I pack Alice's bags in line with the newspaper guidelines, barely speaking a word as we do. I fold her vest, a pair of knickers, a petticoat that she has only just chosen from the dressmakers, two pairs of stockings, a small pile of handkerchiefs, a blouse and a cardigan. My hand hovers on the navy-blue knitted cardigan, before I pick it up and take a deep inhale of her sweet, childish scent. I hug it close to me.

Ma brings in Alice's favourite night dress, a comb, towel, soap, washcloth, and the toothbrush she was so keen not to be parted with. Clothes for the following morning are already laid out, along with her red overcoat that suddenly looks so small and precious.

I pause in the doorway of her bedroom, listening to her breaths. I know I should not risk waking her when we all have such an early start the next day – she is to be at her school by nine in the morning. I cannot resist sneaking in, however. I kneel beside her bed and pull her blanket a little higher to her chin – she has an awful habit of kicking off any coverlets, even in the depths of winter.

Her face looks so angelic in sleep. Skin completely unblemished, no frown or worry lines, but no smile lines either. She still has that baby fat plumped look about her, but it is clear she is leaning out.

I use my finger to gently move a stray curl from her face and kiss her forehead, lingering to breathe her in as much as I can. I wish I could squeeze her, hug her tighter than anyone has ever hugged before, so she has that memory to leave with. If she does indeed leave the next day.

By the time I make my way down to the kitchen my hands are shaking considerably more than they had been. Ma is already making rations for her to take in a brown paper lunch bag. There are two cheese sandwiches, a packet each of peanuts and raisins, a small container of extra cheese, one apple, one orange and, though the guidelines expressed Barley Sugar should be taken instead, we pack a few small squares of chocolate and wrap them in a napkin.

"As a treat," she says, patting them more times than necessary.

I collapse on to the wooden chair at the table and hang my head in my hands. "What will happen to her, if we let her go?" I look up through my fingers when she doesn't answer, and I see silent tears streaking her cheeks. She kneels beside me as I had just done with Alice and places her hands on my knees.

"Should we, let her go?" I whisper.

"There is no right answer. I heard tonight that the people in authority are staying. They are advising people not to act rash but -"

"But it is different for children. We have to choose for them."

"We will go to the school tomorrow," she decides, firmly. "Our gut will tell us what to do, then."

"And then we…" I inhale a deep breath, trying to ignore the burning in my chest, "and then we just leave her there?"

"The teachers will make sure the children get to the boats safely."

"It seems cruel, doesn't it, to just leave her there? To walk away, and know that she will be watching our backs as we go…Ma, how will we not run back to her? What will we do if she tries to follow us? She is so very little -" I break off as my bottom lip begins to tremble.

She sighs and sobs at the same time – a disconcerting sound from a woman who, for my entire life, has kept her emotions largely suppressed. Lucille La Joie, she of the stiff upper lip. "It would be more of a cruelty to watch her get on a boat and watch, helpless, from the harbour."

I nestle my head into her shoulder then, and allow my tears to fall unapologetically.

When I feel I can, I rise from the table. "So, tomorrow?"

"Tomorrow."

↔

Guernsey folk tend not to panic; we are the ideal people to have around in an emergency, so at the school the following morning it doesn't surprise me that the parents remain level-headed, with an air of approaching a problem head on. The adults silently assess their emotions, only their eyes betraying the deep-rooted pain they all feel. The children are less boisterous than they might otherwise have been, crammed into the school hall, but nevertheless it is still noisy. It has a sardines-tin feel about it all.

It still does not feel real to me, that we are going to just leave her here. I keep expecting someone to announce the entire thing has been called off, that the war is over and no evacuations will take place. Alice has never gone anywhere alone; not even the life at liberty we live on the island would stretch so far as to let a five-year-old girl go off unaccompanied.

I notice that she is shying away from her friends, keeping one hand on the hem of my mother's skirts.

I crouch down to her level. "Are you okay, Alice?"

She looks at her feet *(when will I see those little black Mary Janes with the shiny buckle again?)* and sniffs a little.

"I'm not feeling very brave today," she whispers, in a voice almost lost in the din of the hall.

My mother and I exchange a glance. Should the three of us just leave, right now, go back home and make an early lunch? Forget that we almost put Alice on a boat to England without us?

"I'm excited," Alice continues, "but…when will I see you again?"

Any answer we may have summoned is interrupted by the head teacher – Mr Despres – walking on to the stage to address us. A hush falls over the hall like a cloud and he adjusts his black rimmed glasses. A tall, wiry man with a generous head of curled black hair, I doubt he could ever have imagined he would be stood up there in this moment.

"I am sure at this time you are wondering why we have not left on our travels yet. We are still awaiting news of the boats that will transport us. I appreciate we have been here a while, and how challenging this must be for you all. I will keep -" he is broken off by an incessant rattling of the window glass panes. Every head in the hall moves like one (it reminds me of a herd of wild animals, in synch with one another) towards the windows, and does not move until the rattles subside.

Somewhere off island we know that some heavy calibre bomb has just been dropped. It is a sobering moment, and we all think the same thing. *When will that be coming for us?* I look down at Alice, who isn't cowering against Ma's skirts like I thought she would be, but is frowning rather furiously at the windows. How can we keep her here, at the mercy of those bombs?

"I will keep you all updated, as best I can," Mr Despres finishes somberly.

Three hours later, after many false starts, we are addressed again. This time it is to get the children prepared for departure. *It is truly happening.* They are to be ferried to the harbour by the bus load and we are to say *À bétao - see you soon -* right here. Many have already left, changing their minds at the last moment. Some of those have returned, indecision still wrought on their faces.

I slip Alice into her red button-up coat. Even when I fasten the very top button, which always elicits a complaint of some sort from her, she does not stir. She is smiling, trying her hardest to be brave. I see through the charade; the smile does not reach her eyes.

"And this, Margot?" Ma hands me the small gas mask which all children are required to have with them. I strap it to her shoulders, cursing the German army for making such a ghastly item a necessity for such young children.

I swallow hard but my throat feels suffocatingly restricted.

This is not real. This is not real.

"Ma? Margot? Where do I go?" Alice stands on tip toes, searching for one of her teachers. Lines are forming without instruction and eventually she spots her class teacher – Miss De Garis – waving in her direction.

Miss De Garis is only a few years older than I, and she will be in charge of overseeing ten to fifteen children safely aboard the boat to their landfall in England.

"Alice," Ma gently pulls her in for an embrace, and I see her breathe in the top of Alice's head. "Be brave, darling."

I do not think I can do it, that I can take these final steps in sending her away. My throat burns and my chest aches. Alice makes the move for me, wrapping her tiny hands around my waist and holding tight. Her head nestles against my stomach where, beneath all the layers of clothing, my stomach is still puckered slightly from carrying her.

I bend down, crisscrossing my arms across her shoulders, letting the tickle of her hair and the brush of her coat make imprints on my skin. My lips tremble when she pulls back, and I am suddenly terrified to talk.

"This is not goodbye forever, is it, Margot?" She blinks up at me.

"Of course not," I whisper. It is as loud as I can speak without breaking.

I cup her cheeks in my hands and run my thumbs over the soft skin. I drop my nose and forehead to hers, resting it there.

Will she remember how much we love her?

What if the war does not end as soon as they say it will – what becomes of her then?

Will she truly be safer in the unknown, than here, facing an undefined danger?

Will I ever get the chance to tell her father who she really is?

She moves slowly away and I keep my fingers outstretched, holding on to her for as long as I can, until they caress only air.

Parents naturally fall towards the back of the hall as the children assemble at the front. No one speaks, only their eyes filled with tears betray any hint of what they are feeling. Hands run through loose hair, fingers fiddle with coat buttons, palms rest desolately on pursed set mouths, every face searching the crowd for their child.

Some children look back, some cry, some bounce on their toes, others dance and twirl out of their line. I find Alice and she is being a perfect student; facing Miss De Garis, hands clasped in front of her holding her small, meagre allowance of luggage and rations, awaiting instruction. Her dark and intricate braids trail down the back of her bright red coat. When will I be able to weave my fingers through that hair again, I wonder.

Do my eyes trick me, or are her tiny shoulders shaking?

An overpowering impulse to run to Alice and pull her from the line sets off a conflicting dance between my body and mind. My head knows that this, no matter how heartbreaking or vulnerable it may be, is the most reasonable choice to take. My body sees no reason; it just wants to feel Alice.

My mother, perhaps sensing it, links her fingers through mine. Her hands are clammy and damp, and when I catch sight of the pained resolve on her face I almost buckle.

This is torture in its purest, most tragic form.

12

Late June 1940

Walking through the town of St. Peter Port is like walking through a ghost town. Business as usual. That was the advice once the evacuations had ceased. The final boat left last Saturday; on it the final export of men and women who thought England would be the safer choice.

There are few children left. As I meander through the cobbled stone streets of our town I hear no playing, no games. No little voices at all. The ones that have been left behind to face whatever unknowns await us now are despondent, and afraid. Mothers weep openly.

I weep, too, when I am alone at night. I pull my covers up high to my chin, letting my tears fall silently until the pillow under my head is sodden. Alice went. Pierre, myself, Ma and Papa did not. One way or another, when this war is over, we will either congratulate ourselves for having the foresight to evacuate her or condemn ourselves for letting her go.

And always in my mind, whether tucked in the back behind thoughts of impending doom or at the very front, lies Otto. Still there has been no word from him. It is impossible not to feel alone when everyone around you keeps disappearing.

Mr Rose – the proprietor of a small grocer shop nestled between the historic buildings of St Peter Port – waves as I pass. It is just before seven in the evening, and he is shutting his doors to head home, well before curfew and black out. I return his wave and wonder, as I pass him by, if he is as affected by our restrictions as I am. A curfew of ten in the evening is hardly difficult to endure, but it has been a struggle to be told what to do. A lifetime of freedom has paved the way to somewhat of a resistance against our sudden boundaries. I hope, with all my heart, that it ends soon.

Papa, at least, in spite of the vacuum the evacuations have left on our island, can smile a little easier now. Export of produce has restarted, and many of the growers have been packing like wild animals to redeem some of the losses incurred over the last few weeks.

As we had driven into the town this evening in relative silence, he patted my hand and held it for a while, driving with one hand on the steering wheel and one arm out of the rolled down window. My father would not talk to me of what it felt like to lose Alice; he does not show his emotions easily. We are all trying to pretend as if sending the youngest member of our family on a boat, alone, is normal.

Business, as usual.

He had paused as we approached the White Rock harbour, letting the truck idle by the Weighbridge. "Go for a walk, Margot. I can unload the tomatoes tonight."

"Papa I -"

"Go. Enjoy the evening sunshine," he suggests, covering my protests. "Get us a table at *Home from Home* and you and I can have a light tea together before we go back home."

I did not head straight to the café. I stopped in at the town library on my walk, and this is where I am now. After a quick *good evening* to Ms. Guille, the librarian, I make my way up the grand central staircase, into a place I know just as well as my own home.

I let my fingers trace the spines and the dated wooden bookshelves, inhaling that stabilising scent of old paper and wood so old it is likely riddled with woodworm. There has not been a great deal of new deliveries – a war will do that – but that does not bother me.

Being around books inevitably reminds me of Tomas; it always does. The boy I had come to define as my very best friend had, for all intents and purposes, dropped off the face of the Earth. I had last seen and heard from him when he and the Reid's stopped in at Guernsey on their way to Germany in 1939. Otto had not spoken of him in our letters, even when I had asked very direct questions. They had gone ignored.

Every new week that starts I think will be the week I hear from him. Is he still with the Reid's? Has he found other family, other friends, to take him in now he is back in his homeland? He had never hidden his quiet displeasure at being uprooted to Canada and his desire to move back to Germany, but his sudden silence is deafening. With the war so well established in Germany I can only guess (and fret) at what the country now looks like. The Nazi's will eat up a boy like Tomas; a book reading, placid and introverted type. He is not built to be around a war like this.

I bid farewell to Ms. Guille after loaning a small selection and tackle the steep hill up to the local's favourite café – *Home from Home.*

"Ironic," I sigh, trying to regain my composure before stepping inside. I had perhaps walked up the hill a little more enthusiastically than necessary, and I need to discreetly wipe several beads of sweat from my forehead. The exertion is worth it, however, for the panoramic views it offers out over the harbour.

The cheerful (and somewhat rotund) café owner Jerry Baudains greets me with a smile and leads me to a table at the back, next to the wall of windows. If I squint, I can just make out Papa's rickety truck in line with the others.

"Busy down there tonight, ain't it," he says, taking my order for two cheese and pickle sandwiches, and tea for two.

He is not far wrong; even from here I can tell that the White Rock is a hub of activity, the growers making up for lost time. The sky is the clearest blue and the sun has just begun to set itself towards the West of the island. I imagine our farmhouse is enjoying the beginnings of a glorious sunset. Perhaps Pierre will want to go for an evening swim at the beach, if the tide is right.

I am calculating in my head how many days it has been since the last evening high tide when I hear them. I hear them before I see them. A low rumble fills the café and the noise inside falls deathly silent. The table under my hand vibrates and a drone builds through the walls.

Someone is speaking, asking what that incessant thunder is, but her voice is just a whisper lost in a shout. Just as I think my ears are going to burst, three aircraft shoot into view, far too low for this to be a casual reconnaissance flight. We can do nothing at all but watch, aghast, following the path of the three planes. My eyes flit dramatically between them and the harbour with growing horror, willing it not to be.

There is a scream – *no!* – at the same time the planes open fire, and the café is peppered with the sound of gun fire. For a few painful seconds we are frozen, forced to watch the endless line of trucks at the mercy of falling bombs. We stay that way until the first fires begin to burn, vehicles lost behind a cloud of dense black smoke.

Then, we run.

I have just turned from the window when a sound like breaking ice comes from behind, and the entire wall turns in towards us in a shower of glass. My body is pushed down, and I feel as I do when caught beneath a rogue wave in the shallows. It is just as suffocating inside, in a building, as it is in the ocean. I push my palms into the floor and force myself up. I do not look behind me as I run through the café, but I can feel the cool air on my back - a pointed warning that there is now a void where there once was not one.

"Margot! Down here! Quick! Everyone, *follow me!*" Jerry is shouting from the top of some stairs. I presume they lead down to the store cellar and he tries to grab me as I fly past him. I let his shouts fall to a hiss behind me. I will not shelter in a cellar whilst my father sits like a duck in a pond under a rainfall of bullets.

My steps crunch as I run across exploded glass on the main street, and the air is thick with a smoke so dense it turns my breaths into a wheeze. I fling myself past outstretched hands as people try to stop me from where I need to go. I do not even see their faces.

"Look, ma, more ladders," I hear a boy shouting above an impossibly loud thrum in the air. I look up as I run; descending bullets drop in symmetrical patterns from the underbellies of planes like the rungs of a ladder. *This is organised.*

As I emerge from the street on to the main promenade down to the harbour, I stop, realisation turning my blood to ice. I have run into hell on earth. There are fires everywhere; the lick of deep red caught only in the shadows of the smoke, which has turned everything ashen and black. Alarms ring out in the background of shouts. Some people run, away from the horror, but others stop where they are, hands against mouths, eyes streaming from the smoke, unable to look away.

I pull my headscarf from my head, not caring as my curls unpin, and dunk it in the water at the harbour, grateful that the tide is high after all. I scrunch it together in a ball and hold it tight against my nose and mouth, blinking as my eyes pick and sting.

"Papa!" I yell, but my voice is swallowed.

Through streaming eyes I try and find his truck, but it is hopeless. The heat is relentless, and I can feel it clawing at my skin. A cough turns into a heave; my lungs are on fire and I cannot take a breath deep enough to fix them.

"*Papa!*" I croak, but this time even I cannot hear myself.

Suddenly I am thrown backwards by an explosion so loud my eardrums ring, followed by the *rat-a-tat* of more rapid gunfire. My head collides with the solid floor and I am lost under a blanket of running feet. I cry out as the fingers on my outstretched left hand are trodden on, a stab of pain working its way up my left arm.

No one comes to help. There is too much panic, too much confusion. *Too many people burning alive in their trucks.* I slowly come to stand on legs that feel like those hard sticks of seaweed I am so used to seeing on the beach at low tide, cradling my left hand as if it were a baby.

Alice. Thank all that is mighty that she cannot see this.

I fight back the urge to sob. I have to find my father.

But the trucks are no longer there. In their place are the burning carcasses of vehicles that, only moments before, had carried crates full of tomatoes. The ground is stained with a putrefying mash of pulp and skin, and the street runs red.

From somewhere behind me the siren of an ambulance rings out, followed by more relentless gunfire.

The ambulance falls silent.

They have bombed the damn ambulance.

We cannot get close enough to the remains of the trucks. Firm hands pull the few of us away, each second bringing with it another *pop* and another truck, hidden beneath the smoke, erupts into a volcano of fire.

Someone sits me on a bench and runs back into the inferno.

The Weighbridge clock has been bombed, the hands on the face frozen at three minutes to seven. Time has stopped as hell has been unleashed. Bodies scatter the ground as if they are litter, and wounded figures emerge from the fires stumbling, only to fall to the ground like skittles. I wait for my father to appear.

He does not.

PART TWO

OCCUPIED

13

August 1940

"Christ alive, it sounds like they're strangling a cat."

Pierre twists a cigarette between his thumb and forefinger before throwing it on the floor and crushing it with the toe of his boot.

The German soldiers are marching through the historical, cobbled streets of St Peter Port for what feels like the third time today. Hanging floral baskets on the windowsills of the buildings overhead quiver in a non-existent breeze. The marching we could most likely endure - if we must – were it not for the incessant chanting that accompanied it.

"Perhaps when this war is over all German personnel will be required to undertake singing lessons," I suggest.

We lean with our backs against the wall on a small alley just off of the main street. We hadn't intended to be caught in this latest march of showmanship, but we had been to the Boots store to collect my belongings. I had been reprieved of my role on the beauty and cosmetics counter, much to Mariette's smugness. Pierre had no reason to be with me, but he rarely let me go anywhere alone these days.

"Let's hope there are none of them left. You cannot rightly deliver singing lessons to corpses now, can you."

I knock him with my elbow, displeased with his choice of words but not wholly disagreeing.

"I wonder if they know the bowls they wear on their heads make them look ridiculous."

"Or that their uniforms are the colour of cat vomit."

At this my brother breaks a smile and hops onto his bicycle. He turns back and winks. "Race you to the top?"

↔

It has been one month since we saw the invasion of the German troops, and little more than that since the White Rock Harbour bombings, where thirty four Guernsey men lost their lives.

Including Frank La Joie.

The losses we know, on the grander scale of the war, are little. But on an island so small, with a community so close knit, the vacant hole they have left in their wake is felt through all of us.

The void that losing Papa - and Alice - had left in our family was gapingly obvious. Somewhere along the line of the last month, however, our grief has been overshadowed by the unfairness of our island finding itself under Occupation by the German forces.

We were told to continue with life as normal under German rule, but it was impossible to ignore them when they swarmed the streets like flies on a carcass.

We live in fear daily, wondering when the barbaric monsters we have heard of will rear their ugly heads. So far we had only seen a great deal of arrogant showmanship and strangled singing. They expect preferential treatment, that much is obvious. A simple trip to the grocers for our ration of bread turns into a fierce battle of wits.

Our newspaper is naturally a puppet by some German holding the strings; according to them, the war will be over soon, Germany victorious. The BBC say otherwise.

↔

"Have you heard the latest nonsense?" Ma asks when Pierre and I reach the farmhouse. She is always so quick to greet us now, as if she has been waiting with bated breath by the door for us to return. "They are holding a dance. Listen to this." She scoffs and unscrews a piece of paper which had clearly borne the brunt of her distaste. "The German Kommandantur would like to invite all islanders to a dance at the St George's dance hall this coming Saturday." She throws the paper on to the table and begins a rant that lasts several minutes, barely taking a breath.

This is new. Since Papa's passing Ma has been angry; she has trouble controlling her emotions and regularly unleashes hell on all who will listen.

"Who is actually going to show up to that?" Pierre sneers.

I have my suspicions, as I am sure he does too.

The German troops, though everything they stood for I despised, were undeniably handsome. They were lean, most of them tall, and chiselled. It would be inhuman to think otherwise. Yet whilst I save myself for when Otto returns to me, many of my fellow island girls do not. The exodus of our enlisting young men had left many of them wanting for attention.

"Maybe we should go, just to see who else turns up. That will show the traitors for what they are, don't you think Margot? Mar? *Go-Go?*"

I let Pierre's voice taper off and frown through the kitchen window at the figure walking through the country lanes, passing our farmhouse. It is not unusual to see neighbours passing by or families (what little there is left of them) out for a walk, but this is not just a casual stroll.

"Is that -" I narrow my eyes as if this will help with what I am seeing. "Is that Ms. Guille? Is she *drunk?*"

The town librarian – a woman upwards of her fifties – stumbles into the hedge and struggles to right herself.

"Surely not," Ma gasps, coming to my shoulder. Ms Guille was as typical of a librarian as there could be, everything from the high bun atop her head to the polish of her black square-toed pumps. She is polite but brusque, perhaps a little uptight. Being seen inebriated in the middle of the day was too far out of character for her.

"I don't think she is drunk Mar…she looks…"

But I do not hear whatever Pierre thinks she looks like, as I am running through the kitchen, my shoes still on and leaving an echo on the stone floor in my wake. I catch Ms. Guille just before she stumbles to her knees.

"Goodness! Are you quite alright?" I lead her over to a dip in the hedge, flattening a patch of stinging nettles with my bare hands and grimacing at the instant itch that surfaces on my palm.

Ms Guille is, I notice, far from intoxicated. But she is also far from coherent, her vacant eyes darting in all directions.

"Ma!" I call back to the farmhouse, where the door is still open. "Can you bring water?"

I hold the woman's liver-spotted hands in my own, crouching down to her level. She is muttering nonsense words under her breath. "It is alright, Ms. Guille, it is alright."

Just as Ma hands her the cup of water a low drone fills the otherwise silent sky and Ms Guille cowers, retracting her head into her shoulders like the baby ducklings do.

"*No, no, no,*" she cries in a whisper. "*No more, no more.*"

"They have passed, they are gone now," I soothe, thankful that this plane, unlike others recently, has disappeared almost as quickly as it had arrived.

In time we manage to get Ms Guille to drink the water, and soon she is at least speaking coherently, albeit her eyes still dart nervously from side to side.

Ma steps back a little out of earshot and beckons for me to join. "There *have* been a great deal more planes lately, have you noticed?"

Our farmhouse sits slightly north of the airport runway; we hear the aircrafts plaguing our island like locusts at all hours of the day, bringing with them more troops, more ammunition, more transport. But she is right - in the last week there have been more; if thirty minutes goes by that we do not hear the rattling drone of their engines, we count it a blessing.

"Did you hear about the commando raids a week ago, Margot?"

I look over her face, wondering if I have misheard. She does not meet my eyes.

"I should have told you," she whispers. "I should have, I know. But the less you know the…well, the better, if such a word can be used. Two British soldiers were caught spying and sent away."

"Sent away?"

"To the camps, in Germany."

I gasp. "What were they doing here?"

"Finding out what they could, I suppose. Intent on getting that information back to Britain."

"They haven't forgotten about us after all then." It had been a bitter pill to swallow for the islanders, feeling so ignored and thrown to the wolves by England.

"It would appear not."

"You look troubled, Ma. It is a good thing, surely. We are not alone."

"It is not for that reason. The planes, Margot."

"What of them?"

"There are too many planes. Something is happening out there, *ma p'tite souée*." She looks up at the sky, as if visualising more looming aircraft ready for invasion. "Something big is coming."

14

September 1940

One unseasonably warm Sunday in September – the only day that Ma handed the crops and the few livestock we had left over to farm help – we go to the beach. This simple pleasure, at the very least, has not yet been taken from us by the Germans.

To our dismay there are a small group of soldiers, out of uniform, sunning themselves in only swim shorts. They are being inoffensive – at the moment, anyway – but we sit as far from them as we can. Nonetheless, their clipped talk - none of which we understand - travels across the beach, and each syllable stabs like ice through my veins.

You killed my Papa.

You took Alice from me.

You have invaded my island.

You have taken my freedom.

You have turned Otto and Tomas into ghosts.

To my horror Mariette waves at them before laying down her towel and leaning back on her shoulders, deliberately pushing her ample chest forward. Pierre rolls his eyes. My blood begins to boil. She flutters her eyelashes, and I think of all those soldiers have taken from us. Perhaps she needs to lose someone to them to make her understand what this Occupation means.

I shake off those thoughts. No, nobody deserves that.

"Next Friday, Nellie is having a gathering at her house. She asked me to invite you both. Will you join us?"

A gathering. The concept seems alien.

"I'm not -"

"Oh here we go," Mariette drawls. "You are going to find a reason not to come, aren't you Margot. What else could possibly be occupying your time? Your *cow?*"

I become aware that my mouth is hanging open, so I roughly close it and catch my tooth on my lip, causing it to bleed. It does nothing to soothe the mood that had begun to brew as soon as our toes touched the sand and saw the Germans.

"Mariette," Pierre breathes a warning.

"Well it is true," she points out, with all the lofty arrogance of someone who thinks she is right. "She has always been that way. Never one to *conform* or show an interest, heaven forbid."

"*She* is sitting right beside you," I mutter.

She turns her head to face me and I despise the knowing glint in her eyes. How can someone you hold so dear infuriate you beyond belief?

"Will you be joining us?" She raises an eyebrow, anticipating my answer.

Otto and Tomas are cousins, and they loved and loathed, too.

The thought creeps in, catching me unawares. Oh, those Reid boys. My insides twist and curl and I momentarily forget all about Mariette's theories on my socialisation, or lack thereof. The sensation of a dagger to the chest is the only way I can describe the crippling reaction to the unknown. I can imagine where they both are, together or apart, in one country or another, but the truth in it is I have no idea. They are lost to me, in a world so vast it makes my head spin.

What if I never see them again?

"Well?"

I cast my eyes to Pierre, who shrugs and curls his lip in a way that says *it could be fun*. We had very little else to fill our time with, now that the Germans had taken our liberty away.

"Alright, Mariette, we will be there."

She purses her lips. "I stand corrected."

"Just out of interest, how does a gathering work if you are on curfew?"

"You don't go home. We stay overnight and walk back home the next day once curfew has lifted."

"This doesn't sound like your first Occupied gathering."

"Now that would be telling," she winks in a way I'm sure is meant to intimidate me, an effort on her part to appear the older all-knowing cousin. It does nothing but irritate me.

I soon realise that my unstable mood is not being helped by staying stationary, so I go for a stroll across the beach, relishing how the subtle breeze takes the heat off of my skin but doesn't quite chill it. I find the rocks I had climbed many years before, the summer I had fallen in love with Otto.

And I find *the* rock. The one with the flat top, where everything happened a lifetime ago. I choose not to dwell on that, because if I do, I may never stop. Some books need to remain closed. Instead I focus ahead, pretending that behind me lies only Guernsey, not occupied territory. For me, these are now entirely separate entities. A *before*, and an *after*.

I close my eyes and listen to the swell as the tide brings saltwater into the rock pools. It has a faint metallic sound, I notice, as it crashes against the sedentary rocks.

I have been in my reverie a while when I hear a surprised "Oh!" from behind.

I know without turning that he is German. They carry themselves differently, occupying the same air as us but filling it rather more awkwardly. Perhaps they know they do not belong here.

I refuse to turn. I have every right to be here, on these rocks, on *my island.* They haven't yet taken that from us. It doesn't stop me from a little thrill shot of fear, though. They are barbarians, after all, and who is not slightly terrified of barbarians?

Will he shoot me where I sit, I wonder absently, *if I refuse to move for him?*

Would I care?

This last thought surfaces momentarily but I push it back down, disgusted.

"Scuze me, m'am, are you – are you, vell?"

I suppose I have to acknowledge him now. To deny him that is to ask for a caution against my name, perhaps even a prison sentence. There have been a few of those dished out already in the short time our invaders have been here, if rumours are accurate. The Guernsey-man was fiercely loyal at best, hot-headed and careless at worst.

"I am quite well," I clip back, hoping he hears in my voice that it is not a conversation opening.

"Ah. I zort, well…"

I think I understand what he thought. Really, truly, is that idea so farfetched? An island with a population that has largely lived a stoically independent and free life, suddenly under intense restrictions, rules and harsh penalties. Is it so unbelievable that a person may consider throwing themselves off of these rocks to avoid the unknown fate that awaits them?

I feel that anger bubbling startlingly close to the surface, and the intensity of it surprises me. I turn to storm past but when I face him I almost cry out. He looks nothing like my Papa, of course; his skin is pale where Papa's was sun-tanned and weathered by the throes of our island climate, his hair is blonde and cut short where Papa's was dark and long enough to curl at the ends, and he is much shorter and slighter than Papa was. The age though, is what surprises me. He must be Papa's age.

What age Papa would have *been.*

The German gives me a wary, apologetic smile.

I cannot bring myself to smile back. "Very well," I mumble as I begin the descent down the rocks.

"Ah," he runs a hand cautiously over his closely shaven hair. "You ah – I haz a daughter about your age. She look like you, a little," he holds his thumb and forefinger together.

I blink silently, caught off guard by his frank admission. I feel something else too, something I do not want to.

"She iz in Germany. I – ah – I vorry. Very far away. Az your *vater* – your uh father - must worry of you, yes?"

The tears are instant. I wipe furiously at my eyes, cursing their betrayal. "My father is dead." *Because of you.* But to finish that sentence is to ask for reprimand, so I continue my way down the rocks and back on to the beach without looking back. When I reach our towels Pierre must notice my red eyes but has better sense than to raise it.

A short while later I chance a look back at the rocks. The German still sits atop them, watching the horizon.

↔

The planes continue to swarm our island like bees to a meadow of lavender.

We watch them come, arriving in the hundreds. We watch them go, swelling the air as they do.

We sit helpless, hearing through the wireless of a battle taking place in the skies over Britain, and lay unwilling witness to the cat and mouse game between Spitfires and Hurricanes, Dorniers and Junkers.

I think of Alice every time the humdrum drone of an engine starting at the airport fills the air. I think of her on the receiving end of those planes, of their pilots.

We take some comfort in the lack of returning German aircraft as we near the middle of September, and share solace when the wireless announces soon after that Britain stands victorious in what is being called the Battle of Britain.

Still, there is no word from Alice.

15

Late September 1940

Britain's small victory over Germany during the Battle of Britain did little to wipe the smug looks from the faces of the soldiers walking our town. *A minor setback*, they proclaimed, whilst still convinced they would win the war, and that its end was imminent.

Pierre had a notable spring in his step, even when faced with mundane chores in the fields or around the animals. I often wondered how it must be for him, a young boy on the cusp of manhood, going through the emotional turmoil of being a teenager whilst under occupation. He seemed, overall, to be handling it with far more grace than I felt I was.

I grew increasingly agitated every time I saw the dull green of their uniforms. On more occasions than not I had had to bite down hard on my tongue to stop from retorting, when asked to step aside on a pavement where we met or when expected to fall back in a queue. It was all done with such infuriating politeness that there was little choice in the matter.

Ma continued in her attempt to keep her emotions under check. Her quick temper was always evident, if we left precious food out to spoil or forgot a minor chore in the farmhouse, for example. And yet, she still had a softness and gentle approach to life that reassured us she was still in there somewhere, buried amongst her grief.

I leave the farmhouse early that morning as soon as curfew has lifted. The sky is still heavy with dew and the grass glistens in a nod to the countryside tranquility. We have a busy day ahead of us on the farm and our one remaining cow – Hetty – needs to be milked. We have a small pasture nestled in the cliff paths of one of the western parishes – Torteval - to get to which I require a permit from the German Kommandantur. The soldiers had begun to restrict which areas of the cliff paths the islanders could frequent, and I did not expect to be able to keep Hetty in the field for much longer. With the permit safely in the pocket of my pinafore, I climb into the cab of the ancient truck Ma had picked up to replace the one –

the one in which Papa died.

I mentally remind myself to drive on the right hand side of the road, a move which still feels peculiar despite being one of the first laws the Germans had implemented upon their arrival two months ago.

No matter how many times I approach the wall of soldiers on my route to the field, the knot in my stomach does not lessen. Rumours are rife that all it takes is for one of them to have a bad day and they would find some reason to reprimand you. I show my permit with slightly shaking hands and do not see another soldier until I reach the heifer.

Exhaling into the cool cliff air, I pat her on the back. "Good morning girl."

This part of the island is my favourite. Blue sea glistens against a turquoise sky that is only just beginning to transition from the deep purple and red of dawn. *Red sky in the morning, Shepherds' warning.* Patches of heather and nettles grow wild among the slopes down to the craggy cliffs, where the sea breaks against the rocks in a cascade of white foam.

Hetty is so used to me by now that the process is painless. I am loading the milk into the back of the truck and clipping the rear barrier into place when a strange sound interrupts the morning birdsong.

I turn and scan the landscape. It sounds like a shuffling – a hungry wild rabbit, perhaps. The air feels too still, too stifling all of a sudden, so I hastily open the cab door and put a foot on the booster. Before I can launch myself into the seat I hear the unmistakable sound of a cough. Not a cough that occurs through illness, but one meant to politely interrupt someone in the course of their actions.

Swallowing hard but keeping one hand on the truck in case I need to make a speedy getaway, I turn back to the cliffside. There, burrowed between two bushes of heather, are two men. They lie on their forearms, bellies against the earth, and eye me with caution.

"Do not shout." Their hurried whisper carries across the still air easily and stops me just as I go to cry out.

They are British. British!

They are not dressed like soldiers, but their clothing blends into the landscape by no accident. They have dressed for intent.

I realise I have been blindly staring at them for too long when one of them coughs again. "Come a little closer, m'am, but make it look natural."

I clear my throat. "No one is here. They do not patrol this area."

"Best to take caution anyway."

I take a few steps closer, my heart hammering painfully against my chest, and crouch down near to them, making moves to take cuttings from some of the wild flowering bushes.

"Are you – are you British?"

One of the soldiers – younger than the other – lifts one side of his mouth. "You bet we are." I close my eyes softly and the world seems to stop. *Is this it? Is it over?* "We have been sent to gather information on the German defences. We arrived by boat in the early hours of this morning."

My stomach drops a little. "So it is not over? You are not here to rescue us?"

The older commando sends me a remorseful look. "Not yet. Soon. We are doing all we can. We will get you all out of this soon."

"What can I help with?" I see them eyeing my truck.

"Do you have a tarpaulin back there?"

"Yes!" My hard darts to my mouth in shock. "Sorry. Yes, yes, I do. But there are checks, I have to show my permit just to get through. They have not checked the truck yet, but…there is always the chance."

The soldiers share something silently between them. "There are checks, you say. All along the coast?"

"Just the south coast, I believe. There have been rumours of a commando raid here before, they are cautious now. Appropriately so, it seems."

"Not rumours, m'am." The younger soldier grins again. "The boys got clean away with all the information they needed."

The jolt of electricity in my chest is a thrill. I find myself not wanting to leave these soldiers, so I tell them that I believe their best bet is to get in the back of my truck.

"I can drop you somewhere, you will blend in as you are. But where…" I drift off, frantically thinking of concealed and unpatrolled places I can drive them to.

"I have relatives here," the younger soldier says, and I focus in on his features for the first time. Unrecognisable to me personally, but all of a sudden he looks like any fellow islander. Yes, I can see him walking the cobbled streets of St Peter Port with friends, spending carefree weekends on the beach. Moments of an era that seems so far lost.

I lean over and place a hand over his, which still rests on the earth. His face is dirt-marked, but otherwise there is little evidence that these men have spent the better part of the night hidden on the cliffs.

"Thank you."

He blinks and nods, and I notice his jaw tense. "You are most welcome."

"And thank *you,*" I say to the older soldier. "We all thank you."

"Just doing what we can m'am."

"Do you know La Villiaze, could you drop us to my uncle's farmhouse in the lanes there?"

"La Villiaze? Why, that's near to where my house is," I say, momentarily distracted by how unsuspicious it would look to be seen there. "But it is too close to the airport! They have converted the chapel at the end of the lane to an ammunition store. It is too risky. The area can be riddled with German activity."

"We will be discreet," he nods to me.

I have to take their word for it. Who was I to argue with the heroes risking their lives for us. Covering the soldiers with the tarpaulin and driving in silence knowing that they lay in the back of the truck seems too surreal, so I convince myself that they are not really there. I am grateful for this tactic as we approach the soldiers waiting for me to return. For a moment I think the soldier who checked my permit and let me pass this morning is waving his arms in the air to pull me over. He calls "have a good day" in broken English, and I realise he is politely bidding me farewell.

"Thank the lord," I hiss through the gritted teeth of a false smile in return.

My hands do not lessen their grip on the steering wheel, however, until I have turned into the drive of the young soldiers uncle. He greets us at the door to his barn with a skeptical expression.

"Your Frank's daughter, aren't you?" He calls, and I hush him with a finger to my lips. It takes me a short while to place his face. Etienne. Papa's friend.

He removes the soft hat from his head and holds it against his chest. "I was sorry to hear of his passing, Miss. All my condolences." He pronounces his '*r's*' in the traditional Guernsey dialect, which was steadily being lost through the generations.

"Thank you," I say. "But there is something rather more pressing. Perhaps I could back my truck up to your barn there and offload some rather precious cargo I have."

He moves back in surprise. "Well I ain't expecting any deliveries today."

"*Surprise* cargo."

"I ain't no fan of surprises," he starts, suspicious. "Good surprise or bad surprise?"

"Now that depends which way you look at it. But trust me when I say, you *should* look at it."

He waves his hand towards the barn and I back my truck up as close to the door as I can, offering a wall of privacy. Thankfully no soldiers have decided to grace the lanes today. *Probably off singing somewhere*. The thought makes me laugh, and soon my stomach aches from holding in supressed giggles at the sheer absurd turn of my day.

Etienne helps me pull the tarpaulin back, and suspicion swiftly turns to a delighted surprise to see his nephew in the bed of the truck. I watch them embrace and exchange pleasantries, before realising that the longer I stay, the more at risk I am of someone seeing my truck and questioning my visit to Etienne's farm. I bid them all farewell and start the engine.

"Margot, isn't it?" The young soldier comes to my window. "Thank you. You played an important role today. The British Army thanks you for it. I won't tell a soul of your service, for your own safety but, well, thank you."

I place my hand over his as it rests on the lowered window. "I would do it again in a heartbeat."

"It goes without saying that -"

"I will not tell anyone of what happened this morning, soldier. You have my word on that."

"Not even your family." He doesn't ask it as a question.

"Not even my family," I confirm.

For the remainder of the day I quell an unsettled but not wholly unwelcome griping in my stomach. As I lay down to bed, having taken a quiet supper with Pierre and Ma, I realise what the feeling is.

I had enjoyed it.

I had enjoyed helping. I had enjoyed doing my part for the war.

The unsettling part of it all was, I wasn't satisfied. I wanted to do more.

16

November 1940

"You should really try it, you know. Laying with a German soldier is quite an affair."

Mariette is holding court at a gathering in her friend – Nellie's – house. I suppose now they were our unlikely friends, too. Pierre and I had been initiated a long time ago, and more to have something to pierce the boredom with than anything else, we went along every now and again. Young people were in short supply, most having departed for the mainland or enlisted in the forces, and the company isn't awful – it was nice to have distractions. Our governing body had also advised that, due to fuel shortages, islanders should share their living rooms (and amenities) wherever possible.

The November winds batter at the windows, and I am grateful that we decided to see out our curfew here, rather than battling the winds on the way home.

I watch Mariette, my jaw not hiding in its surprise at her revelations. I had long ago suspected that she had been fraternising with the soldiers after hours, but to have it so brazenly admitted in a room full of people surprises me. She has been drinking alcohol – some ghastly homemade concoction that turned me off it at the first sniff – so that likely went some way to her confidence.

"Of course, you want to make sure that they don't like to get a bit overfriendly with those heavy duty belts of theirs. I have been on the receiving end of one of those before," she grimaces, to which the girls in the room cackle. "But most of them are just a bit thick between the ears."

Having heard enough, I stand to leave. How can she do it, I wonder. How can she let those hands anywhere near her body knowing how many innocent lives they have taken?

"I'll say," calls one of the boys, a little older than Pierre. Ralph is his name. "I heard that one of them had been billeted in a house, and when he went to tell the Committee that he no longer required it, he called the house 'please shut the gate.'"

There are howls at this, and I let a small chuckle pass. The language barrier provides us with some semblance of entertainment, at least. An Irishman – Seamus, I believe his name is – stands then, orating the beginning of what I know is a crude joke at the Germans expense. I stow away into the kitchen where Pierre joins me a few moments later. "She's back into her stories of sleeping with the Germans."

I roll my eyes. "I just hope she is safe. If something should happen to her it would be the final straw for us, I think, for Ma."

"If something should happen to her it will be her own fault. She's not exactly being discreet, Go-Go."

I run my fingertips over my eyebrows, staring into the space out of the kitchen window but not really seeing anything. A thundering drone punctures the air outside, announcing the arrival of another of their cargo planes. I suppress a childish bolt of delight that the plane sounds to be struggling in the crosswinds – whoever is on board will not be having a pleasant journey.

"What more could they need," I grumble. "Our roads are already riddled with their motorcycles and cars. Surely there is no space for much else."

"More soldiers, apparently. They are bringing in the wounded now too, to stagnate here instead of the mainland. Our boys did a number on their airmen, the *Luftwaffe*," he spits.

"*More* soldiers? Good grief. We will be overrun."

"Part of the plan I believe."

"Pierre," I eye him now. "How do you know so much?"

"A boy shan't reveal his sources." He taps the side of his nose.

"Are *you* being safe?"

"You know me, Go-Go. Always."

"I *do* know you and that is what worries me."

I knew Pierre had been chipper lately, too chipper for wartime, some might say, but I had put it down to teenage adrenaline.

When was *I* last that bouncy?

The memory of aiding the commando's rises to the surface with a bubble of thrill, and I scrutinise my brother. *Is that what you are doing?*

↔

Later that night, as Mariette and I turn in to the double bed Nellie has put us up in, I roll over to face her. With her hands tucked under her cheek she does the same. She has always been so beautiful, my cousin. When did she decide that sleeping with the enemy was the way forward for her? I think back on all the summers we had spent as children, squeezed into my bed at the farmhouse like this to free up beds for the Reid's. Would the girls back then have believed what the world was like now, I wonder.

"Why do you do it, Mariette?" I whisper.

She doesn't have to ask what I mean. "It is quite wild. You should try it."

"You know what they are calling those women?"

"Jerrybags. I have heard it."

"Do you not worry?"

"What they think of me? Have I ever?"

It is true. Mariette has never given consideration to much beyond herself.

"But…they are Nazi's. How can you in good conscience commit yourself to them like that?"

She sighs. "Commit myself to them? It is just sex, Margot, not a marriage. Simply a matter of opening your legs. You, more than I, should know of that."

The slight stings, and she knows it. Her face softens and her hand reaches for my arm. "I didn't mean that how it sounded. That was crass of me. And they're not all Nazi's. A shame, perhaps. The Nazi's are a little more…intense, shall we say. Quite a delight."

"How on earth do you tell the difference?"

"The salute." She rolls on to her back. "The Nazi's salute like this," she extends her right arm fiercely from her shoulder into the air with a straight hand. The accompanying scowl is so severe we both end up giggling.

When that subsides, a shadow comes across her face which is so unusual that I want to roll her into an embrace.

"You know an awful lot about them," I whisper.

"Men talk a great deal when their guards are down. They reveal a lot." Her eyes drift away from mine, not willing to share anything more.

↔

On our cycle back home the following morning, I decide to confront Pierre.

"Why do you have such a spring in our step lately?"

"You think I spring?" He asks innocently, and with a glint in his eye bunny hops his bicycle.

"Proving my point."

He shakes his head and after a while says, "to tell you is to implicate you."

"Pierre," I gasp, confirming my suspicious.

"I'm not in some underground revolution, Margot, you can still sleep at night. I just, wanted to do something I suppose. Small things. Things they see more as an inconvenience than an act of sabotage." I narrow my eyes at him. "The worst thing that could happen to me now would be for, you know, you and Ma, for anything to…well…if anything should happen because of something I had done, it would, god, it would just…"

He trails off, running a hand through his hair, and I understand he cannot finish the sentence. He is doing what he can without sacrificing anyone else along with him.

I am filled with a sudden sadness at how quickly he has had to grow up. How quickly his line of thinking has shifted from keeping entertained on a weekend to keeping his family alive.

We dawdle on our way back to the farmhouse without agreeing we would do so. A path of unspoken words often winds itself between my brother and I. As children, those words were swears and insults thrown to each other that would have earned us a clip around the ears had we spoken them aloud.

We are discussing what chores need to be undertaken around the farm, when hurried footsteps interrupt us. Ma rounds the corner of the drive at a run, almost knocking us off of our cycles. I brake too hard and slide off of the seat, my cycle falling to a crumpled heap at my feet. Her hands fly at the air and I notice her perfect curls have unpinned.

"What is it?" Pierre breathes, "what has happened?"

"They're coming for the cars," she pants.

The Germans had already requisitioned a great portion of our motorcars, and banned all civilian driving on the roads unless it was required for their work. On the first day that the war hit our shores, the first occupiers had stolen whatever cars they came across in an adrenaline-fueled panic. It became more organised after that, but every few weeks brought a fresh announcement of some new item to be requisitioned from the islanders. Islanders who needed their cars as part of their trade hadn't yet had to sacrifice their own wheels.

"The truck?" I ask. "But they can't! That's our livelihood. How will we get - "

"Not the truck, his car, *his* car, they will take his car!"

In 1938, mere months before war was declared in Europe, Papa had brought a Morris Eight Saloon. It was painted a deep khaki green, a foreboding giant grille to the front, and curves over the wheels that looked alive. We felt like royalty when we rode in that car. He would take us on coastal drives, though good heavens if sand came so much as an inch within the doors.

We follow Ma into the rarely used side barn attached to the house. The projecting front light pokes out from the sheet covering the bulk of the motorcar, watching us like a rogue lazy eye. The three of us stand and watch the car for a moment, waiting for some sign, some clue as to what we should do next. If the Germans are making house-calls and requisitioning cars, as Ma claims they are, we cannot leave the Morris Eight to their mercy. Papa is all around us; he lives on in the weathered floorboards in the house, in the navy Guernsey jumper that has not been washed since his passing. And yet – I swallow hard – he is gone. This car was his pride and joy, his one indulgence in a life spent working the earth. To let it not only leave our possession but leave it to be ferried across to Europe and used in Germany's warfare was letting a piece of him go that we were not ready to do yet.

I watch Pierre pace around the car, playing with the button of his shirt, thinking. I chew the inside of my cheek. Ma just stands, her hands over her mouth.

There is a simple solution, I rationalise. *Don't overcomplicate it.*

Could we pass to a neighbour? *No, we would implicate them.*

Well we can't drive it anywhere, that would raise more eyebrows, we don't have a permit for it. *No.*

Could we take it apart? Reduce it to a carcass and store the smaller parts somewhere safe? *That would break his heart. It would break Ma's.*

One of the glasshouses, perhaps? *There is no room, every bit of earth needs to be utilised so we don't starve.*

Tell them it has sentimental value? Ask them to leave it? *Are you dim?*

Pierre has paused by a small square bale of old hay. "This could work," he mumbles, distracted.

"That hay has been sitting there for years, you would kill off the animals if you gave it to them. Can we focus, please? Ma, when are they coming?"

"Not for the animals," Pierre says animatedly, and I can sense a plan forming. "We have stores of hay, don't we, from the summer harvest?" He knows we do, had done the heavy lifting himself mere months ago. They are stored in the open barn near the paddock.

He looks at me, past our catatonic mother who has not yet relinquished her gaze on the car. That glint is back in his eye. "Fancy a drive?"

I take charge of maneuvering the car as tight against the rear wall as I can whilst Pierre wheels a large cart back and forth between the paddock and the side barn. He shifts cartloads of dry hay bales and, after recovering the car with the sheet, I begin to stack them in front, creating a false wall and concealing it. Then, we add columns of old packing boxes in front of that. By the time we insert the last box like a puzzle piece we are drenched in sweat and panting like animals. We stand back and admire our work.

"Bit risky, isn't it, having it this close to the house?"

"Not at all," Pierre says, clapping his hands together in triumph. "It's what Papa would have done."

And he would have done it with the same glint in his eye. I give him a sad smile and turn to Ma. She has watched the whole scene unfold around her with minimal notice. Her eyes finally look to us, shining with the glisten of tears. She pulls my hands into hers and rests a forehead against Pierre's. We are joined, skin to skin, a triangle of protection against the world outside the barn.

"Lord what are they turning us into," she whispers.

17

January 1941

The oppressive winter weather makes the occupation feel like a reality. The jarring mix of sunshine and soldiers had felt too surreal, like a child's make believe on a summers day. But there is no mistaking the aroma of war as the relentless rains continue to lash the island and the winds whip at our raw skin.

We had survived a miserable Christmas with an air of relative optimism. *It will be over soon.* By late January the following year, however, not only did the war show no sign of ending, if anything it was in a fuller force than it had been in 1940.

It is obvious to any islander that our food supplies are in peril. Guernsey had thrived on a mutual overseas trade, and the severance of this tie with the mainland means that islanders survive off of what they can grow. We are lucky, if the word could be used; we have fields, we have glasshouses, we have livestock. But the Germans take a majority share in anything grown or produced, and we had handed our land over to our States Controlling Committee. Our independent work-life had long gone; we worked for others, we grew for them, we had a flat-rate wage paid by the government. This loss of independence though, we were willing to accept, for it meant that our supplies were helping save the islands population from starvation.

On a typically overcast late January morning I make my way into the kitchen, where Ma is already at the stove. I sniff the air; tomato chutney.

"This must be the last of them, surely," I marvel, dipping a finger into the simmering concoction and tasting it with a satisfying *pop.*

Tomatoes across the island had been in full season at the time of Occupation. Hundreds of crates-worth, that would otherwise have been exported out, had been ordered by the Germans to be picked and destroyed. The land, they said, must be cultivated to sow an assortment of fruits and vegetables, not just tomatoes. Growers had had to get creative with how they used their tomatoes to ensure they didn't go to waste. Sadly, a lot had. By the end of Autumn 1940, we had given a great deal away for free. We had stored several small crates as best we could - in the dry and the dark - but they were beginning to turn.

Ma points behind me to two small jars of already-prepared chutney. "Would you take these to Ms. Guille at the library today?"

We had not seen our librarian neighbour to talk to since late August. She had been overwhelmed by the sight of soldiers, armies, uniforms and aircrafts when the occupation was in its infancy; I wonder how she is coping now, six months under their rule.

"I will. I'll pick up some new books, too. And I'll collect our bread from the market, whilst I am in town."

Ma scoffs. "*New*. What does this word mean anymore?"

I glance down at our stockinged feet; there are mirrored holes in both of them, our big toes protruding through. Shortly, I will put these holed stockings into shoes with worn soles, scuffed fronts and broken heels.

The war had already taken Europe by force before it reached our shores, and we had been feeling the effects even then. We know there will be nothing *new* for a long time. We have to make do with what we have and endure the wear and tear.

I kiss her on the cheek and go to leave. "Margot? Breakfast?" She gestures to the table, where I longed to see a bowl of cornflakes and fresh milk. My stomach grumbles at what awaits me - a small plate of dried sugar beet. My body repels the thought of putting the dry, rubbery breakfast substitute into my mouth and my stomach grips. Ma would have spent hours picking, slicing, mincing and drying the sugar beet, and I cannot simply turn it away.

I sit down, stomach a few mouthfuls, and tell her to eat the rest. "Keep your strength up, Ma."

I am out the door, overcoat, chutney and umbrella in hand, when I swear I hear "for what good."

I slide the umbrella across the handlebars of my cycle and get started on my journey to the towns library; a journey which, in the motorcar hidden behind the bales of hay in the barn, would have taken me fifteen minutes. Just under an hour later, after taking conscious efforts to dodge the patrols of field grey-clad Germans, I approach the desk of the library. It is vacant so I ring the bell. It echoes around the silent lofty lobby, and it isn't long before I hear the clip-clop approach of Ms. Guille.

"Thank heavens," she breathes, enveloping me into an uncharacteristic hug. "I thought you were one of them."

"Ma made these for you," I say, handing over the chutneys. "Do many soldiers come in?"

Though paler and more lined, her face seems hardened, now. Resilient. *Or resigned.*

"Unfortunately, yes. Not a day passes where another book is not taken from the shelves."

"I did not think them so cultured," I whisper.

"Oh, not to read. Though there *have* been a few among them who take a book for enjoyment. No, we get more coming to remove them from our shelves permanently."

"*Permanently?*" Requisitioning books hardly seemed necessary. "Why?"

"They have been pulling them like you would not believe. *Offensive to the Fuhrer, they reason it.* You would not believe it, Margot. They have taken H G Wells, Vernon Bartlett, Douglas Reed, *Winston Churchill* for goodness sake."

I shake my head, feeling violated just standing in the same building that they had stormed and raided.

"Anyway, dear, can I do any- " she breaks off into a deep, hacking cough. I expect it to cease, but it continues until she is barely able to catch a breath between attacks. She covers her mouth with her hand and I guide her to the stool behind the desk. Thankfully our water is still working and I run to the back room, filling up a small tumbler with tap water. She takes a sip and finally the coughs subside. Her breathing is ragged after, choked and full.

"Does that happen often?" I ask as casually as I can. Ms Guille suddenly looks her age; frail and withered. The reduced food supplies are beginning to take their toll, I fear.

"Only recently," she wheezes. "It passes. It always does."

"If you're quite sure…"

"Go and help yourself to a book, my dear. You know where they are. No new ones, of course, but I am sure you will find something."

I am hesitant to leave her – and simultaneously nervous of inadvertently crossing paths with a German. She folds her hands over mine. "I am quite alright, Margot. Ease your frown, now. This war is aging us prematurely as it is, you do not need worry lines on your pretty young face before your time."

I smile sadly and leave her, ascending the stairs, ready to lose myself in a small semblance of normality among the bookshelves.

My hand comes up, gently fingering a weathered spine, and that is when I see the red stain of blood. A smear of it taints the back of my hand and the perfect imprint of three bloodied fingers coils around my wrist.

↔

I wait in line at the market holding my ration book and trying to ignore the pink smudge of faded blood on the back of my hand. Ms. Guille had seemed well when I had checked out my latest book, but she had surreptitiously avoided eye contact. At what point did one need to worry about blood in their phlegm?

Fond memories of waiting in line for freshly baked bread with Ma comes to mind. It is the same place, the same baker at his stall, but the smell is all wrong. My nostalgia is offended; the bread is some German rye offering that could break a toe if dropped from a height.

Without turning, I know that the next in line after me is a soldier. The air grows thicker around them, colder, like a dense cloud has descended. The smell of starch and a sweet, sickly scent tickles my noise unpleasantly. He coughs. Abruptly, intentionally.

I fix my gaze straight ahead, watching the baker serve those ahead of me with a concentration to be revered. To my side, dawdling near the lacklustre fruit stall, I see two familiar faces with their heads together, willow baskets holding only a few market wares. I send them a wave – Mrs Leale and Mr Nichols. Their respective spouses had evacuated – Mr Leale with ill health, but stubbornly refusing to leave his home to the mercy of the Germans so insisting that his wife remain, Mrs Nichols because her husband had insisted on it. Mrs Leale, so Ma said, had been darning the holes in Mr Nichols' socks.

They wave back, sending a scornful look over my shoulder to the German soldier behind. A few more whispered words, then they approach, coming closer than necessary to pass us by.

"*Baisse mon chou,*" Mrs Leale says pleasantly, nodding to the German with a smile.

I almost choke on fresh air, covering it with a deliberate cough.

"Good day to you too," the German bids the elderly couple.

Whilst many of the Germans plaguing our island have mastered the basics of the English language – enough to get by, at least – they had not anticipated our native tongue, our *Patois*. Most of the time our whispered language infuriates them, you can see it in the hollow glare of their eyes. Often they misattribute our insults as well wishes and good tidings, and this is always a source of great amusement.

Baisse mon chou categorically does not translate as *good day to you.*

You sly little things, I think, stifling a chuckle.

The soldier behind me coughs again, impatient now. My smile fades and I straighten my chin, edging it a little higher into the air. I am two people from the front when he loses his patience and side sweeps me, taking a step in front.

"Ze madam vill let me go virst," he snaps at the baker.

Can their language ever sound romantic? I wonder.

It is not a question.

I glance down at the faded blood on my hand. "The madam will *not*." Before I can stop myself I move forward, side by side with him. "Until there is a written rule saying otherwise, I have just as much right to -" but as I turn to the side to face my tormentor face on, my eyes drift past his lofty shoulder, into the shadows under the archaic arches of the Inner Market.

An alien green helmet tops a handsome face like an ill-fitting jar lid, whilst a right -but wholly *wrong* uniform - befits his body. In the same way that war made no sense in the summer, *he* makes no sense in this soldiers uniform. Not here. Not today.

Yet it is undeniably him.

I would know his stance – the slightly parted feet, cocked knee to one leg – in any place, at any time. My breath hitches in my chest and everything around me stills; the bustling of the market dims to a hum, the bodies blur into a cataclysm of colour and shape, the clouds drift slower in the sky. Inside my body a tornado begins to form. A burning lick of flame roars across my chest at the same time as my stomach twists itself into a coil.

All thoughts of bread and lines and cantankerous German soldiers forgotten, I walk at pace across the market square, my eyes never leaving the soldier by the arch.

Step by step. One foot in front of the other.

Do not run. Do not make any rash moves.

Like stalking an animal in the wild I will myself to move slow, slower than my body wants to go. I cannot raise alarm; I cannot have eyes on me. I use one hand to anchor my body as I swing around the nearest market pillar, ready with shaking hands to finally see him. To hold him. To love him. To kiss him. My lips part but no sound comes out.

He has gone.

I whip my head in every direction, searching the crowds with wide and eager eyes. My body aches with a desperation so overwhelming that my head wobbles, precariously light headed.

"Otto." I let his name dance on my lips, only a slight whisper that is snatched away by the breeze and carried up into the clouded sky.

Still hidden in the shadows I back up to the pillar, allowing the icy stone to break its way through my overcoat and cool suddenly overheating skin. My eyes refuse to close, to accept that he was here - he was *here!* But now he has gone. If I let them close, the image will disappear. He will cease to exist here, in this moment.

I let my knees buckle and my body fold in on itself until I come to sit on the cobbled floor of the Inner Market, arms folded around my upright legs. I rest my head on my knees, opening the doors for the clammy, warm and wholly unpleasant storm grappling at my skin with resignation.

Gentle breaths. I am anything but senseless, but all reason has been momentarily lost on me.

"Were you even here?" I whisper, unsure if I am more afraid of succumbing to hunger hallucinations, or that he may have intentionally deserted me. Left me behind. Again.

Heavy jackbooted footsteps assault my silence, stopping just short of my feet. A cough. *That* cough. I bring my head up with a jolt, finding his eyes straight away. *My bread nemesis.* He is young, the marks of outgrown acne still visible on his cheeks. I question him with my eyes, too afraid to speak. My voice will almost certainly betray me.

"Are you vell?"

"I saw someone. I thought I did," I mutter, laying my head back down. Is this against the rules? I think, idly. Is he here to throw me a fine?

There is a short muffle of noise and then, thankfully, his footsteps ebb away like the tide. When I finally look up and out of my silent trance a loaf of rye bread sits by my feet, carefully wrapped in the crumpled remnants of the local newssheet.

I find him in the crowd straight away, like he had been attached to one end of a string and I the other. He strolls away from the market, into the main town, hands empty.

18

February 1941

Alice has been gone eight months. Eight months of the worst form of ignorance. No islander knows the whereabouts of any children, husbands, wives or friends that had evacuated in the summer of 1940. They could be on the moon for all we know. The moon is likely preferable over other alternatives.

There were rumours, in January, that we would have word from them soon.

No word came.

In February when those rumours resurface, they are taken lightly. Inside, deep down, we all hope for it. My mind, usually so clear on what emotional response is necessary in a situation, cannot settle. I am desperate to hear from Alice, so desperate that tears fall at the slightest memory of her; running barefoot through the cornfields, rinsing sand from little toes, the naturally sweet scent of her skin, the tickle of her hair when we embraced. Yet I only wish for good news. If the messages will bring anything other than that, they can keep them. I cannot even entertain the thought.

At the beginning of the month, news arrived that the first batch of messages had landed and were being sorted at the post office. Jaws dropped, hearts beat faster, eyes widened, hands shook. An air of disbelief rendered most islanders temporarily soundless.

We waited, and waited. We watched as neighbours received messages from husbands and wives, parents got their long awaited letters from evacuated children and farm aides received notice from friends overseas. February turned into March and still, we had no word from Alice.

Almost one month after the first Red Cross messages made landfall on the island there is a knock at the door. We had gotten quite used to the sharp rap of the German soldiers, catching us unawares, no concern of giving us premature heart failure with their incessant tapping. Ma, Pierre and I stop what we are doing and stare at one another. This knock is different.

"Ma?" I tremble a little, unsure of our next move.

She runs a tea towel through her hands, over and over, watching the door as if waiting for it to guide her. “One way or another,” she finally says, “we will know.”

The time it takes her to walk to the door seems like hours, at the same time as not coming quick enough. Pierre has come to stand beside me and he clutches my hand in his. Strong knuckled and comforting, I almost crumble into him. The local boy messenger – one of the very few left on the island, poor boy, he must be working overtime – hands over the blue envelope with a half-smile. He has no idea if it is the good news that warrants a joyful smile, or bad news that requires condolences.

Ma thanks him and carefully closes the door, sealing us in our bubble. We know that the contents of the envelope are not going to give us our message. We know it is simply an invitation to the newly established Red Cross Bureau in town.

But it is *something*. Our waiting is finally over.

↔

The journey to the Red Cross Bureau that evening is slow. Trying to get my body to move quickly is impossible; it feels like I am wading through treacle. I am not sure if it is nature’s perverse way of telling me to wait a bit longer, or if it is trying to dissuade me from going, from finding out Alice’s fate. The fact is irrelevant, really; even if I really did have to wade through a treacle lake of man-eating fish, I would get that letter, one way or another.

It is busy when I arrive. They had nominated me to receive the letter; Pierre was going to milk Hetty (we had had to move her from our pasture near the cliffs – the soldiers had riddled our picturesque landscape with defence mines) and Ma sorted what she could for dinner. She had been lost in thought, peeling and chopping parsnips, as I had left. I found her away with the fairies more often, lately, and wondered if it was her next stage of grief.

The hall hums with the low drone of people – many of them collecting their letters and leaving, to read them in the comfort of their own homes with their remaining loved ones, as I intend to do. Others tear the paper open where they stand, the months of torturous waiting finally unbearable. Most cry tears of joy, some collapse to the floor in a broken heap. I avoid catching the eyes of those people.

Just let her be okay. Let her be safe.

A rare early March sunshine filters through the dirty windows of the hall in a daze, sending hovering dust particles dancing in the beams overhead. It could almost be beautiful, if the circumstances for being here had been different.

I am two from the front of the stiflingly warm hall when I see Ms. Guille loitering on a bench beneath one of the windows. She clutches a small parcel of letters – several weeks’ worth, at a guess. She holds them to her heart, staring wistfully into space. She stifles a cough, I notice, and whilst it is still persistent, the attack ends quicker than the one in the library had. And no blood, from what I can see.

"Margot La Joie," I announce, handing over the blue envelope. "Also for Lucille and Pierre La Joie. I should have some letters from my sister," I stumble, the words sounding like cotton wool in my mouth. I had not once had the inclination to call her for what she is, but now I want to lay all claim on her – my daughter. It raises questions of what will happen when she is back with us, but I push them away.

"Let me see," the clerk mutters to herself. She is peppy, holding a permanent smile. I imagine they have been told to. "Ah, here we are. Frank, Lucille, Margot and Pierre La Joie. Quite a bundle."

My hands shake as I take the letters. *Frank.* Alice doesn't know. I swallow a tear, whisper *thank you* and clutch them to my chest like the smallest breeze might snatch them away. Though it were wholly unladylike, if anyone dared to put a hand to them I was sure I could wrestle them to the ground.

I go to leave in a more subdued trance than I thought I would. *Frank La Joie.*

I pass Ms. Guille, still on her bench. "My son," she croaks, holding up the letters. "He's *alive.* He's been away fighting but he…he's alive." Her face is more alight than I have ever seen it. "And you, dear? Alice?"

"Alice," I confirm.

"Was it…I'm sorry, dear." She pats my knee, misinterpreting my tears.

"She doesn't know." My breath hitches, making me gasp and sob at the same time. Faces turn to me. *She's received bad news.* "She doesn't know about Papa."

She wraps a surprisingly strong arm around my shoulders. "There will be time. Savor what joy you can in this world, Margot. Take your letters straight home. Do not stop until you get there. Smile the smiles, or cry the tears, whatever it may be."

I wipe away at the thin trickle of tears tickling my cheek. That is when I notice the specks of blood on Ms. Guile's overcoat.

19

April 1941

"*Eight* eggs! An omelet with *eight* eggs. I wanted to snatch his plate from under his nose and devour the entire lot, like Hetty inhaling her feed," Pierre grumbles.

I let the foul hunger twisting in my stomach pass before I respond. "When was the last time you saw eight eggs, Pierre, in one household, let alone on one *plate*."

"It sickens me," he shakes his head. "We have barely enough rations to survive, our elderly unable to endure it and our children hardly growing because of it. Yet those cretins sit and scoff their plates like they haven't eaten in a month."

Children hardly growing. It hurt me to the very core of my being to see our young ones so desperately in need of a more fulfilling diet. Our government were doing what they could; children have higher milk rations, for one, but their stunted development – physically and mentally – is not lost on us. It is the only account on which I am grateful Alice is safe in Britain.

She wrote in her letters about the dismal sailing conditions she had endured with a grace that only a child could. I felt sick to my stomach when she spoke of sailing over in the animal hold, of children fainting from hunger and overcrowding. She had been brave, she wrote, even when she had been piled onto a train with hundreds of other children, with no idea where it was headed. She was living in Coventry, with a kind couple and their two young girls similar in age to her. They were teaching her how to braid her hair and play hopscotch. I cannot picture tiny Alice living a life somewhere I know nothing of, under guardianship of a family who are strangers to me. I long for her to be back with us at the same time as thankful she is not enduring this.

The soldiers, on the most part, have been physically amicable towards us. Their disregard for our hunger however, and their hypocritical rations on fuel when they ride on buses only a quarter full, are what fuels the fire in our bellies.

Pierre and I are on our cycles, making a slow and steady return to the farmhouse after delivering produce to our once-favourite cafe *Home from Home*. Jerry still owns the café, his patrons now mostly made up of German soldiers, since people can barely afford to go out to eat. The glass windows have not been replaced since the White Rock bombing and remain boarded up, giving the café a clouded, seedy atmosphere, even without the addition of the enemy patrons. It was there, as we handed over our requirement of produce, that we watched Germans dine on overindulgent omelets and meals made with the food that we were limited to.

Wiping away spots of drool from the corner of our mouths and wrestling with the gut-wrenching hunger pangs, we make a conscious effort to go slow. Our energy, like all the stores on the island it seems, must be reserved.

"Let's go the Blue Mountains way," I suggest, trying to sound casual. "We can rest at the top."

Pierre exhales. "This is keeping us fit, I suppose."

Relief floods my burning chest. *Thank goodness he agreed.* I know that it is futile, and I know that I am putting myself through the cruelest form of torture. I had long ago come to the realisation that I had hallucinated that day in the market. I was not the first to do so. The doctor in charge of the civilian populations' health had recently notified us on symptoms to watch for as we progressed steadily from food scarcities to critically low shortages. Vivid hallucinations were just one of the many ways our bodies and minds could betray us without the correct level of nutrition. I picture the Germans, drool dripping down their chins as they dine on daily feasts, and the thought pokes the fire in my belly a little more.

I have no choice but to believe that Otto had never been so close. I never actively hunt the groups of soldiers down, but at times like this, when we are out on the streets and one of their egotistical parades takes place, I search for him.

We are almost to the top of the steep lane, where we can take rest on a bench and overlook the parade below us from a safe distance, when we see a shuffling figure approaching us. No, not approaching us, this figure has no idea which direction it is taking.

"That's Mr Nichols," Pierre nudges me.

I look again. His beard is overgrown, his hair dangling untidily past his ears. He wears a jacket spotted with noticeable holes and one foot is missing a shoe. He is a far cry from how I had seen him last; laughing with Mrs Leale in the market – my stomach twists at the memory of the day – and greeting the soldiers with defiant and brazen improper phrases in our native tongue.

We gently guide him to a bench, the incoming parade coming closer. It is clear he is not well; he wears the signs of malnutrition on his skin like a cloak.

"They took the bloody thing," he mutters, spitting crudely to the floor at his feet. With alarm, I notice it is tinged with blood. "They took my bicycle. I saw 'em, riding off on it as I came out the pub. How am I supposed to catch 'em, eh? At my age," he shakes his head. "I tell you. If I could curl up in a ball right here and die I would. I won't give 'em the satisfaction of taking 'nething else from me."

"Let us take you home, Mr Nichols. You can have my bike, I'll walk."

"I'll walk," Pierre insists, guiding our patient to his own bicycle. "I can run to keep up with you, I'm out of shape anyway." He smirks at me, both of us knowing this is far from the truth. Neither of us, truly, could do with losing anything else; my fitted dresses already hang like smocks.

The parade is below us now, and before I mount my bike I look down. I can see their faces clearly, and my eyes wobble in my head as I skip from man to man, giving them only a seconds grace. *I'll know him when I see him.*

Pierre eyes me curiously, but doesn't speak on it.

"Don't be insane," I whisper when my brother and Mr Nichols are out of earshot. "He is not there."

↔

We walk Mr Nichols' home. I doubt very much that he has been bathing. Our water allowance has been reduced to a minimal to get by on, and there has been talk the Germans will ban water for flushing lavatories next. I eye Mr Nichols' startlingly frail frame; the elderly would never cope with outdoor sanitation.

I search his kitchen for anything to make a substitute cup of tea with – nettles and brambles had been a considered substitute. I cannot say *popular,* because that would imply it tasted anything more than insipid. On the top shelf there is a lonely, wrinkled and browned teabag. *A real teabag.* Real, and used – multiple times by the looks of it. I put a small pot of water to boil and let the teabag soak, getting as much of the weakened flavour from it as I can.

"There's nothing a cup of tea can't fix," I say, handing him the steaming mug.

"Ah, that it cannot," he says with a wistful smile, smacking his lips. "But how am I going to get around now. My knees can't handle walking these roads, you know."

"Don't worry about that," Pierre assures him, getting in before I can answer. "I will sort it for you." I send him a steely look. *Don't make promises you can't keep.* Bikes have become hot commodities, and soldiers have been reduced to petty thieves, stealing them from civilians in the middle of the night.

"Well, while you're here," Mr Nichols says, shooting a furtive glance through the kitchen window, "want to listen to the news?"

Our wireless sets, by some miraculous turn of events, have not yet been confiscated. We all wait for the moment they will be taken from us, already nervous to listen in on the BBC broadcasts in case we are caught and they decide on a whim to pull them from us. We live isolated in every form; our wireless sets are our only connection to the outside world. We still have Papa's, in full working order, defiantly out on display in the farmhouse.

I check the time – thirty minutes till curfew. "We would like that very much."

So it is that when we first hear of the *V for Victory* campaign we are sitting on the plain brown sofa, in Mr Nichols' small single story cottage, ignoring the odour of unwashed flesh. I listen in on Colonel Britton telling Europe how it can take part in the campaign and show their solidarity with our forces, and I watch as my brothers eyes light up and begin to dance. Paint them on street signs, write them on walls, plant them in flower beds, salute in a hand gesture, tap it and clap it.

The next time I see Mr Nichols' he is winking to Pierre and I as he cycles past on a new bike, holding his index and middle finger up to us in a 'V.'

20

May 1941

We had been told in the beginning to be passive; to refrain from provocation, to comply. We had, by and large, done these things. We had most likely been their most obliging occupied territory. The attitudes from the majority of soldiers helped; most of them seemed to not want to be here as much as we did not want them here.

But almost a year into the occupation of our island - an island rich in memories that we all held so dear - and something has shifted in the air. Our patience are worn out, our fiery tempers quicker to flare, and our resilience to being occupied is faltering. The soldiers' attitude, too, is changing toward us. They are less tolerant, less understanding, less forgiving. Fines are given daily for small, inconsequential things. Prison sentences are frequent. The soldiers no longer pass by us with genteel, welcoming smiles. Their smiles now feel like those of a wolf in sheep's clothing.

I carry a small handful of early blooming flowers as I meander my way through the country lanes to Mariette's house. It has been several weeks since Pierre, Ma or I have seen her. It isn't unlike Mariette to disappear for a little while, she is a slave to the dramatics of womanhood, she always has been. But it paid, in current circumstances, to pay your loved ones regular check in's. Particularly to Mariette, with her undesirable penchant for the soldiers.

Early May sunshine warms the skin on my face. Spring is coming, whether this occupied island is ready for it or not. I approach Mariette and her father's cottage and notice with surprise that the garden lies unkempt and overgrown. Flaccid weeds lay across the gravel path and sun dried flowers hang limp from their stalks, wrinkled. Harry Shaw, Mariette's father and my uncle, is garden proud. A recluse in all senses of the word, his only noticeable presence outside of his home was his garden.

Pierre and I have no relationship with Harry. He had married Ma's sister, for reasons none of us could quite fathom. Mariette's mother had been loud, brazen and confident. Harry, on the rare occasions we had seen him, refused to talk and, we suspected, had had to be bribed to be in the very presence of others. Mariette said little of him, not even now that she was older to recognize his reluctance to be in public was down to something more medical than choice. For the most part, she pretends he does not exist.

So, as I approach their front door, avoiding the threatening nettles lining the path, I am surprised to hear their raised voices coming from within. My hand hovers in a knock – *do I intrude?* They are arguing, it is clear in their tone and level, but I cannot make out the words. It is an odd occurrence enough for me to hear Harry's voice, let alone hear it raised to his daughter. I begin to feel uncomfortable hovering on the doorstep so I take the chance and knock – once, firm. The voices stop, then the unmistakable sound of footsteps receding away from the knock.

Mariette opens the door with a *whoosh*, cool air caressing my flushed skin. Her eyes are rimmed with red, and under them are slate-grey shadows. She closes her eyes – whether in relief or annoyance I can't quite work out – and rests one arm on the frame of the door.

"Margot, you caught me unawares. What are – why – why are you here?"

My cousin, the pinnacle of poise and grace, looks as disheveled as her garden. I do not wait for an invitation in. I stride past her, closing the door behind us. She leans against a wooden pillar that stands at the entry into the rest of the house. I lean against the other.

"I heard you arguing."

I expect her to deny it. Exhaustion gets the better of her, it seems, as she merely nods. "Dad and I…"

"Yes?"

"It is complicated."

I raise an eyebrow. "Complicated how?"

"I wish I could, Margot." For once, I believe the words that escape her. This is Mariette, I realise. Raw, unfiltered, natural. She is not trying to impress anyone. She is the cousin I recognise before womanhood got in her way.

"If you wish it, then tell me," I take her hands in mine.

She looks behind us, into the shadows of her home where, I imagine, her father sits somewhere, alone. She whispers something into the shadows, barely audible.

"Mariette?" I push.

"They will hurt him." When she turns back I notice her eyes are filled with tears. "Please, do not ask anything else of me, not with this. Just," she sniffs, "just let this go."

I quietly check her skin for signs of bruises or marks of violence, but there is nothing. *Nothing visible*, anyway. "If he is hurting you…" I say gently.

She drops my hands as if she has touched a naked flame. Her features twist and she steps back from me, shocked. "Hurting me?" She hisses. "You believe my father is *hurting* me? He would – he couldn't – *god,* no! He would never even dream of such a thing."

Before I can say anything more, there is a furtive knock at the door that freezes us both. Rather, four knocks. Three soft ones to start, one loud to finish. I stare at the door, waiting for the brutish instructions to be barked from beyond.

"Do not worry, Margot, it is not the Germans."

"How do you know?"

"They have a special knock."

It no longer surprises me that my cousin knows so much about the soldiers, but even I know that they all knock with a sharp *rap-rap-rap*. What other *special knock* could they have? I shiver a little, knowing the only relationship my cousin has with them is physical. Was it a particular…*invitation?*

"They do?"

"*We* do."

"*We?*"

"Yes. *We*."

Mariette sighs, moving past me and opening the door. Three people I know vaguely from sight rush in and close the door swiftly behind them. They acknowledge my presence but do not comment on it.

"She was visiting."

"And is she…" one of them asks, side-eyeing me with a glance.

Questioning something silently, Mariette assesses me. She chews the corner of her lips, gnawing at a loose piece of dry skin. It is the only time I have seen my cousin anything less than confident.

"She can be trusted."

There is a noticeable drop in whatever tension had been filling the same lobby we all occupy. Without instruction, the three visitors carry themselves off into the shadows of the house, knowing where to go next with no invitation. Mariette does the same, glancing over her shoulder with a flick of her hair when I do not follow.

"Well, are you coming?"

"I – I, I'm confused…"

"Confusion won't stop you from doing your bit. Come on."

↔

Two days later, I am ready for my first act of sabotage against the German soldiers in the name of the *V for Victory* campaign.

Mariette and her friends had listened to the BBC broadcast and had, along with what appeared to be a great number of the civilian population of Guernsey - both young and old - taken Colonel Britton up on his suggestion. They had been chalking large motifs of the letter 'V' on walls, scrawling it on to Nazi signposts, doodling it in the dust prints of shop windows, had even etched it into the sun softened tar on one of our main roads.

Tonight, we were to take it a step further. My stomach had been in knots for days. Mariette and her friends had not forced me into anything, they had simply allowed me to listen in on their clandestine meetings. It had – I assumed – the desired effect on me. I could never have told them about my interactions with the commandos on the cliff top, but I recognised the thrill deep in my stomach for what it was. I was aching for a chance to help. To revolt.

So, I had suggested that we target the soldiers and their precious requisitioned bicycles. There had been more and more calls of late for islanders to hand over their only means of transport to the soldiers. A prime way to get back at them, I proposed, was to chalk the cardinal letter 'V' onto the seat of their bicycles whilst they wined and dined on *our* food supplies in *our* cafes and restaurants. In the dark of night, they would hop on their bicycles and go back to their barracks or billeted houses, none the wiser that when they stood up again, a 'V' would be imprinted on their backsides for all to see.

Armed with chalk and out well beyond curfew, Mariette and I loiter in the bushes outside one of the pubs in the main town. Our hair is tucked inside dark shirts, in turn tucked into sleek men's pants I had borrowed from the back of Pierre's wardrobe. My heart is thumping so hard against my chest it burns, and swallowing is difficult. The hand holding the chalk is clammy and shaking, but determined. Mariette's eyes sparkle in the dark, and I can feel my own doing the same.

We had observed a group of five soldiers abandon their cycles and enter the pub fifteen minutes ago. Inside it is rowdy and noisy, and my ears ache from listening to endless repetitions of their repulsive chanting. It incentivises us.

I wait for Mariette's go ahead. She gives me a thumbs up, and we know that the moment we leave the hidden safety of the bushes we have only seconds to chalk the letters and run back. We crouch low under the line of the pub windows, targeting as many of their cycles with the chalk as we can get to. When I am three cycles from the end of the row I hear the unmistakable sound of a door opening and the noise from inside fills the still air beyond it. I freeze where I stand, making myself as small as I can in the dark shadows. Mariette does the same.

Without moving I cast my eyes towards the door. My heart thumps into the pit of my stomach with an agonising wrench as I see a soldiers outline illuminated from the lights within (lit from *our* fuel rations) and watch as he leans against the doorframe, igniting a cigarette (*our* tobacco rations). His eyes wander across the dark landscape, adjusting to the murky shadows. In seconds he will see me, no matter how small I make myself.

My eyes quickly shift to the other side of me when I sense movement, and almost gasp when Mariette drops her chalk at my feet and strolls brazenly past with her head held high. I notice she has unfastened a few buttons on her shirt and freed her long hair from the collar.

"Stay there." As she passes, her whisper gets lost in the tidal wave of noise from the pub.

She walks on her tip toes, inventing heels that aren't there, and pinches the apples of her cheeks just as the soldier turns to her. His hand automatically clasps the pistol at his waist. Relief washes through me when his hand changes course and waves in greeting to Mariette, instead.

"Madam Mariette," he acknowledges, with a thirsty look that makes my blood curdle.

I remain as still as I can. Mariette has angled herself so that the soldier has to turn away from where I crouch. *Someone is going to come soon*, I think, *it is too risky*.

"Major Schafer," she purrs, leaning against the exterior wall of the pub and running a hand through her hair. "May I?"

She takes his tobacco and inhales several long, deep breaths in quick succession. She keeps him talking as she does, distracting him, rubbing a hand seductively across his upper arm. Before he even realises, she hands him back the stubbed cigarette, whispers something in his ear and ushers him inside. He is so beguiled by her that he has a bewildered look on his face – *how did that happen?* - as she closes the door behind him.

Mariette momentarily rests her head against the cool door, then strides over to me, picks me up from my crouched position, grabs the chalk and scribbles on the three remaining bicycle seats as quickly as she can. We navigate our way home by darkness, aware that if we happen to meet any patrols we will be fined or arrested, for certain. It is only as we reach the relative safety of our country lanes, where the patrols are fewer, that we both exhale and look to each other. We collapse into fits of exhausted, relieved giggles, until our stomachs hurt and our throats burn.

I leave Mariette at a fork in the road – her house one way, mine the other. I am still smiling as I enter my kitchen, kicking off my shoes, leaning two hands on the kitchen table and breathing. This frantic buzzing in my chest is addictive and intoxicating. Could this be it? Could this be the way to getting my beloved island back?

I am lost in this concoction of thoughts when from somewhere just outside of the house I hear a rustling. My feet stay rooted to the spot – a stray animal, perhaps? *Or a soldier, coming to arrest you.* The noise comes closer until it is outside the kitchen door. Still, I cannot move. I look down at what I wear, at the chalk staining my fingertips. There will be no denying it.

With horrifying clarity the handle of the door twists. My stomach grips with an overwhelming and sudden nausea. Will they turn away, disgusted, if I vomit right here? The door pops open and I throw my hand to my mouth, stifling a scream as a figure clad in black falls through the door. My blood runs icy cold and my limbs have all but turned to stone, for what good they can do me now. With wide eyes and trembling hands I can do nothing but watch on as the figure carefully closes the door, leaning their back against it as it shuts with a click.

A black balaclava hides his features until he whips it off and Pierre, with his unruly hair and bright eyes finally notices me. He starts, throwing a hand to his chest in surprise. His scowl turns to a rueful smile and he raises an eyebrow at my trousers. *His* trousers. The silence between us speaks volumes of its own. He walks to me until he is the other side of the table. My hand still trembles as I withdraw the chalk from my pocket and place it on the table between us, the glistening white like a ghost against the dark grain of the wood. Slowly he shakes his head and, chuckling, puts his hand in his own pocket, pulling out a pair of rusted wire cutters, and placing them beside the chalk.

Our eyes meet across the clandestine objects of sabotage, so foreign in the comfort of our farmhouse kitchen. *We are in this together.*

21

May 1941

The following morning, with the effects of last night's sabotage still thrumming through my blood, I am milking Hetty in the new paddock. She is now just through the field at the back of the house; the Germans had insisted we move her each time they found a new location for their insipid mines to be buried.

I am glad to have Hetty closer. This month has seen the arrival of wave after wave of slave labourers on the island and with them, the theft and mutilation of a great number of livestock. We had barely seen them with our own eyes, but they left their mark in other ways. Animals had been slain where they stood, and meat hacked off carcasses with, one can only assume, the bare hands of desperate starving men.

Rubbing a hand over Hetty's coarse and bristly behind and flitting away the swarms of flies, I rest my head on her. *How much longer. How much longer will we have to endure this?* I quell a rising panic. *What if this is what life looks like now? No more bare foot runs on the beaches, no more quiet skies, no more picnics by the oak tree.*

I finish up with Hetty and stroll across the paddock back home, my joy dulled now by the chilling realities of what a life post-war could look like. I am still in the field when I see two figures in the distance, walking in my direction. One of them drops to the ground, looking for something. Or rather, as I realise as I get closer, inspecting something.

One is a German soldier, though I've not seen him before. This means he is either new to the island or is of a higher rank, therefore spending a lot of his time behind his desk. The other is a local police officer – Officer Martel. Once it is clear that the two men are not looking for me, I can relax enough to breathe again.

"Zis, here, it 'az been cut," I overhear the German saying to the police officer, in horrendously broken English.

My stomach drops, remembering the wire cutters now buried under ground in the allotment at the house. I continue walking but slow my pace. I am yet to pass them.

"Hmm," Mr Martel ponders, and I'm not sure I believe his tone. "Do you believe so?"

"Vell," the German stands and rubs the small of his back, looking around. He must clock Hetty as he says, "I zay de cow must hav ztood on eet. Yez?" He says it pointedly.

There is a moment of such still silence that only my footsteps on the gristly, parched grass is audible.

"Good morning," I mutter, trying to see the wire of which they speak. It is obvious, even to me, that the wire has been cut by human hands, not the hoof of a cow. If I see it as such, so must they.

"Why yes, yes Officer, I believe you are right there."

↔

There is a minor reprimand in the form of sentry duty for sixty civilian men, for the cutting of an internal telecommunications wire, elsewhere on the island. Thankfully, the German who had overseen the cut wire in Hetty's field must have officially marked it as an animal accident, as we heard nothing more of it.

When we hear of the reprimand, Pierre and I share a knowing glance over a paltry breakfast of dry Rye bread, but say nothing.

"Where is she?" Ma stands suddenly, frantically looking around the room.

"Ma?"

"Alice. Where is that girl? She will be late. Look at the time!"

Our clocks have long stopped working – there is nothing left on the island to feed them. Most of us have turned primitive, relying on the height and angle of the sun to determine exact times. Our grumbling stomachs could no longer be depended upon; that discomfort was permanent.

"Ma…" I try, but she has run from the room before I can speak.

Pierre and I look to one another, hearing the *tap-tap* of her feet on the wooden boards upstairs. Inevitably, there is a terrifying scream that rattles our bones, and she races back down to us.

"She's gone! They must have taken her in the night! Her bed, it has not been slept in."

Pierre leaps up and tries to control Ma but her movements are too frantic, too wired. I can see where she is headed; I run to the door and latch it shut just as she throws her shoes on.

"What are you – *Margot*! Move! Alice has been *taken*."

With surprising force Ma pushes at my arm to move me. I refuse to budge, a horrifying combination of fear and grief poisoning my stomach. Pierre holds her back just in time as she scrabbles at my open skin, leaving raw red marks on my forearm. Tears sting at my eyes. With his arms wrapped tightly around her, Ma barely moves an inch. I watch her with a subdued terror creeping at my skin. Her erratic breathing and pumping chest slows, slows. She hangs her head and I nod at Pierre, who guides her back to the table.

"Ma, Alice is -"

"- I know where she is."

We finish our breakfast in silence. Ma does not move.

↔

Handing over our fields to the Global Utilisation Board on the island – known as GUB, locally – meant that I had considerably less farm work that I was able to help with. We had agreed that it was more important to ensure working roles for our fellow islanders who had lost work. It was better for them to be here, on the farm, than forced into working for the Germans. Many had, of course, seen more incentive working for the enemy. Better wages, for one. Perhaps they thought they would have an elevated level of immunity, too. But for islanders with integrity, it was the honest Earth work that kept them going.

I had decided to ask Ms. Guille if she needed any assistance in the library. It would fill my time, give me joy being around what I loved most at a time that was anything but joyful, and would enable me to keep an eye on her. It was obvious she was severely ill. As was the case with most inherently stubborn islanders however, I could almost guarantee that she would refuse to see a doctor. Perhaps if I could be around more, I could convince her that coughing up blood is never good.

Ma cycles with me into town, and I cautiously keep an eye on her as we walk our bikes through the German-dominated streets. I have become so immune to their clipped way of speaking that I barely register it anymore; it drifts like an echo in the distance. And if I walk with my eyes straight ahead, only ever glazing over moving figures, I can pretend that they are fellow islanders.

It has been a fortnight since her episode, and Ma has been almost as she had been before the occupation. *When Papa and Alice were here*. Her temper is slower to flare and she embraces us more, kisses our cheeks, holds us as she used to. *She holds you closer,* I think. We both know it is perhaps too good to be true, but we pretend that she is over the worst of it. This is a new stage to her grief, we say. Perhaps, if we wish for it, Ma will be back.

I leave her to turn into the side street to the library just as a deafening roar tears across the sky over the town. The plane flies so low it looks as if it will rip through the tops of the historic buildings. Within seconds the monotone whirr of the air raid siren sounds, and people dart for cover. I scan the crowd for Ma but can't see her. A powerful force suddenly pulls me backwards. At first I think – in some abstract obtuse way – that I have been hit. Then I notice my heels dragging along the ground, and my hands try desperately to free whatever vice grip holds the back of my shirt. I am hauled into the porchway of a nearby shop. With shock and revulsion I realise it is a German soldier who has pulled me there, his hands still on my clothes. The same soldier who had left me his Rye bread on the day that I saw – *thought* I saw – Otto. Or the ghost of him.

"What do you think -"

He inhales sharply, so his nostrils flare. "Here," he points to the two of us and overhead to the porch, "*gut*." He then points out to the now vacant street. "There, *nicht gut*."

His logic is undeniable, but I am stunned nonetheless by his selfless act of saving me. What with his bread donation, some would even say he bordered on gentlemanly. Yet, he was German. He was the enemy. He may have saved me from a potential air raid, but that did not mean I had to look at him. I turned my back on him, imagining for a terrifying moment what this street would look like if it were bombed into oblivion.

That is when I see her. Ma. Standing on her own, in the middle of the empty street, staring up to the skies. Her arms hang limply at her sides and her bag, ready to be filled with whatever the days rations were from the market, lies in a heap at her feet.

"Ma!" I cry out, about to launch myself from the porch.

The German holds me back in a strong hold. "Do not go out there."

"That is my *mother*," I scream in his face. "Ma! Just – stop – just, argh!" I shout out, scrapping with his hands as they refuse to budge from me, sinking my nails into his flesh.

"*Bitte*, please, do not…"

I spit in his face. Finally, his hands release their grip on me as the foaming white spittle drips down from his eye. "Fine, *fine*," he spits back, "you go."

I curse myself as I race out onto the barren street, the *all-clear* siren now sounding. I reach Ma just as people begin to repopulate the area in a bizarre daydream-like fashion, as if nothing had ever happened. Pulling her close and smelling her hair, I whisper over and over, "what were you thinking."

She does not reply.

22

"Is your mother quite alright, Margot?"

Ma sits with her empty bag upon her knees, staring at the blank wall of the library. I wonder what she sees when she glazes over like that. She is frowning slightly, but the hint of a smile caresses her mouth, like she wishes to grin but cannot remember how.

I swallow hard. "She is fine, Ms. Guille, just a little out of sorts."

She nods, her mind wandering somewhere for a while. Of course she knows. Not so long ago it was her that had had to be soothed. This thought gives me hope; *look at you now,* I think. *If you can get better, so can Ma.*

But Ms. Guille is not better. Her cheeks are so hollow she gives off the air of a grisly skeleton, slowly coming back to life. Her skin is of a pale so ghostly it borders on translucent. Her once bouffant hair has clearly been falling out in clumps, though she has tried to sweep it to hide it.

"And you would not consider…" she trails off, her eyes squinting almost in apology at the thought.

I know what she is thinking. I would be lying if I claimed the thought had not entered my own mind at times. When I watch her walk into a room and stare at a wall for minutes on end, for example, or when I hear her having a one-sided conversation with Papa at night. I often think the best place for her, at least until she gets better, is with nurses who could help her. But then I imagine the farmhouse without Ma at the helm, and I know that it is an idea I cannot bring to fruition.

"I cannot," I whisper to Ms. Guille, well out of Ma's earshot. "Is that awfully selfish of me?"

She rests a withered hand on my arm and I shake off a shiver – it feels like bones against my skin. "This war is making us contemplate things we would never have done otherwise. In your heart, you will know."

I hope and pray that the war will be over before that moment; a magical veil will lift and all will be well again, as if the occupation had merely been a very unwelcome nightmare.

With a new job under my belt and due to start the following day, I wish I could say that our cycle back home was easier, a weight lifted. But Ma cycles in silence, and it is a wonder she makes it home in one piece at all.

As we walk to a gathering with Mariette and her friends – *our* friends, I suppose – later that afternoon, I raise the idea with Pierre.

"Would it be the best place for her, do you think?"

I expect him to revolt the idea. A part of me wishes he would. He simply hangs his head, letting the whisps of his thick hair dangle over his eyes. *He needs a haircut,* I think absently. *We all do.* We are almost to the house when we hear the familiar sound of jackboots marching on our lanes.

"Could we pause for a moment," I say, "I need to lace my shoe."

This is a lie. The laces holding my forlorn shoes together are nothing but a thread; it barely held them together, tied or untied. Pierre sighs, letting me know his displeasure at being caught in another of the soldiers' pompous showmanship parades, but he leans against the hedge, nevertheless. I take my time, and by the time I come to stand, the soldiers are close enough that we will pass them before our turn off. I watch their faces closely, scanning them all for any sign of familiarity. *He is not here.* The thought briefly enters my mind that perhaps it is *I* who should be entering a facility for the mentally ill, wishing the ghost of my love to come to life.

"I know what you are doing."

He catches me off guard and I struggle to hide the thoughts on my face. Ever since childhood I had been terrible at disguising my feelings; there was no future in theatre for me.

"Hmm?" I pretend I haven't heard him, avoiding his stare.

He stops and puts his hands in his pockets, kicking at a loose pebble just outside of the house. "You can pretend if that makes you feel better, Margot, but it is not lost on me that you stop us whenever there is a parade nearby. I see the frantic glaze of your eyes as you look at their faces. You are searching for someone." I say nothing. To Pierre, this says everything. "What I do not know is *who* you are searching for. It would not be a German soldier, I tell myself, because you despise them, just as I do. I often wonder if you search for the only German boy we know. Are you looking for Tomas, Margot, when you search their faces?" My hands begin to quiver, and he stills them in his. "He will not be among them."

He isn't to know that I look for Otto. Why would he make the connection, after all. Why would *I?* The only connection Otto has to Germany is heritage on his mothers' side. If he has any role in this war it is either from safe shores on the other side of the Atlantic Ocean, or as a Prisoner of War. Both notions turn my stomach to fire.

"I know," I whisper. "I know he will not."

Where Tomas is, I have realised, will remain a mystery to me. Likely forever. He had had time to write me before the war took Europe in her fierce clutches. Wherever Tomas is, he does not want to be found. I wonder with a sickening thought if this is also true for Otto. My best friend had abandoned me, a long time ago. Was my only love now doing the same? Was it time I let him go?

↔

Five more days pass. Life is monotonous.

I wake. Ma makes what she can for breakfast. Pierre cycles to drop me off at the library before returning home to help with the farm aids. I spend several hours assisting Ms. Guille with book loans. I am now, against my wishes, regularly in the company of German soldiers and officers, who see being in the presence of books as a reprieve from the mundanity of war life on an occupied island. Pierre collects me shortly before five, and we cycle home together.

I have finished sorting the book returns on the first floor, placing torn and battered books back on the shelves, and make my way down the bare floored corridor. The wooden boards beneath my feet still show the ghostly signs of the carpets that once warmed the lofty space. The Germans had torn them from the floor a long time ago. Those carpets were likely now warming the floor of somewhere in France, cushioning the bare wood or concrete for a German soldier living in the lap of luxury.

"Ugh," I remark. Every reminder like this pokes at my frustration a little more, making it rear up and hiss like a snake prodded from its slumber. I was assisting Mariette with her minor acts of sabotage where I could, but she had withdrawn again lately, barely leaving her house. I longed to do more.

Ms. Guille is showing me how I close down the library for the evening when the chime above the door rings and a customer walks in.

"Oh," I remark, "we are just closing down for the evening."

The young man – I pitch him at Pierre's age, possibly younger – nods but turns to Ms. Guille regardless.

"Ah, Paul. First floor, row A, fifth book in, *Stuart Little*, by E.B White." He nods again and makes his way up the stairs to, I presume, the first floor, row A, book five.

"How did you know which book he wanted?" I ask, a little bewildered by the entire scene.

She eyes me curiously, as if reading something in me. Then she shrugs, "it is a librarians' job to know what a reader requires," and continues to show me the art of shutting down a library for the evening. She intends to give me my first solo experience the following night; I suspect it is her stubborn way of acknowledging her body needs to slow down.

Twenty minutes later, the young man descends the stairs, bids us farewell and leaves the library. His wide mouthed smile could almost make you forget that outside of the library doors, an enemy runs amok.

He has no book in his hand.

23

"Do you dream of food?" Pierre asks.

I notice drool collecting at the corner of his chin and suppress an entirely irrational smile.

He is cycling me into work at the library, as he has done since I started there a fortnight ago. We had left Ma that morning sat in the kitchen, a small slice of uneaten (inedible, in her defence) bread at the table in front of her, staring mutely at the wisp of clouds drifting across the brilliant blue canvas of a crisp Spring morning. We had tried, and failed, to get her attention.

"Do we force her to eat?" Pierre had whispered as we hovered at the door.

I took in her slumped form and felt the knot in my stomach tighten. *Was it now? Is this the moment Ms. Guille spoke of?* "She won't starve herself," I had said, not quite trusting it. "She will eat when she is hungry. Bye Ma." There had been no reply.

"Every night," I tell him.

And those dreams are the most torturous to endure; a heavenly robust and slick with fat roast chicken usually sits at the centre of the table, surrounded by the softest, fluffiest golden potatoes dripping in goose fat, and complimented by the undeniably crisp yet succulent roasted root vegetables. I would carve into the chicken, the scent wafting into my nose and making my eyes water. The knife carving the chicken makes a slick-slack sound as the juices from the meat run out and just – *just!* – as my fork is fully loaded with food and coming towards my mouth, I wake. Then, I would curl into a ball and cry until I bled my body dry of water.

Three months earlier, before Ma's episodes had become semi-permanent and were still an occasional occurrence, she had crept in to kiss me goodnight and found me awake and restless.

"What is it, *ma p'tite souée?*" she cooed, stroking my head.

I looked into her eyes and, seeing the concern in them, couldn't be entirely honest. I couldn't tell her that, in spite of her best efforts in the kitchen, I was starving. My ribs were visible beneath breasts that were once full and ripe but now hung withered and depleted. The twisting and turning of an empty stomach had progressed into a perpetual hollow sensation. Wrist bones, ankle bones, cheek bones, all of them were so close to fragile and translucent skin that one wrong fall or knock and I feared they would pierce through it. Sunken cheeks and shadowed eyes caught me off guard every time I happened to catch sight of myself in a mirror or pool of water. I had aged eighteen years in eighteen months.

"I'm just a little hungry, is all," I had lied.

There was little she could do to solve that. She had kissed my cheek, squeezed at my upper arm – her fingers reaching all the way around – and wavered at the door. "Lie on your stomach, my darling, it will help."

It had worked to a point, the pressure and weight of my body filling in the hollow. As hunger had turned to starvation, however, even this move failed to cure it.

"It's usually pork in my dreams," Pierre muses, bringing me back to the present. "I'm not going to beat around the bush here, I think we need to eat Chops."

Chops was the pig we were rearing on the farm. He wasn't ready yet, but close enough for the roasted pork dreams to enter my unconscious mind, too. With bitterness I realised that sixty percent of Chops would go to the butcher, whereby most – if not all – of it would be sold to the soldiers before islanders could even get a look in.

"One day," I say.

"One day I will be a bag of bones on the roadside," he grumbles. "At least make sure you suck my bones dry of their meat, won't you, before those cannibals can get a piece of me."

I jokingly hit out at his arm. He may be half the width he was before the war started, but he certainly had not lost his sense of humour.

We arrive at the library to find it still closed. I look around; it is unlike Ms. Guille to be late opening. Using the spare key, I let myself in and begin the ritual of opening the library up to her patrons.

Most businesses had fallen at the knees during the occupation, many had closed and boarded up all together. The library, however, was one of the few places that still thrived. Ms. Guille tells me that member numbers were at an all-time high. Was it the art of getting lost in someone else's story when your own situation is as dire as ours, I often wondered, or were people reading more because there was considerably less to do under such tight restrictions?

Pierre does not want to leave me on my own. I reassure him that, should anything happen, even if Ms. Guille were here it is unlikely she would be any help in defending me.

"It will be fine," I urge him, keen to see him away from the hub of soldiers in the main town. He had carried out low-key acts of sabotage, as had I, but he was young and fiercely loyal. Where I had my head screwed on to fight those dangerous impulses that could end in prison or death, his was somewhat loose. No, the farther he was away from the town, the better.

Shortly after I have pushed him out of the door and watched him cycle off up the hill towards home, I have my first customer.

"Good morning."

"Oh," he says, shrugging himself out of a light jacket and hanging it on the hook.

I wait for him to elaborate but he just looks around searching for, I presume, Ms. Guille. "She is not in yet."

"No, no, quite…"

"Can I help at all?" He eyes me for a moment, until my feet shift and I start to feel uncomfortable. "Was it a particular book you were hoping to borrow? Or I could suggest something…"

"I will…I'll just have a look around actually. Many thanks."

I let him go, taking my place at the counter and watching the doors for Ms. Guille. Throngs of soldiers pass outside and I find myself searching their faces. I miss Otto. That is the truth of it, no matter how questionable my sanity is at this point. I search hopelessly for him because I miss him. It was like waking up one morning to find yourself missing a limb, but having no idea what had happened to it, where it had gone, who had it instead of you. I was no stranger to waiting for him; we had gone two years between seeing each other for most of our lives. I had always known he was coming back, that was the difference. I knew how long I had to wait; I could count down until that moment. Uncertainty stretched out in front of me now until it disappeared to a dot on the horizon. It was frustrating, heart breaking and unfair.

It is time I move past this. It is time I forget him.

"Mariette!" I call, sighting her through the door on the street beyond. She has almost collided with someone and doesn't hear me as she speaks with him. I recognise him from one of the many gatherings she had taken us to – Ralph. Whatever they are speaking of it is clear that she wants no one else to hear. She is doing the talking. He is listening. Typical of Mariette.

I had not realised she and Ralph were particularly fond of each other, but her mouth is perilously close to him. Had it not been for the frown on her face I would have thought she was whispering sweet nothings into his ear. A look of something flashes across his face – uncertainty, perhaps – and she clasps her hands around his shoulders. He sweeps a kiss across her cheek, then, and walks away. I blush watching Mariette stand alone on the street, feeling awkward at having witnessed what was clearly an intimate moment between the two of them. If it were that intimate, I realise, she wouldn't have shared it with the scores of soldiers teeming the streets around her.

I open the door and usher her in. Her eyes flash for the briefest of moments before she composes herself. By the time she joins me in the lobby of the library she is calm and…Mariette.

"Was that Ralph you were with?"

"Not Ralph, no," she says, looking up to the lofty heights of the room.

I frown. "I could have sworn…"

"Well, you swear wrong," she says, shrugging. She does not meet my eyes.

"Mariette," I say slowly, not quite understanding what there is to hide by not admitting she had been with him. "I know that was Ralph."

"And I am telling you, Margot, that that was *not* Ralph." She levels her eyes with me and they are as cold as steel. "Do you understand?"

"I'm not sure I…"

"You saw me with *someone*, but you cannot say for certain who it was. It could have been Ralph, but it could just have easily been Matthew, an old friend from school. It could even have been Joseph, who lives just around the corner from here."

I am stunned into silence. With a start her hand darts out and grabs my wrist, holding me firm. "You cannot trust what you saw. Those words, exactly. *You cannot trust what you saw.*"

"You are hurting me, Mariette, and I don't -"

She tugs me closer. "For once in your life," her words are a hiss, "can you accept that things may not be as black and white as you see them."

"I – I thought I was helping you with this," I whisper, keeping my voice low in case the visitor to the library chose that moment to leave. "If this is something to do with the sabotage -"

"It is *not*."

"Well I can help you…"

She lets my wrist go and I hold it against my chest, rubbing it. "This is not just an act of petty sabotage that might land us with a hefty fine or even a short stint in prison. For this, Margot, *I do not need you.* Not because you would not be a valuable asset, but because I will *not* put you in that danger. Is that clear enough for you?"

I study her. I had an uncanny ability to read people; there was little about them that surprised me, because I had always intuited it on some level. Mariette was telling the truth. She had never before in her life put anyone before herself, but this time, I believed her. Whatever she was involved in was something far beyond small acts of inconveniencing the soldiers.

"Okay. I don't know who I saw you with. It could have been anyone."

She watches me, waiting - I'm sure - for me to argue. To fight back. When she is satisfied that I won't, she stuns me once more by pulling me into a tight embrace.

"I love you," she whispers, and leaves like a gust of wind.

I am still stood rooted to the spot, wondering if I have suffered a spot of emotional whiplash, when the visitor to the library knocks me out of my reverie by descending the stairs with a *clump-clump-clump.*

I rush back to the counter. "Did you find what you were looking for Sir?" I glance over his empty palms. "Perhaps not?"

"I did, many thanks, Madam…"

"Margot, Margot La Joie."

"Margot. I found *The Seven Pillars of Wisdom* particularly riveting." He pauses a beat, and his eyes almost imperceptibly widen a touch. "Do pass that on, won't you."

"Pass it on to…?"

The corner of his mouth twitches. "Ms. Guille, when she arrives." He turns to leave, then, draping his light jacket over his forearm.

"Sir?" I call after him. "The book? Are you not borrowing today?"

I was no expert in speed-reading, of course, but even I knew that it would take a lot longer than fifteen minutes to read *The Seven Pillars of Wisdom.*

He shakes his head and, I could swear of it, laughs softly.

↔

By mid-day, Ms. Guille still had not come in and I was concerned. Every time the chime above the door sounded I looked up hopefully, but it was always another customer, of which there were many.

"Madam? Where is Ms. Guille?" Most of them asked, a fretful look crossing their face when greeted by me and not the librarian.

"I am afraid I do not know; she has not made it in yet."

"She has told you of a book I am to read though, yes?" It was always this question, or a variation of it. It was obvious that Ms. Guille was an artful librarian, knowing what book to recommend to which reader.

When I answered that *no, sorry, unfortunately she has not left instructions*, they turned on their heels and left, a sullen, disappointed look visible not only on their faces but also in the slump of their shoulders.

The fact that Ms. Guille was late in was overshadowed by the fact that, had she known she would be, she would most certainly have left instructions. She would have told me what to do. It was not difficult, of course, I had picked up the gist of it throughout the course of watching her work, but it was sloppy and unorganised. Two things that Ms. Guille was absolutely not. By the time Pierre comes to collect me shortly before five o'clock, I almost bowl him off his feet and tell him that we have to visit her.

I sense that something is wrong before I even knock on the door. It is locked, as I suspected it would be – no-one left their doors off the latch anymore, not like they used to – and the black out blinds are still drawn tight across the windows.

"Pierre?" I ask, panic threatening to spill over.

He slides a hand through the letterbox opening in the door and calls in. "Ms. Guille? It's Pierre La Joie. I'm here with Margot. We have come to check that everything is alright." With our ears tight against the gap in the door we wait and listen.

"She's obviously in there," I point out, before calling louder "*Ms. Guille?*" I can tell what Pierre is thinking when his eyes meet mine. "Well, can you?"

"I can try..."

"I am not a fool, Pierre," I whisper in a rush, "if you are capable of cutting a wire in a field watched by sentry soldiers you are capable of picking a lock."

He pouts and I can tell he is torn whether to feel impressed or insulted. With some form of trickery – and with the help of a pin from his pocket – the door opens with a satisfying *click* and we rush in.

The traditional narrow Guernsey long-house opens up to a wide hall with two doors either side of it. Without discussing, Pierre turns left and I turn right, into a small kitchen. What I see surprises me, but does not shock me. There is little furnishing left. I suspect a cold winter in a house on her own, with rationed fuel supplies teetering on the edge of being depleted, meant that she had burnt what she could. One chair is slid neatly beneath a small table, and only one kitchen cupboard remains whole; the rest are missing doors, or shelves, or entire units have gone altogether.

"Margot," Pierre calls, and I run into the living room.

Immediately I cover my mouth with my hands and let out a yelp. She is not dead; her eyes flicker with mild recognition when she sees me, but no other part of her moves from where she sits on the lonely armchair. Just her chest which rises slowly, painfully, with a laboured breath.

It happens in a haze. I fall to my knees at her side, barking at Pierre to call somebody, and I kiss her forehead. I realise with a start that she is already cold to touch.

"He is getting help," I try to assure her. "We will get you to a hospital Ms. Guille, just hold on." A rattle escapes her and my eyes dart up – I had heard about the rattle of death, surely, no – but I realise she is trying to talk. "I can't hear– I don't understand what you…" She tries again but her lips are dry, almost crisp, and another awful rattle escapes her chest. I lean in closer to her mouth. "I don't know what -"

"*Guns,*" she whispers. "*They bring the guns…*"

"No guns, not here, Ms. Guille," I reassure her. "Just the doctor, nurses, they will be here soon."

A look of frustration crosses her otherwise still face, her stoic features. "*Guns,*" she whispers again.

24

The following day, once the *Guernsey Star* broadsheet is delivered to our home by the messenger, we read that a boat with eight passengers had escaped the island the evening before. Of these eight I recognise only one name. Ralph Lisle.

It is obvious that seeing Ralph and Mariette together had been no coincidence. I did not need to search far to understand that Mariette had, somehow, aided Ralph in escaping the island. What I did not know was how, or even why. This had meant more to Mariette than petty sabotage, she had admitted as much to me in the library lobby. And by what means had she gathered the intelligence required to aid in an escape of this magnitude.

"I'll speak with her today," I say to Pierre on our way to the hospital to visit Ms. Guille. "She has to tell me, there might be something I can do."

"Mmm."

He is oddly quiet today. I had watched him as he read the news of the boat escape, just to see if he had played any part in it, but it was obvious to me that he hadn't. It was news to him, too. A frown played on his brows and the corner of his mouth twitched in irritation as he read it.

"She must have a reason for helping him. They weren't involved romantically, were they?" If they had been he can't have been pleased with her sleeping with the Germans.

Pierre shrugs and continues to stare ahead as we cycle.

"Imagine the thrill those men felt on that boat," I muse, wondering if I can get to him through adrenaline, instead. "The excitement, the fear of being caught. And to get clean away! What a feat."

"Uh-huh."

It is clear that he does not want to talk anymore of this, and I wonder why. My brother has played an active role in sabotaging the soldiers and inconveniencing them, and the night-time escape of a boat carrying eight local men was surely inconvenient. It concerns me that he does not share my enthusiasm for it.

I think as we cycle, and I realise that it is envy he likely feels. The escapees are young men, his age, leaving – I assume – for England to join the forces and play a more active role in the war. A far more active role than petty disruption. With a jolt I understand that I could lose him. It had not occurred to me before now that Pierre may not be satisfied with this half-life on the island. He had been a boy before the occupation. He was a man now.

We reach the hospital and walk our cycles into the lobby. He does not speak to me, even as we ascend the stairs to where the porter has informed us Ms. Guille is bedded. I hover with my hand on the door to the ward.

"You are going to leave me, aren't you." I cannot turn to face him as I speak, so I say it to the wood grain of the door instead.

There is a palpable pause in the air between us, and that tells me everything. If he had discussed it with me, I know it would mean his leaving the island was only a possibility, a young man's dream. The fact that he had not, tells me that nothing I say will change his mind.

Then I say something I hadn't even thought of until the words escaped my lips. "Take me with you."

The very act of saying it fills me with a sense of betrayal. Would I be satisfied leaving my island to the mercy of the soldiers? And what of Otto? What happens when he comes back to the island and cannot find me?

You were forgetting about Otto, weren't you?

Pierre makes an odd noise, sort of a gruff strangled noise from the base of his throat. Then he falls silent and I proceed onto the ward, my stomach in knots.

The nurse informs us that Ms. Guille has advanced tuberculosis. In the same breath, she tells us that there is no medication left on the island that could help her. Quieter yet, she tells us that even if there were, the Germans stockpile it for themselves. She is in a poor condition but awake and – at this she eyes us curiously, wondering what part we play in the elderly woman's life – has asked to see us if we visit.

I clutch my chest as we move through the ward, the stench of death hovering in the air like a plague. I avert my eyes, keen to give the patrons their privacy in a room overcrowded and understaffed. The few nurses move from bed to bed like wound up zombies with dark circles ringing their eyes.

A thin curtain offers Ms. Guille some solitude, at least, and she gestures for us to pull it closed as we take a seat at her bedside. She sits up, frail and ghostly pale, but surprisingly alert. As we talk we avoid the obvious, neither Pierre nor I keen to draw attention to the fact that, without adequate medication, Ms. Guille would likely not be leaving the hospital again. She thanks us for finding her, asks Pierre questions about the farm and hands me instructions to keep the library afloat.

"I wonder if I might speak with Margot alone," she says, ending it with a painful wheeze.

"Of course." Pierre tips an imaginary hat and goes to wait, I assume, outside of the ward. I panic; I don't want to give him too much time alone in his own thoughts.

I put my hands over hers. "What is it, Ms. Guille? You can trust me with the library, I promise. *Even if the soldiers require a book,*" I finish with a whisper.

"I know, dear, I know. But I wonder..."

"Yes?"

"Answer me. What do you make of the soldiers?"

I chew my lip, more for show, really. I think of the peace they have taken from us. I think of Papa. Of Alice, stranded in England. Of our young men lost in battles. Of Ma, teetering dangerously on the edge of insanity. "They are insolent. Repulsive. I despise them."

A smile drifts across her mouth and for a brief moment her features come alive, her skin colouring. A flicker of something – decisiveness? – crosses her eyes.

"On Monday you will have a visit from someone, usually an older man, sometimes a younger one, sometimes a woman. They will take themselves off between the shelves of the library. When they return they will give you the title of a book. Bid them farewell and remember the title. That is important. *Do not forget it.* Throughout the day, people will drop in and ask if you have any recommendations. To them, always suggest the book title given to you that morning. Allow them time, and do not question them when they return, empty handed. Act as if this is nothing unusual."

I wait for more, stunned into silence. My jaw opens, then closes again. "Ms. Guille..." I whisper.

"If you despise them as much as you claim to, this will not be a problem for you. *Is* it a problem, Margot?"

My stomach fizzes like an overly sugared sweet. My heart thumps so powerfully against my chest that I feel my shoulders pulse and heave. I recognise it for what it is. Excitement.

"N-no, it is not."

She considers this for a moment. "Remember what they have taken from us, dear. Remember that."

↔

I know I cannot tell Pierre. To tell him would be to implicate him, and it was a rule we had stuck by as we had both been carrying out our minor acts of disruption. Neither one of us knew what the other had been getting up to. He knew something was afoot though, as I all but bounced home to the farmhouse after the hospital. I highly doubted he would guess old Ms. Guille was involved in something underhand. I just wasn't entirely sure what that was yet. But I would find out on Monday.

When we enter the kitchen my thrill disappears like the stubbed end of a spent cigarette. The countertops are filled with every pot and pan we must own and a burnt odour lingers in the air. Ma sits on the floor with her back against the counter, embracing her knees against her chest. Pierre flies to the cooker, where Ma has left the precious gas on and a lurid column of smoke wafts from a pan into the air. I approach Ma with caution. She holds a knife from one hand, the sharp edge glistening at me.

"I couldn't do it," she cries. When she lifts up her head I notice the run of tears streaking her dirty face.

"What couldn't you do, Ma?" I ask, gently.

"I picked them, the sugar beet, I picked all morning. They say to boil them, but it is impossible, they just kept burning. And now they are no good."

I sigh in relief; a housewife's dilemma on feeding her family on limited supplies, that is all this is.

Pierre is quietly stacking the pans around us.

"I have heard that." I say. "There is a knack to it, supposedly. So, we don't have sugar beet syrup tonight, we can sweeten our tea with something else instead."

"This is impossible." She shakes her head. There is a decisive look in her eyes. It only has a second to frighten me before everything happens at once. She ducks under my arm and around Pierre, coming to the other side of the kitchen table. She waves the knife in front of her, telling us in no uncertain terms to keep back. Instinctively, I hold my hands out to her. I'm not sure if it is to ward off the knife or in the hope that she will embrace me.

She swings it in front of her, holding herself back, poised and ready as if we are about to fight her. With a shock I look at Pierre and see that he is leaning casually against the kitchen unit, arms outstretched with his hands on the counter, facing Ma with a look of resignation.

No. It can't be now. This can't be the moment.

"Ma, you need help," he says.

She swings the knife in his direction. Her eyes are crazed, she doesn't look like Ma anymore. *I want you to look like you again. Look like the Ma who strokes my head at night and tells me to sleep on my stomach to ward off the hunger pangs. Ma, who laughs and whose face lights up a room.*

"*I* need help? You two are working for them, aren't you. That's where you disappear to at all hours. I've *seen* you. I see you creep back into the house in the early hours. You're either working for them or you are *sleeping* with them," she turns to me. "Slut."

The tears are instant. Her words aren't her words, that's what logic should be telling me. But in this moment, hearing them from Ma, my confidante and my best friend, the one who shared in my secrets, hurts me like an open wound.

Pierre steps forward. "Put the knife down, Ma. We need to get you some help." He looks at me, gesturing his head towards the door. I understand.

I begin to creep around the table as Ma focuses in on Pierre but she shrieks and leaps to stop me, brandishing the knife like someone possessed.

"You won't use that on us," I say. "Ma, you can't."

"On *you?*" She spits and spittle lands on the table inches from me. "This isn't for you." She sobs, then, but it is guttural, coming from somewhere down low, deep in her stomach. "This is all impossible." She falls to her knees, wiping the sharp edge of the knife cleanly against her open bared wrist. The blood wells to the surface instantly, bubbling, then pooling. Before we can get to her she has sliced through her other wrist, and the knife clatters to the flagstone floor with a hollow clang.

25

July 1941

I hear them before I see them. I always hear them before I see them; their clipped voices and heavy jackboots predate their menacing presence. I grip the handlebars tighter, willing the worn rubber tyre to hold on just a little longer. The war will be over soon. That is what everyone is saying.

Walking the cycle on the pavement is asking for trouble, my logical mind tells me that. I should, reasonably, mount the bike and cycle on the road for the remainder of my journey to the library. My body, however, stubbornly refuses.

So, I continue to walk the bike as the soldiers approach me from the opposite direction. Two of them, side by side, filling the pavement from left to right. Guns hang from their shoulders and beady eyes take in their surroundings: sentry duty. I lift my chin a little higher, meeting their eyes. I don't recognise these two, not that that is a surprise - the turn-over of soldiers is so frequent that the same man is rarely seen twice.

One of them nudges the other, gesturing with his chin at my incoming presence. Perhaps they can sense trouble in the air. The thud in my ears gets deafeningly loud as the soldiers get closer. We play chicken; they do not slow down, neither do I. We are a mere inch from colliding with the other when we both stop.

"Madam," one of them says. He is young and sharp, with chiseled cheeks that in another life would have been handsome. He leans forward ever so slightly, bending at the waist but keeping his feet rooted. "Move."

The bluntness of his directive has the opposite effect to what it was, I assume, intended to have. My hands do not shake in fear, they shake in anger. This is *my* pavement, on *my* island. A gentleman would move aside, let a woman pass. I fleetingly reason with myself; would I feel this way if Ma had been serving breakfast this morning, rather than me? Would I feel so rebellious against these soldiers if she had gone to sleep last night in her own bed, rather than in a facility overseen by nurses?

It had been two months since she moved into a hospital more able to cope with her needs. They had diagnosed a nervous breakdown, all a result of suffering extreme grief in this unprecedented time of war. We were not able to see her until advised by a nurse it was safe to do so. Seeing us too early, they said, would inhibit her healing. *Healing.* As if it were a wound that merely required dressing and rest.

Of course, this response to the two soldiers in front of me could have been down to hunger. Breakfast sustenance had been non-existent; Pierre and I had drunk thrice-stewed tea, reluctantly accepting afterwards that the tea leaves were now spent.

"Did you not hear me, Madam? I zed move."

A nasty smirk plays on his lips. That is the right word. *Plays.* For these two bored soldiers, walking the country lanes of a relatively subservient occupied territory, this was play to them.

"I will not."

The soldier to his right takes a sharp intake of breath, switching feet, getting himself ready. With a jolt I realise I do recognise him; as he lifts his head, I see under his helmet the same soldier who had deposited his portion of rye bread at my feet and pulled me into the doorway during the air raid. He does not meet my eyes.

"Oh," the first laughs, and his face is no longer handsome. "You vill not?"

I set my jaw firm and shake my head. His face is suddenly in front of me, bursting whatever personal boundary I have left. With a grimace I notice he smells like rotten fish. I cannot hide the look of revulsion that must cross my face.

"I could teach you a lesson. I should teach you a lesson, no?"

I force my eyes not to hover on the gun hanging from his shoulder, the faint metallic aroma wafting perilously close to my nose. Was I afraid that he would use it? No. He would not use it. The soldiers that infected our island had, for the most part, been all talk and little action. There is a minute shift from the soldier to his side but whatever he is going to say, or do, is not necessary.

"But no," he decides, and spits on my shoe. "I vill give you a fine, yes, zat is vat I vill do. Look at you, you are disgusting. These clothes, they would be better as rags." He reaches into his pocket and with a short stub of pencil scribbles onto a piece of paper. He flings it at me. As much as I want to watch it flutter to the floor in defiance, instinct takes over and my hand mechanically reaches for it.

I fold it, deliberately slowly, and slide it into the worn pocket of my dress without moving my eyes from his. My fingers brush the bare threads holding the pocket together; he is right, the dress is better suited as rags.

Satisfied with his egotism, he ushers the other soldier forward – his head turns slightly in my direction but his eyes still do not meet mine – and they walk off. I do not look behind me. Neither, I suspect, do they.

Keeping my head held high, it is not until I reach the safe confines of the library that I allow myself to look down. Using the torn hem of my dress I wipe the spit off my shoe, then proceed to tear that part of the dress off, leaving a short and asymmetrical hem. I throw it aside, and cry.

↔

By the time the library has its first visitor I have composed myself.

Jean – he arrives first most mornings – nods to me over the counter as he ascends the stairs. Twenty minutes later he is back, notifying me that *Mary Poppins* is a thrilling read. My face must betray me as his eyes crease in confusion. He cannot know that the last time I had read that book had been in another lifetime.

I am no stranger to the sadness that floods my chest.

"Will it ever end," I ask aloud. "Will we ever just be…happy again." It is not a question, and I do not expect him to answer it. I am surprised, even, that I have asked it out loud.

He purses his lips. A middle-aged man originally from England but a firm staple in island life for decades, I wonder what Jean makes of Guernsey being taken over. Of course he must revolt against it in some way. I do not know the significance of his book drop ins most mornings, but I know it is some act of rebellion.

"You should try reading *Mary Poppins* this morning, Margot." My face must remain blank as he insists, "just read it."

It occurs to me, then, that before today, I had never thought to do this. Each day Jean (or another) came into the library, he would relay the title of the book to me and I would pass it on when asked, as instructed by Ms. Guille. It had never occurred to me that I should find the book myself; I had just assumed these visitors had been told by another to look for something in the text. What was I expecting to find?

The library, however, keeps me busy all day. As I approach five on the hour I find myself more desperate to be home, with Pierre, then amongst the books. This is a first. My hands shake inexplicably as I lock up and begin my journey home. I fear I may be getting sick, something I can ill afford. I divert up the Blue Mountains and, not hearing any parade, still lean my head over the uppermost wall, looking down onto the street below. No parade, no soldiers. It was just a habit.

With a curious jitter I am keen to get home, but as I go to turn back from the wall I hear the almost silent approach of footsteps behind me, and then a voice.

"Would you be looking for me, I wonder."

A feeling akin to being doused in ice cold water stabs at my skin, freezing every part of me. Were it not for the thumping of my heart I would have been sure I had turned to stone. Rigid fingers hover over the cold stone of the wall, unsure whether to grip or not. I close my eyes.

It cannot be.

I tell myself that all voices sound the same, with so few words spoken. But it is a voice so unheard of on the island. Our own island drawl peppers the overwhelming harsh tones of the soldiers. But that is all. We hear no other voice. This lazy drawl – in particular - has not been heard on the island for well over a year.

"Every now and again I look out of my window to see this girl, sitting in the same spot, watching the parades and the marching. But she doesn't look happy. She is looking for someone, it would seem, or waiting for something. She wouldn't be waiting for me now, by any chance, would she?"

I inhale sharp, the breath not reaching my chest. My head whirls like a spinning top. The tears to my eyes are instant. Before I turn, before I realise by some cruel twist of fate that my mind has imagined him, I soak up the idea that he could truly be there.

I imagine what it would feel like to turn and run into his arms. To nestle my head in the familiar crook of his neck. How warm and strong his arms would feel as they wrapped themselves around me. How I would lose myself in his kisses, running hands wildly through his wispy hair and smelling his skin. For a moment, a moment all too brief, I am lost in him, completely and irrevocably overwhelmed by what we have missed in the last two years.

A tear strokes teasingly at the side of my nose. I wait for it to reach my lip before breathing in.

26

Otto

She is still, so still. Only the twitch of her hand on the wall betrays that she has heard me at all.

My chest heaves, waiting for her to respond. I have imagined this moment for weeks, for months. Fate cruelly dealt its hand, billeting me not only in a house that looked out to the Blue Mountains viewpoint where she looked from most days, but in a room that, as I lay in my bed recovering, had the perfect view of *her*. She was in sight but so out of my grasp. The pain from my shrapnel-wrecked leg had been nothing to how it felt to see her and not be able to hold her, for her to not know I was there, watching all along.

I have waited a long time for her to be alone. Pierre walks with her most days, for which I am grateful, I suppose. Many of these soldiers are leeches, hungry for only young women and blood. Where she comes back from, so routinely, I have yet to know for certain, though I have guessed. A workplace seems the most logical answer, and if knowing Margot almost my entire life has taught me anything, it is that the logical answer or solution was most likely the correct one.

I did not dare to speak with her whilst Pierre was there. He is - *was?* - one of my closest friends in life. But that was before the war. Before I was wearing this. He is a young man, fiercely loyal and, justifiably so, prone to rash behaviours. One look at my uniform and there was a chance one of us would end up dead before we had even given any thought to what we were fighting over.

I was relieved, then, to find her alone today. I had thought lying in a bed and seeing her just beyond my fingers grasp was torture, but waiting for her to turn around in this moment is worse. Suspense hangs in the air between us. Will she balk and run? Will my uniform frighten her in the same way it so often frightens me when I catch sight of it? Will she be able to see past it? What will I do if she cannot?

I focus on her hands, now. They are shaking but she does not try to hide it. She thinks this is a dream or a nightmare, conjured up by a bored and discouraged mind.

With no prewarning she whips her head around and suddenly, overwhelmingly, her eyes are locked with mine. A wrought tension she has been holding cripples her as it breaks; her shoulders slump forward and she steadies herself on the wall behind. Instinctively I step forward, ready to catch her if she falls. She is skin and bone, barely the weight of a feather.

At my step she holds a shaky hand in the air. *Wait.*

I cannot decipher her expression. There is fear, and it almost breaks me in two to be on the receiving end of a look such as that. But there is love. I could see it in her eyes before her mind caught up with her. *There is still a chance.*

She is shaking her head, clutching at her stomach with one hand.

"May I?" I ask. I cannot stand to watch her like this. I take another step forward, but this time onto my wounded leg and I stumble a little. This extra movement startles her, and she ends up falling down. Tears fill her eyes, but I know she is not hurt. Not physically, at least.

I walk to her, this time not waiting for an invitation. If she notices my newly developed limp (a result of exploding aircraft shrapnel, and the reason for my being here at all) she does not say anything. I hold out my hand and almost cry in relief when she takes it. The feel of her hand in mine is like golden Guernsey butter to bread – real bread made from white flour, not the substandard German substitute. It is slick with sweat but soft, so soft. Time has not changed that. I entwine my fingers with hers and help her to her feet. I do not let it go when she comes to stand. I do not think I will ever want to let her go again.

"H-how?" She breathes, and I marvel as her eyes flicker over my face. I do the same to hers, taking in every small bump or shadow in case fate cruelly snaps her away from me again.

"How?" I ask.

She nods. "How. Why? When?" A smile flickers on her lips, and I recognize that this is the pivotal moment she understands I am not a dream. Do I spoil this moment now by revealing all the sordid truths of what has brought me here, today, dressed as I am? I would be a fool to do so.

"It is a long story, my love."

She exhales at this last part. "So I still am? Your love, that is. You still love me?"

I hold her hands tighter in mine, the small distance between us all of a sudden too unbearably wide. How do I tell this girl – this *woman*, now – that she is the only reason I have kept going since the war broke out in Europe? How so often I wanted to be the next soldier killed in action, or simply to accept death knocking at my door as I slept, never waking up. Only for her face to come to me when those thoughts almost swallowed me. She saved me, in no uncertain terms. How could I allow myself to die before I knew that she was well?

Her eyes drop to my lips and I realise I have been edging closer, my body reacting to her instinctively after too long apart.

"You cut your hair."

"I had no choice." I had no choice in anything, at all.

"You are bigger."

I smile as she takes in arms that swell against the seams in my jacket. "You are smaller."

But then her eyes dart off to the side of us and she drops my hands. Like I have been plunged into a bucket of the coldest ice, my body screams to have her back. I hear a cough from the direction of her glance; not a cough that signifies an illness, but one that is very much intended to interrupt something.

I turn to find an elderly man with a long, wild beard paused on his bicycle, watching us through wide, disbelieving eyes.

"Margot," he gasps, and then starts as if his own voice has frightened him. "Well I never." Then he spits on the ground before us and cycles off.

Margot pulls at my arm as I make to follow, a rage tearing through my chest like a tornado. "Stop," she says feebly. "Let him go."

"But Margot," I shake my head. "What is the world coming to?"

We share something then; the answer to my question lies in the look that goes between us.

"Look at you," she says gently, running a finger along my uniformed arm. Beneath the starch it leaves a trail of tingles. "And look at me." She takes my hand and holds it up to her face. I notice, however, that she breaks the lock between our eyes briefly and looks around us before returning to me. "I suppose it wouldn't be right to embrace you?" She asks, her voice hoarse.

I sigh. "What I wouldn't do to be able to pull you on into me right now, like such a reunion merits. But there are eyes everywhere; you've just seen that. I cannot do that to you." Suddenly my plan to find her does not seem so sensible. "You will have a label above your head. I have seen what happens."

The unimaginable picture of women with shaved heads and spittle on their torn and worn clothes, being paraded through the once quiet residential streets of northern France like animals, still haunts me.

Her chest heaves. I fight to keep my eyes focused on her face. My emotional responses to being with Margot again are shifting into physical ones at an alarming rate.

"You have seen a lot?"

A film reel of the last two years plays through my mind, most uninvited and unwelcome; countries on fire or left desolate, so many bodies that I have become immune to the effects of seeing the sightless eyes and grey mottled skin. The end of the world as we know it.

"Not now," I say, and it surfaces more as a croak. "May I walk you home?"

She starts to nod, then frowns.

"Pierre? Your mother? Frank?" I ask.

"I'm not sure how he will react to seeing you, to seeing you like this. I wonder…" she chews the skin on her lip. It is as endearing now as it had been when we were children.

"Could I come to you tonight? Once you have had a chance to speak with them and explain…this." I am filled with a sudden longing for that homely farmhouse of my childhood.

"Explain what?" She asks. "I myself do not know how you are here."

I release a breath I did not know I had been holding. "This is pure torture."

She studies my face for a moment, assessing me in a way I do not hate. "Pierre is a teenager. My home is not…" she battles something, then. "It is not what it once was. But I may know of a place. The old fisherman's hut, near the valley in the cliffs, do you remember? We used to keep Hetty in a paddock near there, but it is swarming with guards now. It would be too difficult…" she looks away, already deciding against it.

Could I risk it? Could I risk revealing to her who I really am among my comrades by facing the guards with her? This all seems so senseless all of a sudden. By coming to her have I put her in more danger? *No,* I think. *I am with her now. She is not in danger so long as I am with her.*

She runs a finger over her lips in thought and her eyes drift off somewhere absently. This simple action decides it for me.

"Leave it to me. They will not bother us."

Is it pity, the look she gives me then? Fear? There is a question in it, but she does not ask it.

27

Otto

Shortly after curfew that night, I idle a truck at the end of her lane. I keep one eye on her drive, one eye on the windows of neighbouring properties. Thankfully they stay well hidden behind their black out blinds; once night falls, the islanders tend to take themselves off to bed, for lack of anything more exciting to do with their time.

She is late. I convince myself that something has happened; that whilst I sit here idling in a truck and tapping a nervous hand on the steering wheel she could be laying in the farmhouse in a pool of her own blood. I give it one more minute before I abandon the truck and go to find her, irrespective of the problems that would arise by my simply being seen to knock at her door, let alone storm through it only to find her lifeless body…no, it is no good, I have to see her. I open the truck door and have one foot on the floor, the other braced to run to her, when I see a figure exiting the farmhouse drive and coming my way. Relief almost blinds me.

Margot has covered her head in a shawl of some kind and wears more layers than necessary. With all the extra material she looks almost at a healthy size, not the walking skeleton that had faced me earlier at the Blue Mountains.

Under cover of darkness, I beat her to the other side of the truck, opening the passenger door and ushering her in. She places a hand on my shoulder and bolsters herself into the seat. The top of my shoulder is still warm from her touch as I get back behind the wheel.

"Did they question you?" I ask.

We had run through possible reasons she could give for being out past curfew, if caught, but she had been unusually vague with details. She said she could handle whatever was asked.

"No."

"Was everyone in bed?"

"No. Pierre was not home."

Her answer confuses me. She seems distant, and I panic. I cannot imagine a life in which Margot does not love me.

"Have I done something?" I ask. I regret it immediately. *Done something? You are wearing the uniform of her enemy*. Fear seems to have replaced the blood running in my veins and my chest burns.

I sense her turn to me then, and she rests a hand on my leg, just above my knee.

"I love you, Otto. You could be Hitler himself and I would likely still find a way to want you."

The Fuhrers name still, after all this time, causes my insides to shudder. I am back in Germany 1939 then, where his name is either spoken like that of a God or a Demon of the underworld. In the end, though, it did not matter which plateau of the earth you viewed him in – heaven or hell – he got what he wanted, and you did not.

I shake it off. She will ask questions tonight, of that I am certain, more certain than I am that she will tell me where her mind goes when I mention her family.

"You walk with a limp now." So she *has* noticed.

"A minor deviation from the script of my life, but yes."

"Could you have died?"

She speaks of death as if it were still an ordeal. Death is commonplace for me now.

"Yes."

She sucks in air through her nose and it whistles. "Could you not do that anymore, do you think?"

I frown. "Do what?"

"Almost get yourself killed."

That, I cannot promise. I smile, and I suppose a part of me *is* happy, even in talk of death. It has been a long time since I have been in the presence of someone who would care if I died. "I will try."

"If you could."

We approach a hut on the side of the road that has clearly been thrown together as an afterthought. Two armed soldiers – I cannot make them out in the dark – line the road. Others, I presume, lay in wait in the hut. As if these placid islanders are going to give them any reason to ambush.

"As we planned," I say to her in a low tone before we reach them, "keep your face away. I do not want them to see who you are. And Margot, you will not like who I become to do this." I roll my window down. "But this is not who I am. Now turn, go on, turn away now."

I wait until her features withdraw into the shadows, like a sketch artist working in reverse. Then I pull back my mask. Or perhaps I am putting one on. I cannot be certain anymore.

In fluent German I report, "Major Reid. If you could pass me through, I have a lady here that I want to show around a little bit, if you understand what I mean." I wink, and it sickens me. "I will expect you to obey orders not to disturb me, under *any* circumstances. I don't care if the damned cliff collapses or Churchill himself strolls up the bay, *do not disturb me.*"

The soldiers cannot suppress a chuckle, and I can't blame them. Margot sits stiff as a board; was it the mention of Churchill? Or my speaking German?

"Of course," one leers, and I catch his eye as he tries to lean around me and get a look at Margot.

I block his view. "Respect is a learned trait. Do you need to go back to training soldier?"

He must catch sight of the motifs on my sleeve as he immediately stands back.

"Major Reid," he muses, stopping at the window as he ushers me through. I freeze, one hand fingering the pistol at my belt. I would use it, if I had to. If he sees who Margot is, I will have no choice.

"*Die Klinge*?" He asks with awe, as if recognising the Fuhrer himself. This seems to cause a stir, and I hear soldiers from the hut whisper "*die Klinge!*"

"Yes," I acknowledge, hating that my reputation precedes me, that this inane nickname is more recognisable among these cretins than my face or name alone.

The officer lets out a low whistle. "Sure, sure."

We meander through the narrow lanes adjacent to the cliffside until we reach an area that has been crudely laid with stone and hardcore. Trucks like mine are parked in a neat, orderly line; these Germans are nothing but extremely neat. *Even when they are executing innocent people – all very neat.* I pull up next to them, and after a glance around me to confirm no straggling soldiers would see where we were going, I open Margot's door.

She hesitates before taking my hand. I notice it. Her eyes dart around us like a rabbit in headlights.

"No one is here, Margot."

Her eyes settle on the towers now peppering the landscape like monsters, lurking out there in the dark. I can imagine what she thinks when she sees these watchtowers that the Germans have built in lightening quick speed. I feel it too.

"Ugly, aren't they."

"Hideous."

"Do you think you can find the hut from here?" I ask. "I have a flashlight."

Her hand clamps over mine as I go to turn it on, and I notice how wide her eyes are. "No," she breathes. "No lights. Give them no chance to find us, please."

Then I understand. We are in enemy territory. Even with me there, she does not feel safe. These cliffs are not her own anymore. We are no longer children playing army, marching up and down the dusty paths, nestled in among the flora and fauna. She is the lamb, sauntering amongst the wolves.

I want to explain to her, then, just why she has no need to worry. But she is away, navigating the paths one step at a time.

"Go slow. Use your feet and follow my steps, carefully. I'll try not to lead us off the edge."

"Margot, it is pitch black out here…"

Her hand darts from behind her and grabs mine. She places it on her hip and continues to walk; I have no choice but to follow. In Margot's world, this movement makes sense – *he needs to hold on to me to follow safely* – but she has little idea of what it does to me, having my hand on her in such a way.

It isn't long before we are descending into a valley, with only moonlight stopping us from careening over the edge of the cliffs. I stumble on loose stones where Margot seems to glide over them. A few minutes later, and with only minor scratches on my cheeks from overhanging thorn bushes, we reach a place I know well.

The old fisherman's hut is still standing, though the roof is a little more weathered, the boards a little more rotten. Iron tracks run centrally down the stone slope in front of it, stopping and disappearing over the edge, down to the sea below. Margot had told us that the fishermen would store their boats in the hut until needed, then open the door and roll them out on to the tracks and down to the slope where, when the tide was right, they could let it glide out to the sea. I can hear it now, the sea lapping at the slopes edge, not quite high enough yet to envelope it. Thick ropes on pulley's disappear from the upper most part of the slope where, presumably, crab pots hang.

"Is this port still in use?" I ask.

Margot looks at me like I should know. "How can it be? The soldiers have put a stop to most of the fishing."

Is she regarding me as the enemy, then, or am I imagining it?

"I don't know a lot of what happens here." My words are full of apology. "I – well, I was sent here after the operation, for my leg. A lot of soldiers get sent here for rehabilitation."

"Oh how hospitable we are."

"Margot, I am not one of them." I feel I have to say it. I fear, all of a sudden, that to Margot now I am just another German soldier. I need her to remember who I am. I need her to know that this is just a uniform I wear – the person underneath is the same.

She looks away from me, out to the horizon, where we can hear the distant drone of aircraft on patrol, the hum of ships, likely targets. For a long time the only sound is the *slap-slap-whoosh* of the sea against the stone slope and rocky cliff face. Every second she is silent passes painfully.

"Die Klinge. The soldier called you that. What is it?"

I grimace. "A nickname."

She turns to me and there is a crease between her brows. "But what does it *mean?*"

My first instinct is to lie; to tell her it means something other than what it does. But I determine that this will achieve nothing but deception. If I deceive Margot now, if I am anything but truthful, she will be lost to me forever. She loves me, of that I am in no doubt, but she is testing me, testing my loyalty, before she falls deeper.

"The Blade."

Her frown deepens. "Blade?"

"The soldiers often adorn others with nicknames."

"It sounds…specific."

I shake my head. Now I am lying.

"He seemed to admire you, that soldier. There was a respect there." Her eyes drift over the patch on my arm, but if she sees anything there that she recognises she does not show it.

"I am of a higher rank than he is, I suppose that is it."

When Margot looks at me I feel like she is seeing straight through me. But I cannot tell her, truthfully, why the soldiers have given me this nickname. Something in her gives, and she has either resolved to accept my lie, or she has believed it. With no further word she opens the door to the fisherman's hut and pauses in the doorway.

"Are you coming?"

The moment the door closes behind us, sealing us in the hut like prisoners, the air between us changes. She chooses not to ask the questions that still loiter on her lips, but her eyes swim with a fear that makes my heart break. Does she not understand that it is she who holds the power over me, and not the other way around?

Her fingers trail the arm of my jacket. "Do you want me to remove it?" She raises an eyebrow and we both laugh. It does not last, but it is enough to lighten the atmosphere.

I begin to unbutton the jacket, then she surprises me by pushing her hands beneath mine and doing it for me. I marvel at the lightness to her fingers, the way they twist around the fabric and unpick the buttons in a skilled and practiced way. The grey jacket falls to the floor and I take one of her hands in mine, guiding it up my bare arms. I need her to see that she is in control. The gesture leaves my skin with raised bumps, sending a shiver all the way through my neck to the delicate points at the base of my head. I move my neck one way, then the other.

She seems to take a miniscule step back, and when I catch her eyes I notice the fear has released itself like a prisoner free from his shackles. Her eyes, now, glisten, like she is seeing me for the first time. I suppose, she is.

"Otto." She breathes it, and I know that no-one will ever say my name like her again. From no other will my name sound so evocative, so *clarifying.*

"Margot."

"This is better," she nods, "much better."

Her hands trail the white vest where it lies across my neck, following it down my chest, and hovering dangerously low at the hem. Her fingers contemplate something – how unlike Margot, to *contemplate* – then without warning her hand dives beneath the fabric and strokes at my bare skin.

I can barely breathe, the air hitching somewhere between my stomach and lungs. I must emit some sound of satisfaction, as the next I know her fingers are at my lips, hushing me. I refocus from the fingertip to the deep, brown eyes beyond. She is so beautiful, so perfect, that I feel an overwhelming urge to cry, to release every emotion that has built up and been supressed over the last two years.

"You are strong," she notices.

She has moved closer, so my head sits above hers. When she speaks I cannot see her face, but she looks down at the body beneath the shirt. A body that has been to hell and back, that bears the scars of battles she will never know of. It is also a body that has been honed, pushed to its limits by sadist commanders.

"I am not strong."

She looks up, and I marvel at how small she is. Was she always so little? The lightness to her, the lithe set of her body, that is a result of poor rations, of *war*. But she sits now just below the set of my shoulders. Can war do that to a person too? It is not happy breaking people from the inside, it breaks them from the outside, too.

"But you are. I – I cannot imagine what you have endured."

Oh, she could imagine, I am sure. If she were to conjure up her worst nightmare then that, *that*, would be a fraction of the horrors I have seen. But I cannot take that road tonight. Tonight, with the markings of my betrayal shed and lying in a disheveled heap on the floor, I am just Otto. She is just Margot.

"I tried to write you. But I had nowhere to send the letters. I didn't know if you were still in Germany, or somewhere else entirely."

"I was nowhere. Yet, I have been everywhere."

"Did you write me?"

"I wrote you, but not on paper. On each battlefield, in each barracks, I wrote your name, Margot. I etched it into the dirt on the floor, scratched it into the iron bedposts, to the worn wooden floors. Had I written you on paper and tried to send it…" I shake my head, unable to finish. If I had done that then her name, her address, would be out there to be found. Fallen into the wrong hands, my Margot, *my Margot*, could be taken from me by whatever sadist General came across them. To take something from me, to take the most important thing from me, would bring one of these creatures of the night great pleasure.

"Did you ever think of me?"

"Every damn day." My voice breaks, remembering every morning, waking in some new desolate place, where the ghosts of European grandness still lurked behind every corner. Each morning, in that sweet spot between knowing I was awake but not yet opening my eyes, I pictured her. I would trace her features in my mind, gripped by sheer panic when those outlines quivered and I struggled to remember which way her eyes slanted, or whether the tip of her nose pointed up or down.

"Are you going to come closer, Otto?"

I swallow, hard. "May I?" I am frightened now, afraid to scare her off with a movement too rash or forceful. "That is, is it the right time?"

I watch, lost for words, as she sheds her layers, letting them fall to her feet. In just her slip, her body teasingly obvious beneath the thin, sheer fabric, she reaches for my hands.

"I have never known you to be coy, Otto Reid."

"I am afraid," I whisper.

"I have never known you to be that, either."

She brings my hands to her body, resting them first on her hips, then guiding them up, until my hands are full of her. She leans her head back, letting out a small exhale.

That small movement breaks something in me, and the only way I can describe how I feel there, in a disused fisherman's hut hidden in a valley, at the darkest of night, is a pure animal reaction to her. Our hands, then, know no boundaries. We clutch and grasp at each other's body, fingertips getting buried in tangles of hair, clawing at the most secret, intimate parts of ourselves. We lose ourselves to each other.

When we finally come together, and with our animalistic need to re-familiarize ourselves with the others body all but sated, the moment is pleasure in its purest form. It is not long before I fall into her, and she into me, our bodies joining in something even dogs would blush at. I allow the world to disappear for a moment, in a blinding light of white. She does the same; this time not hushing me with a fingertip. As the all-encompassing and shattering sensation beneath my naval ebbs slowly away, I pull away, lengthening my arm and allowing her to roll into me, nestling into the crook of my shoulder as if the only thing that had happened here this evening was an embrace.

The wood of the floor splinters beneath my back, but it could leave shards of wood embedded all over my back for all I cared.

"I hope that was not too *coy* for you," I smile into the dark.

She buries her head into my chest and laughs. Her hot breath on my skin elevates me to a place I haven't been for a long time.

"Most definitely *not* coy."

Then, as I knew she would, she asks.

28

Otto

"'There is a certain poetry about walking through Europe in the wake of war. I don't think I could ever explain the sensation, Margot. It is rather akin to tiptoeing through a town that has been burned and reduced to rubble, its townspeople merely ghosts. But to do it wearing the uniform I do; it is both an invitation and a totem of fear.

Men, women, you see them shrink into the shadows as you pass, sometimes buried so deep in the dark they are only eyes, furtively watching you. The children – rattled, bedraggled children no taller than my thigh – are the ones who do not hide. They stand boldly on the desolate streets, often with ash up to their ankles, seeing us through eyes wide like saucers.

There was one street I walked through wearing my uniform – that part is crucial, I needed to be in that uniform – before I was deployed from Germany. One street, shortly before dawn, where I snuck into a clustered apartment, riddled with damp and the tangy scent of rotting vermin hanging in the air.

I found him passed out on a stained and pocked mattress, one arm hanging off the side, under which an empty bottle of Jägermeister laid upturned on a threadbare carpet so thin I could see the rotting boards beneath.

I sniffed at the musky air and odour of unwashed flesh and that's when I knew. Only one of us would be walking out of there alive."

I lean down to Margot then, and with my thumb gently iron out the creases that have collected between her eyebrows. I can see that this is not the narrative she is expecting.

"Do you wish me to continue?" She nods – *yes.*

"There are only two men in this world that I imagine wearing Satan's horns. This man was one – you can guess the other. So, I stayed there for a while, watching him fester on that mattress, comatose. I allowed him those minutes to take his last few breaths. Murderer I may have been about to become, but I was – *am* – no savage.

I believe there is an instinct within our bodies that makes us acutely aware when we share the same air as another. I expected him to wake. But blind to the drink, he did not. So I nudged his foot firmly, then harder still when he didn't stir. I had to shake him awake, Margot, the feel of his clammy skin getting beneath my fingernails. His blood-red mottled eyes opened and I could tell he thought himself still drunk. When he realised I was real, now straddled over his body, face inches from his, he barely startled.

"I knew you would come," he had croaked, voice still hoarse with sleep.

And that is why he did not flinch when I pressed the cold barrel of my gun against his chest.

"They gave me this," I said, pushing it hard enough to leave a mark.

"Standard issue. You will do great things with that."

I moved my mouth closer to his ear, so there was no mistake of what I was about to say. *"I do not want it."*

His lips pulled back from his mouth, revealing yellowed teeth, some missing. *"You have no choice."*

"I do not belong in this. Canada is my home. I just want to go home."

"It should never have been your home."

"Had you not had such a rotten heart, perhaps she would have stayed." This was important. I needed him to know he was at fault. Men like him, they never think it.

"You can never run from the blood that runs through your veins, Otto. No matter how hard you try, your blood is not Canadian. I can smell it, even here, now. The German blood is strong. Pure. Elka's blood. My blood."

I let this sink in, watching Margot's eyes disappear somewhere for a while, taking stock of my words. When it dawns on her, her face changes.

"Doug is not your father?"

"He is my father, the only one I have ever known. He raised me. Taught me to ride a bike and brush my teeth. Showed me how to shave without nicking yourself. Showed me what it meant to treat the woman you love with care and respect, because she will be the most important thing in your world." My voice hitches – at one time I would have covered it, covered the weakness. But here and now, I want her to see that it is true. She is. "But his blood is not my blood."

She raises herself onto her elbows. "This man. He is your father?"

"Was."

A noise escapes her, so minute, but loud here in this hut.

"Why did you kill him, Otto?"

"My mother told me as soon as I was mature enough to process it. She explained everything, in such vivid detail, that I could see it whenever I closed my eyes. Those Germans, they have no filter. His brutal beatings, the spittle from his mouth covering clothes he did not approve of her wearing. Ripped hair in his clutches when she wore her hair wrong. But none of this made her leave our glossy apartment in Munich – you know mother, perfectly poised and graceful even when underneath she is falling apart. She did nothing, until one day in 1921. When he turned his hands to me."

Margot gasps, clutching my hands in hers, her eyes roaming my face as if for battle scars. "How awful. What happened?"

"I was too small to remember anything. Mother tells me I had just learnt to walk, toddling unsteadily on chubby legs. I was besotted with him, so she says. Never leaving his side. He was a stoic man, intent on solitude, indulging my infatuation with him on his terms only. One day I toddled to him, where he sat in his armchair reading the paper, a bottle of something or other on the table next to him. Mother says she was through the kitchen when she heard the shriek, the breaking of glass and the thud of something hitting the wooden dresser. I had stumbled into the table, knocking his bottle. In retaliation he had thrown me against the dresser."

Her hands find her mouth, then mine. She kisses me with a sudden fierceness, then, unlike her kiss before. That first kiss had told me she wanted me. This one tells me she will never leave.

"She escaped with me that night, under the cloak of darkness. She waited until he was deep into a drunken slumber – much like he was that morning when I found him in his squalid apartment – pulled me to her and ran. For all I can imagine, she ran from Munich to the shores of Canada with me still on her hip."

"But," Margot hesitates. "To kill a man in cold blood, Otto, no matter how awful he had been in life…"

I can see that I am losing her. She has to see. She has to see why I did it.

"When we returned to Germany we knew there was a chance he would still be there. My grandfather – I call him that loosely, I'd never seen him, only written letters on occasion – lived in a small hamlet just outside of Munich. Mother intended to go straight there, collect him and leave again, hopefully flitting through the precursors of war before we were noticed. But he was so sick, unable to move. Or unwilling to. For eight months he lingered between life and death, and we lived a life in limbo. She pleaded with me to go home, but how could I? When he did pass, Mother refused to leave until we had sorted a burial - but it was one day too many. He found us the day before we were due to leave. But he did not want her. He wanted me.

I cannot explain the struggle, Margot, it still feels so far away to me. Like one of those vivid dreams you wake from, your body spent with sweat and tears."

"He wanted to keep you there, in Germany?" She shuffles closer.

"He didn't care where I went. But he made me do it as a part of the German forces."

"*How?* You are Canadian!"

"No, Margot. I am pure German blood. That is all they cared about – who was pure, who wasn't. They were sweeping the country with a fine-toothed comb, building their army with the finest of their breed. I was young, fit, and pure. I had no choice. They came for me before I had chance to escape. So, when I made it through the training and was issued with my gun, I found him, and killed him. I needed to destroy him, as he had destroyed me. For all I could see, he had decimated my future."

She folds her arms across me, resting her chin on my shoulder, and gently squeezes. I take it to mean she understands.

"But how are you here, on Guernsey?"

"My leg was torn to pieces in action. They said it would be quicker and easier to remove the limb from the knee down but I fought it. I did not want to return to you, whenever it may have been, half a man. So I argued my case, over and over. They listened, but it took several operations, each time the recovery taking that little bit longer. They decided, after the final operation, to send me away to heal. I asked for Guernsey. They accepted."

I want to tell her about Tomas, but she does not ask. I sense, perhaps, that the question loiters on her lips. But when it does not come forth, I do not offer it up.

There will be time, now. We have time.

29

June 1942

1941 had been easy. That was the general consensus among us. For by the summer of 1942 we knew what teetering on the edge of bona fide starvation really looked like.

What was left of our island was desolate, obsolete. It was a shadow of its former paradisical self; hundreds of ancient trees had been felled for firewood, entire houses had been demolished to make way for a trainline – *a trainline!* – and the scent of the slave workers lingered in the air even when they were not in sight.

I imagined our landscape like a painting; once so full of life and vibrancy, but now as if the Germans had doused a rag in grey pigment and wiped it across the canvas, obliterating all colour.

We lived under a shade of constant threat; if we did not obey orders, we were threatened with the capture of hostages in retaliation. They paid no heed to the fact that for the first two years of the occupation we had been obedient and compliant. Now, our young men were frequently blackmailed with recruitment into the Nazi regime or, worse, the Organisation Todt, the governing body behind the slave workers. There had been rumours of deportations, waiting for us to put one step out of line so they could throw islanders to the fire raging Europe.

Pierre was agitated, the most I had seen him since the war came to our shores in a wave of field grey regalia. I felt now, more than ever, that I was close to losing him. I could not, however, for the life of me figure out what it was he was planning. Something was afoot, and the constant barrage of threats from the German authorities only served to incentivize him.

Ma was still in the hospital, under the near constant supervision of nurses. We were still not permitted to see her. I suspected this would be the case until the Germans, one way or another, left our shores and she was allowed to grieve in the proper way.

Alice sent regular letters – as regular as could be – and at times there would be a backlog of several of them. I would take that bundle, sit with Pierre (if I could pin him down) and enjoy her tales of life in England. It was frightening, of course, but nowhere near as frightening as having the enemy live under your feet.

Mariette was absent most weeks. She was withdrawn, spending all of her time in her house. I wondered if something had happened with one of the soldiers, but all I saw evidence of was malnourishment and exhaustion - two things every islander was subjected to.

I spent most days at the library, where I was now in full control. I dealt with the Germans daily. At times such as those I imagined a mask, coming down across my face, where I was perfectly polite. Inside, the hate raged. I would make the briefest of eye contact, as I had been instructed to, disappearing into the shadows – figuratively as well as physically – as soon as I was able. Just as he had told me to.

"It would be wise to stay out of their way, Margot. Do nothing to make yourself more known to them. Stay hidden. Please."

I could not avoid them – no-one could, unless you were Mariette who slunk around in the shadows like a creature of the night – so I had taken to hiding in plain sight.

Having Otto back in my life, even at the distance we had to keep ourselves – still gave me hope. We could go days without seeing each other, and we never did make it back to the fisherman's hut. A week after our rendezvous a German, armed with a map of the mines that had been planted in the cliffs by his comrades, blew himself up with a misstep, taking the hut with him.

I struggled to know Otto's place in this tangent of the story. He had come to the island to recover, where a great deal of soldiers - he told me - were sent for rehabilitation after surgeries. He was more than an airman of the Luftwaffe division – he was a Major, a squadron leader. Yet, as far as I could see, he had not set foot near an aircraft since his arrival. We were rarely seen together – we were clever – but on the occasions where we were, his peers acknowledged him in a peculiar way. They did not jest, or jeer with him, as I had seen so many do (though their sense of humour was quite disconcerting). There was a level of respect from his peers to himself, though he never accepted it. He shrank from it, almost. This was not the Otto I knew. Regardless of the circumstances, the Otto of our childhood had been brazen, loud, eager to be the top of the pack. He was still sure of himself, still held his body in a way that made the girls melt as he passed by, but any mention of the admiration his peers seemed to give him was fobbed away.

I did not push him on it. Everyone was allowed their wartime secrets; me included.

Three months after being reunited with Otto and advised explicitly by him to keep off the Germans radars, I had discovered Ms. Guille's secret. It was now mine.

Most mornings, when the first visitor to the library spent some moments upstairs among the books and came back to me with a title, I would find a moment to take myself away. I would find that book, and hidden beneath the cover - sometimes nestled amongst the pages - I would withdraw a neatly folded sheet of paper. On it would be snippets of information that told the truth behind our German-run newssheet headlines, some jokes at their expense, or local news that had been censored from the paper. It was light entertainment, but in the wrong hands, would mean a prison sentence. It was my role to pass this book title on to other islanders if they visited, using the prompt *which book do you recommend today?* Germans – or those working for them – were too pig headed to ask for advice from a lowly library clerk.

It was today, however, that the innocent quibbles at the Germans expense had been promoted to something deeper. I was holding in my hands something that would not only earn me a prison sentence and, possibly, deportation, but something that would also put my family at risk; for one man's crime in German-run Guernsey was not just one man's crime - it was his families, too.

One half of me quivered with adrenaline at finally doing something more worthwhile than acts of petty, inconvenient sabotage. Circumstances now called for more than that – it was one of the reasons I was sure Pierre had something bleaker than wire-cutting on his mind. The other half kept replaying Otto's warning – *do nothing to make yourself more known to them.*

I finger the paper in my hands, marvelling at the delicate crease lines of a piece of old tomato paper that had been folded and refolded numerous times. It was now no bigger than the sole of a man's shoe; this was indeed the way I felt certain my visitor that morning – Pieter – had snuck it in.

It was a week ago that a moment I felt sure would define 1942 for us occurred. It had been the catalyst for this piece of paper I now hold in my hands. Without this, we would be irrevocably isolated.

Maeve, that was her name. She had been one of the few children to stay on the island during the evacuation that robbed Guernsey of 20,000 inhabitants. For the last year she had been delivering milk to the farm regularly; always with a smile, always cheerful in spite of circumstances. On this particular morning she had come bustling down the dusty driveway as I had been sweeping the front porch. What alerted me first was the slump of her shoulders and the way she watched her feet as she walked. When she came closer and noticed me, she paused, bottom lip quivering. Had I not come to her then, taking the precious milk bottles from her hands, they would have surely smashed to the floor.

"What on earth is the matter?" I asked her, wrapping an arm around her shoulders and feeling nothing more than bone. I tried to remember if she had a father on the island, or a brother – it was usually a matter of the men folk that brought us to our knees.

"We are to lose our radio-sets." Her eyes swam with tears. *"I heard them laughing about it."*

I was not surprised then when, two days later, a notice went out requisitioning all wireless radio sets. In the same way that the looming prospect of evacuation had been the source of much deliberation amongst islanders, it was now debated in hushed tones whether you would be obeying the order or not. Most, with heavy shoulders and sunken jaws, trudged their wireless sets – often heavy and cumbersome objects – to the depot.

I simply could not do it. Otto had begged me to. *"Margot, please. If they find out…"*

"They won't find out," I assured him. *"I can hide it."*

"You don't think they will check? They want people to disobey these orders, that's why they set them in the first place! They have a thirst for blood."

"I will hide it well."

He had shaken his head, raised an eyebrow. *"Where?"*

I had hesitated to tell him, and the hurt on his face almost broke me.

"You still don't trust me?"

"You are still one of them."

"I am not!"

"Then take off the uniform."

"If I do that, I die. And you cannot marry a dead man now, can you."

This had given me reason enough to assure him that I would hand in the wireless set. I did. I made sure I was in receipt of the proper paperwork to prove I had done so. Then I went straight to one of my neighbours whom, I had been told, was not keen to keep his set but did not want to deliver it to the hands of the enemy. I offered him a good price and, right now, that wireless set is hidden in the eaves of the farmhouse, behind a beam. Otto does not know. It makes no sense to tell him.

But back to the paper in my hands. Right now I hold one of the first prints of the remodelled G.U.N.S newssheets – an acronym for *Guernsey Underground News Service.* Since the confiscation of our wireless sets and our blanket shut-off from the outside world, the small group of anonymous islanders had changed tact with their daily bulletins. The papers concealed in books on the library shelves no longer held examples of grievances with our occupiers, or humorous cartoons at their expense. They had been listening in to the banned BBC broadcasts and summarising them in type. Put to paper, these articles would then be printed and circulated right beneath the Germans noses.

It had been Pieter who had arrived there earlier that morning, but our contact had not gone the way it usually does. He had leant across the counter and whispered, *"It is something new today. In accepting this you are in effect an accessory."*

I had blinked a few times, caught off guard. He had taken a step back then, and I panicked, thinking he had taken my hesitation as a refusal. I grabbed at his arm.

"Will it work in the same way?"

He had softened. "*The very same way. You have to do nothing else, except maybe enjoy a little bit of extra reading yourself.*" I had nodded, to which he winked and charismatically sauntered up the main steps.

So here I was. Enjoying – if you could use such a word – the exact transcription of last night's BBC broadcast. I refold the paper and place it back carefully between the pages of the chosen book, ready for its next reader.

Otto could never know.

When he comes to the library at five on the hour to chaperone me home, I am surprised. He usually keeps out of sight to stop the locals from gossiping and the Germans from noticing me.

He looks tense as he waits with my bicycle by the front steps.

"How did you…"

"I found the key. You should keep it on you, not under the stone."

"Will you be riding with me?" I eye his bicycle, wondering absently which of my neighbours it had been requisitioned from.

He ushers me forward, and when he mounts his bicycle I do the same. We ride in silence out of the town, pausing at the top of the main hill with laboured breaths and a glistening sheen to our skin.

I meet his eyes. A drop of sweat beads at his temple, and I follow it down his face where it rests on his upper lip. Instinctively I go to wipe at it, running a finger along his skin. His eyes close and his lips part, his heavy breath warming my palm.

"You have something to say to me," I say.

He moans, grudgingly opening his eyes. "How did you know?" To this I raise an eyebrow. "The farmhouse."

The hand steadying my bicycle grips at the handle. "What of it?"

"I overheard talk today, in the headquarters. They are to inspect it for billeting."

I allow my stomach to roll. It is not unexpected. Many houses had already been inspected to accommodate the ever-growing numbers of soldiers being dispatched here. Most families of these properties have been turned out, expected to find housing elsewhere. In most cases, these homes have been in possession of the same family for generations. A lifetime entombed in walls, suddenly ripped from their grasp and invaded by the enemy in field grey. It was only a matter of time for the La Joie family home to be subjected to the same.

"Well, I can't very well change their mind, can I. Thank you, for giving me notice."

"Giving you notice?"

"Yes. I will make sure Pierre is out of the house and I will – well, I will make it as unaccommodating as possible." Should a platoon of soldiers begin investigating every corner of the property when my brother was home, I was certain someone would be leaving it with either a broken bone or a prison sentence.

His hand reaches out for my arm. "You will not be home."

I frown. It is not a question. "How can I *not* be?"

"They will inspect it whether you are home or not. They are not exactly waiting for an invitation in for tea."

"I cannot allow them to snoop around my house without me there."

"Why not?" Something flickers across his face. Knowledge. A suspicion.

"Would you readily allow the enemy to interfere with *your* home?"

His jaw tenses, but he drops his hand from my arm. "I'm not sure I *have* a home anymore. The farmhouse is the closest thing to it."

"Then let me protect it. I will, I don't know, throw manure under the carpets, keep the doors open so it is frigid, do *anything* to make it as unappealing to them as is possible."

He shakes his head sadly, and at first I think he is disagreeing with me. Then I see it for what it is; an act of resignation. "And what if it is not the house that I want them to find unappealing."

"*Oh*." I understand. "You are worried about -"

"*Look* at you." When his eyes meet mine I swear I see the glisten of tears. He blinks, and they are gone. "Look at you. I am surprised they have not sunk their claws into you by now. I want you to stay unseen, Margot, do you not understand that? When they see you, when they see that you live alone -"

"- I live with Pierre."

"You live *alone*, in terms of no husband, no father there. Whilst I would not wish to be on the receiving end of Pierre's fist, he is no match for a gun."

"They aren't exactly going to have their way with me in the middle of the afternoon surrounded by soldiers," I laugh, but trail off when he does not.

"I have seen worse."

"Otto," I say gently, stepping closer to him at the same time as suppressing a shudder. "They have been here for almost two years. They are not interested in raping us." He flinches at the flippant use of the word, and it surprises me. If 'worse' was not rape, what exactly was it that he had seen?

"That you have seen or heard of."

"On an island so small I would have heard of it."

"Would you?" His eyes are challenging, daring me to ask outright. I cannot bring myself to do it – to know the murky underhand movements of his comrades.

"Remember this, I have been the face of the library for a long time, now. I have had countless interactions with them, mostly alone, and yes, whilst the great majority of them are rude and pig-headed, not one of them has tried to be inappropriate with me. Not one."

"That is a library. A house is an entirely different setting."

"Would you like to be there? Could you perhaps ask to come along, and keep an eye out?"

"I have tried that already."

His foresight is touching, and I want to kiss him, but I cannot, not in the middle of the street.

"And they said no?" I wondered, then, if I had overestimated Otto's rank amongst his peers.

"*He* said no. Colonel Köhler." He spits on the floor. "He rather detests me."

"Have you given him reason to?"

I see the boy from my childhood then, rising to the surface. He flicks the ghost of long hair that no longer exists out of his face. "Other than refusing to be a Nazi, you mean?"

I see through it, of course. There is something else. Some other reason this Colonel Köhler does not like Otto. Was he also the reason that Otto, put on a pedestal by his comrades, was being left on Guernsey when each new week brought new soldiers in on a wave, and the old ones out?

"You are not telling me something," I finally say. "I will not ask why; war makes secret keepers of the best of us. But you will have to tell me your secrets one day." As I knew that I would have to tell him mine, too.

He walks me home, leaving me just on the cusp of the parish, before retracing his steps and returning to his billet. A day later, the soldiers come knocking.

30

I cannot see any sign of him from where I stand, at the front door, watching a group of four soldiers parade down my dusty drive. I insisted that Pierre be out; he was reluctant, and I suspect that he is lurking somewhere behind the bushes, keeping an ear out for screams. I wonder airily if he and Otto lurk side by side without realising it, for I may not be able to see my love, but he is undoubtedly out there, watching, waiting to intervene.

I crumple the piece of paper between my fingertips, where the words 'large garden' and 'many rooms' leap out from the page. The letter was waiting for me when I arrived home the day before, as Otto had said it would be. Perhaps it was not wise, I think, as the soldiers' heavy jackboots leave a cloud of dust in their wake, to be here alone.

The man at the front – *Colonel Köhler*, I assume – is a tall, thickset man, his uniform clinging to his body as if a size too small. I half expect a button to pop off of the strained jacket. A smile plays across his lips as they approach, and I do not miss the purposeful rove his eyes take down my body. I suppress a shiver.

"Miz La Joie," he announces. He says it *la jo-ei.*

"*La Joie,*" I correct him.

"Vat I zed, *la jo-ei.*" He pauses a moment too long, raising an eyebrow, waiting for the challenge. I swallow whatever retort plays on my tongue. "Vee are here to inspect ze property - " he searches the front of the house for the stone where the house name is etched above the door " – La Douit." He pronounces it *la dooee-it.*

"La *Douit.*" I correct him, again. *La Dwee.*

Small red circles appear on the overweight, softened apples of his cheeks and he sucks in a mouthful of air. "All zis *la* and *le*, you would think you people are ze French, no? I miss ze French. So *frech*, so feisty. We had much fun in Cherbourg, but now," he sighs, "now we are here." He keeps his eyes on me as he speaks. He folds his arms in front of his ample chest and I notice the belt around his waist struggle to contain him. "You stay out here, while we look."

The four of them have marched past me into the farmhouse before I can say "I would rather show you around, in fact. The letter," I hold the paper in my hands up, "says I should."

His lip twitches. "Very vell." He stops, ordering his men to the side as I move past them. Their eyes burn into my back as I take them to each room, where they discuss between them, in German, the contents. I try to follow their words, but it is so rapid – such a *brutal* language – that I soon give up. I wince as they pick up objects from mantlepieces, from shelves, from inside cupboards, putting them down with a force meant only to break them. They all have to squat their heads under the doorframes as they make their way between rooms, but Köhler's head skims the ceilings, making him look even more grim and ogre like.

↔

"It iz cold, in here, for June," one remarks. It takes me a while to realise he is looking at me, waiting for an explanation.

"It is an old farmhouse, made of stone, it is difficult to heat." I had woken early, five on the hour, to open all the doors and windows wide, letting as much of the little heat the house had retained ebb away.

"Vat do you make of the rooms, Braun?" Colonel Köhler breathes heavily at the top of the stairs, as if he has just run for miles. He defies all of my preconceived ideas of what a soldier should be.

An officer – Braun, presumably – steps forward. "*Klein*, sir."

I bite my tongue. Traditional farmhouses still had small – *klein* – rooms, both horizontally and vertically. Many rooms yes, but small all the same. Köhler nods his head, his eyes wandering across the walls, the floors, the ceiling. I follow his gaze and my heart almost comes to a stop when I realise what he stands beneath. The small hatch to the cramped roof space above sits slightly proud of the ceiling, the small rope I use to pull down the attached ladder and listen to the wireless hidden beneath the eaves dangles dangerously close to the top of Köhler's head.

"Mmm," he grumbles. "Very vell. We have seen it all. Wait for me outside."

I turn to leave with the men, and the thought that Köhler wants to be in here alone fills my stomach with terror. Had he seen the rope? Would he investigate the attic space? Would he think to look behind the beams in the eaves, where he would be sure to see the wireless hidden there?

"Miss La Joie. Not you."

A dizzying combination of hot and cold flashes across my skin, simultaneously burning my skin and freezing me in place. I pause, watching the soldiers retreat without another look back. Only the sounds of their heavy footsteps, then the slamming of the door, fills the silence in the hall.

"So." Without turning back to him I feel his approach, before his hot breath comes close enough to smell the acrid tang of whatever he had eaten for lunch. I doubt very much that he had had a small, unfulfilling bowl of turnip tops, as I had. "You are what Otto has been skulking around in the shadows for, are you."

At his name I close my eyes. *This has to be a dream.* A panic grips me, and I clasp my hands together at my waist to hide their trembling. The only way to face it, I know, is to turn, so I face him straight on, my eyes meeting his.

He takes a step back, an unpleasant smirk twitching at the corner of his mouth.

"I could not understand why any soldier would request to come here. Most of them ask to go as near to home as they can, but not Otto. He ask to come to some *klein* island and recover alone. Hmm. Very odd, to me. So, I follow. Not straight away, you see, that was not possible. But I did. I came. And what do I find? He is not recovering, he is *verliebt* – in love. He tried to hide you, but I do not blame him, we all like to hide our favourite things so no one can play with them."

"I do not know this *Otto Reid* you speak of." I fill my voice with as much distaste as I can manage, hating the way his name sounds in that tone. His name is meant to be whispered, caressed, dancing off of my lips.

Köhler barks, filling the suddenly still hall with a sharp, biting laugh. "Perhaps it would interest you to know that one of my duties before coming to this *scheiße* hole of an island in the ass end of nowhere was to interrogate spies, Miss La Joie."

I do all I can to let nothing show on my face. Inside my heart clamours like the engine of a steam train. "Is that so, Colonel. I fear, then, that this must be quite a demotion, for you. You must be rather bored here."

"Ah, there is no such thing as a demotion when you are where I am." He places a fingertip on his lapel, tracing it with an unexpected tenderness. I do not understand the symbol beneath it, but it sends a chill across my skin regardless.

His hand moves to his chin, then, and runs a stubbly, stained fingertip across his lip. I wonder, briefly, if he is trying to be seductive, but then he fixes me with a stare so cold, so piercing, that his intent is obvious.

"You are lying. I have seen many liars, some of them good at it, some of them not so. Most bodies have a threshold of pain, and when this threshold is broken, the truths just…" he tilts his fingers forward, "…tumble out. What do you think your threshold is like, Miss La Joie. Or can I call you *Margot.* That sounds more familiar." My name rolls off his lips with an unpleasant lurch.

A disagreeable roll of my stomach brings with it a wave of nausea, and I fight against the turnip-tops from lunch that threaten to make a reappearance.

"I shouldn't hope to find out, Colonel."

"No, no. That would be wise. Wise indeed." His finger continues to stroke his mouth. "Perhaps you wish to know *why* I am interested in Otto's taking with you?"

"I would be, if I were to know who he is. You will have to forgive me, the soldiers all look alike to me."

His eyes narrow. My neck is beginning to ache; he is tall, ever so tall, and I wish for nothing more, as my muscles burn, than to look away.

"Ah. But you have been seen together, no?"

"I speak to many soldiers, Colonel. I work with the public."

"The library. Yes."

If it surprises me that he knows where I work – which it does not – I try not to let it show. "Indeed. Perhaps I will see you again, Colonel, should you require the loaning of a book. Many of your men do."

"But you are forgetting, Miss La Joie. The billeting?" He gestures to the house around us, and a sudden fear of this man - and men like him - lurking in the shadows of the farmhouse clutches at me. It would hurt, both in my heart and my head, to leave the house to their mercy and walk away with nothing but the memories.

I have no doubt that Köhler will turn the house over to billeting. If nothing but for whatever vendetta he has against Otto. So I am suspicious and surprised when he speaks next.

"No. This house is not appropriate for billeting to a troop of soldiers." He sighs, and it feels like the theatre. Pre-planned, pre-staged.

I nod. "Have a pleasant day, then." I need him away from the farmhouse. I need Otto.

When he smiles at me and bares his browning teeth, then, I am reminded of a dog our neighbour had when we were children – Ruff. Ruff was far from friendly, and if you dared to get too close to the invisible line dividing our neighbour's property to ours, he would bare his teeth, raise his hackles and emit a low, threatening growl. Colonel Köhler now, baring his teeth, draws himself up, if possible, even taller, ducking his head down to me, stale breath washing repulsively over my face.

"Not large enough for a group of soldiers, no. For one, however, perhaps." Where Ruff's warning sign was a growl, Köhler's is a chuckle. He walks away and I know I should follow, ensure he makes it out of the house, when I can safely breathe again. But my feet remain where they are.

He turns back, slowly. "And Miss La Joie? I never told you his surname was Reid."

A day later, the letter arrives. Colonel Köhler will be billeted at *La Douit.* On his own. I am to remain in residence.

31

July 1942

He gives me a week. One week in which to prepare the house for his arrival. When news that Köhler would be billeting with me travels across the grapevine, friends and neighbours who had had officers billet with them are keen to offer their advice. There are instances, of course, where the officers stay out of the way, preparing their own meals, keeping to their rooms, offering little in the way of interaction but polite, all the same. How I wished Köhler would be one of those soldiers, but I knew to expect otherwise. It was the rarer instances I was interested in. Like the young woman in the town, with two small children, whose husband was away fighting for the British, who had a particularly volatile and narcissistic officer billet with them for little over three months. He was rude, quick to temper and take his hands to her, and expected her to cater for his lavish, indulgent dinner parties. All the while the woman and her children had to continue living off of meagre rations unable, even, to help themselves to the copious leftovers.

When I had handed the letter to Otto he had paled instantly. There was now a fist-sized hole in the door leading into the living room from the kitchen. He had dropped to his knees, with bleeding knuckles, and held his head in his hands.

"We have to run away," he had whispered. I wasn't sure I had heard him correctly, so asked him to repeat it. "*Run away. It is the only way I can keep you safe.*"

I had sat heavily into a wooden chair around the table, and he had come closer, resting his head in my lap. I stroked at his shaven hair.

"You are frightened."

"*For you. Not for me. For you. He knows now that you are dear enough to me that I would ask to come to this island. He wants to take what is dear to me. He wants you, Margot.*"

"Can you tell me why, yet?"

He opened his mouth, and I flew high on the hope that maybe he was finally going to tell me what happened between him and Köhler. But he closed it again, burying himself further into me.

"You will never look at me the same," he whispered.

"Since when is running from our problems the best solution? I am a Guernsey girl, Otto. We face our problems head on."

"And I am Canadian, Margot. We do not."

"Pierre will be here, most of the time." Even as I said it I knew it to not be true. Where I had once suspected Pierre's absences were increasing, I now knew they were. He did not hide the fact.

"Pierre is no match for Köhler."

"Do you think he knows," I wonder, picking at a loose thread on his uniform and trying to change the subject, *"that you are here, yet."*

"I don't think so. He would not be looking for me, not in the way you were."

"He might be pleased to see you..." Neither of us believed that. Pierre would not see Otto, beneath that uniform. He would see a German soldier.

We were playing with fire meeting with each other, particularly at the Farmhouse. It was only a matter of time before someone suspected the soldier visits to the house were for anything other than duty, or Pierre decided to come home early. But when I wasn't working at the library, and it was just me and the farmhouse, I was bored of being alone. As soon as Pierre left the house – usually as soon as the curfew was lifted in the morning – I would wait. Some days Otto would be to me within minutes, emerging from his spy spot in the hedge. Other days he would not come, no matter how long I waited, his call of duty impossible to defy.

Otto's sporadic visits had taken the number one spot on the things I thought about most during the day; it was no longer food – we knew we were not getting any more of that until the war was over, nor was it the eerie vacancy of the house without Ma, Papa or Alice – or Pierre, for most of the time – milling around. So even if he could only spare me an hour, it was an hour well spent; tumbling between bedsheets or, sometimes when we couldn't wait, on the kitchen table, holding each other still under the illusion that each other was a mirage, laughing in our cocoon, forgetting for a short while that outside of it the world was breaking.

Now, I wait at the kitchen table. Pierre left just short of thirty minutes ago. I tap my fingers on the solid wood, marvelling at the dull echo as it rebounds around the deserted kitchen. The winter of 1941 had been difficult, it was cold, starved, and desolate, and I wasn't taking any chances again. I had begun the heartbreaking process of removing the kitchen units Papa had handmade over a decade ago, breaking them into small clumps of firewood, ready for the next winter.

When Otto does not show, I spend some time doing this, taking the new firewood outside to the rear of the house to dry. As I emerge from the woodpile, dusting the woodchips off my hands onto my dress, picking at a splinter that has webbed its way between my fingers, I see a figure running down the drive towards the house.

At first I think it is Otto and my heart soars. Then I realise I recognise her; Maeve, the milk delivery girl. She is running, her dress trailing behind her, falling foul of the dust. She does not slow down as she approaches, a twisted look on her face, and I raise my hands to take the brunt of the force as she barrels into me. I barely stay on two feet, and her hands grip onto my shoulders.

Something has happened to Mariette, to Pierre I think. But then –

"They're coming!"

"Who?" Though the answer was obvious.

"Oh Margot. You have to hide it!"

"Hide *what?*" Again, I suspect I know the answer anyway.

"Your radio set!"

"Maeve I…." It is no good lying, of course. Only last week we had, with a small number of other select, trusted neighbours – Maeve included - gathered around the set in my loft and listened to the BBC broadcast. If we were to believe the censored newssheets, Germany were winning the war. The BBC said otherwise. I chose to believe them.

"How do you know?"

"They came to see me. Well, it was a he, *he* came to see me. All scary looking in his uniform. He knocked on my door, all German like, you know, that *rap-rap-rap* and when I opened it I almost -"

"*Maeve,*" I say, keen for her to get to the point. She is rattled, the fingers gripping into my shoulders tremble.

"He – he said" and she puts on a low monotone voice now which, in any other circumstances would have been amusing and worthy of time on the stage, "your Neighbour was not in. I will come back tomorrow to search her property. Please pass the message on." She stops, breathing hard. Finally, her message delivered, she loosens her grip.

I know that they have been making house calls, finding excuses to search homes where they suspect – or have been tipped off by an untrustworthy neighbour – that the owners are using illegal wireless sets. I also know that I have been home all morning. Raising before curfew ended, watching Pierre depart when it did, making firewood from the cabinetry. I had not left the property, and I most certainly had not had an unwelcome house call.

"He couldn't have meant me, Maeve, I have been home all morning."

She shakes her head wildly, making her eyes rattle. "He pointed *at your house.*"

I turn to look at Maeve's house, a small speck across the fields, but clearly visible.

"I suppose I had best hide the wireless set before tomorrow, then."

Maeve is frowning. "Do it now, Margot. I can help. Where should we take it?"

I suspect her desire to help hide the wireless set has less to do with the potential prison sentence on my head and more to do with her BBC communications being cut off at the source (there was always the G.U.N.S newssheets to supply us with all we needed) but I appreciate her offer all the same.

I usher her inside, where she begins to make her way to the loft. I stay on the front step, scanning the horizons. Maeve believed she was doing me a favour, giving me warning of the German's search. A small warmth spreads in my stomach, and I recognise it as appreciation. But not only for Maeve. It is clear that the German had not visited me prior to making his house call at Maeve's. He was giving me a warning; giving me time to hide the set.

I frown, watching a seagull carve its path against the blue sky. There is still kindness, still humanity, in them.

↔

The day before Colonel Köhler is due to arrive for his billeting, I find myself cleaning the house from top to bottom. I dust, wipe, set the fire, prepare his bedding. My fingers work with surprising stability - inside I tremble. Is it worse to know when something terrible is imminent, or when it takes you by surprise?

I have not seen Otto for several days. I try not to overthink it, to understand that he has duties, no matter how little I think of them. But I cannot do it; I cannot lose him all over again. It had almost destroyed me the first time, not knowing where he was. If it happened again, if he were to just vanish, I was certain it would break me, and I would never recover.

Is he still billeted in the house near the Blue Mountains, I wonder, when I finish setting Köhler's bed. It sickened me to do so, in Ma and Papa's bedroom, but I would give him no reason to find fault with his lodging. I could not afford to. Perhaps I could take a cycle past the house, see if I catch sight of him. I am overwhelmed by a need to prove that he is real.

I find Pierre sitting on the front step as I go to leave. His hands are clasped between his legs, head bowed. He does not look up when I emerge, nor as I take a quiet seat next to him. It is his ragged breath that I hear first, then a sharp intake and the distinct low sound of his sob. It is rare to see my brother cry, so rare that tears instantly spring to my eyes, too.

He does not need to tell me. I know already.

Yet, I still need to hear the words from him. So I wait, one hand lightly on his knee, the other tucked underneath me to stop the trembling.

My brother. Younger in age but, somehow, grown wiser in years. I could ask what it is that has brought him to this decision, but I do not need to. He has never been satisfied with doing the bare minimum – he went above and beyond in anything he did. If not in talent, most surely in enthusiasm. Once a boy, now a man, but not just any man. A Guernsey-man; loyal to the core, stubborn as a mule and fierce as the wind. He was always going to leave, always going to find a way to make a difference.

"Tomorrow, Go-Go," he eventually says with an effort, before dissolving into more sobs.

"It is alright." I whisper it for fear of breaking. "It is alright."

"There is talk of the glasshouses being returned to us soon, all that extra work, all of this," he motions to the land that had been in their family for generations. "How can I do it, Margot? I will be back working all of this while a real war is being fought out there, beyond the horizon."

"You do not have to justify it, I understand."

"How can I?" He turns to me. His eyes are red, rimmed with purple. He has not been sleeping; this has been playing on his mind for a while. "With one of them coming to stay here, how can I leave you now?"

Would it make a difference, I want to ask. It would not. If Köhler wanted something other than my hospitality, he would take it, whether Pierre was there or not. Köhler is a mountain.

It is then that I realise I have to tell him about Otto. If I do not, if I continue to hide it, he will believe he is leaving me unprotected.

"I have something to tell you."

His head jerks up. "I thought this was my moment for revelation. Stop trying to steal my thunder, will you."

I laugh sadly, nudging his elbow. He nudges me back, and I rest my head on his shoulder, soaking in his scent of perspiration. *Boys,* I think sadly. *I used to loathe them. Now I love them.*

"Otto is here."

My head falls off his shoulder as he turns his body to face me, an indescribable look on his face. "*Otto Reid?*"

"The very one."

He stands. "Wh – h – how? How is he? Where is he? *How?*" He spins his head wildly, as if expecting Otto to emerge from the bushes on cue. I half expect the same.

"It's a long story."

Otto had described it all for me of course, that night in the old fisherman's hut on the cliffs. How he had been enlisted with no say on the matter, what he had seen, what he had done. The marks he had left on a ravaged Europe. He hadn't told me it all, I knew that, and he knew I knew. It was only a matter of time before he told me it all.

"Goodness. Well bring him here! I don't know how this happened but what a miracle. Let's get him here, have a knees up celebration for my last night! I would love to see my old friend."

I smile, enraptured by his joy at hearing Otto is on the island. It must not reach my eyes, however. When Pierre stops trilling, his eyes narrow instantly.

"Just *how* is Otto here?"

If the brain were a mechanism, I was certain I would have heard the cogs in his whirring into action. His eyes blank momentarily, taking him somewhere where he can figure it out.

"That's the thing…"

"Oh gosh," his hand slaps to his mouth and at first I think he has worked it out for himself. Then I see that his eyes are full of sorrow, not scorn. "He is one of the slaves? Did you – did you see him on a labour march? I can't believe – how *horrific*." He sits back down next to me, wrapping his arm around my shoulder and bringing me in close. "I can't imagine how that was for you to have to see. I'm sorry, Margot."

I take a deep breath in.

"He is a soldier."

A ripple of confusion crosses his face. I remember that feeling, I still have it. No matter how illogical or unfathomable, it is true.

"He is a soldier? A German?"

"A soldier in the German forces, not a *German*."

"I don't see the difference!"

"But don't you see, Pierre, you can go now." My words tumble out in desperation. "You do not have to worry about leaving me here now. I will be okay. I have Otto. I am not alone."

His face scrunches up. "That is not better."

"It is *Otto*. You love him like a brother. He loves *you* like a brother."

He eyes me then, an odd mix of fury and suspicion warping his features. It is not his best look. "You have seen him?"

I swallow. "Of course I have."

"You have seen him to talk to?"

"Yes."

"How often?"

"Not often enough."

"When? Where?" When I don't answer he lets out a sharp laugh. "Here. Of course. I should have known. Under my roof!"

"*Our* roof, Pierre."

"You let a German in willingly."

"Not a German. Otto." He doesn't seem to be understanding that part.

He paces the dusty drive and I have little choice but to watch him. He looks young then, just a boy riddled with angst, running a finger through his wayward hair wondering what the meaning of the world is. Eventually, as the sun passes the highest point in the sky and begins its descent, he sidles up next to me.

"I am pleased for you, that he is alive. I am pleased for *me* that he is alive. I will not begin to understand how or why he wears the face of the enemy now. But -" he puts a hand up as I go to interrupt – "it *does* make me feel better, I suppose, knowing that he is here, that he will be watching out for you. I know, I know," he stills my protests, "you do not *need* watching out for. Just, for once, allow me to be the brother. Allow me to worry a little. Allow me to *admit* that I worry," he laughs sadly. "I know you are capable of coping in this war, you have proven yourself over and over again, particularly with G.U.N.S." I start a little – I hadn't realised he knew of my role in the underground news service. "I think it is highly admirable, that you are doing your bit, Margot. So I hope you can understand me needing to do mine."

Later, we make our way on our bicycles to Nellie's house. I had not wanted to go, but Pierre had insisted I be there to give him a hearty sending off. He did not want to spend, he admitted, his last night on the island cooped up in the farmhouse surrounded by the bleak memories of people that were no longer there. It is only as we are walking that I realise he does not mean to return to the farmhouse at all before he leaves.

"By what means are you leaving?"

"I would rather not say," he admits. "Less to implicate you with."

"Will you say goodbye?"

"Do you think *this* could be our goodbye, Go-Go? I hate the theatre, the dramatics, the *scenes*. Let us just go to this party, go to sleep, and when you wake I will already be on a new adventure."

"What will you do, when you get to wherever you are going?"

"I will be heading to England, that beautiful Isle – not more beautiful than this one, of course," he winks. "I will enlist, start fighting the war with force rather than sitting back and letting them take what is ours. When I can, I will come back to you Margot. I hope the next time I step foot on this island is to liberate it."

"I will miss you."

"As I will you."

Pierre stays true to his word, and shortly before midnight he is asleep, obliterated by the strong – and, I suspect, homemade - alcohol flowing freely at Nellie's house. We could not conjure food from anywhere, no matter how we tried. Yet we did not seem to have the same problem with alcohol. Mariette, I notice, is not present. It is a shame; I would have liked to check in with her. I decide, then, after the library closes tomorrow, I will detour to her house.

I wonder briefly, as I mount my cycle to get back home, how Pierre intends on escaping. Boat is the only logical option, unless he intends on swimming to England. But it will be difficult; the Germans have sentries on all the harbours and potential escape points. Thinking about it too much brings the bile up to my throat so I choose not to. I choose to have faith in him and believe that he knows what he is doing. He has surely been planning it for long enough, if his prolonged absences have been anything to go by.

Mid-way between Nellie's and the farmhouse, nestled safely in the shadows of rarely used lanes, just me and a few dark, looming houses for company, I become aware of a scraping metallic sound from near me, which only gets louder the more I cycle. With horror I realise the sound is coming *from* me; the rubber on my tyre, which has barely survived after nearly two years of continuous use, seems to have finally succumbed to the war. The tyre is running on the exposed metal. I cannot continue to cycle it, particularly not tonight; in the still of night the Germans would hear me over a mile away. Even to push it would make a ruckus so loud I may as well hold a beacon over my head and call *"come and find me, I am out after curfew."*

We had learnt by now that the people we were reluctantly sharing our island with were creatures of habit. Their patrols during curfew were regimented to the minute, each route taken exactly the same, each step of the soldier matching his partners. We had observed the safest times and safest routes to take home if you chose to do so during curfew hours. As was the case back from Nellie's house. I had left the party at the correct time, to the minute. I had stuck to the lesser travelled lanes, to the shadows. I should not have encountered another soul, let alone a German. Which is why I am surprised – and a little nauseated – when I hear the footsteps behind me.

Thlunk – thlunk – thlunk

At first I think it is a trick of the night, but the steps continue. Perhaps they had heard my scraping bicycle after all. My rational mind kicks into action and I realise I have two choices; to stay and face whatever fine or punishment the soldier approaching me – for I am almost certain those jackboot footsteps can belong to no other – decides to hand out, or I can abandon the bike and run deeper into the shadows. I grip the handlebars and conclude that running would result in a heftier fine or punishment than would facing up to what I have done and taking it on the chin. I just hope that the soldier is in a good mood.

I wait, but the steps have stopped. I am dimly aware of someone loitering there, masked by the shadows of the unlit country lane, though I cannot see them. It reminds me of the times as a child my mind would create the outline of some terrible monster lurking in the dark corner between my wardrobe and wall, only to shine a light on it and realise it was just my imagination.

I cannot shine a light on this shadow. My skin crawls. I decide I have no choice for it; I lay the bike down to the floor as delicately as I can, letting my fingers waver just a second longer than usual – a fleeting goodbye to my trusted friend, my only means of independence at a time when freedom has been eradicated for us. Then, I walk away.

Almost instantly the *thlunk – thlunk – thlunk* continues.

I stop. So do the footsteps.

I spin on my heels and stare into the night, my ears thrumming and vibrating in the deafening silence. Cautiously I bend and pick up a loose bit of stone from the floor, appreciating that if I have to use it, I will almost certainly be spending the night – possibly the rest of the war – in prison for causing harm to a soldier. I grip it harder.

"Are you following me?" My voice is but a croak in the night, but it carries.

There is a shift in the shadows, and the thin sliver of moonlight catches the glint of metal from my bike. As if by magic it stands up from the floor on its own. But there is no magic here tonight. As my eyes adjust I can see someone standing at the handlebars, facing me.

"Perhaps I am."

I almost cry with relief. *Otto.*

"I was not expecting you to leave after curfew, however. I thought my duty was done, safely delivering you and Pierre to the house. You are lucky I chose to loiter outside a while."

The ear-piercing scraping sound begins again as he pushes the bike towards me.

"Well you really ought to do a better job of it," I bite, throwing the stone in my hands to his feet and rubbing at the indentation it has left on my palm.

With one hand still on the bike keeping it upright, he bends down and picks up the offending stone, turning it in his fingers. It's more of a pebble, really. Or, if I'm honest, a loose bit of grit.

"What were you going to do with *this? Tickle* me to death? Not quite your usual skimming standard, hey." He turns his wrist out, holding the utterly hopeless stone between his thumb and forefinger, and skimming it towards the hedge. He shrugs. "I still find it impossible."

"You remember that?" I am touched that the Otto of that time – pig headed and overtly confident – remembered such a small moment of our childhood. That he remembered *me*.

"Of course, I remember it all. I have been watching you since the day I met you, Margot. It's always been you. Didn't you know boys always try to infuriate the girls they like?" My breath catches and suddenly the air around us seems to tingle and spark. "And how could I forget the first time I realised a girl could do what I could not."

"Where have you been? I was going to come to your billet -"

"Don't ever do that." The tease in his voice has gone. "You must never come there. There can only be trouble when a lamb walks in to the lions den." He must notice me stiffen, as his voice softens. "Of course, one could also warn the lamb from walking anywhere alone, in the *night* of all times, where lion's roam freely." He raises an eyebrow in scorn.

"Yet here she is, facing that lion, alone, in the dark."

When our eyes meet the charge is almost magnetic. I barely have time to hear a distant *clang* as the bicycle clatters to the floor; his arms wrap around me with an urgency so frantically that I struggle to stay upright. His fingers spider down my waist, pulling up my skirts and raising my hips to him in one swift move. I do not even have time to admire his agility as he grabs hold of the top of my legs, wrapping them around his waist and walking with me, deep in his clutches, to an opening in the nearby field.

"I am sorry, Margot, that I haven't been able to see you," he breathes into my ear. "I have tried every loophole I can to prevent Köhler from being able to billet at the farmhouse."

I press a finger to his lips, not wanting that name to spoil the moment. He carefully lays me down on the grass and we move together, his breath hot on my neck, with the stars above us. The tiny pin pricks on the midnight sky seem to shine brighter as he lies against me after, spent.

He raises himself onto his forearms, and I can hear him fumbling with something near my ear. He takes my left hand – which has been gently tracing his upper arms – and bends a blade of grass into a circle around my finger like a ring, kissing it.

While the rest of my view blurs, his eyes, inches from mine, glisten and sharpen into focus. "One day, Margot. One day I will marry you, just as I promised."

↔

"I cannot believe you were going to just leave this in the road. You do realise how valuable bicycles are now?"

"I have little choice," I argue, waving at the glistening metal. "I can hardly ride it now. It is beyond saving."

"Nothing is beyond saving."

"What do you propose?"

He looks around us and his eyes settle on the farmhouse and glasshouses just beyond the field we had just made love in. Without another word, he high jumps over the low wall and disappears from view.

I settle on the hedge beside it, absently wondering how I would explain my presence should anyone find me. My body tingles in the aftermath of us, and the memory of his scent sends another wave of shivers across my skin. In the distance I can hear the drone of German aircraft at the airport, getting ready to depart. Wrapped in Otto's embrace, I could always momentarily forget that a war was happening on our doorstep. I could forget about what war has taken from us.

I startle when I hear a scuffle from beyond the wall, but then Otto jumps back over, holding a hose pipe in one hand, what looks like offcuts of wire in the other, and a small bale of hay tucked under his arm. I watch in fascination as he deftly stuffs handfuls of the hay into the hosepipe then wraps it tightly around the rim of the bicycle wheel. Finally he secures it in several places with the wire. He moves it back and forth on the wheel, nodding with approval when it works. He holds it out to me to try.

Sitting on the seat and marvelling at how seamless the substitute rubber seems to glide over the loose grit on the road, I turn and kiss him on the cheek. "I trust you will replace that. I know Mr De Garis. He will not be best pleased to wake in the morning and find that a great length of his hose pipe has been stolen."

"Naturally," he says, pulling me along on the bicycle, my feet resting on the pedals. "Though somebody had already taken a length of it. My guess is Mr De Garis' bicycle tyre ran out of rubber long before yours did."

The only thing to break the silence as we walk and cycle is the departure of several aircraft. Loud, rattling and leaving a thrum in my ears, they fly almost over our heads. I follow his gaze. Do I see longing there?

"You miss flying."

He shakes himself out of his reverie, dropping his eyes back to ground level as the drone fades away.

"Why do you not fly anymore?"

A deep sigh, but he does not pause. I can see the farmhouse now, breaking into the shadows like one of those bedtime monsters of my childhood. "I am not permitted to."

"Not permitted to?" Would I rather Otto be allowed to do what he had been trained for, to be a fighter of the skies, to drop bombs on innocent civilians? I cannot imagine it is any safer on the ground, at the front lines. Because deep down I know; I know that Otto cannot possibly spend the rest of the war on Guernsey. I wish for nothing more, but wishes do no good in wartime.

"I made a choice once. Köhler was my superior at the time, and he hasn't let me forget it. That's why he is desperate to claim ownership of you, Margot. He wants me to pay for choosing wrong. Köhler has never forgiven me for what I did. What I nearly *didn't* do, I suppose." He sighs, turning to me. "I don't think you could ever forgive me for it, either."

"War has made us all do things, Otto," I say, picturing the G.U.N.S news sheet I will be reading at the library tomorrow, and helping distribute. "I will never hold you accountable for something that you were coerced into doing. You have no choice, I see that. I understand it."

"Choice, what a funny old sentiment. War has taken choice away from all of us, hasn't it." He continues walking. "Lucille, your Ma, is she any better?"

"Still no word." The knot in my stomach when I talk about Ma, about any of my family, still forms.

"And your Papa…" he drifts, going into territory we haven't yet spoken of. He knows Papa is not at the farmhouse, he knows he is not around. He has made his own assumptions, I presume, and I have never been able to correct him.

Perhaps now is the time to do that. A secret for a secret.

"Dead." I release a breath I didn't know I had been holding.

His head snaps up. "Margot. You never said anything! Why didn't you? My love, if I had known…"

"In this war you are either dead, fighting or just about surviving. I assumed that you – well, as he is not around I thought you would know. It is just not that easy to put into words, I suppose."

"Frank," he whispers, shaking his head to the air. His fingers fold over mine on the handlebars. "Well, shit. Shit. *Shit.* I suppose I just assumed he was in England, that he managed to get away. Perhaps with Alice."

My eyes prick at the mention of her name, but I wipe them away.

"No, not with Alice. Alice *is* in England, but Papa died."

"Can I ask how…"

I scan the skies, as if by imagining the aircraft that had dropped bombs on Papa's truck I would bring it back into fruition in the skies.

"Friday, June 28th, 1940."

Otto's eyes narrow, his mind clawing at something. I wonder if the dates all blend into one for him, wonder if June 28th holds as much of a significance for him as it does for us.

When he exhales, I realise he has resolved himself to what he had probably anticipated – knowing someone who had died in the bombings. He had been a part of this island once, after all.

"The harbour bombings? Before the Germans landed?"

He still refers to his soldiers as '*the Germans*.' Not '*we*.'

"He was parked at the harbour with the other drivers, waiting for the tomatoes to be unloaded, when it happened."

His hands trail up to his face, almost clawing at his cheeks. The look on his face is pure horror, and I cannot help but relive that day. I am back on that bench, lungs clouded with smoke, the scent of burning flesh thick in the air. I gasp, as if my body has forgotten it is no longer suffocated.

"This can't be true." Otto has seen his own war horrors, though clearly not immune to them. Perhaps he feels it more. Guernsey had been a second home for him. I find myself gripping his hand now, instead.

"It was a nightmare, but what bombing is not? Aren't they all unfair, unjust and cruel? I will never get the memory of that day out of my mind. I can see it all when I close my eyes, as if I am back there laying witness to it. But how can I move forward if I do not try. What I am saying, Otto, is not that it is alright, of course it's not, but we *will* move past it."

His hands had been covering his eyes but now they slide down his face, bringing the corners of his eyes down with them in a torturous, drooping motion.

"You were there*?*" He whispers, voice thick with emotion.

"It was hell on Earth. But I suppose you have seen several versions of your own hell by now."

He shakes his head. "You were *there?* You saw it all. You were close enough to it to...Why were you at the harbour, Margot?"

We had all heard the rumours of life after duty, that boys who went off to war never returned as the same men. Stories of mental unease punctured the picture perfect propaganda of men fighting for their country. Was I now seeing this for myself? A cloud has come over Otto's face, something inhuman. I watch him fight to catch a breath before something in me clicks and I hop off the bike, pulling him into an embrace.

"I went with Papa," I whisper, hoping that the calm, low level of my voice will combat whatever fire is raging in him. "He told me to take a walk. All I could think of was Alice, and of you. I missed you so much, Otto. He saw that – he knew I needed the space. Ironic, isn't it? That missing you saved my life."

He buries his head deeper into my neck and for a moment I worry he is going to burrow all the way into me. Then his shoulders begin to shake, and the strong boy I am in love with falls to pieces on me.

32

End of August 1942

I loiter in the doorway of Pierre's room, holding a pile of scrubbed linens. Or, I suppose, what was once his room. Pierre has been gone for a month now, and I wonder every day if he made it safely to England. There have been no news reports of escapees, as there had been with previous failed escape attempts by islanders. I cling to the hope that the Germans would be gleefully reporting on failed attempts, but keeping it to themselves if one were successful.

I want desperately to ask Otto if he has heard anything from the soldiers, but I have not seen him since the night when he fixed my bicycle. One month, without him. It seems like so little, when we have gone so much longer, but it makes it no easier. By coincidence or not, I have seen several bikes since with stuffed hosepipe in place of the worn rubber tyres.

I allow myself one long, hard inhale, letting the fading scent of my little brother fill my tired, aching and starved body with a little comfort. I close the door gently then wonder why I bother, when my houseguest thumps around downstairs like a baby elephant.

Somehow, at some point, I have developed a limp not dissimilar to Otto's. I could not recall an injury, but one way or another my knee now weakened on impact. Malnourishment, perhaps. Not satisfied with breaking our island, they are breaking our bodies too.

On Köhler's first day I made it clear that my door had a lock installed (Otto's work, the night before) and I would be using it. My hands trembled as I said it, and my body poised ready for defence against an impending attack, but the attack did not come. Whether it was my warning or some long forgotten respect of his (I doubted it) he had not made any advances toward me. But then, he has seemed somewhat preoccupied, holding regular hushed conversations with soldiers around my kitchen table.

A kitchen table covered with food. It makes me sick to think of it now, as I fight off another gripping twist that feels like my stomach is turning itself inside out. I clutch the linens tighter to my chest.

We are starving. With a torturous slowness, our bodies are eating themselves, or what little is left of them. Every other night I have had to cook meals with ingredients ferried over from the mainland, ones that never find their way to the tables of islanders. With a mix of white hot fury and agony I had, just last night, prepared a roast chicken dinner with potatoes and vegetables. The smell had ripped through my body like fire. There were leftovers, there always are. He makes me wrap them in an old, dirty linen cloth and then he takes them to dispose of. He watches. Last night he had stood at the other side of the kitchen when his soldiers had departed and licked the bones of the chicken carcass clean whilst staring straight at me. If I hadn't known the biological impossibility behind it, I would swear that he did not blink for those three, excruciating minutes. With a *thlurp* he had sucked it dry and thrown it atop the cloth of leftovers, then carried them all away.

I delay as much as I can, exhaling with relief when I hear the door out of the kitchen close. Running to the landing window that overlooks the front of the house, I watch as his monstrous form thunders up the drive.

By the time I arrive at the library my chest has loosened somewhat, and it is easier to breathe. When Pieter strolls into the lobby I all but throw myself on him, asking for any news on escaped islanders. I have had to abandon my BBC broadcasts (the wireless set, with Maeve's help, is now hidden beneath a pile of idle packing boxes in one of the glasshouses) as every waking moment of mine now seemed to be required by Köhler. I have become reliant on reading the G.U.N.S news sheet.

"Nothing in there today," he whispers back. "The news is positive elsewhere though, Margot. You can read it all, but I think we may win this war." His smile is contagious, though it drops almost as soon as it appears.

"What is it?"

He drops his eyes. "There are rumours on the island, not good rumours. More deportations. They are beginning to panic." *They*. The soldiers.

"For *who?*" I exclaim, wondering just who was left on the island to deport. The Germans had already sifted their way through every person of Jewish descent and deported them to camps in Europe. They had become possessed with the need to do so, to the point where I had even caught them looking at the dark-haired islanders in a way that can only be described as hungry.

"You should read it. Perhaps, perhaps this will give them a chance to get away, or at least prepare them for it." He sighs. "Sending more of *us* away and bringing in more of their own. They are like the plague."

"I would welcome the plague more, I think. They are bringing in more soldiers?"

Pieter nods grimly. "The latest regiment is a nasty bunch. The 319th Infantry Regiment." He puffs out his chest as he does so, talking as if he has a plum in his mouth. "Commanded by Major General Müller – a nasty, tyrannical man from all accounts. If you ever want to watch something oddly satisfying, you must try and get a view of the regiment on parade."

I catch him just as he is leaving, thinking of something. "Could I get an extra copy," I ask with a whisper. He raises an eyebrow. "For my cousin."

Giving the vacant lobby a conspicuous glance, he reaches down to his ankle, lifts his trouser leg and raises his foot slightly from a worn shoe that looks a size too small. He pulls out a tiny fold of tomato packing paper; when he hands it to me it nestles into my palm.

"Very clever," I admire.

He winks and says over his shoulder, "perhaps this war is bringing out the best of us where it brings out the worst of them."

↔

Where I had once suspected Mariette was drawn and hallowed, I now know for certain. Whatever she is up to in the wings is showing in her appearance. She is thin, but we all are. It is her skin, covered in a mix of fresh purple bruises and fading yellow ones, that shocks me to the point of nausea. Her bare arms are pocked with open welts.

I push my way through her front door; she is too weak to put up much of a fight.

"I know," she admits, collapsing into the chair around her table. "You do not have to say it."

There is silence from the rest of the house. *Is my uncle still here*, I wonder. If he is, I cannot see how he can keep to the shadows when his daughter looks like this. If ever there is a time to show your face, it is now.

"He got away, Margot."

I have opened my mouth, about to dwell on her fragile state – *she looks as if she has just walked away from a torture chamber, for goodness sake!* – but I snap it closed. "Pierre?"

She smiles, and it pulls a deep bruise around her left eye into a sinister and disturbing shape. "He made it to England."

"H-how do you know?"

"Who do you think arranged it?"

There was a time when Mariette would have said this with gusto and glee, bold and forward as she is. Now she is merely resigned - a slight raise of her eyebrow the only indication that she takes pride in her actions.

I sit across from her and clutch her hands in mine. I want to thank her, for aiding Pierre's escape, grateful that he is now away from this place. But at what price has she saved my little brother?

"Is this what you are doing? Is this why you -"

"- look like a human pin cushion?" She laughs sadly, without a smile. "This is not the result of torture, Margot. The Germans have no idea that it is me helping islanders get the fuck away from this god forbidden place. This," she waves absently at her bruises and welts, "is a result of some rather fucked up fetishes these soldiers have."

"You are still *sleeping* with them?" I ask, keeping my voice as low as possible and eyeing the ceiling.

She follows my gaze. "He is still here. And yes, I am. I need the information, you see. Without the information, I cannot help. Give a soldier what he wants in bed and he is surprisingly loose lipped."

She rests laconically against the back of her chair. Beneath the bruises, she appears to be smirking. It no longer reaches her eyes.

"That's what *this* is for," I retrieve the extra copy of the G.U.N.S news sheet from my shoe – as I had seen Pieter do – and throw it onto the table. "You do not need to be doing that. We can get our information from here."

She unfolds the paper with trembling fingers and her eyes scan the contents. Pieter had been right; it was a tale of two halves. The first, positive news from the BBC broadcasts, that Germany were failing on most fronts, the world starting to push back against them. The second, however, brought the disturbing news that all English-born islanders were to be deported. Our friends, some more established in the community than those of us born on the island, were to be sent to Europe. Sent to a hell worse than this.

Mariette lazily pushes the paper back towards me. "I knew this already."

I scrutinise her as I carefully refold it and place it back in my shoe, finding some comfort in the way it makes my heel sit more proudly. "You knew?"

She nods and purses her lips. It looks painful. "Next week, I believe. Possibly earlier." She tilts her head back, exhales and moans at the same time. The sound echoes off the walls of the bare kitchen. "It is for him. I needed this information. No matter the consequences."

I follow her eyes to the ceiling. "Your father?"

"*Papa*," she calls up, surprising me.

There are a few tentative steps on the floorboards above, then I hear the creak of the stairs and Harry Shaw emerges.

It has been over two years since I set my eyes upon my uncle, so I suppose I could have been forgiven for not noticing it. Now, I view him with fresh eyes and chide myself for not having seen it before.

Dry and coarse though his black hair may be, the curls that it forms itself into only stand to make his face look pretty. His nose sits off-centre to his face, as if at some point in its history, it has been broken. Large black eyebrows meet in the middle and stand like thick caterpillars above small, conservative and ageless eyes.

"Margot," he whispers, and his arms hover beside his body, unsure whether it would be appropriate to embrace the niece he hasn't seen in such a time.

Mariette goes to stand next to him, and I do not miss the meaning behind the move. *Us* against *you*.

"In 1920 Harry Schreibman travelled from his home in Lithuan - "

"Mariette, perhaps *I* should tell Margot my story." His voice is hoarse, cracked with disuse. "Come, let us sit." He puts a fatherly hand around Mariette and I, guiding us back to the table.

I watch on as Mariette rests her hand in his lap and, as she shuffles closer to her father, am filled with an indescribable longing for my own.

"I will not fill you in on the long, sorry story of my upbringing. That is a tale that I will be grateful to have follow me to my grave. I was born and raised in Lithuania, in a town so desolate and broken that I travelled weeks by foot to escape it. My parents were strict to the point of abusive, and as soon as I was able, I left. Simply rose one morning, packed a satchel with enough coins to sustain me for a while, and walked away. No siblings to say goodbye to, no friends to ask to join me. I reached the nearest coastline and did not look back as I snuck on to a boat intended for England. You will have guessed," he says, looking to me from beneath bushy eyebrows, "that I never made it."

I swallow hard, trying to stop whatever strange emotion is rising in my throat. This is the most I have heard my uncle talk. I suspect it is the most he has *ever* talked.

"A necessary stop just off Guernsey's shores was all it took for me to get a glimpse of the small island in the Channel. A smaller boat was leaving the ship for the island, for supplies, so I talked my way onto it. Yes, it is true," he says, noting the surprise on my face with a small laugh, "I could once talk myself out of a paper bag. The moment my foot landed on Guernsey I knew I was home. Only three months later did I meet my Lily, a hurricane wrapped in a white dress." He looks to Mariette, and all of a sudden I feel an intruder to their moment.

"You won't remember, of course, Margot," Mariette starts, her eyes glistening. Her face appears to have settled; she looks relieved of a burden. "I barely remember myself, a time before my father was – well – before he was -"

"A recluse?" Harry adds, helpfully. "When I arrived in Guernsey I abandoned any name that would tie me to the home I had left behind. It was easier, back then, to do so without raising questions. So from that day on I became Harry Shaw. Harry Shaw is who Lily married. For almost a year we lived blissfully, the talk of the town, two confident and brazen people destined for a great life of social hierarchy. And then Lily gave birth to Leon, a boy born sleeping among the stars."

"You had a brother, Mariette?"

She waves her hand in the air. "One cannot miss what one does not know. Of course some days, growing up, I saw what you and Pierre had and I longed for a brother of my own, the big brother I should have had. But father isn't telling you this for sympathy, Margot. He is, I believe, justifying his absence in your life. And mine, to some degree I suppose."

Harry nods. "My life changed that day. A year later Lily gave birth to Mariette, and my beautiful daughter – so like her mother – went some way to healing a broken heart. Alas, I never fully recovered. Being around people, even family, was difficult. I retreated into the shadows of my own thoughts, and life – or the absence of it – made sense there."

"Inside of the house, well, I never admitted it, Margot, but father was wonderful. Truly." A tear falls from her eye, and I follow it down her cheek until it drops onto her stained dress. "But how can you explain that to a world outside of it. I wanted to scream and shout every time someone called him rude or reclusive. He was neither of those things! He was broken. Within our walls, though, he could be a father." She turns to Harry and rests her head on his shoulder. I want to cry with them; cry for her, cry for him, cry for me and my own lost father, a relationship that will now, for evermore, be frozen in time.

"Schreibman," I say finally, though it had made sense to me the moment Harry had walked through the door. I had seen him with fresh eyes; his was a profile that had been used mercilessly against him for several years.

He holds his hands up in a gesture that says, *what was I to do.*

"It was a step ahead of my time, anglicizing my name. One that has, so far, saved my life I believe. If I had remained Harry Schreibman, I would not be here right now."

"For several months I have been helping arrange boatloads of islanders to leave under the cloak of darkness. Father has always refused. So I have continued my…dalliances, in the hope that one day we will receive information that he cannot deny."

"Mariette," I breathe. "You should have said something to me."

"And implicate you more? I can see the fire in your eyes Margot, but I could never allow you to be a part of this. You are already doing what you can."

I look to Harry. "Will you…has she convinced you to…"

"Tonight," he confirms. "I can refuse her no longer. I gave a false place of birth in England when I arrived in Guernsey, and it will not take long for the Germans to realise this when they begin their investigations on the deportees. What that may lead them to, well, let's just say that to learn that a man of Jewish heritage has been living beneath their noses would humiliate them. And a humiliated German soldier is a dangerous one indeed. I have stayed under the cloak for long enough. I do not want to leave the only place I have ever called home," he looks around at the kitchen solemnly, then to his daughter, "but I am left with no choice. Mariette will be able to return to living a normal life."

Mariette laughs sharply. "There is nothing normal about this place anymore, father." Harry thankfully does not see what I see; for the briefest of moments, Mariette's features had twisted into one of hate and disgust. Nothing in that moment frightened me more than what that might mean.

By the time he faces her again, her face has returned to normal.

"Please do not ask anything else, Margot. The more I say the more -"

"- I can be implicated, yes, people seem to be saying that quite a lot to me."

"It is for your own good. You have one of them living with you now."

"I hardly call it living."

Mariette's face falls serious. "Has he -" I shake my head. "Good. Good. Remain wary of him, I have not heard good things."

I want to argue that it is impossible to be anything *but* wary of him, of all of them. But I catch Mariette and Harry look to one another again, and I realise that the more I sit here and talk with them, the less time they have to say goodbye.

So I do something I have never done before. I embrace my uncle, and I thank him.

I never see him again.

I never see Mariette again.

33

October 1942

They allow us a funeral, though it is overseen by a small group of German soldiers. There are not many of us there; those of us who are, ignore them. I can only assume that she had achieved what she set out to do, as Harry Shaw is not in attendance at the service. He had simply vanished from the island one night, as he had done from his hometown over twenty years earlier. There were no reports of escaped islanders; I will never know if he made it to England.

When news reached me that a young girls body had been found hanging from the branch of the old oak tree in the purple meadow, I was not surprised. Grief, as it always does at the moment, threatens to engulf me, but I never allow it. Mariette did not lose her life at the hands of someone wielding a gun or a knife; she chose to take it herself. She was never a person to shy away from her actions or disclaim them, no matter how willful they were, and a part of me understands – if no-one else does – that this was just another of them. She would not want me to grieve her. She would want me to revere her.

So, I can do neither. To grieve her would be to open doors that I have shut firmly in the last two months. To revere her would be to condone the selfish taking of her own life.

The weather is beginning to turn. We had been blessed – if one can use such a word – with a late, prolonged summer, but the grey clouds roll in daily now like warning signs, and as I walk back to the farmhouse after the funeral service I cannot help but feel that the weather is a sore reflection of my mood.

Köhler is at the table when I arrive.

"Firewood," he barks, without looking up from his papers.

For a moment I wrestle with the idea of taking his meaty throat in my hands and twisting and pushing until it snaps, of what it would feel like to stick my gnarled and worn thumbs into the sockets of his eyes and pulse until he is blind.

"There is none left," I say, trying not to let emotion seep into my voice. I have become quite good at it.

He slams the papers down and I back away. This will not be the first time he has raised a hand to me. The beatings I can endure; they had started when I returned from Harry and Mariette's house the night before Harry escaped and were, I suspected, a ploy to get at Otto. To lure Otto to the farmhouse to defend my honour.

It had not worked. Otto has remained out of sight. A part of me believes I understand why; he brings with him an undefined danger of which I don't understand. If Köhler should see for himself that Otto loves me, Köhler will use me as bait. A larger part, however, understands that he already is.

I swallow hard. *Do not think of him now, not here. Not yet.*

His nasty breath is close enough to warm the skin of my face. "My men are felling trees down by the meadow. Tell them I sent you. Bring what you can carry."

I want to yell "*more trees? There will be none left!*" but of course I cannot do that. My cheek still throbs where only yesterday he had hit me with the back of his hand when I did not come into the room quick enough when called.

The only satisfaction I now get is that the soldiers seem to be suffering a little of what we are. They still find food to eat, though there is less of it. They still wear uniforms, but they are no longer starched and clean. They find means of washing with no water restrictions on them, yet still reek of perspiration and grime.

I go to walk around him, holding my breath, but he grabs out at my arm as I pass. I do not meet his eyes. His mouth comes close to my ear and my instinct is to flinch away – his grip tightens.

"I am starved."

Hot liquid runs down my throat at the same time as my stomach lurches. "I will make you something to eat when I return."

But I know. It is not food he longs for.

I begin to fear that my luck in escaping Köhler's leering advances has come to an end.

He releases his tight hold on my arm but his fingers remain. A girl cleverer than I would run away and never look back, but how do you run away on an island where you can always see the ocean? There is nowhere to hide.

"That would be a wise idea. You should never leave a man hungry." There is a stomach-turning *smack* as his lips clamp together over my ear and a wave of rancid breath makes my eyes water.

When his hand releases and pushes me away towards the door, I do not look back.

↔

I run to the brow of the hill that overlooks the purple meadow, where only a few days ago Mariette's limp body was found hanging from a branch. I can smell it in the air before I see it. Their bodies take to the oak tree – *my* oak tree – like ants attacking discarded food. They swarm it, climb it, attack it with tools that make noises and those that do not.

Falling to my knees is the only way I can think to catch a breath. Branch by branch, the tree falls. Branches that will be cut and sliced to service the fires of the soldiers.

I do not hear the soldier before he is behind me. I never turn. I never see his face.

"I have a beautiful garden such as zis at 'ome. When the war is over, for God's sake, kill every Nazi zat is left."

↔

When I think back to this moment, I will know that Otto had been watching the farmhouse. Almost as soon as Köhler leaves with his dutiful pack of dogs following behind him – one of whom, I notice, is the soldier who pulled me into the entry of the shop during the earlier days of the occupation – there is a knock at the door.

It is dark out, far beyond curfew. We have reason to suspect every knock that arrives on our doors. More often than not, a soldier stands on the other side, come to investigate something. We have come to learn that investigate means steal.

So it is with caution that I unlatch it, opening it just a crack at first.

Otto has never looked more handsome. And more beaten. He looks unharmed, for which I breathe a sigh of relief I did not know I had been holding. Did I think he had been attacked? Killed? Of course I did.

But he is all wrong, and it overshadows my relief. He looks half the man he is. Strange, considering he is all of him at the same time.

"May I speak with you, Margot?" He slurs. *May I schpeak with you, Margot?*

"Are you hurt?" I ask, suspecting the answer when a distinct scent washes over me. "You are drunk."

He stumbles in and I have no choice but to catch him in my arms when he trips over the step. Clumsily, he rests his forehead against mine.

"I don't know how to say it. It is something, and nothing, and everything at once. It is going to change it all – it will change *us*."

I guide him to the kitchen and sit him down on the chair where only moments before Köhler had been holding court with his dogs.

Otto sniffs the air theatrically. "It smells like him in here."

"Have you been drinking?"

"I'm a German soldier, Margot, all we do is drink! And smoke! And…"

I drop my gaze; it is the first time he has referred to himself as a German soldier. "Is this what you have come to tell me? Is that where you have been all this time? I have seen your men outside the houses of ill repute. Your whores are imported from France, so I've heard."

"That's what you think of me? No!" He cries, suddenly sobering. "If you only knew the truth you would *wish* all I had done was lay with another."

"Then what is so awful that you cannot tell me? There is only so long I can pretend that you are not lying to me."

I am suddenly angry. Angry at him. Angry at Köhler. Angry at the world.

"Wallowing in my misery." *Mishery.*

"Well perhaps you should go back and wallow some more. I do not wish to see you like this."

I am no stranger to seeing drunks. Say what you like about a Guernsey-man, but he can hold a drink stiffer than most, and has a stomach lined with lead. But it looks wrong on Otto.

"Don't look at me like that, Margot," he whispers. "Please, god, don't look at me like that."

"Like what?"

"As if you hate who I am. I already hate myself enough."

"I do not hate you Otto. Really, truly. I have been worried. How was I to know you were not injured, or worse! Who would have thought to come and tell me? No-one, that is the truth. And my *god* I have missed you," I admit, all the words that had gone unspoken tumbling out as one. "But this -" I have to stifle a laugh as he hangs his drunken head between his knees, "this is just something you need to sleep off. It was incredibly reckless coming here; Köhler could come back at any moment. Please. Go and sleep this off."

He rises as if to retaliate, then slumps back down into the chair with a thud. The air around us tingles. "You have heard them call me the blade? *Die klinge?*"

I nod, remembering the way in which he had been recognised by the guards on our night at the old fisherman's hut. Now I recall it, it had been whispered on several occasions when we had been seen together. The way he was treated by his comrades – revered, as if he was iconic – was surely in some part a reason for the nickname *Blade*, but I had not allowed myself to dwell on what it meant. I couldn't.

"You said it was a nickname."

"That part was not a lie." *That part.* "Make no mistake, it is not a nickname I enjoy. A moniker is a sign of companionable mocking – an enjoyment. A sign of inclusion." His eyes find their way to mine and their sheer blackness chills me. "I despise it. I *loathe* it."

"You were fast? As an airman, I mean, you were fast? Is that why they call you the blade?" *God let it be that.*

"Whippet fast. The fastest." That explains the way he is looked up to by his peers. I hope. "Yes, a blade is fast. But do you know what a blade also does, Margot? It destroys. It cuts. It *desecrates.*" His voice is thick with hate.

I lower myself to my knees and wedge myself between his legs. I hold on to the upper part of his thighs and he buckles, his head falling on to my shoulder with an ungraceful loll.

"I can imagine that you have been forced into doing things that you do not like in this war…" I swallow an unwelcome rise of bile in my throat. I cannot allow myself to go there, I cannot begin to imagine what he has seen, what he has done. "You had no choice."

He groans into my shoulder. "That is what I told myself, in the beginning. This uniform, this symbol, do you know what it means?" He scans my eyes for any sign of recognition in them as I focus on where he points; the shapes on either side of his collar mean nothing to me. "No, I did not think that you did. Otherwise perhaps you would have asked questions before now. I was never just an airman; I was too damn good at it. They promoted me. I am – *was*, I suppose now – my squadron leader."

This means something to him. This is the root of what he has been hiding from me.

He swallows hard, shaking his head to the floor. With a great inhale of breath that borders on a gasp, he leans back from me, resting his forearms on his knees. Then he tells me. Everything.

34

Otto

"Each time I got into my aircraft I could pretend I was a different Otto. An Otto who could see past everything that was happening around him – all the atrocities and horrors. Because I had to, if I wished to survive it. Until I could hold up the pretence no longer. Something altered my blindness to the war. Something changed my wish to live through it.

I have a conscience, you see. Something so many of my comrades lack. They see fire, they see blood, and they thrive on it. They flourish on the misfortune of others. I just wanted to fly, Margot, because when I was flying, I could forget. The walls of the aircraft were so thick, so dense, that I could pretend nothing existed outside of that bubble of mine.

Köhler dislikes me because the last mission we were called to, I did not just hesitate on an order. I refused it. I refused to shoot. I tried to turn my squadron back. I need you to understand that - it is vital. *I tried to turn us around.*

On June 28th I was stationed in northern France – Cherbourg. I was given my orders to fly out over the channel with my unit and recce the military status. I did so, and I did it without a second thought. If I were to choose a moment when I felt most human in the wave of inhumanity I had been caught in, it would be on a reconnaissance flight. There was little chance, you see, of injuries to innocents, of death. I have long since come to terms with the fact that death in action and on the field - fighting soldier to soldier – is to be expected. But I could not – *cannot* – endorse the taking of innocent civilian life.

On that Friday we approached Guernsey, just as the glorious sunlight was reflecting off of the glass houses. I could almost *smell* those tomatoes. I allowed my mind to drift; were you down there, somewhere, watching my plane fly over in a cruel twist of fate? Had you evacuated? I had no way of knowing where you were, but I wished you were down there, I prayed that you were seeing me, that we were connecting in an opaque and alien way. All I could think of, at what I deem my most selfish and egocentric moment, was that I might get to see you again. That maybe, just maybe, I could start to feel like the old Otto, like *me* again. And if I was down there on the island, I could protect you and your family.

There were three of us in aircraft that day -

- please, don't cry, Margot. I must finish. You can hate me after but please, my love, allow me to finish.

One of the other airmen pierced the silence inside my bubble with barks so fierce that I almost lost control of the aircraft. I could not decipher what he was saying right away, and when I did, I pleaded ignorance. It was a dangerous yet instinctual move of mine.

Over and over I heard cries that military vehicles had been spied, even though the island was supposed to have been demilitarised by the British government. There was a lot of shouting over the radio - a great deal of confusion, of anger, of injustice. A German soldier does not like to be fooled, you see. I swooped low and spotted what the other airmen could not have known; they were not military vehicles, but trucks full to the brim with ripe and ready tomatoes for export.

Do you remember that summer your dad let us ride with you both? I knew it was not military, but no-one would listen. I tried. I screamed until my throat was hoarse and every word dissolved in my throat. I god damn *tried* Margot.

Köhler was barking at me to shoot, to drop the bombs that sat like lead in my aircraft hold. I have never heard names like those he called me, most of them something to do with swine, all of them German in origin.

He got louder, Margot. He was *so loud*. I still hear his roars at night, echoing through my ears like wind in a tunnel. The air around me buzzed with sound. And in that moment I knew I would never be whole again, no matter which course of action I took.

Ignoring them, flying away, I would have been dead in seconds. They would have forgotten about the trucks and turned their guns on me. But to go through with it, to open the hold and drop bombs onto an island that was my second home, on to people that I had likely known for most of my life…how could I?

So, I waited, and I waited. I ignored them. I welcomed death with open arms. Dying there, above the skies of an island and a girl that I loved more than life itself, seemed like a poetic way to go.

I tried desperately to break myself out of the formation, but there was just no way.

When I realised that a poetic death in the air was not an option, I did the only other thing I could do. The other aircraft had already begun to drop their bombs on to the trucks, to shoot their machine guns at the moving specks on the ground. It was as though my heart had doubled in weight; my entire chest heaved with the pressure. It felt like suffocation. I *welcomed* suffocation. Yet with each breath I was still alive, and I hated myself for it. I closed my eyes as tight as I could, aiming my guns to anywhere that would do the least damage – the open fields, the small stretches of barren land. Above the skies it was chaotic, but on the ground…I can still hear…sometimes I wonder if it was my mind imagining the cries I could hear, or if they really did reach my aircraft that day.

Then I left, with the island burning behind me and a reprimand ahead of me.
I left, with your Papa in the truck. And you, Margot…
I left you all.

35

On his knees with his arms wrapped around my legs, I open my mouth to speak. He must feel the contraction of my stomach, the tensing of my body before I say what I must, as he gasps. It is a great sucking of air that feels so final that for a moment I listen for his next breath to make sure it comes.

His voice is muffled, barely a whisper, mouth tight against my clothing as if breathing me in. "Don't say it. Please…don't say it."

"Otto -"

"*Please*, Margot," he begs.

"You should -"

"*No*, please, do not say it."

"I think you should leave." The words – they come out as more of a question, really - are barely a tickle on my lips, the inaudibility of them the only sign of the torture behind saying them.

I try not to look down into his face, I really do. But it is an impossible wish. His hands tighten into my clothes and when I meet his eyes they glisten and shine in the shard of moonlight piercing through the kitchen. A thick cloud passes across the moon, and for a moment the room is pitch black as well as silent.

"I will come back tomorrow." His voice is thick with hope.

"No, Otto." I try to push him away from me, raise him to standing, but he is as solid as brick. He holds me tighter. "I need some time - some distance from this. I just need to think. I don't blame you, *god* I don't, but it could have been *your* bomb that…"

"It wasn't, I swear it," he heaves, shaking his head from side to side. "I aimed *away*, and I did all I could to stop them! I have tortured myself, over and over. Margot, I have nowhere else to go. You are my home, *this* is my home," he sobs, burrowing his face into my dress so deep I can feel his tears on my skin.

It is hopeless to try and bring him to his feet, so I sink to my knees with him. With a hand on either side of his head I raise his face to mine. His cheeks are streaked with tears and dirt. My tears now flow in thick streams down my own. I rest my forehead to his; it is slick and clammy.

"Give me this, my love. I need to make sense of this." With the saltiness of my tears stinging a path down my cheek and caressing my lip, I take a deep breath in. "You have to go now, Otto." I stand and pull his hands with me. This time he does not fight it. He has no fight left in him at all. "It is time to leave."

36

Otto

Nobody ever tells you that the hardest part is physically leaving a person when you know that you will not be returning to them. Knowing that you must leave, that there is no way back for you, but physically pulling yourself away from that moment, putting one foot in front of the other, breaking the tie between you…no, it is impossible.

It is a stretch of such delicate fabric, pulled taut, tearing at the edges as you walk away from them. Next to her I am whole, but with each step taken I get ripped and shredded apart, by a sinister and sadistic seamstress.

But it is taking that first step, that first actual movement away from her, that is the hardest. The most challenging move I will ever make, steepled in complications and fear.

I do not wish a moment like this upon anyone.

She walks with me to the gate at the end of her drive, where the shards of moonlight patterning the ground would have, in another lifetime, been beautiful. Now they just taunt me with their freedom.

I must be the one to move. I must be the one to walk away. Someone has to, and I cannot let it be her. That would seem more final, somehow.

I cannot let this be how it ends.

I manage two steps before turning back. In the whisper of the wind I like to think I hear her say my name just before I turn. My lips find hers at once as my body barrels into her. I wrap a hand around the back of her head, letting my fingers sink into her thick hair, finding a comfort that she will have to pull away from us first to part. I can never let that happen. Her mouth parts and mine explores the welcome darkness. It feels like the final time. A saltiness tangs the taste between us, so one of us must be crying. Perhaps we both are.

We ran the gauntlet, didn't we? We found each other again, against all odds.

God gave her to me, years ago on a beach with sand between my toes and a salty breeze in my hair. Now, he is taking her away.

37

October 1942

Our death rates have been rising to alarming levels as the cold sets in, particularly among the elderly and infirm. Each new day brings with it the unwelcome news of another neighbour or friend passing, and I am numb to it all. Ms Guille…Mr Nichols…they have all gone. I have tried to reason with it, as has been my nature for all of my life. But there is no reasoning with war. I have lost too much. Deaths are published in the G.U.N.S news sheet only – the German-censored newspaper no longer runs them - and this source to a life outside of the occupied island has become a lifeline for so many of us.

I know Otto is watching me. I feel his eyes fall upon me as soon as I lock the library at the end of each day. It has been that way for the last week. I know he is waiting for me, waiting to see what happens next, what move is to be played.

I make my way towards the doors now, ready to bid the library goodnight, and I can sense him out there already. With the key to the door I am suddenly pushed backwards onto the lobby floor as the door slams open.

"Zorry," a soldier clips, holding out a hand.

I stare blindly at his jackboots before moving to his hand, studying it. To refuse his hand is to defy him, which is naïve at best, suicidal at worst. To accept it feels like handing over control.

Reluctantly, I take it and let it drop as soon as I am back on my feet. I brush my hands on my overcoat, hoping he gets the point that I want rid of his touch, however brief it had been. I refuse to meet his eyes, staring instead at the lobby floor now trodden with dirt and grime.

"Ah," he says, following my gaze. "I vill help. First, I have a list."

"A list?"

"Why, of books."

"Yes, I assumed as much. For whom? The library closed five minutes ago, perhaps if you could return in the morning -" I try to look beyond the doors to the street outside and wonder if he is still out there, watching. Would he leave, if

I didn't come out on time? I can see nothing but the lobby reflection, however, the sky already darkening at an alarming rate.

"It iz important that we have these now. *Sehr* important."

I glance at the clock on the wall, set to German time - one hour ahead of ours. Anything to make life more convenient for our occupiers.

"You are vorried about curfew. Zat is okay," he waves a hand in the air, pulling a piece of paper from his pocket and handing it to me with a flourish. "A pass," he points out, when I hold it in the tips of my fingers like a bomb about to detonate.

"I gathered."

"So. Ze books?"

I cast my eyes to the doors one more time, but I still see no sign of him. With a sigh I take the list from him and lead the way to the first floor.

He must sense my unhappiness, as he quips "you vill be glad to see our behinds, I bet."

However inappropriate it may feel, I laugh. He looks stung, but not angry. "To see the back of you, you mean?"

"Oh," his face falls. "Zis language, it is *sehr* difficult, no?" It rolls to the tip of my tongue – *go back to Germany, then.* "Well, we vill all be speaking German soon, so."

"Perhaps not."

It would be easy, I realise, to get angry at this soldiers' blatant arrogance towards the pending outcome of the war. I feel less angry, and more sorry for him; the BBC tells us that we will win, Hitler tells his men that we will lose. This man – for really, he is just a man – in all likelihood has a family back home in Germany waiting for him, just as the women and children on Guernsey wait for their men to return home.

He purses his lips and raises his hands to either side of him. "Perhaps. We vill see, *ja*."

The sun is far past setting by the time I finish finding the obscene books the soldier requires, plunging the eastern sky over the library into an eerie orange and purple dome. I wheel my bicycle out from the safety of the locked side room beside the main building, lock everything up, and begin my cycle home. I feel his eyes on me almost as soon as I set off.

The cobbled streets of the town are still busy even though curfew looms - everyone intent on getting their essential vitamins from the dwindling daylight. But as I meander through the streets and into the country, the lanes begin to empty. Out west, the islanders would already be in the safe sanctuary of their own gardens, away from the prying, steely eyes of the soldiers.

A strange sound punctures the otherwise silent air when I am a short way from the farmhouse. A regular low drumming vibrates underfoot, and I look around for the source. Riding over the crest of the hill an undulating shadow moves like it is alive. I see the dots of grey and green among them first – soldiers

- but it isn't until the shadow creeps closer that I have my first horrifying experience of the slave workers inhabiting the island.

We had heard rumours of their arrival. We had seen evidence of them in the road gulleys and in the camps set up in large unoccupied spaces. There was a house – *Paradis*, ironically – that housed a great number of them. We could only imagine what it would be like to witness the whispered horrors first hand, as the guards were clever; they usually marched the slave labourers out of camps before curfew ended in the mornings and waited until the curtain of our curfewed night fell before returning them.

It is worse than I could have imagined.

We are hungry. These people are starved. We lack luxuries. They lack basic human rights. We, though patched and barely fit for wear, wear shoes on our feet. I see no shoes on the prisoners, just a lucky few with straps of newspaper under foot, feet almost beyond recognition for what they are.

They are little more than bones. I think back to many years ago, when I met the boatload of French refugees at the Harbour, fleeing a war which, even in its infancy, had already shortened their supplies and wrecked their homeland. These people are worse; worse than any nightmare. They lack any animation that would define them as human. Their eyes stay fixed to the ground, trained and conditioned to obey and subserve, like dogs.

I watch frozen in place, my knuckles white from their grip on the handlebars, waiting for them to pass. Not one of them acknowledges me.

As the last body shuffles past, dressed in sodden rags and smelling like a decrepit sewer, I abandon my cycle and vomit into the hedge. I continue this way until my stomach is empty, my throat is raw, and all that is left are dry, guttering heaves. I wipe the back of my hand across my mouth, letting my tears mingle with the sweat on my face.

The worst thing - the worst of all - and the thing that remains imprinted into my mind long after I have left that damned road, is the guards.

They were smiling. Grinning like the Cheshire Cat in Alice's Adventures.

38

I stumble through the kitchen door in a semi-catatonic state, the horrors of what I have seen stamped and marked in my mind, forever.

"There is no coffee," Köhler barks from the table.

Is it a bark, I wonder, similar to the one he used on Otto in 1940, as their aircrafts bombed Guernsey. I shiver.

"I will grate some parsnips, let them dry out and crush them. They will not be ready tomorrow, though."

"And what of dinner?"

"I was waylaid at the library. One of your men required books. I picked up some animal blood from the butchery yesterday, I shall mix it with potatoes."

"Peasant food."

"It is all there is."

It is then that I notice the *tap – tap – tap* from the table. He is rolling an envelope between his fingers, letting it tap onto the wood, and repeating. He watches me with those devil eyes of his. His poise is calculated and intent; he has forced himself to laze against the back of the chair, with one leg resting at a right angle on the other. The arm not holding the envelope rests idly across the chair.

Without asking, or trying to sneak a look at the address, I know it is for me. What would the Red Cross be writing to Köhler for, anyway, for that is what the letter is. In two years, those blue envelopes have come to embody emotion, and seeing it in the thick and grubby fingers of a German makes me want to tear his limbs from his body and watch him squirm.

"I know something you don't know," he sings.

I tear my eyes from the flip-flopping envelope and force them to stare into his. There is only cold and black there. He is the Nazi of which stories will be written in the future.

"Do you want me to beg for it?" I ask, exhausted, feeling no need for pretense or games.

"This?" He looks at the letter in mock surprise, as if puzzled to find it in his hands at all. "Oh, not this, you can have this. I know of something else."

"The letter…" I start, very little concern over what else he wishes to taunt me with.

He stands and holds it well above my head height. "Jump."

I want to kill him. The thought comes to me with such overwhelming clarity. "I will not."

"Then you do not get your letter."

"It is from Alice, please, just give me my letter." I hate the sound of my voice, filled with a desperate begging that leaves a foul taste in my mouth.

His cold eyes twinkle. "Then jump."

I raise my hand high towards the letter, bend my knees and allow myself to jump, despising every moment. The feeling of degradation will never leave me, I fear. But what choice do I have? My fingertips dust the edges of the letter but fail to grasp it.

It all happens so fast; before my feet can touch the floor he raises his knee, like a venomous snake rearing itself ready to attack, and brings it to my abdomen. Any control I have had over my body disappears in that split second, and it folds in on itself. My forearms wrap around my stomach as any air left in them leaves my lungs in a whistling breath. Curling into a foetal position on the cool flagstone floor of the kitchen – a kitchen where I had taken my first steps as an infant – I feel broken. I close my eyes and pray that he will leave me now, leave me to recover, but I sense him before I hear him. He approaches slowly, but not with caution – his lack of speed is premeditated, intentional.

He is the lion. I am the lamb.

The air sucks itself away from my body – the only warning I have before his foot blows into my bruised stomach. He kicks once, twice, three times, each one rising a guttural groan from somewhere deep inside of me. Still, my eyes remain closed. It is this, I will think later, that is the reason I do not have the chance to run away. I do not see as he changes position, as he stands over me, straddling my broken form. His strong hold around my wrists surprises me just as much as it pleases him.

This is it. I cannot avoid it this time. I have no fight left.

"You have no choice, Margot. Something for me, something for you. You will learn, by the end of this war, that we are the superior nation. You have no choice in what you do, at all. Do you hear my words? *No choice!* Now, open your eyes."

I pinch them tighter. I do not want to see how he looks as he sits atop me, pulling the layers of my skirt higher. A moan of pleasure fills the silent kitchen as he exposes my bare thigh.

"When we say jump, you ask how high. When we say fire, you *fire*," he spits. "Were you there that day, Margot, at the harbour? Did you see the havoc Otto Reid reaped upon your people, how close he could have come to killing you, to spilling his beloved's own blood. Now, I said," his voice is closer now, sickeningly close to my ear. "Open your eyes. *OPEN YOUR EYES!*" He shouts. The words reverberate through my ear until I can feel them in my chest. Spittle dampens my cheek and the air rings with a repetitive hum. My ears feel broken, just like the rest of me.

I open my eyes when I feel a swelling wave of air in front of my face. I do not focus on him, but the letter he holds.

"So, something for me," he leers, "for this. Or I burn it."

Alice. For Alice.

I nod, weakly, and brace myself.

No choice. I realise that now. He had no choice. Otto lost all hope to an autonomous life when he was forced to enlist. He had to let those bombs drop. *He had to do it.* Because what was left for him if he did not? He did what he could, didn't he? He aimed for nothing, let the bombs fall where they would do the least amount of damage.

Köhler's belt unbuckles. His trousers drop. His clumsy fingers find my underwear and pull them down toward my knees. He folds himself over me and a bead of sweat falls onto my upper lip. I leave it. He roughly moves my legs and –

– then a knock. A knock that changes everything.

My eyes fly open, as do his. He stills, but the look of shame I had expected on his face does not appear. He shakes his head and sighs – frustrated.

"*Wer ist da?*" Who is it?

With growing horror I realise that he has no intention of moving. This is not a position he finds shame in – he has merely been inconvenienced by an interruption. He presses himself against me but leaves me intact. It is a warning. *Do not move. Do not speak.*

Irrationally, I wish for it to be Otto on the other side of that door. I imagine, in the quick-fire way that the mind can work, him throwing open the door, murdering Köhler with a knife across the neck, raising me up and into his arms. Köhler's blood will be on me, and will inevitably stain the flagstones, but I will not care. I will be safe, back in his arms.

It is not Otto's voice that calls from the other side of the door.

"Heinkel, sir."

"*Lass mich.*" Leave me.

There is a pause, a moment hanging in the air, before he responds.

"*Es ist dringend, Sir, sie werden gebraucht.*"

It is clear from the tone of Heinkel's voice that he is as happy to be delivering the news as Köhler is to receive it.

"*Es ist wieder die Organisation TODT.*"

I did not understand the words, but recognised *Organisation Todt*, the word for the slave labourer guards who, by all accounts, were more malicious and viler than the soldiers themselves.

"*Arschloch,*" he grunts.

I do not allow myself to hope until he stands and redoes the buckle on his belt. I crawl to sitting, leaning my back against the remaining cabinets, fighting to catch a breath. My stomach throbs, making it almost impossible.

The door opens and Köhler leaves.

↔

I do not realise the soldier – *Heinkel* - still stands in the doorway until a short while later, when the cool air of the open door caresses my skin.

"Do not ask me how," the voice whispers hurriedly. "I have seen the next roster for deployment. Otto Reid's name is on it."

I look up sharply. It is him. The soldier that I could – lightly – call friendly.

"Where are they sending him?" I grab a hold of the cabinet behind me, and with a wince struggle to my feet. "When will he be back?"

The soldier stumbles on his own feet, his hand hovering ever so slightly, as if toying with the idea of helping me steady myself. He thinks twice and it falls back to his side.

"They are going to the Russian front."

The words are like blows to my chest. The Russian Front. To death. No-one comes back from there.

"When does he go?" I repeat, clumsily sliding my feet into my shoes, each small movement like a thousand needles into my sore stomach.

"Madam…"

"Please." I am in front of him now. I do something then, that restores perhaps both of our faith in humanity. My hands find his shoulders and clutch gently. "When is he leaving me?"

I watch the soldiers throat working and wonder if he is swallowing the words that I desperately need to hear. "He is already on the runway."

My body is on the run before he finishes his sentence. Somewhere outside of my body I sense his arm raising towards me as I pass, the whisper of a hand gently brushing against my arm.

"The curfew!" He warns.

"I have a pass!" I call back, the slip of paper sitting like a paperweight in my pocket. I silently thank the arrogant German at the library and his urgent insistence for books as I run.

The farmhouse sits slightly to the north of the airport, a mere five minutes' walk away. Three, if you run it, as I do now.

Run, and do not stop.

He is on the runway. Words that sit like rock in my bruised and battered abdomen.

I run until my chest burns; until each inhale slides down my throat like fire. Cool night air stings at my eyes and I blink away tears. My legs turn to lead, pulling my body down into the ground. Heel to toe. Keep going.

It doesn't occur to me to think about what comes next. What do I do when I reach the airfield? A chain-link fence borders the perimeter, what did I suppose to do? Jump it? And that is supposing I can get close enough to do so. There will almost certainly be soldiers on duty, guarding insane civilians from doing this very thing.

A low drone fills the air. It could have been there all along, but I had selectively chosen to ignore it. As I close in on the land bordering the airport, however, there is no denying it. Before an aircraft takes flight it has a presence in the air, not just in sound. It sits in the air, pregnant and swollen. It turns stationary objects to vibrating hubs. The thrum gets into the far reaches of your body, through your skin and into your very fibres. The taste of the air changes, momentarily filled with a metallic tang. For a blissful second, everything around an aircraft about to take off freezes. It stills. But I keep running.

The noise increases, reaching a crescendo as my feet break ground on a patch of road with a clear view into the aerodrome. Like the grim reaper, the only aircraft on the runway rises, almost vertically.

"I wish I had realised it earlier," I whisper in its wake. It gets lost in the drone of Otto's plane. "I wish I had realised earlier that you had no choice."

39

On a small, unassuming island nestled between the coasts of Northern France and the Southern tip of England, a bruised and beaten girl packs a small case with what few personal belongings she has left. She takes herself – and the case – off to a vacant cottage, once owned by her dead cousin and fugitive uncle. She hastily scribbles on a scrap of paper - *this house is occupied* – and rests it in the window. She knows it will not last. She knows that he will come and find her and finish what he started. But for now, she is alone, and that is how she needs it to be.

She opens the blue envelope and unfurls the crisp, slightly discoloured paper. She reads –

ALICE LA JOIE

KILLED IN COVENTRY AIR RAID

AUGUST 1942

40

November 1942

For a week I live amongst the ghosts of Mariette's cottage, spiraling dangerously between grief and exhaustion. I inhale every last morsel of food and drink that lurks in the corners of the cupboards. I find a particularly potent batch of aged alcohol that goes some way to blissfully purging my mind. I do not open the library. I do not leave the house. I have held myself hostage, and that is just fine. There is nothing outside for me now, anyways.

↔

It takes seven days for the first itch of desire to hit; desire for fresh air.

I find a surprisingly healthy-looking cache of clothes in Mariette's wardrobe. They are barely worn, albeit a little outdated. Apologising to the ghosts of my family, I begin to layer myself in coats and headscarves and hats until I look unrecognisable. Quirky, but unrecognisable. Also, thanks to the alcohol, still a bit drunk.

↔

So here I am. Stood on the brow of the hill in the purple meadow, looking down on the ruins of the oak tree. I imagined it would look like a plucked chicken, bare and barren, but those soldiers went one step further. All that remains now is a knee-height stump. Good for a child's jumping game, perhaps, but not a great deal else.

The meadow is eerily silent, suspiciously vacant.

Beneath the layers of the perfectly preserved clothing – clothing I now realise once belonged to my aunt – I begin to perspire. It is an odd sort of heat when you perspire in the November air. The chill nips at my exposed cheeks, but at the nape of my neck, under my arms and between my thighs a painful heat gathers.

I eye the little stream – the *Douit* – that runs through the purple meadow. Whilst the seasons may be different, the method of our childhood should still work. So, as I had done many years earlier alongside my brother and cousin, I make my way down the shallow bank, this time alone.

I stumble and almost lose my footing on sodden and unstable ground. I curse feet that had once seamlessly molded themselves to the contours of the earth.

I plant my feet on protruding rocks as best I can, but the flowing water still finds its way through my pocked shoes, tickling at my toes. I cup my hands to the water and my body instantly cools in all the places it needs to. I long to splash the water beneath my arms and feel the relief, but I settle for bringing my hands to my face, instead.

The ice-cold water sits cupped in my palms and I am about to splash it to my cheeks when a movement to my right makes me pause. My eyes scan the length of the Douit, but the movement is small, in the water with me.

At first I think it is a water rat come to investigate, but with a growing horror I realise the moving object is not so much moving as it is floating. It is not alive. It never was. The water trickles back to the stream through my frozen parted fingers as I fold over on myself and vomit into the water. The vomit joins the faeces floating mere inches from me.

Only one of the soldiers or slave workers could have done such a thing. No islander would deface the island in such a way; no, only someone with little respect for the ground on which they walk could have done it. We had heard the warnings of such a thing – typhoid was spreading at an epidemic rate – but I would never have believed it until I'd seen it. What was the world coming to? Were we travelling backwards, to a time when we were more animal than man?

I want to scream. I want to hear my pitiful cries echo from the lonely remaining trees in the purple meadow, the ones that now pierce the treescape like the last teeth in a mouth of rotten ones. I want to feel the burn in my throat and the tightness in my stomach beneath the bruises. I want to do it for Papa, Ma, Alice, Pierre, Otto, Mariette, Harry – every single one of whom has left me here, alone. Because that is it now. I am wholly alone.

But I am not insolent. Whilst I cannot see any Germans, they will be there, always lurking, watching, waiting. Drawing attention to myself is the last thing I want.

"*I want you to stay unseen, Margot*," Otto had whispered, words I have lived each day by since the occupation, even before they were spoken to me.

So I do the next best thing. Silently I hold my fingers to a *V* and hold them up into the air. I make a turn, loving how free my arms feel. I do it again. Then, I am dancing, my victory sign aloft against the empty autumnal blue sky.

I am certain I do not laugh. I smile – how could one do this *without* smiling? – but other than the crunch of crisp grass and squish of doughy moss underfoot, I remain silent. I am sure of it.

Thus when I hear it, I am not prepared for it.

"Halt!"

My hands freeze in the air in the most incriminating position they can be in. I force them down, pinioning them to my sides, but by then of course it is too late.

41

Tribunal of

Feldkommandantur 515

Margot La Joie

By virtue of a Judgement of the Tribunal of Feldkommandantur 515 you have been sentenced to nine months imprisonment for anti-German political actions.

The chief of Tribunal has confirmed this judgement on the 4th November, stating that the sentence is to be served in the Caen Prison, France.

The judgement is thus enforceable and final.

42

I have just enough time to find Maeve and ask her to cover the library for me – the last thing I wish is for it to fall fully into German hands. The most important thing is to show her how the procedure works for distributing G.U.N.S to the islanders; I fear for this lifeline the most.

I watch her face as she takes in everything I say. She makes a face somewhere between awe and surprise. "You have been doing it the entire time?"

"Not the entire time, no. Ms Guille enlisted my help when she fell ill."

I recall that day vividly, as my brother and I had broken in and saved her from the brink of death in her living room. She had been whispering "*guns…they bring the guns*." I had assumed she had been referring to the infiltration of armed German soldiers to our shores, but now I understand her to mean the clandestine deliveries of G.U.N.S to the library. Though of course the contents of those underground news sheets have now changed to something more unlawful in my hands, and the implication of Maeve in this is not lost on me.

"If you would rather not continue with this Maeve, I can inform them. You mustn't do anything you don't wish -"

She places a hand on my arm and squeezes gently. "We must all do our bit. Of course I shall continue this on. How else will we spread the word that we are winning?" She winks then turns to the main door, where a troop of soldiers silently marches past. "They are *rotten*, every last one."

Not every last one, I think, picturing Otto in his uniform. A panic fills me then, that should he return I would no longer be here, on the island. Would he know where I was? Would he ever track me down, should I perish in the gaol?

The time for the soldiers music and singing appears to be over. They feel the shift in the air, as do we. I have not heard their music – their strangled renditions of *Deutscheland uber Alles* still appear in my nightmares, on occasion – in months. Now, more than ever, it is imperative that the islanders' spirits remain lifted, when theirs appears to be faltering.

I show Maeve how to lock up, then dismiss her, telling her I need to finish off some chores. This is a lie. What I need is a moment with the books.

With a smile I allow the echoes of my wooden-soled shoes to fill the cavernous lobby, taking each step of the stairs with a slow satisfaction. *How long until I hear this sound again? What if I never do?*

I cannot allow myself to think this way. I did wrong, and I have been held accountable for it. Grief is no excuse, not to them. No matter how inane the so-called crime is, I must accept the fact that I did it. Where there are actions there are consequences. Nine months is not a long time to sacrifice for my small act of rebellion, in the grand scheme of things. I would do it again tomorrow. My consolation is that this overpriced punishment seems to be a knee-jerk reaction to their war losses. I can cope with that.

I walk the rows and rows of books, occasionally running a finger down a weathered spine, every now and then opening one up just to smell the aged pages. The thick, musky scent fills me with a strange comfort. Even in a world of uncertainty, there will be books.

But then my mind begins to turn, and Köhler's form starts to emerge from the shadows at the end of these rows, and when I pull a book from the shelf I pull one of his grubby stained hands with it.

I had expected to see Köhler at the farmhouse when I was marched back there by the German soldier that day in the purple meadow. I couldn't rightly give him Mariette's address as my own; it was far too risky. So I had had to accept the fact that I was going home. I found the house silent, with the stale air that encompasses a vacant space. I could not bring myself to enter his room, to see if his clothes still hung in the wardrobe or his small personal effects littered the bedside table. It was not our bedside table; it had appeared one day with a truckload of other – stolen, I assumed - furniture that his soldiers had delivered.

Sleep did not come easy that night; I was alert to every small sound, wondering if it was him returning and how long it would be before he realised I was there. How long it would be before he came back to finish what he had started.

A part of me understands that I see Köhler now, in the shadows of the library, because I still cannot say for certain that he will not be at the farmhouse when I return. The only way to rid him from my mind is to see if his room is clear. I am also mildly aware, as one would be looking in on someone else's life, that my mind is fragile. The books have now lost their appeal, so I whisper "goodbye", lock up for the last time, and cycle home. I am half-way into my usual route when I get diverted by a line of soldiers.

"This is my way home," I point out, seeing no evident reason for the blockade.

"Find another one."

I turn with a huff, then realise I am not all that upset about a delay in getting back to the farmhouse. So when I pass a wide expanse of uncultivated grass, I pause. It is unusual, in war-time Guernsey, to see such a thing, but as I slide off the seat of my bicycle and concentrate more, I realise why.

A number of soldiers are being put through their paces by an officer on a horse, who rides around them like a dog herding sheep. I am too far away to make out faces or words, but something in the stance of the officer astride the horse tells me this was perhaps the regiment Pieter had told me about - *"if you ever want to watch something oddly satisfying, you must try and get a view of the regiment on parade."*

Whilst they are not on parade, I can do with something to make me smile. Keeping my bike close, I walk a little further around the corner of the fenced off expanse. A small hill works its way closer to the soldiers, so I lay the bike down and crawl up on my stomach like a commando, until my head just appears over the crest. I am fairly certain no one can see me, but from here I have a much clearer view. And if anyone were to walk past and see me nestled on the hill, clearly watching? Well, as far I am aware, the Germans have not made that a crime – yet. I am sure having a young woman watching them perform will nurse their ego's, if nothing else.

The officer – the *Major* – sits astride his horse much like a doll would a toy one. If that doll had legs the size of small sausages, of course. They look peculiarly disproportionate to the rest of him, and I wonder if the reason he is not on the ground, in front of his men like I had seen other commanders do, is because the minute he gets down he will be a foot below the rest. Power is in perception, after all.

So, this is Major General Müller, the man Pieter had told me about. His face is the colour of puce and even from a distance I can see thick eyebrows set over his eyes. I watch him for nearly ten minutes undisturbed and his eyes never leave his men, not once. He barks orders at them that I do not understand, and in response the men run, jump, press and haul. I am exhausted just watching. I have to suppress a laugh when Müller must spot something amiss in the perfect formation of his men; he leaves behind him a wake of mud and dirt as he gallops at the offender and barks in a voice so high and shrill I would swear it were a woman's. The soldier at fault evidently does not find it humorous as he flings himself to the ground, face first, and lies so still that I believe him dead from fear. Müller trots off and the solider remains there.

My eyes drift past the crumpled soldier face first in the dirt, unsure whether I should laugh or pity him, and the formidable – if small – form of Major Müller. They do it of their own accord, like opposing ends of a magnet being drawn to something – or someone – that it cannot pull away from. There is a soldier, standing tall and proud with a knowing smile on his face. His eyes, now, recognise the magnetic pull from my own – or perhaps he senses himself being watched from the trees – and click into mine in one seamless motion. His smile falters only a little, mixing in with something – confusion, perhaps - before it spreads back across his face tenfold. He is keeping one eye on Müller, I observe, keeping one half of his body turned in his direction. Even from here I can see that he is stronger than he ever was; arms that once hung limply like branches from his skinny adolescent body now fix themselves to him with a confidence, jawbones that sit so sharp I could slice an apple on them.

It is a peculiar moment when you come face to face with an old friend; life seems to roll in reverse, and you see through the mask of age that they wear. You do not recognise them, not immediately, but they are familiar to you. A warm feeling wraps itself around you like an embrace.

It is more peculiar, however, when you come face to face with someone you used to love, who disappeared off the face of the earth without a trace. It is like meeting with a ghost; a coolness like ice running through your veins, a sudden jolt of disbelief to the heart. There is an internal struggle happening inside my body at this moment. I want to simultaneously pull him to me and push him away.

His eyes reluctantly pull from mine as Müller approaches him. The soldier says something, something that makes him laugh so hard his large round stomach shudders up and down. Did I see correctly? I squint. Did Müller just run a tender hand over the soldiers buzz cut hair? The soldier takes a moment, seems to stare into the distance in Müllers wake, before bringing his eyes back to mine. His body may have changed, resurrected itself from the earth as something stronger and more defined. But his eyes...well, his eyes remain the same. Those never change.

The next time I see Tomas it is as I disembark the boat back from Caen prison, half the shrunken woman I already was when I left, and he twice the man.

43

March 1943

The human body is capable of wondrous things. Childbirth, self-healing bones, even a graze that heals itself and fades to nothing on the skin - they are all acts of miracle.

I think this as I watch the skeleton attempt to climb the prison wall. The French guards wait at the bottom with minimal interest, their guns remaining holstered. They see what we all see; a desperate woman's ill-fated last attempt at survival.

It is no better out there, I want to scream. But I have learnt better. The lashes on my back are testament to that new knowledge. You obey in a place like this - obey or die.

Inevitably, the skeleton scales the wall only so far before she falls back, landing with a sickening crunch in the soil. No-one runs to her. No-one comforts her as she takes her last rattling breath. The courtyard full of prisoners barely even acknowledges her.

↔

I am midway through my prison sentence. I am sure of it, because I have been scratching markers into the underside of the small metal table in my cell. It is the only way to tell the days apart in this place. It is the only thing that keeps me going.

Sometimes I sit on the metal-frame bed, ignoring the instant swarm of lice that attacks my skin, and imagine that a newspaper reporter back home is asking me questions about my time in Caen prison. I wear flawless make-up in these visions, and a long, elegant dress the colour of lavender. I am always lying idly back on a chaise-longue, one hand draped across my thighs and the other dangling over the edge of the chair, languidly holding a cigarette.

"What was the worst thing?" She asks, flicking a lock of blonde hair away from her blue eyes. I always imagine her this way; perhaps the German propaganda on the ideal form has wormed its way into my mind, after all.

"Hmm," I muse, before taking in a long inhale of the heavenly cigarette and twirling it between painted fingertips. "I would say the boredom was the worst. The hunger was unimaginable, sure, but you can die from that. Starving, to the point of wondering if you could chew on a loose flake of concrete, you can be assured that you *can* die. There is hope for it. But you cannot rightly die from boredom, can you."

"And what of the food, Margot?"

"You mean the scraps of animal feed they left us? Inedible. Insipid cabbage soup, so watery it was like trying to chew on urine." The reporter always flinches at this, as if my time as a prisoner has made me crass and vulgar. "Crumbs of bread were offered on occasion, but most of the time they were so hard and stale that you could drop it to the floor and it would bounce back."

This will make her chuckle, a little, which always surprises me. Only someone untouched by the war would laugh at such a thing.

"And to drink? Was there tea?"

Such a British thing to ask. For if I think this, I can forget the desire for a strong, fresh brewed cup of tea that isn't of the acorn variety.

"We were given one cup of tea – acorn mostly, but sometimes mint – in the mornings. And do you know," I lean in in a conspiratory whisper – she joins me, and I can tell she is waiting for something off the books, something secret and perhaps headline-worthy. Something that will propel her to the top of the journalism career path. "We learnt from one of the prisoners to pour the tea, piping hot – don't even blow on it – straight down your throat."

"Why is that?" the reporter asks, leaning forward, her eyes darting across my face ready for the climax.

"Once scalding hot tea reaches your stomach it blows it out and makes you think," I tap my head for effect, "you are full."

The reporter leans back slowly, and I can smell the disappointment on her. "Alright, I suppose that would work. How did you curb your boredom whilst you were incarcerated?"

"I didn't."

Flustered, she grapples for her next question. "You must have done something to pass the time? A day is a long time."

"For twenty three and a half hours we were locked in our cells. You do not need to tell me that a day is a long time."

"I have spoken to other prisoners; they say they played cards or games…"

"Then they were lucky people indeed." She frowns a little at the word *lucky*. Perhaps I have used it too loosely, but the prisoners who found the energy to play games were the prisoners who had not been incarcerated long enough. "In the beginning we made playing cards from scraps of cardboard we picked up in the thirty minutes we were permitted outside. Our minds couldn't think much past dreaming up childhood games of Snap or Sevens. But in the end even that felt like an effort."

"Was it the disuse of your body that caused that, do you think?"

"Were we dumbed down, do you mean?"

"Well -" she flushes again. I always quite enjoy this part, when she starts to lose her perfectly curated poise. "Yes, I suppose."

"Sometimes," I take another drag on the cigarette, riding high on the kick I get as it gets into the far reaches of my lungs, "we wished that we would be allowed to work hard labour. I would often imagine taking a spade to my unused hands or using fingertips for something other than flicking lice off of skin. But my offence was political, you see, not criminal. So no, there was no work to be done, and yes, I believe my mind suffered terribly for it."

Our eyes meet across a cloud of smoke and she shifts in her chair, uncomfortable. Frightened of me. As if being in the very room as someone who once made removing lice from her privates a part of her daily routine - morning and night - makes her dirty.

"Perhaps you could tell me a little more of your room, your private space."

"Would you call it private if someone could slide open the window and peer in whenever they pleased?"

"I suppose not."

"My *cell*, then, was identical to the others. White-washed, if you can imagine that, but horrendously dirty. I could tell that some effort had been made by the staff there to cleanse the walls and floors before my arrival, but sadly some parts of my predecessor remained – blood stains mostly, still red in colour, not yet dried to a burgundy, but hair too, gathered in the corners like dust bunnies."

She gulps and I smile before continuing. "Imagine, if you could, your last shit." This time noticeable red patches flush the reporters cheeks. "I suppose you did it in a flushing toilet, like any other civilised human being? What you must remember, here, is that we were not intended to feel like human beings. They wanted us to feel like animals. Oh sure, they provided us with a sanitary bucket chained to the wall, but it was never scoured, never cleaned. Emptied, naturally, by ourselves once a week, on a Saturday, which is ironic because Saturday used to be my favourite day. But even when I had emptied it, the smell never quite goes away does it."

"No," she will say, in a quiet voice. "I don't imagine it does."

"Just a bedframe and a mattress that undulated on its own with lice. Sure, you could flick them off at bedtime but what is the point, really, when you will have to do it all over again the next morning? I had a table -" I always pause here and break my vision to look across at the real life table-come-calendar, "- but I used it for very little. On occasion, if I was feeling fancy, I would set my bowl of cabbage soup down on it and eat as if I were in a restaurant. The walls, whilst dirty, made for fantastic acoustics, and if I spoke just right it was as if I had a fellow patron in there with me. Or a waiter, perhaps, come to ask if I wished for a top up."

"Bathing – how did you – were you able to wash?"

"Do you recall those days of childhood when you felt particularly *sticky?* You know the ones, where you have spent all day in the summer running on the beach and swimming in the ocean, where the salt and the sand and the heat come together in a -" I slap the palms of my hands together sharply. "If you could choose any part of your salty, sandy and overheated body to wash, what would you choose?"

The reporters eyebrows always shoot up, surprised by the notion of putting herself in my place. "My face, I suppose."

"Uh-uh," I wave my finger at her, "wrong. It will always be the feet. If you can wash your sticky and grimy feet, even a little, the rest of you feels somewhat cleaner. Just a little tip, if you ever find yourself in that position." She squirms again. "One and a half pints of water was all we had, each day, for everything. That's drinking *and* washing. Not quite enough is it, and you people all wonder why so many of us walked out of there with some form of dysentery. But, we got clever," I will say, flicking my cigarette and watching the ash fall to the floor, "and learnt that we could strain the globules of limp cabbage from the soup and wash our feet in the water, which left more water for other uses. Quite an educated move, don't you think?"

"Very. Did you share your cell with anyone?"

Did you have company, is what she means. *As you seem a little like a lunatic.*

"I did. For a part of it. The Germans pulled off her fingernails with a pair of pliers."

She emits a high pitched squeak, but shakes off the ruffle in her composure. "You never considered escape, Margot?"

"*Considered* it? Oh darling, I thought up a thousand different ways to escape, but each one had already been tried and tested by some inmate before me."

"And what of them? Did they manage it?"

I will pull my chin down then, so my eyes level with hers. "I saw seventy people, on different days, pulled into the courtyard and shot. No, they did not manage to escape. What is the point, I often wondered, of escaping one hell just to run into the clutches of another one?"

"Quite right," she mumbles.

"A lot of the time we couldn't even see what happened outside the windows," I say with a forced sigh, as if I longed to see a courtyard littered with dead bodies. "Whenever there were signs of an air raid they would nail wooden boards from the outside across our windows so we couldn't peek. As if we were children on Christmas Day, longing for a glimpse of Father Christmas."

"Did you write to your family?"

"Ah, but writing would require paper, and a pencil, two commodities very hard to come by in a prison where they do not want you to partake in activities of human socialisation. You could pay, sure, many people did, bribing the guards in some way or another." I flick an eyebrow at her so she understands my connotation. "There will always be a prison guard who can see past the filth of a female prisoner. A hand is a hand, after all."

This time the reporter shakes her head. *No.*

"Not for me, of course, as I had no-one to write to."

"No family? But what of your mother, your brother? It says here -" she consults her imaginary notepad, fumbling a little on the paper, "- Lucille and Pierre La Joie? There was also a…Frank and Alice La Joie, both deceased during the war."

I flinch a little here, remembering Papa and Alice as 'deceased.' I shake it off. There is no time for grief in this vision of mine. "A mother in a mental asylum, who was likely far past reading?" I say, with more than a hint of contempt. "And a brother for whom I had no address? No, I had little inclination to write, though I did miss the *act* of holding a pencil." I will wave my cigarette – almost depleted now – through the air like a pencil, leaving smoke trails in its wake instead of lead.

"That must have been lonely."

"I had the girl with no fingernails, at least for some of it. But I suppose it could be, at times. It says a great deal about human nature that when you are made to feel like an animal - to eat like one, sleep like one, be manhandled like one – you suddenly start to *behave* like one, and you embody their pack tendencies. So we tended to stick together, when we could. If you were an animal in that prison, what would you be?"

Having another question bounced back at her frazzles the reporter even more. "A bird, I suppose, so I could fly away."

"Useful," I say, nodding. "But the guards have guns remember. They would wave them around like giant -" I wave my hand between my legs and she blushes again "- competing for who had the largest. So, a bird would not be a good animal to be. They would shoot birds."

She nods beneath her crimson cheeks. "Very well. A lion, perhaps, so I could attack them."

"*Guns*, remember. You are not approaching the question correctly. You are thinking of an animal that could flee the prison or attack the guards, neither of which was ever going to happen."

The reporter always holds her hands out here, and a whiff of expensive perfume tickles my nostrils. *Perfume…when was the last time I dabbed that on my collarbone and wrists?*

"Then I do not know, Margot. What animal should I have been?"

"A monkey, of course!" I say with a chuckle, throwing my arms up in the air as if I had just delivered the punchline to the best joke of all time.

She laughs along with me, but I suspect it is out of politeness. "A monkey? Why on earth would you have been a monkey?"

"Why, so that you could pick the lice off of your cell-mates privates and no one could batter an eyelid. Now *that* would be very useful."

Rather amusingly, the reporter freezes with her mouth wide open. Her eyes are wide with – I can't quite work it out – shock? Revulsion? Empathy? Colour blooms on her cheeks – a deep and full bodied red – before turning into the thick, oozing liquid of blood. Right there, pouring from her skin. It patters onto the concrete floor – *wasn't that carpet a moment ago?* – with a delicate *pat-pat-pat.* A fly flitters skittishly around her open mouth before coming to rest on her bottom lip. I watch in fascination as it hesitates a moment, wondering if this is some sort of trap, before plunging into the dark abyss of her mouth. Then another comes, and another, until a swarm of them glide gleefully into the frozen reporters open mouth.

I sigh. I horrified her to death. I always do.

If only it had been that easy to die.

44

August 1943

"That is my home, right there," I say, pointing like a proud child passing their house on a school outing. "Isn't she beautiful." I ignore the concrete pillars that sprout up on the landscape like unwelcome pimples. Or the swarm of green-grey figures that pick at the landscape like termites to wood.

The sun – that *glorious* sun – which seemed to have forgotten to shine on France is shining on Guernsey, who is steadily coming into view from the boat. I turn to the person I am sitting next to - the young girl who had accompanied me on the boat trip back from the mainland, who was travelling on to goodness knows where - about to point out roughly where my farmhouse sits, but then I realise two things.

One. I am not even sure I have a home to return to. Köhler's belongings had still been in his bedroom when I had left; he had probably assumed full control of the property by now and I could not return.

Two. The girl next to me is now dead.

↔

For some passengers it is noticeable that the salt air and cracked lips are unwelcome gifts of sea travel. They moan, pick at the flaking skin on their lips and smack them together as if someone is going to come and pour water down their throat. Sure, the salt air burns the throat and leaves it with a thick, crackled coating, but I welcome that salty presence on my body with wide open arms.

I stumble to the decking to see Guernsey in clearer detail as we come into port. My gnarled and bony fingertips clamp themselves around the railing of the deck, slick with sea spray.

"Home," I whisper and lick my lips. I let out an involuntary groan as the salt tingles on my tongue. I lean my head back and close my eyes. If I keep them closed, I can un-see the German soldiers swarming the harbour. I can pretend it is just an ordinary summer and I am returning from a trip to the mainland. When

I open my eyes I will see a welcoming committee of Otto, Papa, Ma, Pierre, Alice and Mariette, waiting with open arms and bated breath for my return –

They open now, and the surprise at what I do see knocks me clean off my feet.

No passenger seems able to summon the strength or inclination to help raise me to my feet, and with my own weak legs it takes me longer than usual to find the railing again. With a great heave I force myself up, force myself to face him.

The August heat reacts with the concrete jetty, giving off a hazy mirage wave on the surface; the ones that disappear as you approach them, vanishing into thin air. It almost convinces me that what I see in the midst of the mirage is also not real. At first I think it is Otto, my imagination putting the two of them together, as they had been for most of my childhood. One of a pair.

Tomas.

I could not trust my memories, my recollections of a time so close to my incarceration in Caen. I had long since believed that seeing Tomas, smiling and proud, dressed as a soldier and chummy with the demonic Commander of the 319th Infantry Regiment, had been a figment of my deprived imagination.

My legs tremble, embodying the vibrations of the boat as she comes to dock. I expect his eyes to scan across the other passengers but they fix themselves firmly on mine. He came here for me, no-one else.

It is with a great effort that I hold myself straight as I depart the boat, unlocking my body from the rigid hunched position that had lately felt more comfortable to adopt. I am aware of his eyes on me, of being on show. It is slightly un-nerving, but *why*, I ask myself. This is Tomas! I should be overjoyed to see him here, to see him so obviously waiting to meet me.

My stomach flip flops as my feet hit solid static ground. *Home.* I wiggle and stretch my toes, fighting against the damaged wooden soles of the shoes.

"To hell with it," I whisper, sliding my sticky and overheated feet from the cramped shoes that were a size too small anyway, and relishing the instant flood of coolness on my soles. I continue on with the shoes in my hands, aware that I would likely never wear them again. I was *home* – I could walk around barefoot if I wished, unless the German authorities had conjured up a new inane rule against it in my absence.

The thought of the German plague on the island sends my eyes back to the top of the steps, where sure enough Tomas waits at the waist-high railing, watching me. With a jolt of unburdened reality I remember similar hot and clammy summer days, years ago, where I would wait in the same place as he disembarked his own ship. How the roles had been reversed. Did he think of himself as the islander, now, and I the visitor? Did *I*?

I cannot stop my head from swimming, and I battle with my concentration on the slippery steps, keen to avoid a spectacle of myself with Tomas watching so intently. Tears come from nowhere – were they from relief, or exhaustion? I swallow them away. *No tears, not today. This is a good day.*

He saunters casually to greet me at the steps which I am grateful for; it strikes me, halfway up the steps, that I have nowhere to go when I reach the top. A firm hand takes my arm and guides me away from the steady throng of passengers disembarking, none of whom I recognise. Where were they all going? Why do I not recognise a face? This is Guernsey, I *always* recognise a face.

Neither of us speaks, and for a moment it feels as if we are frozen rigid on the spot whilst the world continues to move around us. My head feels too light, wobbling on my neck like it no longer wishes to be attached. Then his composure breaks and his face splits into a grin. I watch it happen, fascinated. His features are so finely tuned now, his edges sharp enough that I can imagine them made from stone. To see the stone split, to see it animate, surprises me.

"Margot."

I swallow, wincing against the salty grit in my throat. "T – Tomas."

"Welcome home." I become aware, then, of his hands on the tops of my arms. He is holding me up, I am sure of it.

"I don't know where to go," I mumble, not ready to ask him the *how* or the *why* he came to be here.

"Come home to the farmhouse." I stiffen and my head swims with confusion. *Did we speak, before I left for Caen? Am I forgetting a conversation?* "I hope you don't mind," he continues, "but I have been looking after it for you, whilst you have been otherwise occupied."

Otherwise occupied? He makes it sound like I have been gone on holiday.

The skin in the nook of my upper arms and beneath my breasts gets warmer and slicker. I wish I could fan my face, but my arms remain pinioned to my sides by Tomas.

"Köhler?" I croak.

"Deployed elsewhere, I believe. He left the island several months ago."

I close my eyes. *Thank goodness.* When I open them his eyes have narrowed, his mouth no longer in a grin. "I was not pleased, when I heard him boasting of what he did."

"*Almost* did," I correct.

He frowns. "The two of you did not…?"

"The two of us would have done nothing, but *he* would have, if he had not been interrupted."

The corner of his mouth twitches but his eyes remain like steel. "Then it is a lucky thing indeed that he is no longer on the island."

Lucky for me? Lucky for him? Lucky for Köhler? No, that felt wrong. Tomas did not threaten – he diffused tension, he did not build it.

"I need – uh – w-water," I stumble over the words, each one feeling like a razor blade as it reached my mouth. I needed cool air more; the breeze from the open sea had all but disappeared and the hot island air now felt suffocating.

His hands loosen on my arm but I can still feel them lingering there like ghosts. I am only mildly aware of his fingers clicking in the air and the rapid footsteps of someone near us.

"*Wasser, schnell!*" I hear someone bark. Tomas?

The edges of my vision waver, a darkness creeping slowly in like a demon. A bottle top to my lips – "*trinken*, drink, Margot" – arms beneath mine, a hand to the back of my head, fingers embedding themselves into my matted and coarse hair. My eyes, in and out of focus, looking at that one thing on his lapel. The small burst of colour on a sea of green-grey.

"*Cat vomit,*" I whisper. I hear a giggle somewhere. It sounds like me.

My centre of gravity shifts so violently that I swallow hard on the rise of bile. I am flying. Floating. Still, I cannot look away from it. That shiny badge, glinting in the sunshine.

A band of textured red on the edge. Like blood. Two intertwined thick black lines, like lovers entangled in the bedsheets. Tomas is a Nazi.

45

My body sits at the table, watching him work his way around my kitchen like an expert. My mind, however, has rooted itself in the omelet he whisks together, slopping smugly amongst the butter, eggs and cheese; food that I had come to believe no longer existed in the world.

"I thought there was a fuel ration," I say to his back. I realise that I am sitting stiffly in the chair, as if it were not my own, so I shift and lean back as I had done so since Papa made them fifteen years ago.

"Yes."

"But it does not apply to you." I try to keep the bitterness from my voice, but I am not sure if I succeed.

"No."

The sweet and indulgent smell of butter sits thick in the kitchen air. He slides the finished omelette across the table to me, then takes a second chair and places it next to mine, so our knees almost touch. He places his elbow on the table, resting the side of his face on his upturned palm, and watches.

"Eat," he urges.

I fear I have forgotten how to. Carefully he takes my hand and places a fork in it – a knife in the other. "You look like you need food," he says. "Let us spend the next day here, at the farmhouse, getting you better."

"It is horrific in there…" I whisper. "A day will not…it cannot make amends for…"

"Of course," he strokes a hand on my hair. "You are safe, now, Margot. I am here. I will take care of you. Please – eat."

My eyes drift down to the pin on his uniform. He follows them. His fingertips deftly unclip the badge and turn it face down on the table. He nods silently in the direction of the plate again, and I know my stomach can no longer resist it.

I cry as I eat, letting the tears fall into the coagulated mass of cheese and egg, part of me grateful, part of me guilty. Tomas says nothing, but one hand soon finds its way onto my knee and pats it, ever so gently. It makes me cry more.

↔

"Were you trying to die?" He asks in a quiet voice much later, when darkness has fallen.

He has assembled a nicky lamp; a jam jar filled with diesel oil, a hole pierced into the lid through which a piece of old bootlace has been threaded and lit, acting as the wick would in a candle. He sits beside me on a sofa which is not my own, his long legs stretched out on to a coffee table I was certain belonged to a neighbour three doors down. The light from the lamp sends his features into a slow flicker.

You have gotten handsome, I think to myself. *You have grown up.*

"Margot? Were you trying to die?" He repeats.

"I wasn't thinking straight. I had just had word that Alice…"

"Alice?" He asks, straightening.

"In the Coventry air raids."

His eyes glisten in the lamplight, and it is my turn to hold his knee. *You need to tell him.* The thought comes to me as soon as I touch him, as soon as he softens under my touch and visibly deflates. *You need to tell him what she is to him. What she was.* I often believe the role I had chosen to play in Alice's life so implicitly that I forget the truth. She is my daughter. She was family to Tomas. She was family to Otto – though I may never get the chance to tell him.

I make all the moves to tell him. My mouth opens, my chest constricts, but in the end I cannot bring myself to say the words. *One day.*

"And Otto had just left-"

"I know."

"I was alone."

"Yes."

"I felt like I had nothing to lose."

"You had me."

"I did not know where you were," my voice rises. "Where have you been?"

He runs a hand across his short, stubbed hair, as if the very act will conjure up his memories. "I thought it would have been obvious. I enlisted."

"*Willingly?*"

"Is there any other way?" Innocent eyes level with mine.

I dance with the idea of retelling Otto's story, but then I wonder if he already knows, and then my mind collapses into a state of exhaustion and whatever energy is needed for such a conversation can wait.

"You have learnt your lesson now, though."

"Lesson?" He raises his eyebrows and my stomach turns when I realise what he means. "There was no-one around, Tomas, I would never have dared do it if there were. I did not mean to provoke."

"Come on now Margot, the victory sign? Of course it was done to provoke. Not that I am laying blame, but -"

"Alice was dead. Otto was gone. I was wearing my dead aunts coat and hiding in my dead cousins cottage…"

He sits forward, bringing his hands together and resting them between his knees. He lowers his head. "I am not blaming you for the reasons behind the action, Margot." He seems to chew on the words. "But one does not go against the authorities for sheer fun, do they?"

My head throbs and I rub violently at my temple. I look around the living room; it no longer smells the same, but I do not loathe it. It smells of Tomas, there is an air of familiarity to it. But the furniture fit out is a jumble of other islanders' belongings; the soldiers – Tomas? – had picked their favourites and played swaps with other billeted soldiers. The juxtaposition of familiar and alien makes me feel not quite here. The feeling you have, I suppose, when you are dreaming.

"You could have *died*," he whispers. "It would have broken me." His sudden sharp gasp fills the room with a haunting echo. It brings me back to reality – this is not a dream.

I put a hand around his jarring, jerking shoulders, ignoring how full they feel in my palms. He sobs in my arms until he has exhausted himself. His hands find my cheeks and cup them, gently, resting his forehead against my own. He pulls back with a gasp.

"You are hot!"

"I have a headache," I say, weakly. My forehead feels cold without him there – already, he is my comfort blanket once more. My familiar in an unfamiliar world.

He retrieves his jacket from the floor and fumbles in the breast pocket. "Here, take these. I will get you some water."

When he returns I still hold the two small pills in my hand like poison. "Where did you get these?"

He pushes the water into my hand. "Aspirin? The black market," he shrugs. Indifferent.

It is on the tip of my tongue to ask him if he is aware how many lives could be – could *have* been – saved with aspirin. Instead, I swallow the words along with the pills and let him roll the cool tumbler across my forehead.

↔

He stays true to his word. For three days we stay in a bubble, just the two of us. Occasionally a soldier will come to the farmhouse for Tomas, but he ushers them into whichever room I am not, and speaks with them in hushed voices. I wonder if he speaks so quietly so that I do not overhear, but when he returns and tends to me, I strongly suspect it is because he does not wish to disturb me.

He sets warm water in the bathtub, leaving me a bar of gently scented soap on a small wooden stool, with a towel that not only looks clean, it smells it too.

He sits behind me on the floor and untangles my washed hair with a gentleness that would soften even someone with the hardest edges.

He feeds me, waters me, tenderly rubs feet that rest in his lap on the strange sofa.

He tucks me in at night and sends me off to sleep with a warm kiss on the forehead.

He looks the other way when the delayed effects of mild dysentery make themselves known in explosive and bloody ways, then cleans up without a word.

He holds me when I cry, when the realities of what I am to live with take hold.

46

Early September 1943

The early September sunshine beats through the glass of the library lobby, warming the side of my face as I sit at the desk. Maeve had gone home over an hour ago; we were now so busy that I had asked her to stay on upon my return. She had done a brilliant job with keeping the library afloat in my absence, especially considering how many visitors we now had daily, even with the lack of new materials to read. I suspect most islanders visited for the G.U.N.S news sheet alone, which was now so popular rumours had begun to float as to who was at the helm.

I am getting my dose of the banned BBC broadcast transcript at the desk. It is just after closing and I have locked the doors from the inside. If anyone (any *German*) questions it, I can merely feign that I had not wanted to encourage customers in when the library was closed.

My hand painfully cramps as I turn the thin sheet of tomato paper, and I have to span my fingers out wide to relieve it. It is just one of the many issues my body now has to contend with after Caen. Tomas will often take my hand in his when he can see the muscles begin to seize and gently massage the joints. I fold the paper, wondering if he will be home to do such a thing this evening.

It has been one month since my return and Tomas is now such a staple in my life I cannot remember there ever being a time when I thought him gone forever. The logical part of me understands he is a Nazi (even though he now removes his badge in my presence) and I am fully aware that he could have found some way to contact me in the years he was missing, though he chose not to. I understand it all, but I have slid it into a far reach of my mind, closed the door on it, locked it and thrown away the key. Because I do not wish to listen to the logical part. Tomas is my best friend, the only family I have left. I must keep him close, because there is no one else.

In return for how well he cares for me, I on occasion have to cook and serve some members of his regiment. They are unlike any soldier I have come across since the occupation, and I despise it. They leer, they make rude gestures with their hands, they are loud and brash, they wiggle their eyebrows in a solicitous way. Once a particularly amorous soldier wedged his hand up my dress when I was serving them dinner – it was only a matter of seconds before Tomas had him pinned to the kitchen wall by his neck, a knife pointed dangerously close to his skin. Not one of them had laid a finger on me since.

A knock on the main door startles me. I squint and try to make the figure out through the glass; a soldier, that much is obvious, but the interior lights reflect off the glass, obscuring his face.

"May I help you?" I ask, opening the door with a sigh. "The library is closed."

An officer I recognise stands at the door, leaning slightly forward as if waiting for me to move so he can enter. I am knocked off centre, slightly, by his appearance here. I haven't seen him since the moment he had told me Otto's aircraft was departing. I had left him standing on my doorstep. Many of the young and fit soldiers had departed the island since then, replaced with the more elderly men and infirm. I assumed he had gone, too.

Seeing him now reminds me of Otto. The thumps to my chest still hurt when I think of him, they still reach my core and threaten to buckle me. He had left thinking I blamed him for Papa's death, and the demise of so many other innocents, at the harbour on the day of the first raid. Two years ago I had felt much the same way, an anxiety filling my bones every time I imagined where he was or what he was doing, if he were even still alive. But so much has changed this time; Caen broke me physically - and, I fear sometimes, mentally – and Tomas keeps me so occupied that my mind rarely wanders. But Tomas is not Otto. He cannot hold me the way Otto does or kiss me so hard that I feel it in my toes. He cannot lie with me in a tangle of bedsheets and promise to one day make me his wife. No, I still love Otto, and seeing this officer – Heinkel – just brings it all back up to the surface.

"May I?" He pushes forward again.

I chew on my lip and look behind into the semi-dark library. "I was about to leave for the evening…"

"This will not take long." His words are firm – I really have no choice in the matter – but his tone is friendly.

Was it really two years ago that he had pulled me into the porch of a shop to protect me from an air raid threat? I remember clawing at his skin and finding remnants of it beneath my fingernails after. I blush, guilty, and move aside. "Very well."

He removes his helmet when he enters, like a gentleman would remove a hat. I expect him to make his way to the stairs, but when he stops and turns back to face me I suspect he is not here for a book after all.

"I am sorry that my words came too late."

"Otto?"

"Yes."

"Do not apologise. You gave me the chance to realise something that I wouldn't have, otherwise." He raises his eyebrows, and I find myself trusting this soldier implicitly. "He did something during the war that he thought I would blame him for. But I do not blame him, and now it is too late to tell him so."

"He told you?"

I stare, incredulous. "He told *you?*"

Heinkel breaks into a sad smile, then, and when he meets my eyes they sparkle with something I haven't seen in a long time – hope. "Otto is a close friend of mine. He told me a great deal. I knew his feelings on the war, and I knew there was only one thing he wanted – one *person,* rather. He did not wish to fire that day but he had -"

"- no choice," I finish. "He trusted you?" My words sound harsher than I intend them to be.

"I cannot say for certain, but I believe Otto would trust me with his life. I believe he already did." He looks pointedly to me. "You." When I shake my head, not following, he continues. "Otto and I began our training in Germany together, but we got separated – he into the Luftwaffe and I into the Infantry. We spent many nights in training, our bodies broken beyond repair, talking. He told me of a girl – Margot – he would one day make his wife. We kept in touch with one another over the years, and I began to grow reliant on his letters. I was drafted into the war from an orphanage, you see, I have no family. Most orphans like me long for the companionship of war, but not I. Otto and I bonded over our dislike for the inane barbarity of it all. My skills, these hands," he holds them out in front of him and studies them, "these are meant for whittling wood, I was particularly good at dolls houses. They are not for killing people. Otto and I became friends in an alienating world. One day, shortly before I was dispatched to Guernsey, I received a letter. He told me to find the girl and look after her as best I could. So I did."

I blink as my mind rapidly rewinds over every interaction I had had with Heinkel. "You did?"

He nods. "For my best friend. As it turns out this Margot is one of the good ones, so it was not difficult to do." He smiles, then, and flicks his foot back and forth.

"I – thank you. *Thank you.*"

"Please," he waves me away, "if we cannot do things for our friends than the war has caused even more destruction than I thought. If I hear from Otto – *when* I hear from him - I will be sure to let you know. Could I ask you the same? If he writes to you, would you tell me? For my mindful peace, as you say."

"Peace of mind," I correct gently. "Of course." But I know Otto will not choose to write me. He is a loyal man. A loyal and respectful man who thought I did not wish to see him ever again. He may have watched me from the shadows before he was deployed, but there was a reason he would not come into the light without my say so first.

I walk him to the door, ready to lock up for a second time that evening, when he turns back on the doorstep and fixes me with a firm stare. "If I may suggest one thing? Keep that hidden." He points to my side.

I look down at my hand, where cramping fingers still clutch the partially folded paper, then back to him. I hadn't realised I was still holding it. He nods, without a smile this time, and walks away.

The thin tomato paper is folded in such a way that the large, black letters – G.U.N.S – are on clear, unmistakable show. In a panic I stow it into my shoe, rather than back upstairs in the book for Pieter to retrieve it from tomorrow. It feels safer on me, somehow.

↔

I make dinner for Tomas and his soldiers that night with the news sheet still wedged beneath my heel. There had been no chance to remove my shoes when I returned home – Tomas and his men were already seated at the table.

"You are late, Margot," he says softly beside me as I begin to chop the food. The Germans are still receiving indulgent boxes of food; tonight, it is a large leg of lamb, potatoes and cabbage. We, in return, still receive nothing. At least Tomas will allow me the leftovers.

"I had a visit from a soldier, I could not refuse him," I whisper back.

He places a hand on my waist. At first it feels oddly intimate, but then I realise it is because he wishes to draw closer so as not to be overheard.

"Do I need to speak with them? It is not safe to have you there longer than necessary."

His eyes narrow as he speaks, and I see something there that I do not like, some fire.

I subtly wrestle myself away from his hand, feigning a retrieval of salt from the cupboard – I fight the temptation to dip my finger into the salt and lick it off. *Hunger can turn you into an animal,* I think.

"I do not believe it will happen again, Tomas, it is quite alright."

He smiles – it makes him look sixteen again. "Excellent. I must return to these men," he lets off a theatrical sigh and sits back down at the table.

It is not until much later, once I have eaten two potatoes and the fatty gristly leftovers of the lamb from the plates, that I can remove the G.U.N.S news sheet from my shoe. There is a loose floorboard in the downstairs hall, that opens up straight into the foundations of the farmhouse. There is a space of perhaps ten inches before you hit hidden ground – it used to be a wonderful hiding spot as small children, if you didn't mind the spiders.

I roll the news sheet into a tube, securing both ends with hair clips. I hover at Tomas' closed bedroom door, listening in for his heavy breathing. He lets out a snore and I creep downstairs, avoiding the squeaking treads. I raise the floorboard with a grunt and slide in the rolled news sheet.

I could confess to Tomas. He would be displeased but he would not disclose it. Would that be the safest course? Else I risk him coming upon it on his own. Though studying the floorboard now in the moonlight that shines through the hall window, it looks rather unassuming, practically identical to the others. He would have no reason to look beneath it. No, I shan't trouble him with it.

47

Late September 1943

"Have you heard of Otto yet?" I ask Tomas as I hand him a plate of rye bread and an apricot from a jar.

"Not yet," he muses with a detectable sigh, skim reading some papers at the table.

Though Tomas has not admitted it to me, I have long suspected that he could find out where Otto is stationed, perhaps even obtain an address for him. The reasonable part of me, however, understands that there is more to war than simply picking up the telephone and asking where a soldier is based. Otto is just one of many men currently fighting on the Eastern Front in Europe. He would not be the first man to go missing in action. But reason does not always win, so I continue to ask Tomas if he has heard of his whereabouts, even if just to keep the mention of his name on my lips.

"I am going to the bread stall at the market today, to collect my ration," I tell him as I walk out the door, "then I will be at the library, should you need me."

He offers me little more than a grunt, still engrossed in his papers, and it unnerves me so that I want to go to the hall and ensure the floorboard is as I had left it two weeks ago. Tomas has had a lot on his mind, of course, I know this – all of the soldiers seem to have of late. But living with the G.U.N.S news sheet under the house still feels decidedly reckless.

"As soon you can reasonably light a fire without raising an eyebrow, burn it," I tell myself, casting a hostile eye to the clear and brilliantly blue sky.

When I reach the bread stall there is a small queue.

"I wonder when we will smell freshly baked white bread again," I muse quietly to the lady in front of me. She has a familiar face – I went to school with her daughter, Elizabeth. She turns and I can see the signs of rapid weight loss, wrinkled skin hanging in sheafs under her chin.

"Oh yes, dear, and the smell of a slow roasted joint of lamb," she adds wistfully.

I guiltily ignore the memory of last months' leg of lamb from my mind. "How is Lizzie?"

"You haven't heard?" Her face drops. "I thought you would have. Lizzie died a few months back. TB."

"My condolences." Lizzie had been only a few months older than I. "I must have missed it. I – I was in Caen."

Her mouth opens, but then she does something quite curious. She looks me up and down, focusing on my breasts, my waist, my thighs. Then she turns back without a further word. When she reaches the front of the line she leans over the table to the baker, speaking with him in hushed tones. When she turns back with her black rye bread she does the same thing, this time with an upturned nose.

"Did I say something wrong?" I ask the baker, baffled.

I expect him to shrug his shoulders, offer me sympathetic eyes, perhaps. What I receive, however, is a hard bread thrust to my waist and ruffled eyebrows.

It is as I turn to walk away, stunned into a silence, that he says coldly, "You look awfully well fed for a girl who is not long out of Caen gaol. Could it have anything to do with that German you are residing with, I wonder."

↔

Since the night, almost ten months ago, when I had my first encounter with the slave workers that now shared our island, I had made a conscious effort to leave the library promptly. If I did not finish my job list, it waited until my next shift. It is fifteen minutes to five on this particularly sodden late September day, and I am eager to leave. The blue sky had evaporated to grey shortly after midday and clouds rolled in from the distance swollen with the threat of rain. I could most definitely justify lighting a small fire to welcome Tomas home. Or to burn the G.U.N.S news sheet hidden beneath my house.

The nights are beginning to draw in, my bicycle on the very last of its legs. If it gave in on my journey home I would have to walk, and walking in twilight can be just as dangerous as walking in the dark; sometimes it is your imagination playing tricks on you, sometimes it is the devil himself.

The library phone rings and my stomach drops. Chewing the skin on my thumb – a childhood habit that has come back in nervous force during this occupation – I consider leaving it ring out. But what if it is a German? Would I get reported? Would I get thrown back into prison for not accommodating a soldier?

I sigh and pick up the handset. "Town library, how may I help?" *Please be a local needing a book,* I silently pray.

"Madam." The short-clipped English is recognisable, and something in my stomach drops. "Ve need you to open zis evening. A zargeant vill be to you in zirty minutes."

"Certainly. I look forward to serving him." I replace the receiver and quell the panic. How long can it take, really, to choose a book? I should still be home well before nightfall.

At seven o'clock, with the library doors only just locked behind me, I still fight the urge to panic. I fly through the streets on my cycle, pushing the poor machine to its limits. It isn't until I reach the familiar country lanes, in a spot not far from my first sighting of them, that I hear the drone of incoming slave workers, moving as one, shuffling eerily down the lane. I dart into a corn field before I can be seen. Before I can see them.

Refocusing my bearings I work out that I can travel a fair way to the farmhouse unseen, simply by meandering through the fields, possibly climbing a few hedges. From where I stand, it looks as though whoever farmed this field deliberately left a row of corn unsown – it makes a natural path through the fields, meaning I could potentially make my way through with very limited damage to the crops. I look down at my bicycle, then at the precious crops towering over me almost ready for harvesting. The bicycle would trample too much of it, I could not risk it. But if I leave it here, it will not be there in the morning. Even with dusk falling there is a chance it could be seen.

I tuck it against a hedge and give the handlebars a kiss. "Get a hold of yourself Margot," I whisper. "It is a bloody bicycle."

But my eyes drift over the wheel, where a year ago Otto had attached stuffed hose pipe to the rim in place of rubber. It is something so silly, so small, so inconsequential in the grand scheme of things. The tears, however, fall. It is a small reminder that Otto is not here with me, may never be, again.

Perhaps it is this, this cycle of reliving every moment I can think of with him in it, that means my wits are not with me when I navigate the fields. In the second field, following my narrow path deep among the towering crops, I almost stumble upon them. Two skeletal bodies crouch low, feasting on unripe corn like lions over an antelope's body. Drool and stiff corn kernels drip down their filthy chins, leaving wet streaks in the dirt. The only sound in the silence is the gnawing and slopping of their feast. I intend to leave them to it. I intend to silently retreat into the shadows, but one of them spots me and instantly draws a knife from his rags, one hand still holding the corn to his mouth.

"Back!" he cries. "Back!" He waves the knife at me and I spot the crumbling rust at its tip.

I hold my hands up in defence, slowly stepping backwards. *If that knife cuts me, I am as good as dead.* There is no medicine left on the island to stop an infection like that.

"I'll go," I say, repeating it over and over as the men – *were* they, men? – stand, knife still raised.

There is a moment of such stillness that it almost feels unreal, before the bodies move as one, dropping what little is left of their gnawed corn and stumbling in my direction. I half-turn but stumble over my clumsy criss-crossing feet. I scramble on my knees with my hands in the slippery fonds of trodden cornstalks, trying to get a grip to hoist myself back up. The ground is dense and wet, too buried beneath the canopy of corn towers to ever dry out.

Desperate men, I keep thinking. Desperate men are capable of desperate acts.

Finally, my grip holds, and I roll forward and up onto my feet, stumbling as I right myself. I dare not look behind me. I run for seconds before a hard push hits my back and I am flattened once more. This time the weight pins me down, face first into the soft wedge of ground. A suffocating force on the back of my head grinds me deeper, and every sharp gasp draws mud further into my mouth. My arms flail helplessly, blindly behind me, trying to attack something I cannot see. All the while I wait for the slice of the rusting knife. But it is not a knife they require for what they have in mind. My skirts are lifted and my stockings pulled down, a rough and calloused hand grabbing hard at my bare buttocks, rising me up. I cry out but my shout is muffled and lost in a void of mud and dirt.

And then, nothing.

The dead weight on my back disappears, my face no longer forced into the ground. I lie still for a beat, turning my head to the side, resting my cheek against the wet earth. *Inhale, exhale.* Then I remember my lifted skirts, my bare buttocks, and I scramble to sitting, scooting into the shadows of the cornstalks and righting my skirts. I cross my arms over my body. *Inhale, exhale.* Then I see them.

Lying mere feet from me, their throats slashed and open eyes staring blindly up to the heavens. Blood seeps into the sodden ground and the *pit-pat* of rain makes its way through the corn canopy. One of them still holds the gnarled core of his death snack in his grubby hand.

I wish I could cry, to feel like I could make some sound at all. In truth all I can do is stare blindly at the men who had tried to attack me. I do not even notice that there is someone else in the cornfield with us until a hand finds mine and pulls me to standing.

"I have got you," he whispers, drawing me into his chest.

"It's just a cornfield," I sob. "I've always gone through the cornfields."

I lay a cheek against his starch stiff uniform, dropping my eyes to the blood soaked knife dangling from his hand. The dagger curves and undulates beneath where his hand grips it, before tapering to a perilous point so thin it appears to vanish seamlessly into the air. *Not an ounce of rust on that one,* I think.

I hear a click of his fingers somewhere in the distance. "Away with these." A bark. An order. I close my eyes at the point one of his men drags the limp forms of the slaves away. Tomas cups his hand under my chin and raises my head. "Let's get you home."

48

December 1943

"Have you heard of Otto *yet?*" I ask Tomas, almost as soon as he wakes on the morning of December 24th, 1943.

"No, Margot, not yet," he sighs with an obvious impatience.

But you are *looking for him, aren't you?* I want to ask.

Stress lines shroud his face like an unwelcome mask, dark circles under eyes that droop and cloud. If we had not heard and read the BBC broadcasts professing that Germany were making great losses in the war, it would have been obvious in the soldiers faces alone.

It is only a matter of time until Germany accept defeat, but then what? What happens to Tomas? What happens to Otto?

"I have some gifts to deliver today, will you be needing anything from me?"

"Gifts?"

"Some small, handmade tokens, mostly jars of preserves that I have been storing. It seems wrong to celebrate Christmas without an offering at all."

"May I see these?" I pick up one of the jars and wave it in his direction. His eyes take in the contents then drop back down to the papers on the table. "The peaches."

"Yes."

"The *imported* peaches."

I roll the jar in my hand. Tomas had brought several small boxes of peaches home one evening in September and I had set to work on preserving them in a (very) light sugar syrup.

"Yes."

He ruffles his papers but does not raise his head. "I gave you those as a gift, Margot. I did not expect you to pass them on to anyone else, even as a preserve. Let us hope that no-one finds out – I may be reprimanded. Who, may I ask, are these gifts going to?"

"Neighbours, mostly, a few friends in the town."

"Very well," he says, as if I had been asking permission. "Please be mindful of the light, it is getting dark earlier, it seems."

My eyes linger in the hall as they always do when I leave. Tomas has barely left me alone long enough since the night I was attacked by the slaves to even consider retrieving the stowed G.U.N.S news sheet. What did it matter now if, according to the underground news reports, it was only a matter of weeks before Germany renounced?

As I go to pick up the several jars of preserves – the peaches and hedge-picked berries, mostly – my hand stiffens painfully and my fingers stick out, frozen in peculiar angles. I gasp and almost drop the jar.

Tomas leaps from his seat and skilfully places the unbalanced jars on the table behind him with one hand, taking my stiffened palm in his other. Tears spring in my eyes as the pain travels to my arm.

"Here," he sooths. "Let me."

He rubs tenderly at the tight joints, his thumb and forefinger kneading in a rhythmic motion. It seems like minutes before the pain subsides and my fingers unseize.

"Thank you," I wince, the ghost of pain still lingering.

Our eyes meet in silence. "Quite alright," he breathes. "I would do anything for you, you know that."

An uncomfortable tension suddenly fills the kitchen, the air tingling loudly in my ears. He does not look away. His intense gaze makes me blink, and I get the unpleasant sensation that he is going to kiss me. The air continues to thrum but neither one of us moves. Then, I withdraw my hand, careful not to move too quick.

"I know, Tomas, as would I for you."

The distance between us is now too great for him to be able to kiss me, if that was what he had intended.

↔

By the time I reach the small grocery store in the town I have reasoned with myself. Tomas was not going to kiss me. Tomas is *Tomas.* He is my very best friend. *Friend!* I had interpreted it all wrong. Beneath his Nazi uniform he was kind, gentle, thoughtful. If I were to read every kind gesture as something deeper, than I would assume everyone was in love with me. How very convoluted. Besides, Tomas would never allow himself to feel that way – I am betrothed to his cousin, for heaven's sake.

Ms. Leale, the small grocer owner, is jittery when I hand over the peaches, and she takes the jar with shaking hands. I hold them steady with my own.

"Is something the matter, Ms. Leale?"

"Did you – did you want to listen to the news? In return for the peaches." She keeps her voice low, clandestine.

"Yes, yes I would very much like that," I whisper back.

She beckons me behind the counter with her, sits me down on an upturned crate before taking her place on an empty apple box. I watch in fascination as she leans into the idle cooker beside the serving counter, removes a false wall at the back and switches on her radio set. In broad daylight. All the while her hands shaking like the last leaves on a tree in the middle of winter.

Less than five minutes later the door atop the bell gives off an unwelcome *ting* and we jump to our feet. There is no time to hide the set, to reset the false back to the cooker, or for it to look as if we are doing anything other than listening intently to prohibited news.

A soldier I have not seen before enters and immediately takes in the two of us with a look of surprise. A stillness hovers in the air as we wait. I place a hand over Ms. Leale's – anything to stop her quivering.

At first I believe he is going to leave; he turns his back to us and makes his way to the door. Confused, I watch as he bolts the latch closed instead, and turns the *open* sign to *closed* with a rather flamboyant flick of his wrist. I swallow the bile rising in my throat, and Ms. Leale shivers so hard I fear she is going to pass out.

My mind frantically fights to work out the correct course of action, here. We cannot deny it – any fool can see we had been listening to the radio. One more step and he would see the set for himself, open to the heavens for all to see.

"Is quite alright. I no mind."

I force myself to meet the soldiers eyes. Do you know, you can always tell by someones eyes what lies beneath? Some are like windows into a deep, dark abyss, and I had seen an alarming number of those since Tomas had been living in the farmhouse. Broken souls. Rotten souls. But this soldier…his eyes are not like theirs. His remind me of Otto's – warm, welcoming, kind. Perhaps he isn't going to kill us on the spot, as I had (in a forgivable moment of dramatics) assumed.

"I vill listen also." With a spring to his step that feels bizarrely out of place in the gloomy side street store, he turns a crate next to mine on its side and sits down with a thump. He looks to the quivering Ms. Leale first, than to me, both of us still standing, unsure if this is a trap. Had we just danced with death and escaped it, or welcomed it in with open arms?

"Please. Sit."

When a soldier tells you to sit, you sit. I have to hold Ms. Leale still with an arm across her lap, her knees audibly knocking together.

He sits with us. Listens. Wishes us *Merry Christmas*. Leaves.

I resume my rounds of delivering my small gifts as if nothing had happened. I do sometimes wonder how long it took Ms. Leale to stop quivering.

↔

I am a quarter mile from home when Tomas strides down the street towards me, a look on his face that momentarily terrifies me. He has found the hidden newssheet. Will he expose me here, in the street? But then his stiff face breaks and softens into relief, a smile gracing his lips so welcome that I sigh. He embraces me with such force that my knees buckle, and even in the frigid December air my cheeks warm.

"Where *were* you?" he breathes into my hair. "I expected you back an hour ago."

I pull back and glance around – thankfully there is no-one to see his overzealous display of affection. They were already talking enough. "Ms Leale needed my assistance. She is frail, and alone, I couldn't rightly refuse."

"Of course, of course. You are deathly pale," he holds me from the shoulders at a distance. "You need to wrap up warmer in this weather. A typical Guernsey winter, hey. Here, have these."

I cannot stop him as he pulls off his gloves and instructs me to fan my fingers whilst he places them on my hands. Then he takes my arm and links it in his, walking us down the empty street back towards the farmhouse. My face continues to flush, this time for an entirely different reason.

"Tomas, if someone should see us like this…"

"I clearly need to fill you up, more," he continues, cutting me off. "Put some more meat on your bones."

"Actually, on that matter…perhaps you should stop. Giving me leftovers, I mean."

"Now why on earth would I do that?"

"It is noticeable. People are beginning to talk."

"Which people?"

"Well…the baker, for one. And a woman, I cannot remember her name. I used to go to school with her daughter."

"That's half the island," he quips, but his words come out stiffly now. "This baker, you say."

"Yes. But Tomas it is quite alright, it does not bother me, but perhaps for *your* sake…"

But he is not listening. "Hmm. It is quite the case of pot calling the kettle black."

"What do you mean?"

"Oh, just some black-market dalliances of his. He can hardly claim to be innocent. Anyway, irrespective of *who* said it, I am not going to stop providing for you."

Providing for me, or stealing for me? I am under no illusions; the food that supplies the Germans comes from either mainland thievery or food intended to supply the islanders.

"Then I will stop eating them," I try to keep my tone light. "It is only fair, Tomas, you understand. Fair to you, too. People may think that you and I are more than friends. They don't remember you from before the war, when you were a boy…"

"It makes little difference to me what they think. Does it, to you? Consider what you are saying. I am still going to bring the food in and provide a meal for the soldiers, a reward for their hard labour, they need it to sustain themselves.

Why shouldn't you benefit from that if the food is already in your home? Do you think your friends and neighbours would think twice about it? The food is better inside of you than it is as waste."

At that moment, the haunting dulcet tones of *Silent Night* ring out from a house ahead of us. In the fading light the melodic sounds seem to echo sweetly from the facades of the houses lining the street, sung by soldiers usually more akin to the brutal renditions of their parading anthems. Unwillingly, my eyes fill with tears. Tomas tightens his hold on me as we stroll down the deserted road.

"Are you crying?" He asks softly. I cannot speak, only nod. "You do not know your own strength, Margot. This chaos, it all has a purpose, and you will overcome it."

He places a hand to the side of my face as we walk, lightly moving it down towards his shoulder. "When the war is over, I will move here, I will help you to rebuild. It will be a new era, you will see."

As I lay in bed that night, the day shifting silently between Christmas Eve and Christmas Day, the transition unassuming and unapologetic, I realise that Tomas thinks a life after the war is one in which the Germans win.

A week later, the baker is sent to prison for black market profiteering.

49

January 1944

"Have you heard of Otto yet?"

The morning beyond the kitchen window is miserable, hail the size of small balls threaten to crack the glass and a ghastly breeze whistles through the cracks.

Tomas places his elbows on the table, bringing his palms together and resting his pointed fingers against his forehead. "It is unfortunate…"

"What is?"

"…but perhaps this will give you what you need. It will provide clarity, for you."

The world slows as he slides a discoloured sheaf of paper across the table toward me. In that moment I must separate my mind from my body – it is the only way to make it. With hands that do not belong to me, and fingers that are not my own, I unfold and read the words.

On this day, I read the words that stop my world altogether.

There is no catching of breath, no pause. It simply…stops.

A tear falls onto the wooden table from where Tomas sits, also broken. The water sends the grain into a dark spin, spreading its tendrils slowly outward, like an ink stain.

Otto has gone.

50

January 1944

True to my word, I do not eat any of the food that finds its way into my home courtesy of German thievery. As a result, my skin hangs gaunt across my cheeks, sending the deep hollows into a colour so dark I look barely alive.

In truth, I no longer wish to be alive. I wish to join Otto.

Sometimes, as I crawl into bed at the first sign of the fading sun, shivering under the meagre blanket, I wonder if it could be as straightforward as throwing the blanket to the floor, removing my clothes and simply freezing to death in my own bed.

Tomas tries. He warms a pair of bricks on the fire each night, removing them when red hot and wrapping them tightly in old blankets. He gently places them at the foot of my bed, and the heat goes some way to keeping me alive. I despise it.

There was a moment, a week ago, when I caught him trying to set the letter informing me of Otto's death in combat alight. He held it so close to the flame in the grate that the edges had begun to smoulder. I cannot remember what happened. It ended with Tomas sprawled on the floor, spread eagled like he were a child making angels in the snow. I had the paper clutched to my chest, my back against the wall and legs outstretched in front of me. There was a deathly silence hanging in the air.

"This has to stop," he had whispered.

I had slept with the paper every night since then, feeling its warmth against my naked chest beneath my clothes as if it were all I had left of Otto.

Then, a fear. A fear that Tomas would try again. With heating supplies so dire, he would try again to light the paper and sustain a fire, I was sure of it.

So here I am, the moon sending shards of sharp silver light across the hall, prising at the loose floorboard as Tomas sleeps. If he cannot find the paper, he cannot set it alight. He cannot take the last remnants of Otto from me. But as the wave of cool air from the foundations hits my face, all the air leaves my lungs in one swift exhale. The G.U.N.S news sheet lies unraveled, the two clips I had used to secure either end lying away from it, as if thrown in a rage.

He has found it.

51

February 1944

I wake one morning in February the same as every other of winter. The thin and threadbare blanket pulled tight to my chin, last night's hot bricks – put there by Tomas – now cool and grainy on my toes. The frost has infiltrated my nose, and I can feel the tiny inconsequential hairs holding on to the cold air as ice. There is always a moment before I open my eyes when I wonder if today will be the day. Will I finally die and join Otto? Or will I find something to live for?

↔

Unusually, Tomas has a spring in his step as he moves about the kitchen.

"Coffee? Only parsnip, I'm afraid, but hold your nose and it can pass as the same."

I sit cautiously at the table and accept the coffee he puts in front of me. The taste is rancid, but remembering the tricks from Caen I gulp it down. Almost instantly my stomach bloats, and it tricks my foolish and idle mind into believing it is full.

He sits opposite me with a satisfied – and somewhat smug – smile. "Beautiful day out."

Outside the window the gale pounds at the weakened stone walls. Papa would have repointed by now, I realise. The house is crumbling without proper maintenance.

"Well," he reasons, following my eyes, "it is *dry,* at least."

That is when I see that he has readied my thickest overcoat and set my weathered shoes below. A scarf – stolen from somewhere, no doubt, as my own had worn down to the threads two months ago – sits with it, alongside a pair of gloves.

"We are going for a walk."

"No. I do not feel up to it."

"Up to it? Margot, you have hardly sustained an injury. What you are suffering is -"

I shake my head but before I have had a chance to take my next breath he stands so suddenly and his voice spills over with such vehemence that it makes my ears rattle.

"– MARGOT! For Christ's sake, this *has to stop!* Are you trying to die? *Are you?*" I open my mouth, likely to confirm his fears, but he holds a hand up. "Don't answer that. We have to get you out; we have to get you back out there into society. You are withering away, wasting before my very eyes. This is – this is *irrational!*" he spits.

I blink but remain silent. I fear antagonising him more, but he softens.

"This is *me,*" he says gently, coming to sit beside me. "I helped you overcome your fear of the ocean, do you remember? Let me help you overcome this. I will help you through your grief but you have to *want* me to. You have to want me, Margot. Can I say nothing to make you smile again? I have been your companion for most of your life, your best friend, and -" He claps his hands together. "- that is it! Books! The one thing you love more than me, right?" He laughs, but it doesn't sound right. "So, that's it. We *will* walk. We will walk to the library."

My instinct is to refuse. I wish for nothing more than to continue withering away in the farmhouse, peacefully. But evidently Tomas is not going to allow that to happen. And, if he is going to force my going anywhere, the library is the one place he would have the most luck. He *does* know me well, I suppose.

"The girl covering you is insolent at best. So what do you say? Will you walk with me to the library?"

"Maeve does a wonderful job."

"How would you know? You have been hiding under the house foundations for a month."

My eyes shoot up to meet his, working to see if he has any inclination of his words. Was it just a mistranslation of *hiding under a rock*, or had it been intentional?

"Shall we?" His eyes don't leave mine, but I cannot fathom if it is because he so desperately wants me to walk with him, or if he knows that I know.

Logic, Margot, choose logic. So I do. There is no doubt that Tomas knows about the G.U.N.S news sheet hidden beneath the house he is living in. He must also know that I put it there, if he has had any sense to check the date on it. He has, however, chosen to feign ignorance. To save me? To save himself? It matters not.

I pull myself up to standing and wrap my arms around his waist, nestling into the crook of his neck and breathing in his scent. The move shocks him, and he stiffens for a moment. I realise then how distant I have been, how much I have pushed my friend away. He relents soon enough, bringing his arms around me.

"I cannot squeeze too tight," he chuckles, sadly. "I do not wish to break you."

"The library?"

"The library."

"And we are walking. To the town."

"You cannot rightly cycle, can you. You left it in the cornfields. We have no choice. Besides, the walk will be nice. Fresh air in the lungs, that is what the doctor always orders."

It does not occur to me until much later that I never asked how he'd found me, hidden beneath the towers of cornstalks, buried so deep within a field of green that I could not have been seen from the road.

↔

We leave the library with two newly borrowed books and a promise to Maeve to be back tomorrow. Getting back to work, busying my mind with ordered tasks and being surrounded by one of life's simplest pleasures – that was what I needed. Besides, Maeve *had* allowed standards to drop in my absence, and I couldn't risk the library being shut down to the islanders as a reprisal. On top of all that, I could wait no longer to catch up on G.U.N.S. Tomas had not left my side throughout the visit, and I had been unable to ask Maeve anything about it.

He takes my hand half-way up the steep incline, the very one Pierre and I had raced to the top of a lifetime ago. The side street has undergone a transformation of its own, as well as the girl walking up it. Gone are the overflowing window boxes of brightly coloured flowers, and the smell of fresh, indulgent cooking wafting through the open windows of the terraced houses lining the road. The doors opening to street level now have bright crosses painted on them, and the scent of death lingers in the air like split milk.

"What does that mean?" I ask him.

He purses his lips. "Quarantine, perhaps. There are all sorts of diseases breeding among these animals."

Who are the animals, I wonder. Did these houses no longer belong to my fellow islanders, the ones who had stood true to their pride and stayed loyal to their isle during this occupation? Or did he refer to the slave labourers – were they taking up camp, here?

There is a mutter, so quiet on the still street that it could have barely been there. But I hear it. I hear the intensity behind it.

"*Jerrybag.*" It is a hiss, travelling through the air from one of the open windows above down to my ears like a snake. Then it is gone. It could have been a whisper of the wind, but I know better.

I drop Tomas' hand. His head swings in alarm, but he does not say anything, and he does not try to take my hand again. Not until we head off the small side street onto a bigger lane, that is. Following this one will take us home on a fairly straight road. I wiggle my fingers from his grasp, and settle for linking his arm, instead.

He looks left, right, left again. Over-cautious. Or looking for something. "This way."

"I know it is this way," I mumble.

Tomas' body jitters gently under my arm. More of an undulation, really. I make to ask if there is something the matter, if he is ill, but the squeal of a car's tyres rebounds off the terraced houses and cuts me off. The car accelerates towards us at an alarming rate for such a small road and I freeze, tightening my grip on Tomas' arm.

As it passes us I exhale, but that, too, is cut short. The car comes to an abrupt stop behind us and before the tyres have even silenced, three of the four doors fly open as if on springs. Emerging from the car are three heavy-set Germans in plain clothes. No uniforms, no insignia.

"Gestapo," I whisper.

"Indeed."

There is a thickness to Tomas' voice, and do I imagine it when he angles me slightly to the right, clearing my sight line towards the car and the Gestapo?

A lone man emerges from a nearby house, as if he has been waiting behind the closed door for the car. When he walks directly toward the three men, I *know* he has been waiting. He holds himself straight with his head held airily high, but even I can see it is forced. The Gestapo could frighten even the boldest of men. He waves in the direction of a nearby house, toward where Tomas and I stand, fixated. There is a particular smell in the air. They say that animals can sense incoming danger, and at this point in time, I am all animal.

"Can we go?" I tug at Tomas' arm. "Let's go. Please?"

If he hears me, he ignores me. Watching only Tomas you would be inclined to think he was watching a football game, waiting as his team walk to the penalty spot, place the ball, stretch their limbs, flex their feet.

Something between the four men is said, and suddenly they break. Heading in our direction one of the Gestapo notices their audience. His face screws into a ball so tight it looks inhuman, but as he nears – about to tell us, I expect, to move on – his eyes drift from the young lady to the man at her side. I see a mother entertaining her small child by swinging a hand across her face, from happy, to sad, and back again. This Gestapo man was furious at being watched. Then he saw Tomas.

"Ah Tomas!" He acknowledges with a smile. "You are here."

It is a strange statement to make. There is no question as to why Tomas is in the middle of this unassuming street, with a young lady companion, mere doors away from a house they are clearly here to investigate. Tomas nods but does not speak.

"We should go," I pull more forcefully at his arm now. I may as well have been pulling on stone for all the good it does.

The three Gestapo men and the fourth – have I seen him before, he looks familiar? – walk briskly past us to a blue door behind. Tomas swivels on his heels, almost sending me spiraling. I am grateful for the movement – I do not want to see what happens next.

And yet, Tomas stays where he is. Is he holding my arm tighter? I am reminded of the day of my return, with arms pinioned to my sides. I am irrationally frightened to look at him, I realise.

So I fight the irrationality. I expect to see some signs of stiffness, but Tomas is soft. His features glow even in the absence of sunlight. His eyes sparkle. I see a thirst in them that I do not like, as if someone has pulled a mask over his features.

With growing horror the Gestapo obliterate the door with first an elbow, then their entire bodies. I do not even see them knock. The fourth man follows behind, stepping over the splintered wood.

"*Tomas,*" I whisper, and it very nearly becomes a weep. "I do not wish to watch."

There is a sound from beside me that sounds unnervingly like the smacking of lips. I close my eyes.

A short while later a man emerges, caught in the net of two of the Gestapo's, thick hands wrapping themselves like pythons around his upper arms. They move so fast his feet can barely keep up. He reminds me of a paddling duck; serene and peaceful atop the water, but beneath it his feet fight to keep him afloat.

The fourth man – the man I now understand to be an informer – drifts out behind the two Gestapo and walks away. His job is done. If this were a play, we would end scene here. But there is more to come.

Once the arrested man is in the confines of the car the two Gestapo stand with their backs against the closed door. The one who had spoken to Tomas looks now in his direction and tips his chin forward. To my horror, Tomas does the same.

"Do you know him?" I breathe.

"I know most people."

"But it looks like -"

"Ssh, Margot."

After a while, the final Gestapo man emerges and treads through the remains of the door, holding a large black typewriter. A slowly growing pain in my stomach threatens to double me over as I see what else they are holding. Several sheets of thin tomato packing paper, one of them already emblazoned with four large letters, awaiting the next morning's news.

G.U.N.S.

"This is what happens when people do not abide by the rules we set." His voice is not dripping with malice or scorn, as I would have expected the words to be.

I am under no illusion, then, that this has been carefully orchestrated for me to see.

Tomas has given me a warning.

52

April 1944

We feed off of the earth, but the Earth in turn feeds from us.

That is my theory, anyway, to explain away the miserable fog hanging over the island in – what should be – the turning of spring. We – islanders and soldiers alike, now – are in a sorry state, and it would be unfitting for the sun to shine on a people so broken.

↔

My mind drifts more often, nowadays. I can be in the middle of a task, and it simply wanders from me, until I am no longer folding the ragged and worn linens in the kitchen, I am with Otto in the East, during his final moments, holding his hand, stroking his head. Would I have been able to lessen his suffering, I wonder, had I been at his side?

A piercing crash knocks me from one of these impromptu reveries, and I look up just in time to see Tomas barreling through the farmhouse door, a face of fury.

"*Arschloch*," he bites, kicking his jackboots off. They rebound off the kitchen cupboard, making a mark in the rotting wood.

"What -"

"*Don't*," he warns, holding up a hand to silence me.

I watch, then, as the tangled marvel of human emotion consumes him. He paces back and forth, a furious hand flicking over stubbled hair in need of a tidy. His face contorts into a frightening wildness, eyes blazing into nothingness and chest heaving in rapid short shallow breaths. This goes on for five minutes – I count, silently, in my head – before the pacing slows, and finally he gives in and sits on the chair. His breaths are longer, I notice gratefully, as the rage slowly leaves his body. It is quite a show.

"Can you believe," he says slowly, through gritted teeth, "the sheer audacity of some people." He doesn't wait for me to answer, perhaps he doesn't need me to. "He left me waiting for thirty minutes, serving *every* single customer in there before me. I was there first! Where is the respect, Margot."

Tomas' fiery temperament is new. He seems to be living in a permanently panicked and disorganised bubble. Neither one of us mentions the fact that even the air sings with an imminent invasion. Germany is losing the war. Even if I had not known this, I would have been able to tell by Tomas alone. I would have read it in the constant clicking of his fingers, the new twitch he has accrued when talking, the fact his knee bobs up and down when he sits, as it does now. I place a hand over it, and it stills.

"Who did, Tomas?"

"The barber," he spits.

My eyes rove over the patchy growth on his head – yes, he does need a haircut. "Perhaps he was busy."

"Oh he was busy alright. I expected to wait for a while – I was *willing* to wait my turn – but I watched civilian after civilian walk into that place and leave before me. He did not even look in my direction."

It is his pride that has been injured, that much is clear. But a man with wounded pride can be a dangerous man indeed. To soften him I offer to take my hand to it, but he refuses. There is a look in his eye that I do not trust; I just cannot work out if his mask has slipped, or if he has just put one on.

"He will regret it."

↔

The following day there is a notice in the local newspaper

I am directed by the Feldkommandantur to warn all concerned that he has ordered that members of the German Forces must be given prior attention in all shops and other establishments frequented by them, and that severe punishment will be imposed on any who disregard this order.

↔

"*Inselwahn*, that's what they say he has."

"Who has?" I ask in a whisper, though the three customers we had seen into the library were on the upper floors. There is just something about libraries that makes you feel the need to tiptoe.

Maeve leans over the desk in the lobby. Dark circles frame her eyes and I notice for the first time that she looks so much older than her years.

"Hitler."

His name sends an involuntary shiver up my neck. The devil himself.

"What does it mean? *Inselwahn?*"

"Island madness, so they say. He is obsessed with keeping us."

"*Our* island?"

Maeve frowns, and she looks her age again, just for a moment. "*Is* it ours, still?"

"Of course!"

Her eyebrows jump and she chews the inside of her cheek. She says in a small voice, "I don't believe it is, not anymore."

My eyes drift through the library doors, to the street outside. An island usually bathing in the first signs of spring and not even one colourful flower has popped above the surface. Perhaps she has a point.

"No," I say, firmly. "If you want something it is because it is worth having. Our island is still special. Ignore the heavy fortifications and artillery. She is still ours."

"Madam?" A call from one of the upper levels.

"I'll go," I say to Maeve, who looks too light on her feet to still be vertical. "Have a rest. Have you eaten today?"

She raises her eyebrows. "No-one has."

Having dealt with the customer I make my way back down the lobby stairs a short while later. I run a finger over the splintered wood balustrade, astonished at how it is still standing. It looks as rotten as I feel.

Maeve is speaking with someone at the desk. Flame red hair and a freckled complexion. I pause on a tread, recognising him. The informer.

He grins wildly, one elbow resting on the desk and a hand in his pocket. "I thought I recognised you the other day. Margot, isn't it?" I silently make my way down the remainder of the steps, conscious of feeling like a watched animal. "Mariette's cousin, aren't you?"

At the mention of Mariette my eyes do a double take. It clicks; the reason he had seemed familiar on the day I had watched Charles Machon - the brainchild behind G.U.N.S – get arrested. Seamus, the Irishman, who had been holding court at one of the gatherings early on in the occupation.

"Did you require a book?" I come to stand behind the desk so he has to remove his elbow. Has to stand to face me like an equal.

"You know," he looks up at the lobby ceiling, but I doubt he finds any interest there, "rumour has it that Charles Machon's web spread a little wider than first thought."

"Are you the police, Seamus?"

Maeve lets out a small squeak and I nudge her knee. *Not now, Maeve.*

"Would you have any idea about that, Margot? Working in a people facing business, and all that."

"I would not."

He brings his hand up, rubbing a fingertip along his eyebrow. A small, black mark is noticeable on his wrist. A swastika. Maeve must notice it, too, as she begins to tremble.

"Was there anything else you required, if you are not here to loan a book?"

He clicks his fingers in the air, as if something has just occurred to him. "That's it! Your brother – Pierre? – he got rather drunk at a party, started raving about, now what was it," his taps his temple. Any fool can see he has not forgotten. *Get to the point.* "That's it. A car. A – Morris Eight, was it? He found it quite the laugh that it was hidden in plain view."

I keep my face as indifferent as manageable. I do not allow my body to freeze, or quiver. *Damn you Pierre, damn you.* "What of this car?"

He smiles, and the air around us cools. "Good day to you, Miss La Joie."

↔

I know then, more than I have ever known it before, it is a race against time. When I reach the country lanes, I run. I dodge overgrown hedgerows and leap over holes in the pockmarked road.

"*Stupid, stupid,*" I repeat, horrified at my carelessness. It had never once occurred to me to check on the car, hidden behind the wall of hay and packing boxes. In truth I had let it slide sloppily from my mind.

I slow only when I reach the driveway. Pausing at the entrance to the open sided barn, I study the packing boxes. They are still stacked, albeit less neatly than when Pierre and I had arranged them, and I can see loose strands of hay from the bales behind emerging between them. They look a little messy, but undisturbed.

There would only be one way to know for sure. A quick look toward the house tells me that Tomas is home; his shadow moves through the kitchen window. I cannot rightly look beyond the boxes and bales now. Then I see it. A black car is parked out front. Someone is in the house with Tomas.

It is with caution that I open the door. What I hear makes my blood run cold. There is a thrum to my body, moving in the stillness only because of the blood that pumps through it. An Irish lilt sings from beyond the kitchen. I follow it, careful with my steps, hopeful to pick up on some stray words. If he had already told Tomas of the car, he would be out there confirming it, would he not? Would this be the final straw for him? Would he hand me over?

My head swims as the two men come into view. Seamus' cocky façade has noticeably dropped, and he stands before Tomas like a student being reprimanded by a teacher. Tomas sits languidly back on the sofa, one foot bent over the other knee, a ream of papers resting in his lap. The floorboard beneath my foot creaks and both their heads whip to face the intruder. With irony I realise the floorboard is the very one below which I had hidden the G.U.N.S news sheet.

"Ah Margot, the very woman."

Seamus has the decency, I notice, to lower his head somewhat shamefully. From my angle in the doorway I can see the hands folded behind his back fidget.

"Come in, come in," Tomas beckons to me. To my surprise he moves the papers off of his lap, stands and comes to me. He leans in to kiss my cheek. "Follow along." The words are just a whisper, dancing across my cheek. "Sit, Margot," he says louder, patting the sofa beside him when he resumes his position. "Seamus here has come to me today with some rather alarming news."

I shoot my eyes at him. *Traitor.* "Is that so?"

Tomas' hand rests on my knee – reassuring. "He claims that there is a car on the property, hidden in one of the barns. As I am sure you are aware, Margot, all of the cars were obtained by mandatory requisition years ago, when this war was in its infancy."

"I am aware, yes."

Seamus' eyes fall on the hand resting on my knee, and I see the callous hope fall out of him like sand from a child's clenched fist. "Perhaps I was mistaken -" he begins.

"Please do not interrupt me," Tomas sings. "As I was saying, the cars were requisitioned for the greater good on the mainland. It would be a crime, now, to withhold any vehicle on your property that the authorities have not already been notified of. You are aware of that, too, Margot?"

I lift my head to face his and his eyes shine, a faint smile playing at the corners of his mouth.

"I am, yes."

"You do not have a car hidden on the property, do you, Margot." It is not a question. "A – what was it, Seamus?"

Seamus clears his throat. "A Morris Eight."

Tomas waves his hand through the air, as if details are inconsequential to him. "You do not have a Morris Eight hidden on the property, Margot."

I am ten years old, then, Tomas sat beside me as Papa drives the car along the coast road. The windows are down, the tang of salt and the fluttering of wind working together to render us speechless. My whole body tingles with pride as he nudges me with his knee, eyes streaming and a wide smile on his face.

His finger squeezes ever so gently on my knee, now. "No, I do not."

"Because that would be a criminal offence."

"Yes."

"Well!" Tomas claps his hands together. "That settles it. Seamus, you may leave. Margot has nothing to hide here." He waits until Seamus reaches the doorway. "Once you have apologised to Margot."

"Apologised?" He turns, eyes widening.

"Yes. You must apologise. You have threatened her good name."

Tomas stands now, gently pulling me to my feet with him. I want to tell him that this is not necessary, that I do not need an apology from an informer, but I stop myself. The informer is, after all, telling the truth. And Tomas knows he is.

"I – s – sorry," he grumbles in my direction, the words barely escaping as a hiss through gritted teeth.

Tomas tuts. "Call me old fashioned, but where I come from, that is not an apology."

Seamus coughs and turns to face me, eyes full of anything but regret. "I am sorry," he forces, ending with a sneer.

"Nah," Tomas drawls, "not quite. You can do better than that, Seamus. Did your mother teach you no manners? Did she not tell you how you must treat a lady? Or has war robbed you of them?"

Seamus raises his hands in injustice but must think twice when he realises who he is raising them against. They drop to his thighs with a slap.

"Kneel at her feet." Tomas' voice has lost its joyful melody. It is as cold as steel.

"Are you – are you serious?" Seamus says, at the same time as I mutter "that is not necessary."

"Kneel. At. Her. Feet."

For a beat he looks at Tomas, motionless. I watch uncomfortably as he breaks, and walks toward me, one knee, then a second, making contact with the floor at my feet.

"I am sorry," he mumbles.

"Clearer."

"*I am sorry,*" he says.

"Now kiss her feet."

"*What?*"

It happens so fast that I do not even have time to move. Tomas whips his hand across the back of Seamus' head and he lunges forward, just saving himself from barrelling into my knees at the last moment.

"Now. Kiss her feet."

A small trickle of blood drips from Seamus' nose. *How hard did he hit him?* He leans forward and my insides curl when a loud *tsk* pierces the living room air. To Seamus' due, he does not stand again until instructed to by Tomas. It is surprising how quickly one can learn their lesson. When no further instructions come his way Seamus, slowly at first, makes his way to leave. No-one follows, and he speeds up. The living room stays silent long after the thud of the kitchen door and the roaring of the black cars engine outside have disappeared.

"Do you have any other skeletons in your closet that I should know of?" My face must convey everything. "Don't look so surprised. I discovered that car behind there the first week I came to stay at the farmhouse."

"But you did not say anything?"

"You had your reasons for hiding it. Your Papa's car, if my memory serves?"

"Is it…still there?"

"Of course not. I had it sent away to the mainland, where there is a dire shortage of vehicles for the services. It was the right thing to do, you understand."

The pain in my chest is irrational, I understand that, yet it does not lessen because of it. Papa's car. The mainland. Tears threaten to spill. I want comfort from Tomas at the same time as knowing he is the reason I need it. My body and mind fight a silent confliction between themselves.

"I will ask you once more. Is there anything else I should know? I can only tidy up what I know of."

"Tomas…"

"Please, Margot. Let me help you."

"You could – you could get into trouble."

His hand goes to his chest, then, fingering the swastika pin he has not yet had a chance to remove for my benefit. "I will not get into trouble." He fixes me with a deep stare, then, and I think of the wireless set sitting untouched in one of the glasshouses. Still hidden, as far as I was aware, behind the discarded packing boxes.

I swallow hard, looking at my feet. "There is a wireless, in one of the glasshouses. I haven't used it," I rush on when Tomas leans his head back, summoning patience from somewhere unseen. I feel like a child being scorned. "I promise I haven't. I – well, in truth, I haven't had a chance…"

He raises his head slowly. "I thought Caen would have taught you a lesson. I thought your days of rule breaking were behind you."

"They are," I say, hurt.

"You cannot continue to do this if there is any hope for us. Margot, you have to obey." He holds my hands in his and kisses the top of my forehead. "I will fix this. But no more, please." He cups my chin and raises my face. "For the love of Christ, no more."

I think back to that morning at the library with Maeve, at my insistence that the island is still ours. I do not think it is, not anymore.

53

June 1944

Approximately 57 nautical miles south of Guernsey, St Malo falls under British bombers.

I lay awake as wave after wave of aircraft fly over the island, the heavy engines making the windows rattle in their frames. Some of them will return. Some of them will fall. Some of them will end their days as rust at the bottom of our ocean.

Bombs drop. Cannons fire. People rush to paint red crosses above hospitals and places where innocent bodies lie like sitting ducks.

I close my eyes and cross my fingers beneath the bedsheets.

Let this be it. Let this all be over.

↔

In the streets the soldiers appear in full battle wear, sure of an imminent attack.

They openly carry rifles slung across their shoulders, hand grenades readily accessible at their waists.

Rumour abounds that officers demand transfer to the mainland, but Hitler refuses.

Inselwahn. He the selfish child, the allies the unruly sibling, and we the treasured toy. He wants no-one else to have us. He has made us untouchable.

We will be free, soon.

Free.

54

September 1944

Still, we await our freedom.

As the allies action their advances through France and Belgium, we sit, and we wait. Patiently. Supplies incoming from the continent cease altogether. We starve. The elderly and infirm die on their doorsteps, unable to continue, unable to wait for a liberation that we fear will never arrive. The RAF, on occasion, drop news sheets to us from the air. Sit tight, they tell us. We are coming.

Brave men sacrifice their lives on mine-strewn Normandy beaches as anxious Germans stand in packs on the island, sick, tired and hungry.

Schools are closed. All places of leisure shut their doors, riding out the storm above our skies. Heavy caliber bombs drop on our harbour, attacking German ships and rumoured submarines. Streets fill with glass.

In a world full of darkness, the searchlights sweep the skies and flares from aircrafts bring in the light. I lie in bed, watching them, imagining Otto behind one of them, coming to find me.

I fall asleep with tears staining my cheeks.

Otto did not get to see this.

↔

Tomas does not allow me to leave the house. He is rarely home, prepared for the allies to land on our shores. When he is here, he tells of quiet, desolate streets.

One night, when he comes home, he stands in the doorway of my bedroom, watching the light show on the walls.

"Are you awake?" he whispers.

"Yes."

"We have been ordered to fight to the last man." My stomach drops. "One way or another," he breathes, "this war is going to end."

55

December 1944

"See that, do you see them? Right there. Do you?"

The German police officer follows where I point, to the unmistakable jackboot footprints in the mud. They surround the mangled carcass of Hetty. She has been stripped almost straight to the bone. I look away when I spot what I hope are not teeth marks gnawing her stained red bones.

He holds his hands up. "What is to say."

"What is there to say?" I snap. "Aside from the savagery, this is theft!"

He merely shrugs, turning his head and looking over the hedge and down the valley, finding something interesting on the horizon.

I fight to keep control of my temper. "You agree, though, that these are the footprints of German soldiers?"

"They could be."

"They *are*."

"Well," he withers under my glare and looks down again to the prints. He holds his own foot out, clad in a similar boot to the print. "Yes, it most likely is."

"And what will be done of it?"

"I can tell them not to."

"Will they be reprimanded?"

"I cannot reprimand a troop for what looks to be one soldiers doing."

He is referencing the troop of soldiers who had taken billet in one of the nearby farmhouses. It is most likely these heathens who slaughtered and savaged Hetty in the night, but of course he cannot pinpoint which – or how many – it was.

Clearly feeling like he needs to give me something, however, he removes his glasses and begins to rub at them with the hem of his shirt. "Now that soldiers cannot buy in the shops, they have hunger, they steal. I will send someone to…" he waves at Hetty's remains and casually strolls away.

I sigh. Now, now is when I wish Tomas were here more often. I could have avoided calling in the German police altogether. I hear him sometimes, coming in late at night or in the early hours of the morning, crawling straight into his bed. More often than not, he is gone before I wake. On the glimpses I do have of him and the fleeting minutes we share together, he is pale and withdrawn, eyes sinking deeply into a face marked with long hours, sleepless nights, and the inevitability of losing a war.

↔

Autumn 1944 had not been difficult. I see that now. Nothing, up to this point, has been difficult. December - the now - this is perilous. It is what most are calling the coldest winter of our time. As I hold the bellows in my calloused fingers, willing the smallest of flames into the fire, I can see why. It is the 23rd December, and the library closed its doors for the year two days ago, on the same day that our gas supply came to an end. Cooking meals now consists of a small open fire and a single pan, the likes of which usually contain nothing more than carrot tops or cabbage.

The nights are dark. I had not appreciated how dark night is without any form of lighting; the sky so dark that you cannot see your own hand if you wave it before your face.

A spark jumps from the grate onto my bare leg and I do not even flinch. Emotions, physical feeling – neither are welcome here anymore.

↔

"It's coming!" Maeve calls from the end of the drive.

I am in the paddock gathering twigs and dried up dead leaves from the ground, hoping to start a fire. I drop them all and limp to meet her. This is the moment we have been waiting for.

Liberation no longer at the forefront of our minds (they have forgotten about us, haven't they?) it was the Red Cross we now waited for. A ship – the *S S Vega* – laden with relief supplies had left Lisbon at the start of the month, carrying four tons of soap and seven hundred and fifty tons of food supplies, so it was said. I maintain that it was this small glimmer of hope on the horizon that kept the islanders alive through the most haunting and depressing Christmas there has ever been.

It is just after six in the morning and Maeve is looking more alert than I have seen her in months. Could it be the cloudy film that has taken to creeping across my eyes, or is there a certain vivacity to her cheeks?

By the time we arrive at the harbour the queues around the outer walls are ten people deep. With surprise I notice the work of unloading the parcels had been assigned to the Germans. Maeve and I watch, marveling at the sight of our occupiers – those very men who had brought us to our knees for four years – carrying the precious brown parcels and sending them off for distribution.

Four days later, we walk together to the small parish shop that was to act as a delivery centre for the parcels. We reach the break in the lane and Maeve asks if I want her to stay while I open it. I shake my head, biting back tears. I want to do this alone.

"Tomas?" I call to the farmhouse. My voice echoes back, but that is the only noise to greet me. He is not home. "Good."

First I lay my hands on top of the parcel, taking in the haunting sight of withered fingers almost to the bone, and wrists so small Tomas could wrap his thumb and forefinger around it. I weep, softly at first, then realising I had no-one to be quiet for, louder.

You are going to save my life, I think.

Everything is tinned or packaged neatly, and I find myself squinting at the colours of the labels, such vivid brightness in a world that had long been devoid of it.

"Real coffee," I breathe, holding the tin of Mother Parkers Tea Company to my chest. "Thank you, Toronto."

Nestled within the parcel are such delights as I never thought I would see again. Powdered whole milk, biscuits, canned sardines, corned beef, sugar, cheese, marmalade, chocolate – *chocolate!*

↔

"Please, Tomas, let me make you a coffee, a *real* coffee…" I try again one morning the following week.

He waves me away. "I cannot."

"No-one has to know."

"We have been ordered not to touch the contents of those parcels, Margot, and I will do as instructed."

Guiltily I heap a teaspoon of the magic into a cup and ladle some hot water from the pan over the fire. I repack the Red Cross parcel and place it on the top shelf of an otherwise bare cupboard. It really is a lifeline. When I turn back, Tomas is watching me.

"Not even a sip?"

He laughs but it catches somewhere around his chest and turns into a cough. "Not even a sip. You, it is all for you."

↔

Before he leaves for the evening he places a wrapped brick at the foot of my bed, as always. He kisses my forehead and I take his hand.

"You are the best friend I could have asked for, Tomas. Thank you, for caring for me. Whatever happens next -"

His face is obscured in the darkness but I feel a finger lightly touch my lips. "Not for now."

↔

I cannot tell you what time it is when I hear the first sounds from below in the farmhouse, but it is a night of the darkest darks. Only a slim shard of moonlight pierces the black through the windows.

A noise has woken me, but I lie still in bed waiting for another, just to confirm it hasn't been in my dreams (can you call them dreams, if nothing good ever happens in them?). In the silence of the house the slow squeak from the kitchen – is it, the kitchen? It must be – sounds like thunder.

It will be Tomas, returning then.

Footsteps across the floorboards, slow and deliberate.

Tomas never takes this much care to be quiet. Sometimes I wonder if he wants me to wake, just so he can speak with me. I pull the blanket up tighter to my chin, making myself small, invisible.

Someone is coming up the stairs. No, not someone, it is Tomas, it must be Tomas. A thief would have lingered in the kitchen, invading the cupboards, helping themselves to whatever they could find. Oh! My Red Cross parcel. That thought alone is enough to fully awaken my mind.

If the footsteps pass my bedroom, it is Tomas, only Tomas.

But the footsteps do not.

They come to an intentional halt outside of my bedroom door. Even without the aid of the wooden floorboards to pinpoint their location, I would know. The animalistic side of the human body is fascinating like that – the air changes when more than one person breathes it. It is instinct to know when you are not alone.

The doorknob twists and I clamp a hand across my mouth. I locked it – didn't I?

A locked door means nothing to whoever it is that stands outside of my bedroom. There is a pregnant pause, then a *thud* so loud that I jump from my bed. The frigid air creeps across my skin and even the strands of my hair erupt in goosebumps. Backing into the corner of the room, making myself as small as possible, I wonder if I can hide in the shadows. I whirl around on the spot – is it dark enough? But no, that sliver of moonlight casts everything with an eerie silver tinge. They will see me. Another *thud* and I realise now that they are kicking the door. I glance at the window. I only consider jumping from it briefly – I am on the first floor, and broken bones could be ill afforded with the lack of medication on the island.

"Wh-who is it?"

A deep and throaty laugh comes from the other side. It is the most frightening sound I have ever heard. I curl myself into a ball when the third and final *thud* sends my bedroom door splintering into a thousand shards. I simultaneously want to look up and stay hidden, in this little cocoon my arms are making, wrapped around my knees and head.

He gives me no chance to decide. He grabs me by the hair and drags me along the rough boards. My body flies through the air like a ragdoll, rebounding off the doorframe then taking each hit of the steps as he pulls me down the stairs. He shoves me into the kitchen chair, one arm pinioned across my chest as he deftly wraps ropes around my wrists and ankles. I scream until my throat cracks, but when I see the tightly clenched fist coming towards my face out of the darkness I realise he does not care that I have no voice left. He stuffs a wadded ball of foul-smelling linen into my mouth and takes a step back. It is then that I can see his face. Or lack of it.

A black mask covers his entire head, not even a strand of hair is free. Two sets of tiny holes have been made for his eyes and nose. He crosses thick arms across a broad chest.

Tomas, I silently beg, *come home now.*

He looks from my wrist to my ankles and, seemingly satisfied that I can make no escape, steps away and begins to investigate the kitchen cupboards. I close my eyes. *Fine. Take it. Take it and go if you are that desperate.* He finds it easily and places it under his arm. *Just leave me alive. But…the chocolate…*I shake my head and let out a low, guttural moan.

This is a mistake. The thief turns and stands in front of me, a thick black wall.

"Zis is for us, now." *German. I knew it.*

He moves like lightning, his hand coming towards me before I have a chance to ready myself. His fingers claw at my neck, taking it in a firm grip and pressing so tight my breath hitches and gasps. My eyes widen, in shock or fear I can't quite pinpoint it, but behind the chair my hands fight tirelessly on impulse. I wriggle and squirm, pulling on my hands. White specks start to dot my vision, an agonizing pain now radiating from his palm as he crushes my windpipe, when one of my hands suddenly springs free from behind me. It glides from behind my back like it has lost all weight, before instinctively clawing at his mask. It is only a thin material, so sheer I can see the outline of a large nose and thick lips. I put as much power into that one hand as I can muster, imagining his face is a sand sculpture on the beach, melting away beneath my fingers. I must draw blood, as a sudden warmness gets beneath my fingernails. He cries out and clutches at his cheek. I may have even gotten his eye.

"Zis is not worth it," he bites, kicking out at my chair and sending me flying backwards. One free arm is no match for the heavy wooden chair, and I have only one thought as the back of my head makes contact with the edge of the kitchen unit, before the edges of my vision turn black.

What a peculiar comment to make.

56

When I come around I find myself lying on the sofa, unbound, cradled in Tomas' lap. It is perhaps closer than we should physically be but I cannot, in that moment, find the strength to care. He has been sleeping, I think, as the moment I start to rouse he jerks and holds me closer, like a child takes to their teddy bear before he falls out of bed.

"Ssh," he soothes, and I get the feeling that he is picking up where he left off, before sleep came for him.

"I was so frightened," I croak, my throat still hoarse. "No one came Tomas. I called but no one came."

It strikes me then that it is the first time, in all of the occupation, that I truly have been frightened. A little unnerved at times, naturally, but not frightened. Until last night. Or tonight. I look out of the window but cannot say for certain how long I have been like this.

"When I came home you were…I thought you were…I am *sorry* Margot, that I was not here for you. God knows I could have stopped…"

But I do not need to hear it, and he does not need to finish saying it.

I nestle into him, soothed by the rhythmic beat of his heart. "He stole my Red Cross parcel," I muffle into his chest. "I was saving that chocolate."

He chuckles, sadly. "Were you now."

"The bastard stole my chocolate." I dissolve into tears and Tomas holds me tighter. "How long will I have to wait for another, do you know?" I lift my head and ask, suddenly, mid sob.

I have caught him unawares, and there is a look to his eyes - a hunger - that twists my stomach. It is only there for a transient moment, before his features rearrange and soften.

"I will find out for you," he promises, delicately.

Then I feel it. Nestled alongside my thigh, an obvious sign of how much he is enjoying this embrace. I steadily extract myself.

"I - I should try and get some rest, now."

If Tomas is aware of what is going on beneath his trousers, he does not show it. He glances lazily out of the window. "It will be daybreak soon."

"Yes."

"Do you not think that you ought to light us a fire? They have predicted a cold start to the year."

↔

I do not hesitate in returning to the library. Tomas tries his hardest to get me to stay home and tend to the house, but ultimately he loses when I point out that the soldiers would be unhappy without their books. Damned the whole educated lot of them.

There is also an odd tension in the air of the farmhouse that I am keen to avoid. Since that night, when I thought Tomas had merely been comforting me, I have felt my every move watched. When the paranoia gets too much, I have to reason with myself. The boy who is my oldest friend was inevitably going to grow into a man, and there are simply some things a man cannot control. I should have been more considerate, yes, I should not have assumed we were still children seeking innocent comfort from one another. Still, the confused tension lingers, and I know he senses it too.

I am on the second floor of the library, noting with pride just how many gaps there are on the shelves, when a polite cough behind me makes me jump.

"Major Heinkel!" I exclaim. "You startled me."

Though it would appear it is I who has startled him. His eyes widen as I turn, taking in first the bruises along my hairline, then the bind marks around my exposed wrists.

"What on earth -" he takes a step towards me, closing the gap.

"Oh. This. The farmhouse was robbed. The thief stole my chocolate. And the rest of my Red Cross parcel but really it is the chocolate I am most disappointed about."

"This is more than a robbery." His eyes roam over me, searching for the glue that holds together the broken girl in front of him. "This is savagery. Did you report it?"

"Tomas did."

"He did?" He scrunches his nose unhappily and I place a hand on his arm to settle him.

"I survived, Major Heinkel. It could have been worse."

"This is not right," he mutters, sulkily. "Now I shall have to explain this to Otto."

My hand stills on his arm. The mention of his name is so unexpected, so startling, that I have no time to control the tears. Heinkel pulls a handkerchief from his pocket and offers it to me.

"Please, call me Werner, Margot. I think we are past last names now, are we not? I am sorry to mention Otto. It was thoughtless of me. At a time like this, when you have just been through such an ordeal – I am an idiot. An idiot who must apologise for more than one reason, it would seem. I promised I would inform you, should Otto write. He did, madam, but then the war took a turn and I have been busy, so busy that I overlooked -"

"Werner." The name plays awkwardly on my lips. "I cannot believe that you don't know…and I have to be the one to tell you -"

"Margot you are babbling."

"I suppose I am." I take a deep breath. "Otto died in combat last year. It has been such a time I am surprised you have not received news of it." A lot of men have lost their lives, I realise; the world cannot be notified every time another falls. But a best friend as good as family? Surely, he ought to have been notified.

His face falls, crumpled in grief, and something else that I cannot yet put my finger on. "Surely not."

I clasp his hands between mine. "I am afraid so. It is true. I am sorry to be the one to bear you with this news."

"Just – uh - just allow me a moment…" he pulls away and sits on a chair against the wall, usually reserved for patrons who find the long walk up the two flights of stairs a difficulty. He sits with his legs wide, elbows on his knees, hanging his head down low.

It is necessary, at first, but soon I become all too aware of how awkward I feel, hovering silently at his side. Do I leave him? Do I stay?

"Did you need something to drink?"

"I couldn't."

"I shouldn't have told you that news here, it was insensitive of me. Perhaps I should have come to find you as soon as he received the letter."

"Insensitive? Of *you?* Margot, when finding out that your betrothed has died in combat, in a war he wanted no part in, you are not expected to find everyone he may have had associations with. *You* need to contend with the grief. The news, it came as a letter, you say?"

"Yes."

"Would you mind – purely for my own memories – perhaps it is improper to ask –"

"Now *you* are the one babbling, Werner."

"If it wouldn't be too much trouble, I would like a copy of the letter. I can get it copied and returned back to you, immediately? Call me sentimental if you wish, but Otto…well, he means a great deal to me. Something like that – I need it, to close a chapter."

"Oh – of course."

"Very well. Thank you."

"Would you like to come by the farmhouse?"

His brows furrow and almost blend together as one. "Perhaps you could bring it with you to the library, tomorrow. I will invent a reason to stop by."

↔

"And this came for Tomas, you say?"

Werner is propped against the library desk, still dripping wet after navigating a heavy downpour to get here.

"Here, let me take this." I point at his sodden coat and he shrugs out of it. "Yes."

"But it is addressed to you."

I pause in the process of hanging his coat on the stand behind me. I had never realised that, though I had read the letter time and time again. I bring my head closer to his across the desk and scan the contents. Yes. It is addressed to me. I look to him and his eyes brim with something…what is that? But I know, as does he. Tomas must have opened my post. He drops my eyes.

"Do you miss him, terribly? Otto?"

"Always."

Reminders of Otto will come at peculiar moments, most of them from our childhood together. A smooth pebble, the scent of pines, a walk down a lane we had spent summers cycling down. In the beginning, just after his passing, I avoided the triggers. I could not bring my head to rise above the parapet, there was too much pain. But time is a healer, and now I seek these reminders out simply to keep his spirit alive.

"Tomas – does he help?"

I blush furiously. "No! Not in that way!"

He stands back and shakes his arms wildly. "I was not implying -"

"He is a friend, Werner. My longest friend, in fact."

"Of course."

"He is here because – well, he took care of the farmhouse when I was in Caen, and it would have been rude to evict him." As if eviction were even possible from an islander to a soldier. He would have gone though, if I had asked him to, I know it. "He is not – will never be - a substitute for Otto."

Werner looks crestfallen. "That is not what I intended, not at all. *Is he helping your grief,* Margot?"

The fire on my cheeks subsides. "He does." Werner nods and resumes his lean across the desk, crisis averted. "He looks after me, comforts me in times of need. He is an angel."

His face twists, just a miniscule amount. Had he not been so close I may well have missed it. "Very well."

"That look…" I briefly wonder if it needs to be pursued. Yes, it does. "Tell me what that look was, just then, Werner. Please?"

I expect him to deny it – wasn't there a soldiers' oath to honour thy brother? – but he fixes me with a steely look. "Tomas is no angel, not on the field."

"The field is different, is it not? Is it the same man you present to the world walking down the street as it is in battle? I know he is tough," perhaps that is the right word, "loyal and…" I remember Seamus, humiliated at my feet, "…*strict.* Are they not the makings of a good soldier?"

Werner looks me level in the eye, a cool blue that could so easily be cold but is rather welcoming. "He is a barbarian."

57

January 1945

I suppose there is no way of knowing for certain, but if there is anything poetic about the human life it is that you leave a piece of you behind on everything you touch. It is for that reason, that instinctual sensation alone of having touched it before, that I know the Red Cross parcel lying in the ditch at the side of the road is my own.

Crouching down to the road, I investigate the contents. Or lack thereof. The chocolate is gone – *of course* – but the powdered milk is still in there, untouched. In fact, I crouch further, *most* of the supplies are still there. I sit back on my heels and look around at the deserted lane, just a little way south of the farmhouse.

"Why would he have dropped it here?" I ask aloud. After all the trouble he had gone through to get it - at my expense - why would he simply have dropped it, virtually intact, here?

I am still sat there, gathering up the supplies, slightly bewildered, when the trotting of a horse sounds along the lane. Standing up I can see a soldier approaching me. There is a familiarity about the way he holds himself, but as he gets closer I still cannot put a name to him.

"Is everything quite alright, Miss La Joie?"

So he knows me, then. "Yes."

His eyes drop to the Red Cross supplies, half in my arms and half still on the ground. He raises an eyebrow, but I do not rise to it.

"I am leaving today."

"Oh?" Should this mean something to me? I fight again to try and place him.

He reaches into a bag slung across his body – next to the rifle, I note – and withdraws a handful of books. "I have these to return. I will not make it to the library, I thought perhaps you could return them on my behalf?" He must mistake my confusion as reluctance, because when he speaks next it is quick and rambled. "It is presumptuous of me, certainly, but I will not find the time to get there, and I did not wish for you to be questioning where they had gotten to when you balance your inventories. You were so kind offering your recommendations for me, and I would not like you to think me no manners. I enjoyed them, very much so."

The books are still hanging in the air between us like a pendulum when it comes to me. "Oh!" I exclaim, taking hold of them. "Of course. Thank you for returning them."

I had all but driven that night from my memory, so haunting as it was. When I think back to it now, it is not the soldiers face I remember, enthusiastic as I reel off book suggestions for him in the library. It is the cut throats of the slave workers, who had attacked me hidden in their towers of corn. I shiver, then take the book.

"Good luck." I add, weakly.

He shrugs. "The war will be over soon. And I can return to my home and read the books there." We look to each other. We both know the likelihood of his town library still standing as it once had is unlikely. He may well be returning to a mountain of rubble.

"Very well." He tips his helmet towards me and turns to retreat up the lane. "He was quite right. You *are* knowledgeable on literature."

"Who was?" I blink, my mind already finding its way back to the parcel in the road.

"Tomas. I had barely arrived on the island that evening and he had me shipped off to the library."

"That very evening?"

"When I came to visit you," he explains. "He was quite insistent. A good friend, yes? He tells me you knew each other before the war."

"We did. We do. I mean – we are, friends, that is."

He trots away, leaving me alone with the depleted Red Cross parcel.

Would that not have been something to mention? Tomas had been the reason, it now seemed, that I was caught in the corn fields at all. Could he have taken accountability for it, even offered an apology for keeping me at the library late? I shake myself. *Don't be ridiculous.* It was not *all* his liability; he did not know that I would encounter slave workers, that I would divert through the cornfields to avoid them. No, what Tomas must be feeling is guilt over what could have come to pass.

↔

"They've eaten my cat!" Maeve sobs as we walk through the town to the library the following morning.

"How can you know that for certain? He has likely run away," I reason. "Trying to source some food, if he's clever."

"No," she grabs my arm, "they *have* eaten my cat. I saw them!" I screw my face up in disgust and she waves at the air. "Well, I didn't *see* them eating him.

But I was in the doorway, minutes before curfew started, you know, getting in as much fresh air as I could, *anything* to feel less hungry, and I spotted Whiskers in the field. I put my fingers to my lips, going to whistle him back, but he was having fun, pouncing on a mouse I suspect. Good on him, I says, envious of *Whiskers,* Margot, because he was going to get a good meal tonight. Then they just emerged from the tall grasses, like tigers, you know, like you read in the books. Just a pair of eyes at first, and I goes to run back inside and lock the door, but it weren't me that they wanted." She dissolves into sobs and I have to guide her to a nearby bench, the once green paint flaking and patched. "They just swooped him up, like he was nothing. They held him under their arms and disappeared back into the grass. I tell you, I aint *never* walking through grass or corn or fields like that ever again. Lord knows what is hiding in 'em!"

I think back to the slave workers nestled comfortably amongst the cornfields, and I understand. Never again.

"Anyway, Whiskers aint returned, and I just know they ate him. I – I get so *angry,* Margot, like I want to hit all of them, like skittles, one, two, three," she gestures at the air. "They're losing, aint they? Why can't they just go home."

"Tomas says they have been ordered to fight to the last man."

Maeve looks horrified. "God no. We're never going to be saved, are we. They're just going to leave us here to rot alongside these…these…*animals.*"

"Besides," I say, patting her frail knee and helping her to standing. "You can't hit them, as much as you may like to, because you will get fined or sent to prison, and…" I drift off, a thought occurring to me.

It is a thought I raise with Tomas later that evening, whilst he delves deep into yet more papers.

"You reported the theft, didn't you?"

"Of course I did. What makes you ask?"

"I found my parcel at the side of the road."

"And what leads you to believe it was your parcel?"

"Intuition." He scoffs at that. "Why didn't *he?*"

"Who?"

"The thief. I attacked him." I put my fingers to his cheek and gently draw my nails down. "Like this." The wispy hairs on his cheeks stand on end. He still does not raise his eyes from the table. "He was German. A soldier. Is it not odd that he did not report me?"

Tomas shrugs. "He probably did not want to admit to stealing from a civilian. The authorities are strict on that, you know."

But he could have lied. He could have said that it was *I* who attacked *him,* unprovoked. It was not unheard of. I had already spent time in Caen gaol; it would not have been difficult to make me appear guilty.

"Regardless. They are looking into it but as he was wearing a mask…"

"It should be easy," I huff, walking away. "Just look for the soldier with claw marks to his cheek."

It is more than that that bothers me, though. Tomas had not looked at me once as he spoke.

58

February 1945

I live with my questions surrounding the events in the cornfield and the robbery for a month, in a certain state of ignorance that the war would end before I had to raise them with Tomas. In the end, it is not the cessation of war that brings me the answers I need. It is Tomas himself.

I turn the key to the library and switch the *open* sign to *closed* with a sense of mild satisfaction one evening in February. It has been a long, laborious day with thick-mannered Germans and only a handful of islanders, the latter preferring to stay out of the formers irritable way. The sky is already a blanket of navy blue, the stars and their dust trails out early tonight. I can feel the cold threatening to seep in through the thin windows and doors, so it is with resignation that I begin to layer up my outer clothes as I turn off the lights, leaving only the lobby switched on to save me plunging into the same darkness that awaits me outside.

The scarf Tomas had accrued for me is on my neck, one arm working its way into the sleeve of my overcoat when I hear a frantic knock at the door. With a heavy sigh I shrug my arm back out, leaving my scarf on in the vain hope my visitor will understand I was leaving.

Halfway across the lobby, with the sound of more frantic knocking ricocheting off the stone walls, I realise who my visitor is. "You?" Confusion is such a prevalent emotion that it outweighs surprise. "Had we arranged to walk home together?" It is a possibility – I cannot trust my mind as much these days.

I turn from the door, eager now to get into my overcoat against the chill that follows him in.

"We did not."

There is a sound - a click - that holds with it far more than just a sound. The air no longer feels right. It brings me to pause, one hand outstretched for my coat. I look behind me, squinting past his form, to the place where the key should be dangling from the lock - but the key has gone.

"Tomas?"

He strides toward me with purpose, closing the gap between us with an air of intention. I know, in that moment, that whatever questions linger in my mind like unwanted houseguests are about to be answered. Something is wrong with how he holds himself, his face contoured into an inexplicable pinch. Truthfully, what troubles me is not how he holds himself – I have learnt of late that whoever the soldiers were nine months ago, they no longer are today - it is the intuitive sensation creeping across my own skin. If I were a dog my fur would be standing to attention, my tail rigid, my ears flat to my head.

"What has happened?" *What have I done?*

"Heinkel."

"Werner?" I cannot hide the surprise in my voice. Of all the things I had expected, a conversation concerning Werner Heinkel was not it.

"You know of more than one?"

I pick up my overcoat and walk past him, toward the lights. "Why don't we talk about this on the way home?"

A hand shoots out, folding itself around my upper arm with such deft skill it does not matter that my other hangs free – he has me in a vice hold. "I cannot go back to the farmhouse, Margot."

"Why on earth not?" I ask slowly, meeting the steel cold glint in his eye, suddenly unsure of the person they belong to.

"It would appear my loyalty to my men has been called into question. I am being dispatched. Immediately."

He does not elaborate. I'm not entirely certain, in any case, if I wish him to.

"Is this goodbye, then?" It feels like no goodbye I had expected. His fingers squeeze tighter on my arm, nails sinking into the flesh.

I wonder at the irony of saying goodbye to someone in such a way, when the one person I longed to have given a proper goodbye to had left without a single word.

"They'll come looking here, first. We must make this quick." I take in the shine on his forehead, the small line of perspiration sitting above his top lip, the nervous twitch in the corner of his left eye.

"Who is looking for you, Tomas?" I ask, slowly.

"Please, Margot." He lets go of my arm and at the same time as he grabs me roughly by the shoulders, his composure slips. Desperation bleeds from him. "Quickly."

"Quickly?"

"Kiss me."

"*Kiss you?*" I cry, incredulously. "Tomas what on earth has happened. Surely this is a misunderstanding."

He steps back, stung. "Is the thought quite so terrifying?"

I take a slow, deep breath in an attempt to steady myself. Tomas is undulating with something. "You do not look well. Perhaps we should speak with your superior, explain that -"

"I said, is the thought quite so terrifying?"

"What thought?"

"Of kissing me."

"This is absurd, you are clearly unwell, I am calling for help." He allows me to walk to the desk and dial the hospital. It does not occur to me that this is at all unusual, until there is no tone meeting me on the other end of the line. The line is dead. I meet his eyes across the lobby and I realise he has been waiting.

"There is no line."

"How peculiar."

Though my heart thuds against my chest, I calmly reset the receiver. *This is Tomas*, I reason. *My Tomas*.

"Is this about Heinkel, or the fact that I will not kiss you?" The words sound absurd out loud.

"He can hurt you and still you love him," he says, sadly.

"I do not love Werner."

"Not Werner Heinkel, Margot. *Otto*."

"Otto is dead," I say levelly. "His hurt has hardly been intentional."

"When will you stop thinking of him as the hero, Margot? What will it take? He pulled the trigger, do you not realise that? He was the catalyst behind this whole invasion!" He gestures wildly around the library, spinning on the spot. "He hurt you long before you realised it."

"He told me about the bombing."

"And still you love him!" he cries, exasperated. "He leaves you without a word on the first aircraft out of the island and still you love him. He *dies*, and *still* you love him!"

I take a deep breath in. *Logic, Margot*. "So this is about Otto, then?" I ask, struggling to understand. I walk carefully across the lobby, the haunting *clip-clop* of my shoes on the floor sounding too eerie, in this moment.

I rest my hands on his shoulders, scolding myself when the touch of them sends a shiver down my spine. How many times have I done this before? He stiffens for a moment, then folds into himself as his shoulders slump and his head droops forward.

In a small voice – a voice so small that it is little wonder the words shock me – he says, "When will it be *me?* I do everything for you and still, it is him."

"You wish for me as more than a friend?" My hands are clammy atop the fabric of his uniform.

His head snaps up and he fixes me with a stare so intense I feel as if he can see into my mind. *His eyes truly are beautiful*, I realise, abstractedly. *Dimples that I could swim in*. "That depends. Am I going to *get* you as more than a friend?" He hardly even blinks.

In the blink of an eye I go over my life with Tomas. A kindred spirit, a best friend, a child into a man - a *beautiful* man, a man with a soul so deep and complicated. The child who brought me books and helped me overcome my fear of the ocean, to the man who placed heated bricks at my feet and fed me forbidden leftovers. The man who put himself on the line to cover for my rebellions.

"No," I whisper. "Tomas I love you in a different way. Our love is unique, distinct in itself, a rarity -"

The blow to my temple cuts my words off abruptly. I wrestle to stay upright and manage it – just - pressing a hand to the pain, but to little effect. My ears ring and my mind rattles, as if someone has placed a ball in it and jostled me around.

Tears spring to my eyes. I look up to him – bewildered, shaken – just as his hand is resuming position at his thigh. He raises his eyebrows in a challenge. *Go on*, it presses.

Barbarian. That is the word Werner had called him; a word I had so convincingly assured him was wrong.

I realise, then, that I recognise the hungry glint in his eye. I had seen it on him before as he humiliated Seamus the informer, or as he watched Charles Machon get arrested by the Gestapo. It takes just a split second for something to pass unspoken between our eyes.

No, I do not love you like that.

Then I am going to have you anyway.

I sprint for the stairs before my mind has even had a chance to decide its next move. Why the stairs, why not the front door? Because, I reason in that quickfire way your brain is capable of when under pressure, he locked that, didn't he. My foot has just made contact with the third step when a hand wraps itself around my hair and pulls with alarming strength. My head flies back, quickly followed by the rest of me, rebounding with a dull *thud* as my body hits the raw stair edges on the way down. I land in a ball, bright sparks of pain shooting from my back, my stomach and the back of my head all at once.

Gasping, struggling to catch a breath, I plead with him. "Don't do this…"

"*Don't do this,*" he repeats in a high, mocking voice. It is so foreign to me that I have to check it is still him. Still Tomas. But no, this monster cannot be my Tomas.

He circles me like a lion. A foot strikes out and hits my stomach. I cough and a tangy, metallic liquid fills my mouth.

"This hurts me more than it hurts you, Margot."

You have to fight, don't just lie here and take it.

The voice is strong in my head and seems to send an unseen power coursing through my blood. He creeps closer, wrongly sensing weakness as I still. *Closer, closer…*He stands with one foot either side of my head, loftily straddling me. I shoot a hand firmly between his legs, curl my fingers around him and grip as hard as I can, pressing hard and pulling down. *Pull the damn thing off.* He follows the motion and crumples forward. I roll to the side just in time to avoid coming face to face with his crotch. I hesitate for a brief moment, watching as his body folds over itself. I almost feel sorry for him, writhing in pain. Then I spit out a mouthful of blood, and it passes.

I sprint back up the stairs. I won't have long. He will be back on his feet soon enough, so I run to the first floor, through the learning room, curling my body around the desks as I do, across the exotic animals section and heading for the rear exit. It opens on to a small back alley which I will have to navigate in the dark, but it will be better than –

I throw myself at the door but it does not budge. In the fruitless way you read about in novels or watch in films, I rattle the door handle to no avail. If anything, I have just made it easier for him to find me. I screw my eyes shut tight. *Think.*

Silence rings through the library but this brings me no comfort. Tomas is a barbaric Nazi, this will not be his first time stalking prey. He will know what to do, how to move his body, how to stay unseen. How naïve of me, to think I could never be on the receiving end of it.

Unseen. I have to hide. *But where*, I want to scream. *Where do you hide in a library?* I scan the room and my eyes settle on the knee height cupboards lining the walls. I fling the doors open but they are full of historic texts, cleaning fluids, ledgers. There is no room for me. Spinning on my heels I find the central displays of books, back to back, a void in the middle. There is little time to wonder. I drop to my knees and set to work carefully removing three, six, nine, twelve books from the lowest shelf. I place them on the floor as I shuffle into the gap left behind, then I pause – listening. In the distance I hear a pained shuffle up the stairs. *Good, I have hurt him.* Sliding in backwards and lying flat on my stomach, I reset the books, filling in the gap. I wait.

He doesn't come into this section, not straight away. He must have turned left at the top of the stairs where I turned right, and the thought enters my mind that I may make it back to the lobby by doubling back on myself. But he has the key. I have no way out.

Then. Footsteps. Slightly quicker this time. *Thud-thud-thud.* He is not trying to be quiet. He knows I am still here, somewhere, and he knows he will find me. He has the power. And yet, I reason, he will never think to look here. Why would he look *inside* book shelves? He is hardly going to start pulling books carelessly off the shelf on a whim. I will wait it out. Sit tight. He will get bored, eventually, or he will come to his senses. He will remember that I am Margot. *His* Margot. Whatever madness has inflicted his mind will rectify itself. He will come back.

He is here now, in the room. The *thrum* in the air alters somewhat, to accommodate another body.

Then I see something that makes my blood run cold. I slam my fist into my mouth to stop from screaming. There, on the floor just feet from me, lies my shed scarf. Waiting, like a beacon. His feet come into view then, and they pause at the scarf. Well kept, nimble hands pick it up and bring it to his face. I hear a sniff - a moan.

"Come out come out wherever you are," he sings.

Puzzled terror courses through my veins. How is this Tomas? *How?*

The war changes people. It is as simple as that.

I barely breathe, staring at his stationary feet. Eventually he moves away but the burning in my throat is raw and red hot. I need to breath, I need to –

Something grabs at my feet and wrenches me out with a force so violent my stomach still feels like it is in the void between the shelves, not crumpled in a heap on the cold wood floor. My hands grapple for something to hold on to, to pull myself up to standing, but his foot makes contact with my mouth before I can. It knocks me backwards and a pool of blood gathers in my mouth, dripping down my chin. I spit out something hard.

"You – you knocked my tooth out," I breathe. It is stilted, unsure. My body is forgetting how to work.

A thought drifts into my head then, lazily, like it was just taking a slow afternoon amble. Suddenly, I am not so certain of what Tomas wishes to do to me. A cold, creeping sensation tickles up my neck. He does not want me, here, in the library. He wants to kill me. He wants to make it so nobody else can have me.

He is over me, tenderly picking up my head in two hands, cradling it in his palms. Thumbs stroke my wet and bloody cheeks.

"Oh Margot. Margot, Margot, Margot," he whispers. Then pummels the back of my head down into the floor, sending splintered wood into the air and dazzled stars into my eyes.

It is a fight to keep them open. I want to ask why, but my mouth is congealing, melting away at the edges. *Why are you doing this.* But I know why. Because I said *no.*

He tenderly lifts my palm into his, splaying my fingers out wide. He croons to me as if he were doing nothing more than singing me a lullaby. "One, two…" he counts off my fingers. I hear the sound first. A cracking, a tearing of muscle and bone. Then a blinding pain rockets from my knuckles to my shoulder; something has been severed, something irreparable. "…skip a few."

The agony is like nothing I have felt before. Childbirth? So distant but so fresh. I would take that over this.My head swims, losing consciousness. I will it to. *Hurry up, get this over with.* The edges of my vision cloud, hazing over, but he roughly pulls apart my creeping eyelids.

"Why?" I splutter. "Why are you doing this?"

Blood sprays his uniform and he wipes it away casually, like a droplet of unwelcome rain, but does not answer. That terrifies me more than any answer he can give.

"I have done everything for you, Margot. Everything. I cleaned your ass after Caen! I have been here to comfort you after everything that has happened. And you still cannot look at me as more than a *friend.*" He spits the word like venom. "This is all I ever wanted," he touches my chest, then his. "*This.* This intimacy. But you reserved it all for him. Even though *I* was the one to break you first. You were fourteen, do you remember, Margot? Just before you fell in love with my idiotic cousin. That is why they call it falling, because it is a stupid misaligned thing to do. People do not *fall* in love, like stumbling over a misplaced pebble.

They drift gently into the all-encompassing ideal of being with their love. Yes, we were young then, weren't we, but I knew even then that you were my sun and Earth. I had you, physically, that summer on the rock when you allowed me to break beneath the surface and make love to you under the stars. But you would not allow me in here," he taps my temple with surprising gentleness. "You reserved that part of yourself for Otto. He became a part of you like I longed to, for so long. So, I continued to wait. One day, I knew, he would mess it up. He would overlook how important you were. I just had to be patient." He laughs darkly, and with it I lose all hope of making it out of this unscathed.

Unless.

"Alice," I whisper.

His hands still on either side of my head where, I suspect, he was preparing to finish me off. "What of Alice?"

"Did you never question it?" My words are beginning to slur together, and I see his face crease in concentration, deciphering. "How alike you both looked?"

His mouth, set into a grimace, salivating with satisfaction, suddenly drops. A droplet of saliva loses its grip and lands on my cheek. "No." His hands withdraw, coming to rest on his thighs, fingernails digging at the flesh beneath his uniform. "You are lying."

"Am I?"

Watching realisation dawn on a person's features is one of nature's magic tricks. But in this place, in this moment, I gain little fulfilment from watching it happen. It has stopped him in his agenda – but for how long?

"You would have said something."

"And what would you have done differently, if I had?"

He slides off of me to the floor, pulling his body into a ball, head hanging loosely between his knees. Inhaling short, sharp breaths of air, I eye the corridor – *I could make it* – then I look back to Tomas. No. I have opened a wound, I intend to close it.

"I loved that little girl."

I try to stand, but from the waist down my body is tingling with impending numbness. Conscious of keeping a distance from him, if this is part of his act, I sit and shift my body against the nearest wall with excruciating slowness. The quiver in his voice sounds genuine, but I can no longer trust him. This thought alone brings tears to my eyes – a string between us, severed.

"On some level I thought you might have always known. Your bond with her was powerful."

"She – *god…*"

There is a prolonged silence so deafening that my ears thrum. He, grieving for the daughter he did not know he had, the one string that - unknown to him - tied him to me more than any other. I, frantically thinking up ways to get out of here alive.

"You can run, if you like. There is no way to escape. All means of escape are either locked or blocked. You will kill yourself if you attempt the jump from a window. And as you have proven, there are only so many places you can hide in a library." Something is off kilter in his voice now, like a perfectly precise line has been notched.

Logic, above all else. If escape is not an option, what can I do?

I swallow a rising knot of fear. "I do not think I am able to walk, let alone run from you. So tell me what happens next."

He looks across, through outstretched fingers; unsure, but curious. "Why are you doing this? If you know you will not make it out of here alive?"

I have intrigued him. I wonder briefly what his years of the Third Reich have entailed, what he has seen, what he has done. I imagine, with misplaced glee, that I am the first of his victims to ever turn the tables on him.

"What other choice is there? I ran, I hid, and you found me. I have very little left to live for, Tomas, that is the truth of it. This war will never come to an end, it seems, and each day that it continues brings with it the loss of someone else I love or care for. I won't cower, Tomas. Though I will admit, I never thought I would need to be cowering from you." The words catch in my throat. "Has it always been this way? How you feel for me?"

"Ah, I do admire that about you – the simplest and most rational approach likely being the correct one. This brilliant mind of yours. Far beyond this island, for sure."

In an unsettling modicum of hindsight, I remember the book he had gifted me, one with the sole purpose of helping me overcome my fear of the ocean.

"You told me once, that I should be afraid of nothing. You wrote it for me, do you remember?"

He shifts to rest against the wall opposite. To the casual observer, we are two friends, sharing stories by moonlight in a deserted library.

"Dear girl, I did not mean *me*. The Tomas before the war was a meek coward, hiding in literature and turning the other cheek in light of conflict. The only time I ever dallied with conflict was warning you away from my cousin. Even then it fell on deaf ears, did it not? I hated him, for getting you. For I never loved anything before you – I have not loved anything else since.

When we returned to Germany I felt something in me alight, I was like a little lost lamb returning to his fold. But my hatred for Otto – his emboldened confidence, the frustrating ease with which he glided through life getting everything he wanted – that emotion was at the forefront. So I found his father."

"*You* did that?" I try to keep my eyes fixed on him, but he is blurring at the edges, the sharp colours contracting, fading into one another. He is eerily reminiscent of a watercolour portrait. Blood trickles down the nape of my neck like perspiration on a warm day.

"I had no choice, if I wanted to put an end to his perfectly curated life. I had heard the stories of his father, the way Elka and Doug spoke of him in hushed tones, as if we couldn't hear or understand. I knew what he was like. So I found him one day, and I told him that Otto and Elka were back in Germany. I was correct in my assumptions – he was involved in the party – and for a man like that, laying claim to a young man pumping full of pure German blood was irresistible. It excited him, riled him. And he came for him, as I knew he would."

"The Tomas I knew would never have done such a thing."

"That is precisely my point Margot. I am not the Tomas you knew. I am better. Sometimes we have to make choices, and sometimes those choices are not sunshine and roses. But it is for the greater good."

It is getting harder to breathe, harder to keep my focus on him. I lay my head against the wall gingerly, finding some relief in the coolness – something is burning back there. "I think I am dying."

"Yes."

"Why do you wish for someone you love to die?"

"So that no one else can have you. I am as sure as dead when I leave this library, Margot. My own men have turned against me. This war, it is reaching an apex, for all of us. You will not allow us to be together in life. This way we can be together in heaven."

"You are not going to heaven."

He laughs – it could be my delirium, but it sounds melancholy. "Who is, truthfully?"

"If I am dying, and you will be dead before long, I wish to know…" I break off, breathing in a sharp rattle that terrifies me. "…I wish to know, how did you find me in the cornfields?"

"You followed a path, did you not?"

"I followed no path. There was a -"

"- missing line of sown corn? I went through and pulled it up. Enough of a gap to be irresistible to someone who would not want to waste good food, but not so obvious that she would question it."

"Then how did you happen to be in the right place, at the right time?"

"Clever girl." He shifts, and I sense that he is getting himself comfortable. Perhaps this is what he wanted all along. "I wanted to be the one to rescue you, comfort and fix you, Margot. Everything I did, it was from the heart. It was to make you see how much I love you. Honestly, I often felt like I was pressing my face to glass, screaming, showing you everything I could offer you, and you did not hear me. You passed by me, oblivious." He sighs. "I bribed the Organisation Todt guards to let me play with some of their pets. You had made it clear you never wanted to see another march again – all I had to do was engineer it. I found out which officer was newest to the island and, in an act of dutiful obligation," he holds his hand to his heart, "I showed him just how wonderful our local library was. You were kept at the library just long enough that I knew you would intercept the march. I marched with them, that day, feigning a discussion with one of the guards. I saw you, a miniscule speck on the horizon making your way home, and I knew you would divert into the fields. I hung back, picking out two of the more desperate looking leeches. I promised them free corn if they were to frighten the island girl a little. Then I heard the cries – and I came for you, the hero."

Bile threatens to rise from my stomach. "That was a risky plan."

"If you had chosen to backtrack your steps, or turn another way, what did it matter to me? I would have killed the slaves anyway – they were never going to tell."

"I believed you had simply followed me. Your plan was far more convoluted than that."

"Oh I have been." I lift my head as much as I can, but it hangs heavy, a feeling of fullness so peculiar I can barely keep it aloft. "Following you, that is You are a creature of habit, darling girl, it is so easy to predict where you will be and when. I set the roadblock that day you first saw me training in the field with Müller, did you guess? I needed you to see me, to know I was here, to know that I would be waiting for you when you came home from Caen."

Somewhere far away I remember knowing Otto was following me, protecting me, whenever I walked amongst the soldiers. What if it had not been Otto after all, intent on my protection, but Tomas, intent on following, stalking his prey. Things tumble, beginning to make sense in a way they had never clicked before. He had come to the island with the 319th Infantry Regiment – he had been on Guernsey long before I saw him in those training fields.

"You knew I was going to Caen?" I want to know if he could have stopped it, used the power he seems to wield to keep me from suffering in the very clutches of hell.

"Did I know? I arranged it all."

Had my body not been so broken, I expect the rising lump in my chest would have surfaced as vomit. But it has no strength left; instead, the sensation creeps up my chest, warm, heady, and dissipates somewhere around the base of my throat.

"Wondering how? It was excellent timing on your part. I thought I was going to have to plant some anti-German propaganda on you somehow. But you and I, Margot, we have always been so in tune. It was as if you *knew* what was needed of you."

My mouth opens, but no sound comes out. There is no sound left. That part of my body has shut down. The edges of my vision darken to a deathly black, steadily embracing my vision of Tomas.

"I was the one to welcome you home, after nine months living like a rat in a cell. And I did, did I not? You felt safe and loved. That was all real, Margot. Do you see now, my love, the efforts I have gone to for you? Did Otto ever do that?"

I think he has come to sit beside me. I cannot be sure, other than the shift in air temperature at my side. There is only a pin prick of light left in my vision.

"I am sorry, for the night your Red Cross parcel was stolen. I told him to leave the chocolate."

"*Barbarian,*" I breathe. The feeling is raw, leaving open wounds down my throat.

I welcome it.

"I am holding your hand," he whispers from somewhere faraway. "This is how they will find us. Together."

Alice – I will be joining Alice soon. A smile plays on my lips. And Otto. My love, I am coming.

59

Heaven is all wrong. It isn't supposed to look like this.

There are no black cars in heaven, or that feeling of weightlessness that comes from being driven at high speed. It makes my stomach lurch. Heaven isn't supposed to make your stomach lurch. There are small eruptions of fire beneath my skin, and I don't like that either. There is a lot of noise, too, and that's not right. Heaven is supposed to be calm, just me and Otto, at least at first. But there are too many people, too many loud voices.

So, you're not in heaven, then?

But I am, I protest. I am! I *must* be, because my head is most definitely nestled into Otto. I would know his smell anywhere. It is tainted somewhat, obscured by musk and grime, but it is him, and he is my heaven.

Except. It can't be. Otto in my heaven has both arms. This Otto only has one.

60

There are a few phrases I hear, as I weave along the plane between conscious and unconscious.

" – lucky to be alive -"

"- she was dead, when we found her -"

" – how can she come back from that -"

" – see if she wakes up first -"

It is one voice, whispered in my ear, that breaks through the layer of phrenzy. "He hasn't left your side, not yet, not once. Please wake up so he can go and bathe. He is ripening out the ward."

I will my eyes to open, but I am afraid. Right now, the pain is manageable. It is all in my head, really. But once I open them, once I see where I am and what damage there is to overcome, it will all be real.

It is his voice, though, that finally raises them. That finally brings me back to the living. "Do not dance with death anymore Margot. Come back to me."

Fingers interlace with mine, the tips so familiar, the tender flesh of his thumb rubbing along the back of my hand. I cannot believe it, cannot allow myself to swim with the possibility. It is this very impossibility that forces my hand to it – I have to see for myself. Now is the time to wake up.

A breath hitches somewhere in my chest. Only one eye can open, the other still too tender…but it is him.

"How?" I croak. The words are raw in my throat, sore from disuse. He does not understand me – all he hears is a pitiful, sorry sound, not words. "*How?*" I try again.

Otto rushes forward and lightly kisses my forehead. His eyes swim with tears, some of them already falling silently down his cheek, leaving delicate streaks on a face lined with dirt. He is whispering something over and over. It sounds like *thank god.*

"Gently, Major Reid." But this voice is thick with emotion, too. There is a shift of colour to my side, and I realise the nurse in the curtained bay has left us.

A sob catches in my throat, unable to rise. It is a transient pain, the burning radiating out from the core and sizzling out. My insides have been broken. That part must not be fixed yet.

"You are wondering how." It is not a question. Unable to move my eyes from him, I nod. He is really here. Or my mind is elaborately fractured. "Werner." I try to raise an eyebrow but even they do not appear to work. "I owe him everything. He had to move heaven and earth to find where I was stationed. The ass end of nowhere springs to mind. Tomas knew exactly what he was doing when he sent me away; he sent me to die. By some miracle – by you, Margot – I kept surviving. Heinkel showed me the letter, the one claiming me dead. It was a forgery, my love. Tomas devised it himself."

"How did he know it was not real?" Otto's eyebrows crumple as he watches my mouth work, and I can tell he is deciphering my broken words.

"How did he know it was not real?" He asks. "A month after Tomas supposedly received the letter of my death, I endured a…an injury, on the field." My eyes skim over his missing arm, something hard falling into my stomach. "There was a nurse, she was kinder than the others. She asked if there was someone she could write to, to inform them. My first thought was you, and I transcribed an entire letter to her with your name at the top. Then I made her tear the paper to shreds and start again. I thought any letter from me to you would go unread, I did not think you wanted word from me. My name being put forward for dispatch I – well, I thought that was fate. Cruel fate, but fortune all the same. So I had the letter sent to Werner. I suppose I hoped that word would get back to you.

When you showed Werner that notice of my death in action, he knew the dates did not tally. He just needed to confirm it. He fought tooth and nail to find me. Tomas had hidden me well under no paper trail. How he did it -" he cuts off, shaking his head, swallowing the quiver in his throat. "– I am forever indebted to him. He did not give up on me. He did it for you."

The thought of Otto abandoned somewhere, in the passive hope that he would be killed by the beast of war, is both deceptive and cowardly. Two things I never thought possible for Tomas, not until tonight. *Wait -*

"How long have I been here?"

"How long have you been here?" He deciphers. "A fortnight, Margot. The longest two weeks of my life."

"We have had to serve him food on that very chair," the nurse saunters back in, smirking at Otto and grinning at me. "Perhaps now he will go and wash."

"What do I look like?"

He visibly grimaces, so I know it cannot be good. "Do you really wish for me to answer that?" But he is smiling. Crying, and smiling. It is an odd but satisfyingly thrilling combination.

He is here – he is really here.

The nurse leans close. "For someone who lost her life on the table, you look beautiful. A miracle brought you back, Margot. That, and Otto's refusal to let you go."

↔

A broken leg and a cracked rib, both on their way to healing themselves.

Two broken fingers that have been splintered but will never again be straight.

A swollen eye, a face beaten beyond recognition.

A split lip, lost tooth.

Major bruising to the skull, but nothing broken there.

When Otto returns after leaving to bathe in the hospital washroom, a fresh aroma washes over me. "Soap?"

"The hospital have a small supply. The nurse said I needed it," he smiles sheepishly. "I suppose if anywhere needs soap it is a hospital."

"I have to tell you something."

His eyes drop and I realise he has been waiting for this. "I cannot make you love me Margot, not if you no longer wish to after what I did…but my world without you in it is inconceivable. I wonder if this would have been different, had I had the nerve to tell you about Tomas in the first place. I wanted to. I should have. I should have told you that he left to join the party almost the minute our feet touched German soil."

"Alice was my daughter."

His head stops shaking. His eyes flash up to meet mine, visibly processing my words. And so I tell him, about the night on the rock many summers ago, when Tomas and I had come together as one beneath a blanket of stars. How it had taken that night to confirm that what ran between Tomas and I was nothing beyond friendship. I watch as his face - lightened by the prospect of having such ties to Alice – darkens into one of loss. He holds me, I hold him, my grief surfacing now, ready to be shared with one who can hold my hand through it.

Sometimes, I realise, you must open the gate and let the enemy in. Only then can you heal.

61

May 1945

"The Queen and I desire to convey to you our heartfelt sympathy in the trials which you are now enduring. We earnestly pray for your liberation, knowing that it will surely come."
King George VI
Words from an RAF leaflet, dropped on Guernsey by aircrafts
September 1940

↔

"...our dear Channel Islands are to be freed today."
Winston Churchill
May 1945

↔

Maeve's hold on my hand swells and ebbs with every bump in the road. The open-backed cart we have hitched a ride on is far from road worthy, the taint of rotten vegetable skins still loitering on the wood, as if it has sunken into the very grain. Nellie, steering the cart with hair blowing behind her in a non-existent breeze, joins us to a convoy of similar shaky trucks. The convoy trails down the *Val Des Terres*, curving, swirling, like an eddy. There is singing from a distance down the hill, making its way up to us like a whisper, until we catch the words and join in.

"Can you believe it?" Maeve breathes into my ear, before it gets lost to the wind. It doesn't matter – we are all saying the very same thing, in one form or another. Islanders from every parish have put their differences aside, coming together as one, thronging into the harbour like a pulsing, unstoppable wave.

For days our island has been swarmed by RAF aircrafts, flying over the island like a welcoming beacon. *We are coming*, those flights said. *We are on our way*. With every drone and magnetic thrum in the air as they approached, the soldiers walking among us shrank, retreating into the shadows. They had no fight left.

They offered us their wireless sets to listen in on Winston Churchill's speech.

Yesterday, our authorities told us to fly our Union Jacks high. Proud.

Last night the soldiers had thrown a party in our honour. With blazing torches in one hand, bottles of champagne in the other, they sang. "If the British cannot celebrate their victory, we had better celebrate it for them."

There is a swell in my chest as I look beside me, into the thousands of shrunken faces who have walked perilously with death, a pride so deeply profound I fear it will break me.

We have been stubborn. We have been loyal. We saw it out, Papa. We did it.

"Leave the cart. Let's walk!"

Bumper to bumper, the carts are stacked. We jump down, joining everyone doing the same. We hold hands with people we know by face, not name. We link arms with neighbours we held petty grievances with a lifetime ago. That is tomorrow's problem. For now, we move as one. We have come to welcome our liberators.

↔

The Weighbridge clock, still frozen to the time of the harbour bombings, sits behind me as we watch them. An incoming wave. A salvation.

Flags fly from arms so thin I wonder how they keep them raised. *Strength.* It is in all of us, if we know where to look. The Union Jack flies from a crane in the distance, flown by a German soldier, who had climbed it the night before.

A man beside me, arm to arm, skin so taught I can see his bones, opens his mouth a little and starts to sing. Quietly, at first, a voice meek with uncertainty, growing louder as our liberators come closer. The haunting melodies of *Sarnia Cherie* – our island anthem banned since 1940 – fills the air. Young, old, we unite in song.

The first soldiers pass us, signs of the islanders gratitude visible in the lipstick marks on their cheeks, hats knocked askew. They swing rhythmically along the jetty, our army of liberation. They send us smiles and hearty laughs, they throw oranges to the children in the crowds, who hold the strange objects in their hands, throwing them to the floor expecting them to bounce like a ball. I pick one up, press my thumb into the flesh and peel back the bitter skin, handing a nugget of juicy fruit to a child beside me. His face, as the fresh juice squirts down his chin, is so eerily reminiscent of Pierre's many years ago, doing much the same thing, that tears fill my eyes in an instant.

I scan the faces of our liberators, much as I had done with the faces of our enemy, recognising with a jolt of familiarity and alarm the young commando from the clifftops. *He survived,* I think. *We* survived. My ears, my body, falls prey to the flurry of sounds around me. We have woken up after an endless night of slumber. An almighty cheer undulates through the crowd, rising into a crescendo, never quite ceasing. We cheer until our throats run hoarse. Tumultuous applause mingles with guttural sobs. British planes fly over our shores in formation. Evocative church bells ring out in the background.

I hear it all, long after I am home in my bed, Otto's arms tight around me. It thrums in my chest, inciting a fresh wave of tears.

He will kiss them, never wiping them away. "You deserve this," is all he will say, one hand resting on my stomach, where a small round fills his palm.

62

September 1945

Four months later, I sit in the cool respite of the farmhouse kitchen, hiding from an unseasonably warm September. My legs lay out on a chair, taking the pressure off of my ankles, hands clasped over a swollen stomach. The door behind me opens with no warning and I still, fingernails digging into the flesh on my palms.

"Easy," Pierre says, kissing my forehead as he passes, placing a rough and calloused hand over my hands.

It is only when he leans against the newly installed kitchen units and pours himself a glass of water from the tap that I allow myself to ease. *How long*, I wonder sadly, *until the sound of a door opening no longer fills me with dread?*

"The minesweepers have been out on the sea again this morning. I heard a few explosions out there."

Three days after the liberation, we noticed the Royal Navy ships on our shores, clearing the seas around the island and eradicating the legacy traces of the German forces. They had been intermittently returning since.

Pierre is on leave, due to return to Britain next week and continue with his service. He had enlisted at the tail-end of the war, and evidently hadn't had his fill of the fighting. I was fond of his company, having spent the last three months in the farmhouse alone, only the sounds of my own movements echoing off the wooden floors and stone walls.

Otto, as with all the soldiers on the island at the time of liberation, had been shipped to Britain as a prisoner of war, shortly after May 9th. I knew, in time, that he would come back for me, but it offered me little comfort in the meantime. There was a long stretch between here and Germany, a lot of uncertainty, a lot of warpath to cover.

"I heard something today." Pierre regularly brings me snippets of life outside of the farmhouse. I rarely venture out beyond the parish, now; there is enough to do here, fixing what the soldiers broke. They may be gone, but their presence still lingers in the air like an acrid smell. We are picking up the pieces, slowly, but surely. Loyally, as we have always done. "Tomas was killed before he even left the island. At the hands of his own men, no less. The soldiers turned against those they knew were Nazi's. There are rumours of several attempts on the lives of the barbarians before the Allied even came for us."

From somewhere deep down in my stomach, I feel the stirrings of what could be grief, if I were to give it conscious thought. I refuse to. Tomas had killed me, that day. Physically, he had broken my body as such that it was a near-miracle I had come back from it. Mentally, he had destroyed whatever semblance to the boy I once knew. I would mourn for the Tomas of my childhood, who died in 1939, when he returned to Germany, but never for the man he became.

"Good riddance."

"I thought you would say that."

"Do you have news on anyone else?"

"Otto?" I shake my head – I wish for news of him, every day, but our paths are so intwined now, so inbred in each other's, that I know it is only a matter of time.

"Werner."

"I am keeping an ear to the ground, Go-Go, but there were a lot of soldiers sent to the mainland, it is almost impossible to know…"

Werner Heinkel had saved my life that day, then had simply vanished. Bit by bit, I pieced together what had happened, coming to the understanding that Werner's revelation of the forged notice of Otto's death had opened up the long list of war crimes Tomas had committed. Whilst the soldiers were not innocent, by any means, he had manipulated, bribed and slaughtered more than any other. I often imagine Werner and Otto together, reunited in the aftermath of war, as they had been in its infancy.

A rap at the door makes us both startle.

Pierre looks to me with one brow raised. "The bastards have made us all jumpy." He shrugs it off and goes to greet our visitor.

"I am looking for my lamp."

"Is that so?" I can hear the smirk in Pierre's voice.

"I've hunted down through four parishes already, walked every street, and I can't bloody find it. They said you had a soldier billeted here – truckloads of furniture delivered to your door, so they say."

"You are welcome to look, Mr De Carteret," I call to my elderly visitor. "If you find it, I won't quarrel. I have little desire to keep anything he saw fit to bring here."

Once the elatedness of our liberation had subsided, homeowners began to hunt back their belongings, so recklessly stolen from their homes by the soldiers when they left their billets, and taken on to their next. In truth, I recognised little of what Tomas had left in the farmhouse. I was quite content to remove it all and start again.

"I'm going to get to work in the fields, see what I can sort before dinner," Pierre says, when Mr De Carteret leaves the room and starts his investigation elsewhere in the house.

"I can help -" I start to get up but he places a hand gently on my shoulder.

"Just keep my nephew safe."

"So sure it is a boy?"

"Without a doubt." A pause fills the air, both of us aware of the child who should be here, but is not.

The evacuees had returned in dribs and drabs, different children to those who had left. Some of them no longer children at all. Parents worked hard to reconnect with these children they no longer recognised with heartbreaking optimism.

"Ah ha!" A delighted cry comes from the living room where, I assume, Mr De Carteret has found his elusive lamp.

↔

Later, after a light dinner (rations were a thing of the past, but our food supply had only mildly recovered from the scarcity), Pierre washes up and I dry.

"Do you think we can see Ma again soon?"

As I had predicted, with the lifting of war and the departure of our soldiers, Ma seemed to emerge from her nightmare. She is not better, by any means; she is still not coherent, but she is calmer, recognising us when we visit. She had light back in her once-vacant eyes.

"I hope. We can go before you leave next week."

"Will you be alright, when I leave? I hate going when you are alone here."

"I am not alone. I have Maeve. And your *nephew*."

He flings the tea towel at me, then slides his feet into his shoes, leaning against the doorframe. "That Maeve girl…is she courting anyone?"

"Pierre!" I throw it back.

"A man can only ask. Look, I wanted to go next door, offer to help plant the crops with them -"

"You do not need to ask my permission. I don't mind."

"Are you sure? I could set us up for cards? You enjoy losing to me."

"Go. Help them. Let us kickstart our economy."

Farming had restarted on a communal basis, almost as soon as the liberating troops set foot on the island. We were all helping one another – old neighbourly grudges staying forgotten, for now.

Almost as soon as I sit down at the table and hear the kitchen door click closed behind Pierre, he is opening it again.

"Did you forget something?" A strange, muffled noise makes me turn, only to find him ghostly pale, opening and closing his mouth like a fish. "What has happened?"

He moves at pace to the kitchen window and looks out. "Margot. Swollen ankles or not, you must get up."

"My ankles are not swollen."

"*Get up*, Margot."

"Must I?"

He is by my side, raising me to my feet, giving me no choice. "Yes."

"Where are we going?"

"Just here." He guides me to the window, where I see two figures ambling down the dusty drive. The very one I had watched countless soldiers walk down, come to requisition something or demand an inspection. The very one Köhler had marched down on his first day of billeting. The road I had watched Tomas come home on. The one I had waited beside, for Otto to emerge from his hiding place.

It is Otto, now, striding at leisure, as if unaware that the girl waits for him in the kitchen window, pinching herself to ensure it is not a summers mirage. His hair, long outgrown from its shaven state, reflects the evening sun.

He is not alone.

I put a hand to my forehead, my own skin suddenly suffocating.

"Don't faint now, Go-Go."

"Is this – are you seeing this?" I breathe.

"Sure as day I am. Why does he always show up when I am about to leave?" He is eyeing me, wondering if he should say what he is thinking.

"Just say it already."

"Will you tell her?"

It is a question I had pondered back and forth on, spent countless sleepless nights imagining, even after I received note of her death.

"Perhaps. One day. Not yet."

Alice, ten years old, with wavy brunette hair chopped to her shoulders, strolls hand in hand with Otto.

↔

The terms of Otto's release stipulates that we must marry immediately. So the very next day, that is what we do. He had fought against the authorities, intent as they were on repatriating the German prisoners of war back to their homeland with minimal disruption. It was Doug, a force to be reckoned with, that made it happen. I ask for few details; it bothers me not how he got here, but that he managed it.

Doug, too, joins us around the kitchen table as we celebrate our marriage with a simple feast. The times for being fanciful are long behind us. Pierre and Otto sit thick as thieves, finally reunited. Alice holds my hand beneath the table, so that we both have to eat one handed.

It is her story that is the most remarkable. She had come across a girl about her age when she was making her way to the public air raid shelter with her evacuation family. The girl was frozen, scared beyond the ability to move. Alice had given the girl her cardigan, in the hopes of bringing life to her limbs. She sat with her, refusing to move herself until the girl joined them. But the father of the family, he fought with Alice, pulled her away, carried her kicking and screaming into the shelter. He tried with the girl, too, but she bit him, clawed at his skin. There was a reason she did not want to leave that spot, Alice claims. Something profound, some reason we would never know. He didn't leave Alice behind. He saved her life. The girl was identified only by Alice's named cardigan.

Otto and I go to bed that night with Alice and our unborn child between us, linking fingers around their cocoon.

↔

Elka arrives two days later, with my mother. In nothing short of a miracle, Ma is Ma again. A veil has been lifted; a fog cleared. There is knowledge in Ma's eyes at times. It sits there, sometimes, when we catch each other's eyes, but we do not speak of it.

Elka had arrived on the island with Doug and Otto, but had gone on to the hospital immediately. Wielding the authority she has always seemed to possess, she had convinced the nurses to let her stay with Ma. I can imagine they had little knowledge of what they were agreeing to. By herself alone, she had brought Ma back to us. Did I intuit it, years ago on the beach, that this strong, powerful woman would save her life?

↔

Mr De Carteret returns one week later, shortly before Pierre is due to depart. He is sheepish as I open the door. Remembering, most likely, the fact that he had laid claim to a great deal of our furnishings, and by the time he had left, our home was considerably lighter for it.

"One of the soldiers left something in my house, and I haven't known rightly what to do with it. I sure don't need it myself, but p'raps you might make use of it, what with your…" he waves at my stomach.

"You really mustn't feel the need, Mr De Carteret…"

"Oh it aint no need. Just seems a shame, t'is all, to have it sitting in my house unused."

He disappears for a moment, and returns holding a large hand cart. "Have you pulled that here yourself?"

"Oh sure. If we can thank them for anything, it's making us walk or cycle everywhere. Fit as a fiddle I am."

Placed carefully in the center of the cart is the most exquisite dolls house I have ever seen. Intricate carvings adorn windows, every roof tile delicately etched into the wood. Familiar diamonds embellish the façade, and it takes me a moment to place them.

"Cigar boxes?" I ask, impressed.

"Sure looks like it. I think the soldier who carved this was some kind of a magician." His good deed complete, he bids me farewell.

That evening, as Alice croons over the dolls house, making characters from linen scraps and ties, I see two words etched into the underside of the roof. *W. Heinkel.*

AUTHORS NOTE

Listening to stories of the Occupation from the mouths of those who had lived it was a big part of my childhood. I remember sitting opposite my grandmother, who was evacuated as a small child, talking me through it all for a school project of mine. I did not appreciate, then, just how valuable her words were. Now, as we pass through this last generation that remembers, it is imperative to pass these stories on.

I set the cogs in motion for writing this novel long before I even realised it. I would read through firsthand accounts and consciously write parts of them down, as I would have done when studying for an exam. I had no idea why; I simply knew they needed to live on past the pages on which I had read them. These facts, statistics and firsthand recollections have formed the basis of *Operation Green Arrow*.

The texts for which I am forever indebted have been noted at the end of this book; they offered insights, no matter how small or large, that formed the foundations on which *Operation Green Arrow* was built. My role was simply to take these real insights and form a fictional story around them to paint an in-depth picture of life at the time.

Historical notes

In Chapter 8, Margot greets a boatload of French refugees. Whilst we do not know for certain who met the boats, or if they were even greeted at the docks, Guernsey *did* receive several boatloads, though the specific number is up for debate.

The barbaric bombing of the White Rock harbour took place on 28th June, 1940, by the end of which 34 people had lost their lives, many caught in inferno's when they sought shelter under their trucks. After the event, the Germans proclaimed to have mistaken the trucks for military vehicles – a proclamation that is hotly debated still to this day.

The Weighbridge clock – still a significant feature of Guernsey's seafront – really was frozen at the time of the bombing.

Once the Germans began their Occupation of Guernsey, they forced islanders to drive on the right-hand side of the road, set their clocks to 'German time' and took control of their newssheets.

In Chapter 15, Margot comes across commando's on the cliffs and provides them with safe passage past the German guards. Whilst the commando's in this chapter are fictional, several raids on the island were successfully carried out. In one instance, a farmer milking his cow on the cliffs was said to have given the commando's he came across fresh clothes and advice on how to pass the guards.

The language barrier between locals and Germans was a point of contention. Whilst many Germans knew basic English, the islanders hoodwinked them with their local tongue, *patois.* The two language-related stories in *Operation Green Arrow* – 'please shut the gate' and 'you'll be glad to see our behinds' – are real accounts.

All examples of the 'V for Victory' campaign in the novel were carried out by brave islanders in Guernsey, including Pierre's wire-cutting sabotage of a telecommunication wire and Margot's chalk on the bike seats.

In *'A Boy Messengers War,'* the author tells of a moment when he is pulled into a shop porch during an air raid siren by a mature German soldier. He later goes on to explain it was because of his likeness to his own son. Similar happens to Margot, when Heinkel pulls her into the shop porch for her own safety.

G.U.N.S *(Guernsey Underground News Service)* came into effect shortly after the wireless sets were confiscated from islanders in 1942, and ran until 1944, when the team behind it were betrayed by fellow islanders. Charles Machon, the brainchild behind the prohibited news sheet, died in 1944, in Hamelin prison hospital. Ralph Durand, in his memoir '*Guernsey Under German Rule'* describes his role in hiding copies of the clandestine news sheet in nominated books of the Priaulx library. In the novel I have taken artistic licence that G.U.N.S was running before 1942, telling jokes at the soldiers expense and sharing news that was no longer distributed in the main newspaper. There is nothing to prove that this was the case.

All references to notices by the *Feldkommandantur* are real, or based on real instances.

The incident where Margot delivers peaches to the fictional shopkeeper, Ms. Leale, is based on a real event that happened to Leslie Roussel, author of *Evacuation*. The soldier sat with them and listened to the BBC broadcast.

When Margot is walking with Tomas on Christmas Eve and hears the melodic singing of *Silent Night,* this is based on a real witness account by the author of *Isolated Islands,* V.V Cortvriend.

The events on the day of liberation, May 9th, are all true. *Sarnia Cherie* was sung by young and old as the liberators stepped foot onto the island. Union Jacks were raised by soldiers and they held parties in our honour. For the most part, the soldiers were just as relieved for the war to be at an end as the islanders were to be liberated.

Resources

A Boy Messengers War, Martin J Le Page
Voices From The Past: Channel Islands Invaded, Simon Hamon
A Silent War, Frank Falla
Evacuation, Leslie E Roussel
Islands in Danger, Mary and Alan Wood
Isolated Islands, V V Cortvriend

Printed in Great Britain
by Amazon

f2a13a2a-cf62-4378-b109-628d0d6e2de7R01